WILL WHITAKER

The King's Diamond

Harper
Press

Harper*Press*
An imprint of HarperCollins*Publishers*
77–85 Fulham Palace Road
Hammersmith, London W6 8JB

This Harper*Press* paperback edition published 2012
1

First published by Harper*Press* in 2011

A catalogue record for this book
is available from the British Library

ISBN 978-0-00-741030-9

Typeset in Bulmer by G&M Designs Limited,
Raunds, Northamptonshire
Printed and bound in Great Britain by
Clays Ltd, St Ives plc

MIX
Paper from
responsible sources
FSC™ www.fsc.org   FSC™ C007454

FSC™ is a non-profit international organisation established to promote
the responsible management of the world's forests. Products carrying the
FSC label are independently certified to assure consumers that they come
from forests that are managed to meet the social, economic and
ecological needs of present and future generations,
and other controlled sources.

Find out more about HarperCollins and the environment at
www.harpercollins.co.uk/green

For Elizabeth and Alexander

HISTORICAL NOTE

It is 1527. The young Emperor Charles V, the most powerful monarch in centuries, rules much of Europe from his capital, Madrid, and is extending his empire in a series of ruthless wars. In Rome, the wily Medici Pope Clement VII has formed an alliance to fight Charles and drive his armies out of Italy for good.

As the powers of Europe take sides in the great struggle, only England holds aloof. King Henry VIII, at the age of thirty-six, is the most glamorous and accomplished monarch of Christendom: dancer, jouster, sportsman, musician, scholar. His Court is a place of untold opulence. He has no intention of involving himself in the Pope's quarrels. Instead his thoughts are on a woman: beautiful and beyond his reach.

PROLOGUE

6 May 1527

The Sack of Rome

He sat and gazed upon the stone. Its surface was smooth and undulating, virgin and uncut as when it first came from the mine. Over it lay a soft and milky sheen, pretty, teasing, allowing no glimpse of what lay inside. To one without experience, it would not have appeared to be a rough diamond at all.

He turned the gem in his fingers until the light suddenly penetrated, and for an instant he had a perfect view into its depths. He saw the tiny flaw that reached down, just off-centre, like a hand plunged into cold water, white against the pale blue transparency of the stone. The ray of light glanced off the flaw and dived deeper, acquiring more intense tints of marine blue and peach-bloom. It lingered on the gem's lower surface, mellowing now, growing frail but exquisite, like the flavours of an old wine. As he turned it a fraction, the light broke, and the timid, beautiful blue exploded with animal wildness into orange, vermilion, carmine, indigo, the turquoise of burning sulphur. The whole body of the stone was alive with colours, jarring, leaping, bursting back up and out, ravishing and dazzling his eyes and making him draw in his breath. A moment later the milky veil was drawn once more over its surface, and the stone lay in his hand, mute and composed: gleaming with promise, and yet maddeningly secret and withdrawn. He shivered with exhilaration. No other diamond, and only one woman, had ever hurled him through such a rush of emotions, the teasing seduction, the passion and fulfilment, the coolness, the seeming rejection and despair. He turned the diamond again, seeking once more for that momentary gleam of light, catching it and losing it again, catching it and losing it.

That flaw fascinated him. It was like a scar on the body of an otherwise perfect woman, a part of her nakedness that he loved almost more than the rest. But he must drink his fill of the sight while he could. Soon the flaw must be cut away. There would be risk. Certainly, it was that pale, slender fissure that had frightened off all the diamond's previous owners from any attempt to cut it. With a rough stone like this, no one could be sure of its properties. You might trim it away to almost nothing, and still find the flaw snaking through its flesh, mocking you. He turned the diamond once more, so that its flaw shimmered in the light. This was a stone among thousands, the stone that would make his fortune: or else bring him to utter ruin.

He thought back to its birth, untold centuries ago. They say that gems are born from seeds, sown by daemons or intelligences underground; the same beings that by their sports create strange effigies in rocks, in the form of shells, bones and trees. The gems grow, slowly over the ages, each in its own secret womb of rock. Rubies in the gleaming red balasse. Emeralds in jasper. Diamonds, most precious of all, in red clay or crystal, or even in gold. The mother stones enfold them, nourish them with their blood, sacrifice themselves so that the gems can live. When the gemstones have reached their perfection, the greed of man tears them from their womb.

There are only three places in all the world where true diamonds can be found. Some come from Borneo; others from the Kingdom of Bengal. But the greatest stones of all are from the mines of

Ramanakotha, beyond the mountains of the Western Ghats, in the lands of the Sultan Kalim-Allah Shah in the heart of India, five days' travel from the fortress and city of Golconda.

He had heard many stories of that broad, arid plain, scattered with rocks and twisted trees, cut across by dry ravines. No crops will grow there. On the tops of the hillocks are the ruins of ancient shrines, and newer ones too: for every time a fresh tunnel is opened, a goat is sacrificed towards its success. Everywhere are the huts of the miners, roofed with straw. Sixty thousand men, women and children work here, dirt-poor and near naked. They pass their lives in debt for food and rent and the permission to be here at all. But having come, no man ever tries to leave. They will work themselves to death sooner than that.

They dig down into the gravel, the red and black clay and sand, which is the womb in which these diamonds are formed. When the miners find the veins where the diamonds grow, half a finger wide and stretching down into the earth, they use long iron hooks to wrench the stones free, and break their way deeper with picks. Often the shock of hacking the clay gives the diamonds fresh flaws. The soft earth can subside without warning. It is a common sight to see the dust and rubble of a fallen tunnel, the bodies carried out and the pyres lit between the mine entrances and the shrines. You will hear the wailing of women, hundreds at a time. They have lost their men, and now they come forward to cast themselves into the flames – or else the mob will drag them to the pyre by force. The diamonds have killed them just as surely as their husbands. Those who survive walk past the fires and back inside the tunnels.

Further off into the hills are the older mines. Some of these were opened two thousand years ago; now for the most part they are dead, empty and haunted. Up here, the diamonds grow in a soft red rock that crumbles easily under the pick. It is a fertile rock, a legend among those who love jewels. The Old Rock of Golconda. Few stones remain. But there are still miners who work these veins, who risk the demons that are said to live here, and the frequent falling-in of the ancient tunnels riddling the hills. For these are the finest diamonds in the world.

Early in the year 1484, in the reign of the Sultan Mahmud Shah, two men walked down out of the hills and into the town square of Raolconda. They were dirty, dressed only in ragged loincloths, and in their eyes was the mad light of those who had lived too long with death and despair. They crossed to where the diamond dealers squatted in the shade with their weights and scales and bags of gold at their sides. Only here, in the kindlier green light beneath the banyan trees, could the quality of the stones be judged. The men sat down before the dealers; one of them opened a bundle and with reverence displayed a diamond. It was a pearl-smooth stone almost the size of a hazelnut, with a white flaw reaching down into it like a hand into water. Three miners had already lost their lives, extending the abandoned tunnel into the hillside. But the two who remained had gone on. They had read the signs in the rock, the brightening in its colour, and the juice that oozed from its fissures like blood. They knew they were approaching their reward.

The merchants leant forward. It was a rarity, this: a stone of the Old Rock of such a size. Their scales proclaimed it at twenty-two *mañjariyañ* and a half: or thirty-seven carats and three grains in the system used in the West. They muttered together, bidding and outbidding one another. Then they looked back at the stone. It was a Gujarati dealer who took it up, of the trading house of Harshadbhai. He counted out two hundred golden pagodas, about four hundred Venetian ducats in the currency of Europe. The miners took their gold and went back into the hills. The light of greed burned brighter in their eyes than ever. No fear of demons or collapsing tunnels could hold them back now. They would penetrate deeper into the Old Rock, and deeper. Within three months, both of them would be dead.

With a stone such as this in his hands, the Gujarati itched for the markets of Surat, where Arabs, Turks and even Portuguese jostled, greedy for the treasures of India. He set off west in a caravan of twenty other merchants, climbing from the plain up into the moist mountain forests, thick with laurel, cinnamon and sandalwood. Six days into the wilderness, brigands surrounded them. His companions agreed on surrender. They would lose their goods; but there would be other ventures. At least they would have their lives. In the past, Harshadbhai would have thought likewise. But he was not to be parted from that diamond. Just as the senior merchant stepped out from among the pack mules, his arms spread in surrender, Harshadbhai put an arrow to his bow and shot down the brigands' leader. In the fight that followed, three merchants died before the brigands fled. The survivors would no longer keep such a dangerous companion in their band. Harshadbhai travelled on alone.

At Surat, he carried the stone about the usual markets. He was offered three hundred pagodas, then three hundred and fifty; but still he kept it back. He met at last an Arab seafarer named Abu al-Husn, a man who traded between Surat and Aden, carrying ginger, aloes and gems to the West, and to the East horses, rosewater, saltpetre and alum. Al-Husn paused, looked, looked again. He weighed the diamond, and tried to value it. But the manner its cut would take, its final weight and colour, all defied him. The man who bought this stone would put his gold and his peace of mind at hazard. He smiled, and began the process of bargaining. The diamond became his for five hundred pagodas. In the days that followed, making westwards across the Arabian Sea, al-Husn took his new possession out repeatedly, and bragged to the other seafarers of the golden profits he would make when he sold it in Aden; how he would accept not less than a thousand dinars, a good sixty per cent more than he had paid. Every night, as the ship rocked in the swells, he played at dice. Gradually he lost every item of trade he had with him, until he had only the diamond. He turned it in his hand so that that curious gleam struck off the flaw like some signal of warning. Then he set it down with care on the table. 'This, against all the rest.'

The other men nodded grimly. The diamond, opaque once more, lay on the table among rubies and sapphires, mounds of gold coins and notes of promise for this cargo or that down in the holds. Hazard was the game; a Turk named Ibrahim shook back his long embroidered sleeves and threw first, a seven. This was the strongest throw he could have made. Al-Husn answered it with a four. Now he must throw, and throw again. If he could repeat his four, known as the *chance*, he would win. But if he repeated his enemy's seven first, the *main*, he would lose. The odds were bad. He broke into a sweat. Unlucky twelves took two of the players out; another threw a six and stayed in, with better chances than al-Husn. All the time the diamond gazed at him like a cold and lazy eye. His hands shook as he made the next throw: four and three, making seven, the *main*, and the destruction of all his hopes.

He sprang to his feet and took the Turk by the neck. He had cheated, changed dice somehow when he shook out his sleeve. Gems and coins went flying. But the Turk had already solved the argument. The curved blade of his dagger slipped between al-Husn's ribs. He fell, and as his eyes misted over, his last sight was of the diamond, which opened itself briefly, rolling in the ship's motion, and favoured him with a last rose-pink gleam from its depths.

Some weeks later the stone landed in Aden, that richest port of all Arabia, where the goods of the East meet those of the West. Ibrahim walked ashore with the diamond concealed in a pouch. He knew nothing of gems. His own trade was in opium, and the dyestuff known as dragon's blood. But the figure stuck in his mind, one thousand dinars, and he would take no less. For three days he walked the city, before meeting an eastern Yemeni named Ibn Hisham. He was a young man, an adventurer, and his usual trade was in pearls of Ormuz. Diamonds lay a long way outside his line. But when Ibrahim opened his packet for a group of traders, the flash of the early sun caught by chance on the place where the flaw shot down inside the stone, and made it burst into sudden music. Ibn Hisham paid down gladly the thousand dinars demanded, around sixteen hundred ducats. He knew he had in his hands a wonder; and it would take him far from his usual roads. The West was the place to sell gems: Cairo, where the Christians came, hungrily clustering to the edge of their world in search of the luxuries of more civilised climes. His pearls too would sell there for more than in Aden.

It was the season of the hot and sudden winds that blow down from the mountains across the straits; but despite that he set off at once. He passed in safety into the Red Sea, and coasted Abyssinia as far as the port of Locari. From there he struck across the desert. Six days' waterless journey, with the only signs of life the distant scudding of the ostriches, kicking up trails of dust with their feet. Then, after coming at last to the Nile, twelve days more by boat downstream, travelling by day, by night keeping watch against the desert Arabs who raided at will along the banks. By the time he reached Cairo he was longing for the tranquil dawns of Ormuz and the sight of the pearl fishers coming in to the shore. For all the diamond's bewitchments, he was in a hurry to be rid of it.

That autumn, in the bazaars of Cairo, a Venetian named Marin Pompeo caught sight of a stone the like of which he had never before seen. Its owner, a nervous young Yemeni, allowed himself to be beaten down to two thousand ducats. Returning home by galley up the rainswept Adriatic, the Venetian turned the diamond in his hands. He soon learnt the knack of catching the light and making it shine. Pompeo was no stranger to diamonds. He had bought and sold them for thirty years, and he had seen them in every size and colour and form. He had handled the rare greens, the common, less prized yellows, the noble whites and blues; he had seen table cuts and pyramids, rough stones with a black flaw at their hearts, strong stones and weak. Once he had owned a diamond that shattered merely with the pressure of his fingers, a beautiful stone with a wild and reckless glint to it. This diamond, he thought, might be another one the same. Again and again he held it up gingerly, by morning light and noon, by lantern and candle. Each time it was different. He yearned to see it cut, and he swore to himself he would do it, whatever the danger. But back home again, walking the Rialto that winter with its jewellers' shops by the dozen, he found he did not dare. When a young nobleman of Florence named Lorenzo de' Bardi offered him two and a half thousand ducats for it he handed it over, grieving, regretful, yet relieved. The temptation was over. He, at least, would not be the one to shatter that stone.

De' Bardi took the diamond with him back to Florence. He had just come into his inheritance. He travelled with fifty retainers, his own suite of furniture, a jester, twelve minstrels, his wife, a concubine and a dwarf. He had come to Venice for pleasure, and he had found it. But of all the beautiful things he bought in Venice's markets, none pleased him so much as this diamond. Pompeo had shown him how to turn the stone and make it shine, and had whispered to him how much greater it could be, if he ventured to have it cut. But that risk was not for him. Why should he wish to share his diamond's beauty with others? It pleased him to think that he alone could see inside its heart; that if anyone else happened to pick it up, the chances were that they would see nothing but a dull, grey pebble. To cut the stone would have meant answering the trust it showed him with betrayal.

Over the years, de' Bardi lost much. His wife left him, and then his mistress. When his family became caught up in the wars of the Borgias, he lost almost everything else; but still he kept hold of his stone. Every night for forty-three years he took it out of its casket and gazed upon it. Those glimpses he allowed himself into its heart were a secret bond, a love that was greater than any he had known.

Only as he lay dying did it finally leave his hands. At his side knelt a young Englishman, a merchant in jewels.

'Who will wear the diamond when I am dead?' murmured the old man.

'A king's lady,' answered the Englishman. 'The most beautiful woman in the world.'

The Englishman rode away south to Rome with fierce exhilaration. He had almost paid for this stone with his life. But a diamond such as this drove away all fears.

He turned the stone in his fingers once again. Since his return to Rome, another man had given up his life for the diamond of the Old Rock. There lay the body in the corner, over by the open chest in a pool of blood, its left arm thrown out, its right clasped over the hilt of a sword. A bloody stain on the back of the green velvet doublet showed the force of the sword thrust that had passed clean through his chest.

Again he caught that deceptive gleam for an instant, and once more lost it. It was exasperating how that window into the diamond's heart was so small, so elusive. He was weak and lightheaded with hunger. His temples throbbed, and yet he felt strangely detached. Nothing in the world save his stone really seemed to matter. At last he had time: time to turn the gem, slowly, lovingly, to see the beginnings of each change, the opening of that chink that led down into its depths, the plunge of the light, the smile of the breaking colours, and then the sudden drawing of the veil across its surface. He could imagine himself dying like this.

Dimly he perceived that he must fight the pull of the stone that whispered to him to stay, look, drink from my waters, just another hour. From outside the room there were the sounds of shots, and running feet. He knew that if he was to live he must leave this place, with the dead body lying in its blood beside the chest. Soon it would be too late. Hunger and thirst would leave him too weak to walk, and too weak to choose. But just a little longer first. Catch the gleam in the stone one more time, and again, and again.

PART 1

Topaz: a Perfect Sunshine Stone

Genoa, 23 January 1527

Now my trembling mind yearns to wander,
Now my joyful feet spring with eagerness.
Sweet band of friends, farewell;
Together we set out from our far home,
But many diverse roads lead us back.

CATULLUS, POEM 46

1

Hammers rang on anvils, and sparks sprayed from the forges out across the stones. Men in flame-blackened aprons held lumps of glowing iron in the fires, then drew them out, refashioned them with more ringing blows, and plunged them into barrels of water with a rush of steam. I watched the new-made halberd heads, the sword blades of their various kinds, the boarding axes that are used in sea-fights. Under the arches of the Arsenal, I could see men forming the finer parts of guns, the twisted serpentines that held the match fuse, and the powder pans, bending the soft metal with their tongs, and I saw the silvery molten lead poured into moulds for bullets. The finished weapons were carried down towards the quay, to be loaded on the Spanish galleys anchored in the harbour, ready for war.

I was in my room in the Angel Inn, late on a cold January after-noon. Since morning I had sat here, unmoving, gazing out at the forges of the Arsenal, fighting a furious battle with my thoughts. 'Go home,' a voice seemed to say. 'Any man of sense would say you have done enough. See what you are in the midst of. Destruction may come to Genoa any day now. Get out of Italy by the safe route, while you still can.' Genoa was a Republic split in two, always prone to revolutions. At the moment, it sided with the Emperor. But the city's greatest prince, Andrea Doria, was an admiral in the pay of the French and the Pope's Holy League, and his galleys hovered out in the blue distances of the Mediterranean, waiting to inflict a stinging blow against the merchant ships of the city that was once his own.

But the road north still lay open. Just two days' ride would take me across the border into the Duchy of Savoy, a region still untouched by the carnage of war. After that I would cross the mountains into France: calm, peaceful France. There were no armies there, roving and looting at will, no plague, no famine; there would be bandits and wolves, perhaps, but they were no more than the common dangers of European travel. A few weeks would bring me to English Calais, that comforting outpost of home planted on the edge of the Continent, and then it would be over the Channel and back to London.

I pictured myself back home on Broken Wharf by the bank of the Thames, climbing the creaking old stairs to the counting house and stepping inside. Here my mother, Miriam Dansey, known to all London as the Widow of Thames Street, directed her many ingenious business endeavours. I imagined laying before her my haul, the emeralds and sapphires, the great ruby, the amethysts and all the rest. I imagined her with her trading partner, William Marshe, the two of them drawing in their breaths and raising their eyebrows in wonder. Yes, I would have a triumph, of a kind. But I would know in my own heart that I had failed. I would have to take my gems to be cut and set by one of the London goldsmiths. I knew these men, and I knew that my stones, that had the capacity to be so extraordinary, would come out looking like all the other trinkets fashioned on Goldsmiths' Row. I might make a profit on my venture, yes, but it would be small, and I would have lost the glory I longed for, that would come only if I could astonish and dazzle a king.

There was another way. I could turn south, and head for Rome. Rome: opulent capital of Christendom, where the finest goldsmiths, artists and dealers in luxuries flocked to make their name and fortune, and supply the endless appetites of His Holiness, Pope Clement VII, his cardinals and nobles. Rome: the seat of a mighty temporal power, for Pope Clement held absolute sway over all central Italy, as well as numerous cities in the north, and commanded Florence through his Medici relations. Rome. Only there would I find the craftsman truly worthy to work on my stones. In my dreams I saw the golden swirls and figures that must surround the gems. I saw something nobler than the common run, something alert and alive, something I had never seen in London.

As I sat, my servant, Martin Deller, paced up and down behind me. He was some ten years my elder, stocky and dark, a useful man with a dagger who had helped me out of trouble more than once. He was also, to my frequent annoyance, the voice of conscience and caution.

'Please, master! We have had good luck. Let's leave while we can for home.'

He was right. Plainly he was right. It was a wonder how we had crossed from Venice overland: first past the army of the Pope's Holy League camped at Cremona, which they had recently won from the Emperor's Spaniards, then across into the Duchy of Milan where this war had first begun. This was Imperial territory. We found the farms broken up, the fields burnt. The Emperor's army, starved of pay and plunder, roved the shattered countryside in bands, robbing travellers of whatever they could get. We had travelled by night and hidden in the day, winning through by a mixture of my boldness and Martin's sense.

The patch of sun on the wall of the Arsenal opposite had shrunk upwards as far as the parapet. It was drawing towards evening. At sunset the *Speranza* would sail. Few ships were putting out for Rome in these days of war. If I was to strike south, this would be my only chance. Perhaps she had sailed already. And that was best, I argued to myself: by far the best. The time had come to call enough, and turn for home. I faced Martin. I was on the point of telling him to unpack the trunk again, and order horses for tomorrow and a guide for the journey inland.

'Well, master?'

A sudden, sick rage swelled up in me. Was I to give up now on the triumph I had sworn I would have, all those months before, when I folded my bills of exchange into the casket round my neck and climbed the boarding ladder on to our family ship, the *Rose*? Now, when I had a casket of gems the like of which had scarcely been seen? Was I to betray them? My blue diamonds of Bengal called out to me, my sapphire that was the colour of pale skimmed milk sighed to me, my fiery garnets and the great dark ruby flashed with rage. This venture had never been for those easily daunted by fears. No, there comes a time when the stakes double: a time when you must either gamble and go on, or else give in, and admit you should never have played at all.

I stood up briskly and walked towards the door. My sword was swinging, my hat already on my head. 'Pick up the trunk,' I ordered Martin. 'We are going.'

I walked out of the inn beneath the painted angel with its wings spread, and into the crowds. I could hear Martin's breath behind me as he struggled to keep pace with my trunk on his shoulder.

'Wait! Master, please! Will you not consider a little longer?'

I did not look back. I skirted the Arsenal, heading east round the broad bay, a mile wide, that forms the harbour at Genoa. Now that I had decided, I was determined not to lose a moment. I pushed my way through the crowds past the wooden piers where the lesser vessels put in, the lighters and flat-bottomed shallops. Here, wine-barrels bumped and thundered, and three men rolled a hogshead up the ramp to the roadway in front of me. I dodged round it with a curse. There was the rich scent of oil, spilling in drops from great jars borne on men's shoulders, and the stink of hemp, its stiff fibres tied in rolls, ready for the rope-makers that twist the long cables in the alleys behind the port. As I hurried on, a mournful chanting struck up from the belly of one of the war galleys out across the bay. Strange and sad, this Mahometan song of the Turks chained at their oars: for that is the rule of the sea, that when a Christian ship lays hold of a Muslim, all her crew become slaves, and when they take a ship of ours we suffer the same.

At the fish market I stopped, impatient, while Martin caught up, the trunk bobbing above men's heads in the thick of the crowd. Red mullet stared up at me, glass-eyed, out of open crates, and a woman in a white linen bonnet chopped the heads from eels and cast them down on the stones, where gulls swooped and flew off with them, crying. Music burst from one of the taverns, a fiddle and pipes, and I heard the clack of the dice, a harlot's laugh, the slap of cards on a table. As Martin came out from the press, I turned and hurried on.

West over the hills the sun broke out briefly through the clouds. It was close to setting. At the last of the wooden piers grain was being landed, passed from shoulder to shoulder in sacks and poured out into bushel measures, sending up clouds of chaff. The men laughed and joked at their work. No one could say how long this plenty might last, or when the galleys of the League might close the sea once more and attempt to bring Genoa to obedience through starvation. I pushed past, bounding up the six stone steps on to the Mole, whose curving arm reached out into the deep water of the bay. The wind blew with full force here, and I reached a hand up to steady my hat. It was a soft bonnet of black Lucca velvet, which had in it a gold medal of the Virgin and Child, in the latest aristocratic fashion. I had paid eighty Genoese ducats for this medal. But it was more than a costly ornament. It was the guiding star of my voyage.

All along the Mole on the sheltered side towards the harbour lay the great ships, bound on far and weighty ventures. Their masts rose tall, clustered like forest trees, flying the flags of all those nations aligned with the Empire. There was the red cross of Genoa, the black and white of Siena, the red, white and yellow tricolor of Spain.

The wind made the ships pull on their ropes and the waves slap against the stone. I ran along the Mole, hunting in agitation for the gilded names on their sterns.

I had sat last night in the Angel with the *Speranza*'s owners, a pair of Genoese brothers named Piero and Federico Fieschi. I had bought them wine and discussed terms of payment for this voyage: ten ducats they asked, for the two hundred and fifty sea miles to Rome. All risks were my own. Piero had looked at me in question. The price was high: some thirty shillings for a journey that should have cost less than ten, even supposing I needed cargo space in the hold. I told them the sum was acceptable; but I could answer at that time neither no nor yes. They went away displeased. 'Remember,' Federico warned me, 'we sail tomorrow, without fail.'

Ahead, men shouted from the decks of one of the ships. Her yards were raised high and clear, slanting out over her sides, and a wooden crane swung goods out from the Mole and down into her holds. Plainly she was loading up to depart.

On the quay Piero Fieschi was standing among a band of five or six men. They had the air of old established merchants, all of them, with grizzled beards and gowns trimmed with rabbit fur and sable. They thought nothing of standing there in that chilling wind, watching with serious eyes as every last bale and crate was winched up from the Mole. Their grave faces showed they knew the risks, putting to sea in times such as these. Doubtless they had prepared well in advance. They would have their servants on board, numerous and well armed. No doubt they had insurance too for their valuables, so that, even if they perished, their heirs would profit. It gave me a sudden sense of my own vulnerability. I had taken none of these precautions. I realised, too, the hastiness and lack of dignity of my entrance. Still out of breath, I swept off my hat and bowed.

'Richard Dansey, Merchant, of London.'

They bowed in turn and presented themselves with their nations of origin: Milan, Lucca, the Duchy of Ferrara. Their eyes lingered on

8

me. Plainly I was a mystery to them. I must have seemed a mere boy, with my light, sand-coloured hair and my beard that was little more than a wisp of down. I was still only twenty-one, and although I was tall, and had gained some skill with a sword, I was not of a powerful build. Too young to be a merchant, in their eyes, and not dressed like one, either. My clothes had more the air of a fashionable young noble's. I wore a purple doublet slashed with white cambric, my shirtbands falling over it from the neck, each garnished with lace and ending in a gold button. My black wool cloak was edged in silver, and my rapier too was silver-hilted.

Piero Fieschi stepped forward from among the merchants with his partner and younger brother at his side. I held out to them the purse I had prepared hours earlier, containing ten gold ducats. Piero looked at me in astonishment.

'Messer Dansey! We sail at once: but do you have no goods to load?'

Martin came panting up behind me. Fieschi glanced at the trunk on his shoulder, clearly pondering whether it might contain anything of value. Martin swung the thing roughly down on to the stones, and sniffed. Fieschi appeared to dismiss the idea. He gestured to the knot of merchants. 'Our companions have loaded silks of Lucca and Genoa, and we have a solid stack of salt barrels belonging to Messer Pinotti here, of Milan: most welcome for ballast. But you, nothing? Truly nothing? You tell us you are a merchant: how will you turn a profit?'

'I have my means.' I smiled, delighting in their disappointed curiosity, and turned from them with a graceful bow. I stepped from the Mole to the wooden rungs of the entering ladder nailed to the *Speranza*'s waist, and pulled myself on board. Martin swung the trunk up on deck, hauling himself after it. While he asked in his London-accented Italian where he should stow my trunk, I strode around the decks, enjoying once more the feel of the planks beneath my feet and the smell of pitch in my nostrils.

The *Speranza* was a great ship of perhaps a hundred and twenty tons, slightly larger than the Dansey family vessel, the *Rose*, which I had left behind at Bruges in August. Peering down the open hatches I saw she had at least two orlops, between-decks where a man could not stand upright; here the goods were being shunted from the hatches and lashed into place. Furthest aft was the roundhouse or great cabin, from which several smaller cabins opened. In one of these I found Martin, sitting on the trunk and mopping his portly face, and cursing gently at the run I had led him through the port. I heard the rattle of the hatch cover as it was fastened into place, and the clank of the capstan as the sailors began warping the *Speranza* out into the bay on her anchor. All at once they broke into a song, a bawdy affair in local dialect, praising the part of the city known as Maddalena, which had the fairest churches, the richest markets, and the greatest number of brothels.

I stepped back inside the great cabin. It was of a fair size, raked back at the stern to a row of fine windows. My fellow passengers were all present, seating themselves about a table, in the high humour of men swept up in the risk and hurry of a new venture. Servants were pouring out glasses of sweet romney wine, and there were fried capons, as well as wafers, almonds and sweetmeats. Martin came out of our little cabin to attend me. This supper was my first meal since the early morning. I ate greedily and drank deep, and all of us talked and laughed more and more freely.

'In Rome we shall buy from His Holiness an indulgence for trade with the Turk,' Piero Fieschi was saying. 'Without that, of course, any commerce with the Muslims would involve us in mortal sin. Then south to Naples, and over the sea to Cairo.'

'Cairo!' his brother picked up. 'What wonders cannot be had in Cairo? We shall bring back silver and cinnabar, raisins, rosewater and sandalwood, cloves, porcelain and pearls, indigo and opium.'

Suddenly the Luccan, Messer Giordano, darted up from the table and into one of the cabins, and returned with a piece of silk some three yards long, shimmering crimson, pirled with a fine thread of silver. 'Do not talk to me of Cairo. Feel this! Smell it! And tell me if the lands of the Turk can boast anything as fine!' He draped it round our heads and we fought free of it, laughing. It had the true tang of new-spun silk, the stink o' the worm, as the silkmen call it, and it was as smooth as the sound of lutes. The others were not to be outshone, and each dived into his cabin. Soon the table was festooned in cloths and colours, blood-red satins, green lustred taffetas, thick black velvets striped in gold with a pile as soft as cats' fur; purple and maroon brocades with patterns stamped in silver that sparkled in the light from the oil lamps. We swam in the silks, laughing at the sheer luxury of it.

They would sell these marvels at the Court of Pope Clement in Rome. Any that were left they would take on to Naples, and offer up to the Spanish Viceroy. Even the Milanese Pinotti held out a handful of his greenish-grey salt, saying, 'Taste it, taste it! Is it not the best?' A Sienese called Basile tipped out a bag of hawks' bells and dog whistles and thimbles, all in silver, that went tinkling and rolling about the table with the ship's motion. One of the bells came to rest in front of me, and I stopped it with my finger. Their laughter was dying, and their eyes remained fixed on me. I was the only one who had not shown off any wares. I regretted that I had not taken on some cargo, just for appearances. A few casks of salt or some dried fish: anything. Their curiosity was a little too sharp. Without my intending it, my hand reached up to my throat to trace the outline of the steel casket that hung by a chain round my neck, hidden beneath my doublet and shirt. The thing was some nine inches long. A key secured it, sliding into a lock under the brass head of a cupid. Its surfaces were polished smooth by long concealment, close against my skin. That casket weighed on me, a precious burden, delicious but dangerous, and unutterably secret.

Martin, who stood behind my chair to serve me, caught his breath, and I put my hand back down on the table. The merchants' stares flattered me, even as they disturbed me; their rich cloths made me feel part of a high and select band. Yes, I could count myself their equal. And soon I would rise higher still. I picked up the empty bottle of wine.

'Gentlemen, should not this poor deceased bottle have an heir?'

Piero continued to stare. But several of them took up the cry of 'Another bottle, another bottle', and others joined in with 'Let it be hippocras, hippocras!'

'But have we a sleeve?' asked Basile. The elder Fieschi went to a cupboard set in the wall and brandished in the air a cone of muslin: a sleeve of Hippocrates, invented by that ancient doctor for some purpose to do with healing the sick, but now used in the brewing of hot, spiced wine, known to all as hippocras. I saw Fieschi unlock a drawer and take out fragrant cinnamon bark and cassia, cloves and grains of musk. These he sprinkled into the bag, which he gave to a servant to take for'ard to the cookroom, along with another bottle of romney. The other men cheered. While we waited for the wine, I slipped out once more on deck, to give their curiosity time to cool. The sun had set, and the air was growing colder. Land was a bare line on the horizon now, black against the indigo of sea and sky. A tiny gleam marked the tower on the Mole where bundles of broom were burnt at night to guide ships into the port. A servant stepped out of the forecastle with a steaming pan of wine and swayed aft over the deck to the great cabin, trailing the scent of warm spices after him. Those smells made me think of home. In a few weeks, maybe, my work in Rome would be done, and then at last I would turn back: back home to the family warehouse, on the rain-soaked stones of Broken Wharf in the City of London. And I would have my triumph.

2

It was seven months since I had set foot in that warehouse, and walked its dim passages between the shadowed mounds of barrels and crates that could contain any merchandise on earth. Here, in the years of my childhood, I had explored along with the other two members of our band. We used to prowl through those mountainous landscapes in the dusty light from the few smoke-blackened windows high above, looking out always for new discoveries. There was John Lazar, bold and fast-talking, big for his age, and my rival for leadership of the group; and there was Thomas, my brother. Thomas was slender, fond of his books, but for all that ingenious in dreaming up exploits. He was never daunted by a wall that had to be climbed or a stretch of riverwater to be jumped. In our hands we carried nails, sticks, even a length of iron bar. We tapped the barrels and prised up the lids. Inside, when we were lucky, we found sweet green mastic soaked in rosewater, and dipped our fingers in for a taste: forbidden fruit from savage lands. There was Baltic amber that gleamed with its dull, orange fire; crates of Turkish knifeblades; pungent cinnamon or peppercorns; oiled canvas packages that hid shimmering rugs and damasks woven with swirling figures.

Outside, before the grey timber front of our warehouse, the stink of the river hung in the air. Water lapped the green-scummed stones where two or three lighters always nudged against the wharf, their single sails furled. This had been my world, the world of Queenhythe Ward. East and west it stretched, the length of Thames Street, from the greasy stink of the cookshops beneath the sign of King David's Head and the Old Swan brewhouse, all the way west to Saint Peter's Parva and the Blue Boar, under the shadow of Saint Paul's. Within these bounds our band of three ran and fought and explored. The streets, unpaved, stank with refuse and the night soil emptied from jutting windows overhead. Gutters ran gurgling down the street edges to discharge their effluent into the Thames, while waterwheels drove bosses, engines that sucked the riverwater back up again and drove it along lead pipes into cisterns scattered along the streets. Into these the serving maids daily dipped their pails to carry into the houses; so that, in my father's phrase, we drank what we pissed just as surely as we pissed what we drank.

'It is a proud name to bear, "Merchant of Queenhythe",' my father used to say, and for much of my life I had believed him. We who were born on Thames Street were suspicious of all those foreigners west beyond Lambert Hill, or east of Towne's End Lane. The ward was a town of its own within the City. It elected an alderman, it had its own Council of Six and its Wardmote Court, nine constables and a beadle, and eight scavengers who slept in the day and prowled the streets at night, shovelling up the multifarious filth of the city and carrying it away into the country, where we imagined it was sold for a great price. There was Five Foot Lane, the narrowest in London; the tumbledown church of Holy Trinity propped up with great oak beams, which I climbed once to the level of its broken eaves, and dared John to follow; there were the poor houses of the packhorsemen and dock hands, and grand hostels with courtyards belonging to the nobles, through whose windows we peered eagerly.

At the heart of the ward was Queenhythe itself, a bay hollowed out of the riverbank between the warehouses, some hundred and twenty feet across. The old people remembered when this had been the grandest of the London wharves, but only barges and small boats could put in here now, thanks to the decay of London Bridge: its drawbridge had grown stiff with age, and would no longer let the great ships through. Even so, the Hythe was a fair sight, when the tide was full and the lighters came upstream and put in, dozens at a time. There was a customs house, with a bailiff who stood before it with his thumbs in his belt. The lighters landed rye and coal, fresh-caught herrings and sprats, eels and mackerel, as well as salt cod, and the dried stockfish that came in from Norway, stiff as a board, which was our fare in the winter. We used to sit on the stones at the water-side, John, Thomas and I, and watch the bakers and brewers come down to buy their wheat and barley. We saw the loads of fish being winched up and weighed by a thin, pale official known as the Meter. After that, the eight master porters took charge, each with his three under-porters. They loaded their packhorses with seven sacks apiece and set off up the steep, winding ways bound for the various fish markets, by Bread Street Hill and Spooner's Lane; and, aptest name of all, when the packbeasts stuck in the narrows between jutting house-timbers, Labour-in-Vain Hill.

West of Queenhythe was the Salt Wharf, and then the bath-house on Stew Lane. Those steamy rooms beneath the brick chimney were about much more than getting clean. Women lived in the house, whores, and on misty nights we could hear their laughter carrying as far as home. Sodom on the Thames, my mother called it, and forbade Thomas and me ever to go near. But curiosity tugged at me, and I knew that one day I must step inside. Beyond Stew Lane was Timber Hythe, where John's father kept his warehouse. We stopped here sometimes to watch the cargoes being unloaded: Dutch wainscot and deals, and clapboards, riven oak lengths that would go to make barrel staves. John did not like to stay here too long. He was ashamed of his father's dull trade: he was restless, hungry for new worlds, just like all of us.

Next along was our own domain of Broken Wharf. Fallen stones spilled into the water from the crumbling steps; the lime peeling from between the ancient paving threatened always a fresh landslide. The firm of Dansey had taken the lease on this wharf at first because it was cheap. Then my father, Roger Dansey, had bought the warehouse and the dwelling beyond it, and we became fixed there. We had built a new oak pier, but it remained a treacherous landing-place, and around the dark pilings river currents swirled uneasily. Here, very often, our band made its camp. We used to perch on the stone edge of the quay with our legs dangling over the water, watching the boats and the men about their business, while we debated our next venture.

'Who has the courage to swim out to the mill?' asked John. He nodded his head to the pair of barges wedged between pilings out in the river, with a waterwheel secured between, perpetually turning with a dull grind and splash. To swim out there at anything other than a slack tide was death. We had done it, John and I, three times already, each challenging the other, and I would have done it again at any moment, even with the tide running, if John thought he dared it and I did not. But Thomas said, 'And what would I do, while you risked your necks? "Who has the courage?"' he mimicked John's voice. 'We've all proved that we can do it. No, let it be Terra Incognita.'

He meant the old abandoned warehouse just upriver from ours. Its grand stone frontage proclaimed that in centuries past it had been the house of a noble, before the relentless tides and currents had eaten at its foundations and driven cracks up into the stonework. Even so, some time in the last century someone had dared to erect a wooden warehouse here. Tall and crooked it stood, rearing up from the ruined old mansion, its head tilting over the river like an old man about to fall.

Thomas was the one who first succeeded in picking the lock. He stood lookout, while John and I squeezed through the doorway into the forgotten stone court, daring one another to leap between the broken arches where the paving had cracked and dropped into dark abysses below. Did we dare go down? We dared. One by one we descended into the dripping cellars, waist-deep in water, rich with the stink of the Thames. Here were slimy caverns and cracked old wine casks, and the shipwreck of a lighter, its rotted timbers glistening with damp. But the real delight of the place was not underground. I found the way up by many a creaking ladder to the attics, where a wooden gantry opened out over the river, far, far below. With a little care and daring I inched out along the timbers and round to the eaves, and so crawled up over the tiles, with a thirty-foot drop beneath, to the roof-ridge itself. John followed, and then Thomas.

We balanced with our legs straddling the roof, hallooed and waved our arms. Beneath our feet ran the great highway of London, the Thames. Every manner of boat was to be seen. There were lighters with their brown sails spread, hire boats steered by a single man at the stern, crossing from one landing-place to another, and the tilt boats with eight oars that carried larger numbers of passengers down to Greenwich. But what really drew my eyes were the great barges of the nobles with their gilt prows and raised sterns, and the heraldic banners flying with fringes of Venice gold. In time I learnt to recognise them all: the crossed keys and scarlet hat of Cardinal Wolsey; the royal leopards and lilies of the Duke of Buckingham, before he was beheaded for ambitions a little too near the throne.

Best of all was when I saw the King himself passing between his various palaces. The royal barge had a crimson awning covering its full length, with flags flying above it and gilded dragons and wyverns on poles. No oarsmen could be permitted in so exalted a craft, and so a second boat towed it, with dozens of rowers all in the scarlet royal livery, using a long tow-rope which dipped and splashed in the Thames. The barge itself glided on, spilling the sound of lutes and shawms and laughter, and the scent of sweet perfumes that drifted even as far as our rooftop, almost masking the stench of the river. The cannons fired from the Tower downstream in salute, and sometimes I could hear the sound of the trumpets as the barge put in at the wharf at the Palace of Bridewell, four landings up, where the King from time to time held court. The others grew tired of this spectacle long before I did. They eased themselves down the tiles and crept back round into the attic, while I stayed, intoxicated. It was dusk, often, by the time I turned for home, and if I had not known the feel of those timbers in the dark I would have met death many times over.

Our house stood immediately behind the warehouse, facing north across Thames Street to the tiny church of Saint Mary Summerset. The street makes a strange sort of a twist here, where Labour-in-Vain Hill comes snaking down to a stop against Thames Street. This meeting-place of three ways forms an odd corner of calm. Passers-by paused when they reached our crooked lane-end, as if to take stock, reconsider their journey and go on. The house itself was like a thousand others in the City: towering, steep-gabled, one rain-bleached oak beam balanced on another, cantilevered ever outwards over the road. This toppling effect, my mother said, served no other purpose but to ensure that when you threw your soil out of your bedchamber it did not end up in your parlour. Behind our windows were the dim, panelled rooms that custom demanded, a parlour and hall and even a small gallery, running along Bosse Lane towards the Thames. To me, returning from the wonders of the royal barge, home appeared a drab place, full of the greys and browns of pewter and kersey cloth, and the stink of tallow candles and rushlights. Pewter might have stood for our rank in life. The vast mass of people in London still ate their meals off trenchers of wood or earthenware; far above them, the gentry and nobility used silver. Pewter was for the well-to-do, the respected, the solid; those who stood high, but not too high. Even though we could have afforded to buy some silver vessels, my mother would not hear of it. 'Once you begin to ape the Court, there is no end to it. Let us keep the way we are.'

In the parlour after our plain supper, I used to question my parents on all the marvels that went into making royalty: where their treasures came from, what they cost, who brought them into England. My father rose to this, his face taking on a look of childlike delight. Sitting by the fire with the flames glinting off the oak panels, he would spin me tales of the furs and the satins that noblemen wore, the cloth of silver and gold and the fabulous dyestuffs, crimson, scarlet and indigo; the perfumes made out of the pungent musk-glands of the Indian civet cat, and the floating ambergris that is said to be the excretion of Leviathan. My mother regarded his stories with cold watchfulness. When my father was not there she beckoned me up to her, squatted down and instructed me. 'Remember this, Richard: never fall in love with your cargo.' I looked back at her defiantly. It seemed to me she might have added, 'Never fall in love at all.'

Already, in those days, my mother was a powerful woman. My father let her run a good deal of the business. He admitted freely she had more sense than he did, and her investments did well. But hers was a cold trade. 'Buy what you understand,' she was fond of saying. 'Buy what you know you can sell.' For her, all the wondrous things that she bought and squirrelled away in the warehouse were just so many ingenious routes towards profit. She enjoyed the chase, and the devious thrill of outskirting the other merchants by means of plans well judged and precisely laid, but in the end she reckoned up her happiness in marks of silver or Venetian ducats. That was her plan in life: to grow richer and even richer, and live all her life on Thames Street within sight and smell of the river.

Thomas resembled her, in character and in looks. He was dark-haired, with brows that frowned while he thought. The careful one, she called him, who always thought before he spoke. I was the quick one, the one with no head for book-learning; I was the dreamer of impractical dreams, with my lithe frame and thin face, and quick, sharp eyes the colour of off-green pebbles. 'Too quick,' my mother said, 'and too like your father.' Too quick to be seduced by the glitter of pretty things, she meant: too quick to desire, and doubtless in the future too quick to buy. A merchant must be slow.

But that was not the style of my father. His purchases were affairs of the heart. When I was eleven, he brought back a bag of Arabian pearls, which he gave me to play with. I remember rolling them about on a broad platter by the fireside, holding them up to see the way they shone in the yellow light of our candles, and then sorting them with tweezers by size.

'Pearls,' my mother frowned. 'Why pearls, in God's name?'

'I bought them because they sang to me,' was my father's reply.

They sang to me too. They spoke of a life beyond what I knew, and for which I was developing a vague but powerful longing.

3

As I grew older, I used to slip away whenever I might and steal northwards up Labour-in-Vain Hill to Cheapside. Here I was truly in a different world. The breadth and openness of the street, the stone paving, unlike most of the city which lay in its own filth, the houses that stood in their majesty like the sterns of great ships, the water conduit with its gilded statues of saints; at all these things I marvelled.

Here, on the corner of Bread Street, is that wondrous stand of houses known as Goldsmiths' Row. Four storeys high they rise, beautified all along the front with figures of wild woodmen riding on monstrous beasts, all richly painted and gilt. There were fourteen shops in all. At the centre of the Row, beneath the largest and fiercest of the woodmen, was the shop of the King's own goldsmith, Cornelius Heyes. He was a man of weight, received at Court with as much deference, so they said, as a great noble. There were others too, almost as grand: Christian Breakespere and Bartholomew Reade, and Morgan Wolf. They knew my family, of course. My father traded with them all, on occasion. Here I came to perch on a stool in a corner, and watch, and learn.

In a goldsmith's shop you are struck, first of all, by the light. The Row faces north, like a painter's studio, and the shelves inside the shops are draped in white cloths, so that there is always the same gentle radiance. Set against these cloths the gems glow, each with its own proper fire. On one shelf stand solitary stones in their purity, rubies and amethysts, garnets and sapphires, some exquisitely cut and polished, others virgin stones straight from the earth, rough like hailstones. On another shelf are rings and signets, threaded on wire or perched on silver stands made to look like the branches of trees. One wall holds crosses and reliquaries, and crystal tablets engraved with scenes of the saints, and the precious things that princes love: little crucifixes for rosaries, jewelled combs, tinderboxes, scent flasks, inkhorns, hourglasses, mirror frames and hawks' bells, all worked in gold and set with agate or enamel or mother of pearl. Higher up stand the great flagons and ewers of gold or silver gilt, gleaming down over the shop like suns, waiting to be presented to the King. I remember in the shop of Mr Cornelius a pair of gilt basins chased with beasts and dragons that weighed over six hundred ounces, and a vase of rock crystal graven with roses and crowns and the cipher of the King and Queen, H and K woven together, sprinkled across it in gold.

In the corners were other rarities: oliphants' teeth, branches of crimson coral, or the horn of a unicorn, garnished in gold. Further back squatted the brick furnace that purred always with a deep-throated fire, and the lapidary's wheel where the goldsmith sat like a potter, pedalling with one foot to polish his stones or grind them down into facets. Close to this, on the workbench, were little jars of pastes and emery powders, and the diamond-tipped rods with which he carved tiny intaglios or signets. Then there were the drills, from the great augers turned with two hands to the tiniest picks for drilling pearls; the pincers that likewise came in every conceivable size, the crucibles, the casting ladles and hammers, the miniature anvils, the moulds, the leather gauntlets and aprons stained black from use;

and high up the blocks of wax and the acids, the *aqua fortis* and *aqua stygia* used for engraving. Closer to the front of the shop was a broad table with richly carved legs, where the smith sat when he was expecting a customer. He would have his scales before him and the minute brass weights, the scruples and the drachms, the carats that are the hundred and forty-fourth part of an ounce, and the grain weights that are a quarter of that again and can only be lifted by tweezers.

What I most loved to see were the stones, in all their varied temperaments and tribes. I learnt the twelve types of the Emerald, with the Scythian at their head, that shines like new spring grass. I learnt of its kindred stones, the jasper and the blue-green beryl that must be cut in a six-sided figure if it is not to lose its brilliance. I learnt of the Diamond: the pure whites of Golconda, the blue stones and the green, and the fair, pointed stones of the Mahanadi River in Bengal. These will cut through armour. Yet if you hit them a blow with a hammer they shatter into shards too tiny to be seen. I learnt too of the cutting of their facets, the stone's eyes, as it were, through which you gaze down into its soul. The principal facet, where possible, will be a flat rectangle or table: the table-cut stone being everywhere the most prized. It has a dark brilliance and a mystery that the pyramid cut can never have. I studied the Ruby also, the great stones and the lesser that incline to the orange of the garnet and the jacinth. I learnt of Amethysts with their delicate peach-bloom shades, that are almost as valued as diamonds, and Sapphires, the true sky-blue, as well as the green, the yellow, the rose and the white.

I studied too their faults and diseases. Some stones are shadowed and opaque; others are washed and pale; others again they call clouded, when there is a whiteness or mist that hovers in the stone's outer regions, even though its heart may be clear and true. Other stones are discoloured, or split, or stained by some alien vein of metal. Again and again I was told that a goldsmith must never show pity for these marred and maimed stones. He must be as ruthless in culling imperfection as anyone else who aspires to the favour of kings.

But it was from Morgan Wolf that I learnt the most. He taught me the tricks jewellers use to improve upon nature; how, if you steep a dull ruby in vinegar for fourteen days it will regain its fire just long enough for it to be sold. He showed me how plain rock crystal can be treated with indigo to make a counterfeit sapphire, and how to set a diamond with a dab of paint beneath to make it shine with any colour you please. He showed me the various foils made of copper, silver or gold, with which the gems' settings were lined. These foils could be tinted, if you hung them in the smoke of burning cloth, or brightly coloured feathers. And so I shall give you this advice: if you have a dead parrot, sell it to a dishonest goldsmith. He will buy it, and give you a good price too. Wolf even kept a wicker cage of pigeons in the back of his shop, and when he had a pearl that had turned old and blind he would coax one of the birds into eating it, and retrieve it the next day from the ordure, bright and restored to youth. But there was always a falseness about these impostures, and in time I learnt to detect them all.

As I sat in the corner of Breakespere's or Wolf's shop with my head resting on my arm, my mind drifted into the future. I knew the life of a goldsmith was not for me. I could not have borne those hours of labour sitting at a workbench on Cheapside, or waiting at the counter for a customer like a spider watching for a fly. No, I decided: I would be a voyager, a prince among merchants. But I would not be selling my goods on Thames Street. I saw myself instead travelling up the river, perhaps in one of those same gilded barges I loved to gaze on, to Westminster Palace or Richmond, alighting at the fabled landing-places with their flags and golden dragons set on poles, and ushered inside, where royalty would await. Such were my dreams. I told no one about them; certainly not my mother.

* * *

The years were passing. Our band of three sat on the highest form in the schoolroom on Old Fish Street, where we learnt the rudiments of Latin, arithmetic and accounting from a wiry young Franciscan. Dust motes swirled in the light from the dirty windows and water gurgled in the lead cistern outside. For six years we had sat there each morning, stifling hot in summer and cold in winter, with the little charcoal brazier in the midst of the room. There were some twenty-five of us, sons of the stockfish traders and other merchants of Thames Street. I yearned to be gone; but I set myself to learn what I thought I needed for the life before me. Numbers were dull beasts in themselves, but when used to reckon up ducats into crowns or for counting profits they acquired a keen interest. Latin, the language of legal contracts, ambassadors and churchmen, I mastered as well as I might; though often, when I should have been committing some verse or other to memory, my mind was drifting restlessly north to Cheapside, and the wonders I would see there later that afternoon.

'I shall beat you,' murmured our master, his voice lowered as if in awe of the punishment he was about to mete out. But he never wielded the rod himself. Instead, he handed us over to a sinewy usher who had an arrow scar on his cheek from the Battle of Flodden some seven years before. Between blows, the Franciscan repeated the verses he was trying, through the medium of pain, to force into us.

'*O dulces,*' he whispered, with tears in his eyes at the beauty of the words. His deputy lifted the rod over my waiting hand. Whack! '... *comitum* ...' Whack! '... *valete coetus.*'

I went home often with red lines on my palm; but pain meant little to me. I was waiting my time. Thomas, the bright star and our mother's darling, always knew the answers. Though a year younger, he had rapidly moved up to join John and me. Miriam Dansey never spoke of him as a future merchant. No, it was the Church for Thomas, and high promotion in it, if she knew anything at all. She had marked him down as the King's chancellor, or at least a great bishop.

As we made our way home, the three of us, the boys from the other, more prestigious schools used to lie in wait for us. These were the scholars of Saint Paul's and Saint Anthony's: pigeons of Paul's and Anthony hogs we called them, after the birds on the great cathedral, and the pigs that wandered everywhere about London, snuffling up scraps until they were slaughtered by the prior of Saint Anthony's for his own and his brethren's enjoyment. These proud boys used to surround us, them in their black velvet gowns as if they were clerks or king's councillors already. They gave us the traditional challenge, *'Placetne disputare?'* Will you dispute? And Thomas, with the light of battle in his eye, replied, *'Placet.'* We trooped all together into the nearest churchyard and perched on the tombs. I can picture Thomas, his thin body straight, tongue licking his teeth, waiting to hear what his enemies would throw down for debate. It might be, 'Whether a hundred petty sins are as damnable as one great one', 'Whether even Lucifer can be saved', 'Whether it is too late for the dead to repent'. He could prove anything, in his schoolboy Latin that became more fluent year by year. His opponents gradually lost their tempers, until it became a battle of satchels and heavy books, and even sticks and stones. Then John and I waded into the fight, and Thomas swung his satchel with a fury that made up for his lack of strength, until the three of us won clear, bruised but triumphant.

Our band still roamed the streets of London, but our interests had changed. We were in love, all three of us, with a certain girl who used to watch from the window of a grand, stone-built mansion on the corner of Bosse Lane, just up the street. Her dark gaze would dart up and down Thames Street as she brushed back a wisp of black hair under her hood, as if she too were restless, and looking for something that was still beyond her sight. We did not know her name, but she looked to be of an age with us, about fourteen. She came from that world I so longed for. The pearls at her throat, the ruby brooch and the silver thread in her gown all proclaimed it, even without the languid ease of her movements and the way she laughed at us and called to her sister, a sharp-eyed little ten-year-old, to come and watch our antics. Plodding home from school we used to throw our satchels down in the street, bow and kiss our hands, whoop and cut capers.

'Sweet sugar sucket, come down!'

'Dance with us!'

'Be my bride!

In response, she would rest her chin elegantly on one hand and smile. Once she even rewarded John with a suggestive pout of her lips, and a finger run along the edge of her bodice and up round her throat. I found a way to climb the sheer face of that house, clinging to the barely projecting stones with fingers and toes, and pulled myself up to her window. Perching there like some strange bird, not two feet away from the soft and suddenly surprised face of the girl, I had not a notion what I ought to do. But with the other two staring up at me, there was no question I had to do something. What a mass of ill-formed scrags of wooing I spun out of my brain! I took her hand and counted off her fingers, this one pretty, that one a little too fat, oh, but that one, I die for it! She drew back her hand and laughed. 'Oh, Susan,' she called through the open door behind her, 'come and listen! This boy is actually trying to woo me!' I was a game to her, a petty amusement, like a lapdog or a juggler. I burned with anger and shame then. If she could only see what I longed to be, and not what I was, a tradesman's son, a schoolboy, one born and bred to the stink of the Thames.

'The Devil carry you off, Richard Dansey,' yelled John from below. He tried to jump and follow me up the wall, but he was too heavy and slid back down again. That recalled my courage. In John's eyes, at least, I was a conqueror. I swung myself forward, and before the girl knew what I was doing, I kissed her loudly on the lips so that John and the rest could see. She drew back with a frown: I had gone too far. Then I lowered myself carefully back down, leaping the last

27

six feet or so. Thomas whooped and slapped me on the back, but John threw himself at me, punching me and knocking me down, so that in an instant we were rolling together in the filth at the far edge of the street. When we pulled ourselves upright to stand glaring at one another, both our faces were bleeding.

'I will win her,' John promised.

'Not while I live,' I replied.

We stood still, wary in case the other made a fresh attack. Then John laughed and held out his hand. 'We'll not let a girl come between us.' He was right. His friendship mattered; though often, as now, our rivalry almost outran it. Slowly I took the offered hand. He nudged me with a mocking gleam in his eye and whispered, 'But I will win her.'

Then we heard the bolts drawn back from the great gate under her window, and the growling of a servant, and we ran off together down the street, laughing and pushing one another. I felt elated at my triumph with the girl, and the dangerous thrill of running so close to losing John's friendship.

For months in the summer we would trudge down dusty Thames Street to stand under her window and find it empty and fastened shut. Only the curmudgeonly servant was left, sweeping the cobbles clean before the great gate. Thomas one day approached him, offered him some coins, stood talking a few moments and then came back to us.

'Her name is Hannah Cage,' he reported. 'Her father is Stephen Cage, a great courtier, with a castle in Kent. The family is off with the King on his country progress: Eltham Palace, Greenwich, Richmond.'

We heard the news in silence. I felt a void open up inside me. There it was again, brutally plain: that gulf between what I wished to be, and what I was. Well, the girl was out of my sphere, and best forgotten.

As we went brooding round London that sweltering summer, John one evening led us past the bath-house on Stew Lane. We stopped and looked up at its brick chimney and mysteriously shuttered windows.

'You dare not take a shilling to the bath-house and buy a night of pleasure,' John challenged me.

My heart began beating hard. The girl might be gone, but I would have my first taste of woman. 'By God, I do,' I replied.

'Together, then? Tonight?'

After dark I slipped from the house and met John at the end of Stew Lane. Fog lay on the river. Lights shone from chinks in the shuttered windows of the bath-house, but all the rest of the waterfront was dark. We handed in our shillings at the door to a smiling old woman with just two teeth, who told us to undress and pass through the curtain. Together we advanced naked across a rush-strewn floor into a cloud of hot steam. All along the walls, in curtained cubicles, were the individual baths, from which came the sound of splashes and laughter. I imagined myself in some fantastic castle out of a romance, where a noble damsel who was the image of Hannah Cage waited for me. I began to tremble with expectation. John, looking at me, winked, and stepped aside into a cubicle. I parted a curtain, stepped into another and climbed into the bath. As I lay back in the warm water, a girl slipped in beside me. She was large, a rounded heap of breasts and thighs that astonished me. She clambered quickly athwart me, red-faced and flaxen-haired, and I braced myself for the exquisiteness of my first taste of pleasure. But lord, she was heavy. As she plunged and gasped I had to fight for my breath, and, instead of being free to explore those unfamiliar reaches of female flesh with my hands, I found I had to grasp both edges of the bath to stop myself from going under. She brought me quickly to my fulfilment, and rolled off with a sigh and a tremendous splash of water. I lay half-submerged, panting. Before I could even think of a new caress the girl leant over the edge of the bath, waved an arm through the curtain and shouted, 'Sally! We're done here. Have that ale and pie for me by the time I'm dry, or I'll baste you.'

I dressed in anger. Even her sigh, I thought, had been a mark of boredom, not of pleasure. Almost I wished I had saved myself. Was this all that women were? No, I knew for sure they were not. As I came out I met John. He too looked disturbed. But he said, 'Choice and dainty. Yours?'

I turned my face into the shadows. 'Paradise.'

It seemed our life at that time would never change; but its end was hurtling upon us. One November, my father returned from one of his long, wandering voyages along with William Marshe. William was tall, droop-shouldered, with long greying moustaches. He had accompanied my father on his ventures for years. They used to come back with wonderfully unpredictable cargoes. On this occasion they unloaded saffron, velvets and the sweet Spanish wine called *vino de saco*, or sack. These, I gathered, had been Mr William's choices. My father boasted of his own share: casks of nutmegs; indigo for dyeing that was dried and powdered and pressed into dark blue cakes; and seventeen small sacks of pepper. I followed him to the spicers' shops on Coneyhope Lane, beyond Cheapside in behind the old Jewry, with a couple of hired packhorses carrying our barrels of goods. 'Foreign lands,' my father called these streets. We were far from the smell of the river. Noblemen's chamberlains and stewards came here to order spices for the great households. The shopmen always had a welcome for my father. With his round, boyish face alight with the excitement of his wares, he sat himself down and told them stories of far-off ports they would never see. He pictured for them the golden light of the sunset in Lisbon, the ships at Antwerp as they came in up the river with the tide, and the lighthouse and bay at Genoa, where in the late spring the coral fishers put out for Corsica in their light, fast skiffs, two hundred at a time. I sat entranced. I promised myself that before many years were out I would see those places for myself.

When he had finished talking, my father displayed his merchandise. The shopmen offered him the best prices they could, but as usual it was not enough. He would take the shopman's hands in his and say solemnly, 'My friend. And so you truly cannot find it in your heart to offer me more?' Then he would sigh and move on to try the next shop, and the next. In the end he smiled and shrugged, and sold his goods for what he could. As we turned down on to Cheapside, opposite Goldsmiths' Row, he reached inside his doublet and pulled out a small leather pouch.

'All is not lost, my Richard. I have one more sale to make.' He loosened the strings and showed me three pale green stones. 'Persian emeralds,' he whispered. 'From a Maltese I met in Naples.' He crossed the road to the shop of Christian Breakespere and went inside. I followed him. He tipped the stones out on the table with a grand flourish. In that first instant I could see that something was wrong. They sent out their beams too easily, barely staining the cloth with a pallid, even glare. Their sheen was all of it on the surface, and not in the depths. The old goldsmith peered forward. He liked my father. But he frowned and shook his head.

I could have wept with frustration. I snatched up one of the stones. Even its touch was wrong. It warmed swiftly in my hand, instead of keeping that coolness which they say makes emeralds a sure charm against fevers. I held it up to my father. 'Do you want to see how far this is from being an emerald? Do you?' I crossed to the lapidary's wheel at the back of the shop, set it running with the footpedal, and held the stone against it using the smallest of the iron tongs. Instead of enduring the touch of the emery, and gaining from it a new perfection and depth, this stone shattered at once into powder.

'Glass,' I commented. 'Beautiful green glass.'

My father went stumping off back to Thames Street, singing below his breath. I followed, angry, and pained for him too. Any man in the world, I thought, could have told the difference between those pebbles and the real thing. In the counting house he entered his sales in the ledger with perfect calmness: *Emeralds. Bought, £38.9s.6d. Sold, £0.0s.0d.* It was his worst calamity yet. The nutmeg, indigo and pepper sold for little more than he had paid. Mr William's saffron made something, but the costs of hiring ships, of inns and port fees and commissions, took up most of it.

Then there was my mother to face. 'You are a madman, a madman,' she screamed, aiming slaps at his face, which my father dodged with a sheepish smile. 'Will you believe everything you are told? Are you an infant? Buy what you hate, not what you think you love. Then you will not be deceived.'

My father never replied to her tirades. But I knew the loss had hit him hard. Some days later he took to his bed. He was trembling, pale and in a sweat, though he promised us there was nothing wrong, nothing at all. The doctor declared he was suffering from a too thick crowding of the humours on his brain. He slid a lancet into his arm, drew off a good half-pint of blood, and prescribed a course of vomits and a purge of rhubarb and brimstone. For weeks his sickness ebbed and flowed. Sometimes it appeared to leave him, and he got up and went back to the counting house, where he prowled around, talking to himself, throwing out fresh ideas for ventures. But after a few days the fever always returned, and after each attack there was less of him. By the start of Lent it was plain he would never rise from his bed.

'One more voyage,' he whispered, as he lay in the dusky chamber that looked out towards Labour-in-Vain Hill. 'Just one more, and I could still have my triumph.' He looked up at us with a smile of fever-ish elation, as if the great venture that had always eluded him was at last within reach. After that he slipped into rambling murmurs and sudden cries which no one could understand. A month later he was buried in the little churchyard of Saint Mary Summerset, almost facing our door. We stood in line by the graveside, and then left the chantry priest to say a Mass for my father's soul.

When we returned home, my mother beckoned Thomas and me to follow her, and William Marshe fell in behind us. None of us knew what would become of the business. I had heard it whispered that Mr William had mortgaged his warehouse to lend money to my father. She led us, unspeaking, down the narrow alley to Broken Wharf. Our footsteps echoed harshly as we trooped in procession between the warehouse's hidden treasures, and climbed the wooden staircase that led up to the counting house. This was a room that stretched along the whole of the southern end of the warehouse, with a long rank of diamond-glazed windows like the great cabin of a ship, looking out over Broken Wharf and the wash and gurgle of the Thames.

On the left was the brick hearth, the fire unlit. Shadows clung round the shelves bearing the company's ledgers, with their page ends turned outwards and the different dates and ventures inked across the body of their pages: *Lisbon Receipts, 1519 to 1523*; *Ventures in Spice*; *Tolls and Imposts – Imperial*; *Customs and Subsidies of the Port of London*. Once we were all inside, my mother seated herself for the first time in the high-backed chair that had been my father's, with her hands spread across the broad, polished surface of the oak table.

'My husband has made me his heir,' she told us. 'There are small bequests for Richard and for Thomas.' We looked at one another. Many women, on inheriting their husbands' affairs, sell them quick, or hand them over to some agent to manage; especially if those affairs were in as tottering a condition as we supposed ours must be. But we did not reckon with my mother.

'Martin!' she called. Into the room came Martin Deller, broad-shouldered, most trusted of the various strong-armed watchmen who guarded the warehouse. He had been in the family's employ for years. I had seen him, in the dusk and early dawn, prowling the wharves without a lantern, moving with surprising stealth. I knew my mother relied on him absolutely. He carried with him a small chest, covered in red-and-white striped velvet, that had stood at the foot of my mother's bed. I had never seen it opened, but had always supposed it contained lace collars or hoods, or stuff of that sort. Martin set it down heavily next to the table. My mother unlocked it and threw it open. It was filled with gold, bills and bonds: the proceeds of her many half-secret ventures. She looked from me to Thomas to William Marshe, and said, 'The way we do business is about to change. We are going to buy a ship.'

Her plans, it seemed, had been laid well in advance; she had even picked out a vessel. The *Rose* was a great ship of some seventy tons. She carried a crew of forty mariners, whom we would have to recruit from the waterside taverns of the City, and had a pair of brass falconets against pirates, as well as a murderer, a light swivel-gun that could clear the decks if she were boarded. Next day William inspected her where she lay downriver, and declared her tight and well-bowed: 'With a good wind, she will truly cut a feather.' My mother nodded in satisfaction. She trusted William, as she had never trusted my father. And so the papers were signed, and bills of exchange handed over. She became ours in the spring of 1521, just before I turned sixteen. A few weeks later, my mother called me into the counting house. She sat stroking her chin with the feather end of a pen. It still surprised me to see her there. My father had been dead for only three months, but already she had transformed herself into that cool and independent business machine, the Widow of Thames Street.

She looked me up and down with a smile: the kind of smile she wore when she was appraising an enterprise which had so far turned out neither well nor ill. From outside the window could be heard the clunk of a ferryman's oars, the whistling of some of our men moving about the wharf, and the suck and wash of the river.

'Richard,' she said at last, 'your schooling is at an end. At the month's close I am sending you to Lisbon, with Mr William. On a venture.' My heart jumped. This was it: the beginning, the first opening of the door. I knew, of course, that this would be her kind of venture, and not mine, and that William would be in charge; but that did not daunt me. I had my plans. And with my small inheritance, I was ready to begin to put them into action.

On a summer's afternoon Thomas, John and I left the schoolroom and walked in silence down Labour-in-Vain Hill together for the last time. At the angle in the lanes outside our door we stopped, and all three of us clasped hands. I had always thought of this crossroads as a place where different ways met. Now I saw it as a place where they parted. Thomas repeated the Latin verse our master was so fond of:

'O dulces comitum valete coetus,
longe quos simul a domo profectos
diversae variae viae reportant.'

John rolled his eyes, and did a good imitation of our master's thin, sharp voice, that for all its severity could be strangely sentimental. 'You are ignorant, and I shall beat you. The sense is: "Sweet band of friends, farewell. Together we set out from our far home, but many diverse roads lead us back."'

Thomas nodded with gravity, and clasped our hands more tightly.

'Swear,' he said. 'Swear that whatever roads lead us apart, one day we shall meet again.'

John laughed, and I did too. To us it was a curious oath. True, John was about to begin a life of voyaging as I was, following his father's ventures into the Low Countries and the Baltic in search of timber and salt. But doubtless our future would have in it many meetings. Why should it not? Thomas, however, was serious.

'Swear. By the Holy Virgin, we shall meet again.'

We each repeated the words. I let my hand fall from theirs and turned away. My mother had asked me to meet her in the counting house the moment I came home, to receive her detailed instructions for the voyage. A new life lay before me, and I swore an oath of my own: that I would snatch the chances offered to me, and turn them to my own ends.

4

Six weeks later I was standing in the steerage house on board the *Rose* as we passed the yellow stone fort and the monastery of Belém on the approach to the Roads of Lisbon. It was a hazy evening. The ship glided into harbour slowly, while I gazed ahead in excitement.

At my side stood Mr William. At sea, he had revealed a different side to himself. He was no longer the rather bedraggled tame dog who followed my mother round and took orders from the House of Dansey. With every mile we drew away from London, he stood a little taller. I saw that he understood gunnery and navigation, how to plot a course and calculate a latitude with the astrolabe, as well as possessing a fair grasp of the curiously pleasing Portuguese tongue. All these things I set myself to learn.

When we landed, William left the ship's master to unload the woollen stuffs we were bound to carry on the outward run, and set off like a hound, sniffing round the merchants' offices in the lanes behind the great market square that fronted the harbour, asking questions and greeting old friends. I saw one man after another shake his head and cross himself on hearing of Roger Dansey's death. William patted them on the arm, nodded at the news he was receiving in return, and moved on. I saw in his strategy something of my father's charm, his absolute attentiveness to the man he was speaking to, that made each one feel he was the most favoured being in the world. I was determined to watch Mr William's methods closely, and learn fast.

These were the days of Portugal's pride: King John the Pious, better known as Spicer John, was sending his trading ships round Africa to the Indies. There they dealt in nutmeg from the Moluccas, pepper from Serendip, ginger and cinnamon from India. The Portuguese were cutting the Arabs and Turks out of this trade altogether. They had burnt the city of Aden to the ground, and William told me that Cairo and Venice were both feeling the pain. The government's Casa da Índia held a monopoly on every peppercorn and cinnamon stick in Lisbon, and they set their prices as high as they pleased. But, William explained, there were certain dark dens where goods came to rest that had slipped off ships unknown to the King's Customs; all it took was a little ingenuity and boldness to find them.

Where William went, I followed. He led me through coiling streets as narrow as any in London, where dogs ran out into blinding sunlight and then back into opaque shadow, and women called out their wares: wine and honey, almonds, figs, fishing nets and twine. We stepped inside a Moorish courtyard ornamented with round brick arches, and a fountain playing in its middle.

'It was your father discovered this place,' William whispered to me, 'and he was the one talked to them until they trusted us. Never think ill of him, Richard. You know he used to say it is not the profit that counts, but how you make it. Your mother thinks I am a cleverer merchant than he was. But if Roger Dansey had never made his losses, I could not have made my profits.'

I pictured them together. I imagined my father, with his quick imagination, his charm and his thirst for wonders, penetrating into every crevice of these lanes. I liked to think of him snatching the best bargains from under the noses of the competition. But I suspected that Mr William had been propping the business up for years; that without his sense, my father would have brought home many more of his profitless cargoes.

While a servant poured us wine, William negotiated with a lean, dark-faced Moor concerning two bushels of cinnamon and one of cloves. He came away rubbing his hands in satisfaction. 'Done! We shall come back with our men to fetch them after dark. True cloves come from only two islands in the world, my boy. We were lucky to find them at the price, excellently lucky.' He stretched. 'A good day's business.' He patted his chest, and looked at me with a glint in his eye. 'Now, my dear boy, it is time we found a brothel.'

I started involuntarily: this animated, cheerful figure was so far from the Mr William I knew at home. With his arm about my shoulder he guided me through yet more alleys to a low doorway which he appeared to know well. I wondered if my father, too, had visited this place. Inside we had our choice between six or seven ageing whores, tricked out as shepherdesses or heathen goddesses, each one clutching a wooden lyre or a milkmaid's pail, as a badge of sophistication or innocence.

'Is this not fine?' William asked, as we climbed the stairs with our arms around our chosen nymphs. 'You must learn to enjoy the sweets of travel, my Richard, as well as suffering the pains. Richard, allow me to introduce you to Woman.' Then, as we slipped together into a darkened room, he murmured, 'Only promise me one thing: never, never tell your mother.'

I did not tell him that John and I had already explored the bath-house on Stew Lane. The whores of Lisbon were in much the same mould, and left me displeased and brooding, wishing to go back and begin again, yet knowing that the next time would be no better than the last. On the couch next to mine, William lay back with a sigh. He was entirely satisfied. The present, with its simple pleasures, delighted him. I rolled over, and felt my purse beneath me. It had in it sixty crowns: all the inheritance that had become mine on the death of my father. I was itching to break free from Mr William and begin to spend. But it would not be easy. He had kept me close every moment, and what I planned would have to be done in secret. No breath of it must get back to my mother: not yet.

The following day we were back in the alleys. William turned to me at a street corner and told me his next associate was of a wary turn of mind, and it was better if he visited him alone: could I forgive him if he left me for an hour or two? My heart jumped. I watched him out of sight and set off swiftly by myself. I knew exactly where I was headed. While following loyally on William's heels, I had kept my eyes open. First I went to a money-changer down on the quayside, and turned in my crowns for Portuguese cruzados. Then I plunged back into the lanes and made for a certain small shop we had passed the day before, in the shadow of the vast, fortress-like Cathedral. I went in. There, just the same as on Cheapside, were the shelves with their white cloths and the ranks of gems that gleamed in the brilliant southern light, fresh in from the Indies, from Burma and Serendip and Bengal. As I looked along them, holding this stone or that up to the sun, I felt the thrill of a deep passion for beauty satisfied. I saw diamonds. I saw Oriental rubies, Persian emeralds and pearls. But I could not yet venture that high. I forced myself to look instead at the lesser stones, the beryls and cats' eyes and cornelians. These stones were within my grasp; but even here it would be prudent not to lay out all my money at once. Buy modestly, and risk little the first time. So spoke my mother's voice within me. But my eyes strayed upwards again to the shelf with the nobler gemstones on it, and fixed on a topaz, of a perfect sunshine colour, without a cloud. The shopman showed me its weight, eight carats, a good size. It was of Ethiopia, I was almost certain: home to the best of this kind of gem. A topaz is almost diamond-hard, and brilliant. If you put it in the fire to leach its colour out, it will make as close an approach to an Indian diamond as you will find. But this stone had no need of adulteration. To my eye, it already surpassed a lesser diamond in beauty. Its price stood at a hundred cruzados: I had a mere seventy-one. I began to bargain. I was stern, then teasing; I lifted the topaz and frowned, pretending to see a flaw, then turned and walked away; but I came back. Some of these tricks I had seen William perform; others welled up naturally, leaving me both excited and alarmed. The shopman's offer came down to ninety, then eighty, then seventy. My palms were sweating. I could buy it. But that would be the end of my inheritance: more than twelve pounds sterling, perhaps eighteen months' salary for a poor priest or a clerk. If I was wrong, I would never see that money again. I knew in that instant that my life could branch in two ways. One way led to safety, ease, and dullness. The other would lead to danger and worries and, yes, if I had enough luck and skill, my heart's deepest desires. I also knew that if I quailed at the risk now, I would never again buy a single stone. I nodded quickly, and counted out the gold.

I was in an agony of expectation until William could complete his buying. He bought furtively and cheap: and that meant he bought slowly. A cask of saffron here, three crates of pepper there. A month passed before the *Rose*'s holds were sealed and we put out once more, and heard the chanting of the Hieronymites in their monastery die away on the breeze as we turned our prow out to sea.

Back home in London I lost no time before taking my topaz to Christian Breakespere. It was of a shade I thought would please him; his shop always had in it a good number of stones with the shades of autumn sun, yellow opals, garnets, amber. The old man lifted the stone in his tweezers and held it to the light so that it took fire, and stained his hand with gold. Then he lowered it and looked at me with his gentle smile.

'A fine stone. Of its kind, very fine. Shall we say sixty crowns?'

I held his gaze. 'I had thought eighty.'

'Had you?' His eyes twinkled. 'Then we had better say seventy. Done?'

'Done.'

'See that you go on as you have begun, young Richard. Do not disappoint me.'

I took the payment there and then, in gold. My profit was ten crowns, but it felt to me like a thousand. I ran whooping back home down Labour-in-Vain Hill and round the corner of the churchyard, the bag of gold clinking in my hand. Then I pulled myself in. It would not do to give away my secret too soon. There was a long road ahead of me first.

On our next voyage William and I went further, southward and round into the Mediterranean. In Barcelona I acquired the small steel casket with its cunning lock and slender chain, which I used, from then on, for my purchases. In Toulon I bought a sardonyx, in Genoa a lesser opal. The time after that we coasted down Italy, to Ostia and then Naples, and I added some jacinths and a small, pale amethyst. Nothing I bought was of the rarest or most prized. But I used my eyes, and always when I carried my purchases back to Goldsmiths' Row I made a profit.

Two years passed. My mother's grip on the business grew. She hired more agents, and sent out fresh ventures. On every ship that left London, it seemed, she had paid for a corner in the hold and was sending out wool or hemp, with instructions to fetch back some carefully chosen commodity in return. An air of excitement hung about Broken Wharf. Our men moved with quickened steps, as if aware they were part of an enterprise that was pulsing with new life. I often thought how my father would have liked to see the firm of Dansey in its new condition, and to set in train that last great venture of which he had dreamt.

On my return home, the first thing I did was to go to the school-room to wait for Thomas. He had opted to remain with the master there, reading deeper and deeper into works of theology and canon law. My mother spoke of him with pride. He had distinguished himself in the annual disputations held in the churchyard of the priory at Smithfield, where all the schools of London competed. Many great men had risen from those contests, Sir Thomas More among them. All that was needed was for Thomas to catch the eye of some man of rank, for nothing was possible without a patron. As we walked together along the familiar route down Old Fish Street past the market, where the gutters were clogged with fish guts and blood, Thomas told me about the plans our mother had formed for him.

'Uncle Bennet, she says, is the best hope. You know that the Cardinal is at work founding a college?'

Our mother's brother, Bennet Waterman, a city lawyer with a beaming face and bald head, and a devilish air of guile, had recently joined the employ of the great Cardinal Wolsey, proudest and most powerful man in the land after the King. Wolsey had need of Bennet's services. He was proposing to liquidate a number of lesser monasteries to fund the largest foundation Oxford had ever seen, to be known as Cardinal College.

'And you are to be one of its first scholars?' I asked. 'That should be pleasing to you.'

Thomas did not answer. That was the first hint, I think, that my brother smarted just as much under our mother's domination as I did. But we were not yet ready to work as allies. That is the worst of tyranny: it divides its subjects. Instead of taking the quick way home, Thomas led me down Labour-in-Vain Hill. Just on the corner, a figure came out from the shadows. It was John. I ran to embrace him; but his air was subdued, just like Thomas's. Soon after my first voyage to Lisbon he had embarked on his family's great ship, *Lazarus*, for Germany and the Baltic, trading in the commodities that had made his father wealthy: tar and pitch, clapboard, iron and salt. Since then I had seen him only a few times.

I said, 'So the band is all together again.'

Thomas gave a wry laugh. 'Is it?'

He was right. Though we were all three present, we were not the same band who had joined hands and sworn our oath in the meeting of the ways two years before. But this was hardly my fault. I sensed there was a kind of shared and obstinate secrecy between my old friend and my brother. I did not know how to break it, and I began to grow annoyed. At the foot of the hill where the lane met Thames Street, Thomas and John turned right instead of bearing left for our two houses. I let them lead the way. In a few paces we found ourselves below the window where we had called and sung to the bewitching Hannah Cage. We stopped. The window was dark, and tight shut. Thomas and John both gazed up at it for a few moments. Then John said, 'She isn't there.'

'You are not still haunting that girl?' I asked with a laugh. I had not been down that way in a long time. Not that I had forgotten Hannah: I still stung from her mocking laughter. I meant to set myself up in the world before approaching that kind of girl again. Still, I resented the way Thomas and John had been looking for her without me. 'You surprise me,' I teased. 'What mysterious men you are growing into.' But neither of them smiled. The friendship that had come to us so easily seemed far out of reach. I was certain John could not be happy, plying the family trade he had always despised. Thomas's malaise I understood less. He had always been private, content with himself and his books, bursting out only in his disputations with wild and quick displays of wit and learning. We walked back along Thames Street as a cold wind blew up from the river. Dusk was not far off. I said, 'Come with me. To the warehouse: for the sake of old times.'

They followed me on to Broken Wharf. At the door to the warehouse we passed Martin Deller, sitting on a barrel with his wooden cudgel across his knee, keeping watch on the comings and goings of the wharf. He watched us through half-lidded eyes, and nodded. We stepped inside the old, familiar dimness, heavy with mingled scents, cinnamon, cloves, pepper. Thomas said, 'And what of you and your trade?'

I still had not dared reveal my new trade to my mother; and that meant it was not safe to tell Thomas or John either. Instead I spoke to them of the alleys and courts of Lisbon, the wonderful bargains we struck, Mr William's skill in trade, my own attentiveness and submission. I knew what I was telling them must sound vague and only half-truthful. It was the story of Mr William, not of myself. Thomas knew well enough that I dreamt of dealing in gems, though I had rarely spoken of it. I tapped the cases in irritation. I ached to tell them everything: the stash of gemstones that even now rested in the little casket, locked in the chest in my chamber, the bag of gold and silver that nestled by its side. Thomas and John were walking on together down one of the dim corridors between stacks of barrels. The sense of isolation was dreadful. I called out to them.

'Wait! I have something to show you.' I ran back out, round the corner into the house and up to my chamber overlooking Bosse Lane and the cracked stone court of Terra Incognita. Breathless, back with them, I opened my casket and set out on a barrel head the small hoard of stones I had brought back with me from my latest voyage. William and I had ranged as far as Naples, where I had acquired a batch of large citrines, showy things that the goldsmiths loved to carve; then there were a couple of Arabian rock crystals, six-pointed, and four or five brilliant red cornelians. John whistled. Thomas reached out a hand to cover the stones, and peered over his shoulder.

'Our mother will kill you if she finds out.'

'But you are not really making money?' John pressed me. His face wore the old, challenging smile, that had a good tinge in it of envy. In reply I set before them my purse, heavy with coins that had all grown out of that first sixty crowns.

'We shall never tell,' Thomas said. 'Now, put them away.'

I tossed a cornelian up in the air. 'Why should I? What makes you so afraid?'

Thomas looked at me. 'You have spent too long off with the seagulls, dear brother. You forget how things are, back here on dry land.'

'Well, and how are they?' I was beginning to be angry.

Thomas stood up. 'Come with me, and you will see.' I gathered the stones reluctantly back into the casket and followed him, down to the darkest end of the warehouse. We passed the various goods Mr William had bought on our last venture, the Lisbon spices, the French woad that was a cheap equivalent to indigo, the Turkish rugs. At the far end Thomas stopped at a case I did not recognise, marked in a curling hand, 'Damascus silk'. I had heard of no such thing coming in. Nothing of the kind would be carried by our other agents, who worked the shorter routes to Flanders, and I was certain it had not been in the holds of the *Rose*. I kicked the case: it was heavy. I turned to the others.

'So it is the old game. Is Thomas daring us to have a look? Shall we?'

I drew out my knife, and John, with a sombre smile, did the same. We worked away at the lid, casting glances back towards the door, where Martin still sat. At last it sprang clear. Inside were a few folds of crimson fabric, but underneath lay something hard. John pulled back the silks to reveal stacks and stacks of books, bound in pale new leather. I stared at them in surprise. The firm of Dansey had never dealt in such things. Books ranked among the goods my mother regarded as poor investments, like gems. And what book could be worth the trouble of bringing from overseas? John picked one up and opened it. The titlepage was covered in strange swirls of foliage. At its foot was a crucifix: but in place of Christ, there was a serpent twining up the cross, and on its head sat the Pope's triple crown. Thomas said, 'Well? Have you forgotten your Latin so soon? Or is it too dark for you? Darkness is best for such things, I promise you.

This is *On the Babylonish Captivity of the Church*. And the author is Martin Luther.' John dropped it as if he had been stung.

To be caught merely opening such a book meant arrest, imprisonment in the Lollards' Tower by Saint Paul's where the heretics go, interrogation by the Cardinal; excommunication and death at the stake. Rumours ran round of the fearsome contents of these books, of the fiery rhetoric that smashed down all you thought was sure. They said that if you once read a book of Luther you would never be the same again. We stood for some moments, staring down at them. Then I reached out my hand, touched the leather of the fallen book and picked it up. The others watched me intently. I flicked beyond the serpent on the cross, and read as quickly as my Latin allowed, jumping from page to page. The Pope was portrayed as a ruthless huntsman, demon of tyranny and avarice, the greedy shopkeeper who released souls from Purgatory for gold. I saw the powers of the priests one by one refuted. There was no such thing as the Last Rites. The priests had invented it for profit, twisting the meaning of an apocryphal verse. Priestcraft has no power to conjure the blood and body of Christ into the sacrament; the Communion is an act of Faith, and no mere Work of man. Confession too had to be Faith, not Work; the task the priests set us, contrition for all our sins, is impossible; our sins are so great, so far beyond the reach of our memories and minds. Even the best works of our lives, of which we are proudest, will turn out on examination to be terrible sins. None of the tyrannical ceremonies of a rotten Church can save us; only Faith, Faith, Faith. I read on, amazed, until Thomas struck the book from my hands.

'That is enough. Now do you see?'

I was beginning to. My mother had no love of Luther, I was sure. But there were many in London who would pay handsomely for those books, and few who dared bring them into the country from Germany where they were printed. The profit for her in that deadly case of books was large and certain: always provided she did not get caught. It was a sign of just how confident she was in her own power, and how far she was prepared to take her policy of ruthless and finely judged risk.

Thomas put the lid in place and began forcing the nails back in with the haft of his little knife.

'You think you can simply strike off on some trade of your own?' he hissed. 'She is the one who decides what is bought and sold. She chooses the risks, and takes them. What will you do if she cuts you off? I promise you, she'll do it.'

'What makes you so sure of that?'

Thomas looked down. 'Because she has threatened me with it. And I am the one she calls her favourite.'

That sobered me. I could not imagine what peaceable Thomas might have done to stir that degree of anger in the Widow of Thames Street. Thomas and John met one another's eyes. That veil of secrecy was back. I was as far apart from them as ever. When the last nail was in the lid we turned swiftly away and made for the door. Martin watched us leave with a stony expression.

'I don't envy you,' said John. 'Not with your family. I had rather take the clapboards, stockfish and pig iron, even though they do bore me to death and beyond.'

He turned away across the stones towards Timber Hythe. It was beginning to rain. Thomas made for the door of our house. 'Are you coming?'

'Soon.' I was thinking hard. Thomas was right. But yet, in our mother's recklessness, I saw my moment of opportunity. I walked quickly back inside the warehouse, crossed to the stairs at the far end, and climbed to the counting house.

Miriam Dansey looked up at me in surprise. She had a sea chart of the western Mediterranean spread out before her, the jagged coasts thick with place names, the open seas scored by myriad compass lines. Without any ceremony I set my casket down on the table, turned the key and opened it up. In the light of her two candles, the cornelians and the citrines gleamed like burning coals. My mother stood up slowly, her eyes fixed on the stones. Then she reached out a long forefinger, poked at them and drew it back as if they were scorpions. At last she looked at me, her face white, the skin around her mouth twitching.

'Christ and all his angels!' She flicked the casket shut. 'I should have forbidden you to travel. I should never have trusted you off and alone. You are just a baby. No: worse, and I know where you had this mischief from. Dead? No, he is not dead. I am looking at him.' She shouted beyond me, down the stairs to the warehouse. 'William! William! Where is he? What was the fool thinking? I told him to watch you and keep you out of folly!'

'What about you?' I answered. 'Do you not think those books in the warehouse just a little bit reckless?'

She sat down again and glared at me with her steely eyes.

'I see Martin has been somewhat lax in his guard duties,' she said quietly. She rapped the table with her hand. 'Those are entirely different. Everyone knows what they are worth. We buy in Antwerp for a crown, and sell here for three. Cash trebled in less than two weeks. Pure profit, if no one talks. And they won't,' she added, with a fierce narrowing of her eyes. 'But these!' She lifted the lid again and took out one of the stones, a pale, gleaming citrine the size of a walnut. 'This might be anything. Yellow glass.'

In reply, I took out my purse, loosened the strings and poured a cascade of silver and gold over her map. The effect was pleasingly dramatic. Covering the coastlines of France, Spain and the Barbary Coast were a dozen or so angel nobles, discs of gold an inch broad worth six shillings and eightpence each. There were nine of the larger royals or rose nobles, at ten shillings, and mixed among them some thirty gold crowns, at four shillings and twopence each, as well as gold half crowns and a good number of silver shillings and groats. My mother's eyes opened in surprise. She leaned forward, and stirred the coins with her finger. Then she looked up.

'You made this? Out of gems?'

'Nothing but.'

'Hm!' She drew back. She tried not to show it, but I knew she was impressed. Money spoke to her, whatever its source. 'Well, you may risk your coins if you choose. But Mr William's is the real trade, and you will learn it. Come back in a year, and show me what you have then. If you have anything left at all.'

5

For the moment, I was content to obey my mother. I was growing, I thought to myself, maturing just like a gemstone deep in the bowels of the earth, that advances slowly to its perfection. I was acquiring a good grasp of Italian, and fair Portuguese and Spanish: accomplishments of value, since few enough men abroad would trouble to learn a lesser tongue like English. My eye for stones was getting sharper with every trip, and my reserves of coin were growing too. Soon I would be able to buy one or two of the dearer stones. It was time I began to look ahead to the next stage in my ambitions. I had set myself to become a merchant in jewels: not a mere retailer who brought in stones to Breakespere and Wolf and Heyes, but a man of standing who dealt directly with the Court. That meant somehow getting close to that wondrous, gilt and tinselled world. Just as for Thomas, I thought, my best hope lay with our uncle.

Bennet Waterman thought very highly of himself these days. He was one of Cardinal Wolsey's audiencers: a legal clerk who prepared chancery bills, and generally took on any business that the Cardinal's labyrinthine affairs required. It brought Uncle Bennet within a breath of the Court. He wore a velvet gown with silk lining, and a silver brooch with a small garnet in his hat. When Cardinal Wolsey was in residence at York Place, his vast house in Westminster, Uncle Bennet often took a boat down the river and paid us a visit on Thames Street. In the winter draughts of our candlelit parlour, while my mother and Mr William discussed the latest tariffs on pepper, Uncle Bennet took Thomas and me aside, his portly belly creaking after one of our generous but plain dinners. He enjoyed playing the courtier before his sister; and even though she might scoff at his posturing and airs, he was a connection she could not afford to despise, at least for the sake of Thomas.

'Ah, King Henry. He is the flower of chivalry, my boy. Have I told you how he came to marry Queen Katherine? He was only eleven when he became betrothed. She was seventeen, the widow of his poor brother, Prince Arthur. For six years after that their engagement lasted, while the late King fussed and grubbed and tried to prise her dowry out of Spain. He would never let his son go, you know. They say he envied him terribly, for his looks and his strength. He kept him locked up, like some poor virgin in a tale. But when King Henry the Seventh died, what did our young King do? Married her at once. Dowry or no dowry. No knight out of an old romance could have done fairer.'

That Christmas of 1523, when I was back in England after another voyage with Mr William, Uncle Bennet smuggled me into a general audience in the King's great hall at Westminster. He whispered to me to keep close by his side, and not to draw attention. I stood among the pages and lesser followers of the Cardinal, and looked at the ranks of great personages where the various factions and powers of the Court were on display. My heart was beating hard. I had never before been this close to the King. There he sat, immobile, a daunting and powerful presence: our sovereign lord, King Henry the Eighth. He was in his early thirties, as handsome a man as there was in the world, large-limbed, with a long, lean face, bearded, even though the common English fashion was to go clean-shaved. He darted his gaze about the hall. He was in a towering temper: news had just reached England that the Turks had driven the Knights of Saint John from Rhodes. An envoy from the Pope was before him and his powerful voice thundered repeatedly, 'I am Defender of the Faith!' The title was a gift of the Pope in which Henry took great pride.

As he was speaking, I took in every aspect of his appearance with a goldsmith's eye. His black velvet cap had a badge in it bearing a large, pyramid-cut diamond. His shirt collar was of gold thread set with emeralds; his doublet was sewn with gold in a lozenge pattern, and at every crossing a cluster of pearls. Round his neck was a gold chain set with great table-cut sapphires and amethysts; a heavy pendant hung from this chain, and in it shone four dark rubies. At his belt was a dagger, its sheath set with yet more stones. He wore rings on the forefingers of both hands, one an opal, one a diamond; and over his crimson silk hose, below his right knee, was the Garter, enamelled and set with pearls. When he moved, a sparkle of jewels darted from his chest, his fingers, his legs, just as if he were God himself seated in his glory.

Beside him sat Queen Katherine, almost forty, with a plump, heavily painted face and a jutting chin. At her bosom she wore a gold cross and several chains of rubies and pearls: doubtless a part of the wardrobe she had brought from Spain. I knew from my friends on Goldsmiths' Row that she seldom bought anything new. Seated with her was the Princess Mary, a small, half-pretty seven-year-old with dark eyes, the only surviving child of Henry and his Queen after fourteen years of marriage. It appeared more and more likely that she would one day be Queen Regnant herself, and so an aspiring merchant would do well to cultivate her favour. But that was far in the future. The real prize was the King.

I knew that Henry acquired mountains of gems each year, and that he had made Cornelius Heyes and the others rich. The trade was there, but how to break in on it? Everything flowed through the hands of those few great goldsmiths. If I only had a patron at Court. I looked along the ranks of the great courtiers. There was Cardinal Wolsey, with two tall priests carrying the silver crosses, nine feet high, that represented his authority as Papal Legate and Archbishop of York. His pride was immense. At a distance stood his almoner, his chamberlains and treasurers, and then in a gaggle round us the constables, the audiencers, the clerks, and even the official whose job it was to melt the Cardinal's sealing wax. I suspected that Uncle Bennet, a humble lawyer, did not have as much influence with the Cardinal as he liked to pretend.

Then, across from the Cardinal, were the other, rival, powers at Court: there was the wise and ironical Sir Thomas More, who had just been made Speaker of the House of Commons; and stern Thomas Howard, Duke of Norfolk, the tough old soldier and veteran of Flodden who had spent years watching, greedily and in vain, for the fall of the Cardinal. He was a figure of little practical power, though much patronage and grandeur. To enter the graces of any of these men was almost as difficult as approaching King Henry himself. What I needed was a chance, an advantage, a piece of luck.

In 1524, on the anniversary of my visit to my mother, I once more opened my casket to her. By now my collection included a small but perfect sapphire, which I handed to her as a gift. She rolled the stone under her finger, then pushed it back to me over the table.

'Keep it,' she said. 'Sell it. You may yet need your pennies. Carry on, my Richard. You have not persuaded me yet.'

Somehow, the old band was never all in London at the same time. In the autumn I was home once more. But by then John had left for Hungary, on a venture concerning salt. The great mines there were threatened by the savage advance of the Turks, and the house of Lazar was looking for a swift profit before the market was closed to them.

'He has found his adventure,' commented Thomas, as we sat together on the wharf, his eyes on the moving swirls of the river. 'If he lives through it.' Thomas was more and more downcast these days. Still he was reading with the Franciscan. The Cardinal's college was not yet ready; the monasteries destined for funding it refused to disband.

'Can you not find a place somewhere else?' I prompted him.

He shook his head. 'Our mother says wait. A little longer.'

The next summer, 1525, I turned twenty. Over these years I boiled with discontent. Ventures with Mr William had lost their savour for me. I had learnt all that I could from him, and my profits were slow. The Portuguese had no real interest in gems, even though their ships touched in at all the best markets: Surat, Calicut, Pegu. No, 'Let it be spice,' declared their King, chief grocer of Portugal, and spice it was. The city I longed for was Venice: that was the place for stones, as well as every other luxury that could give life opulence and wonder. When the day came to display my treasures to my mother again I poured out before her opals and amethysts, garnets, jacinths and pearls, and threw down my three purses of gold beside them with a loud chink. She raised one eyebrow.

'If you would only lend me a little money,' I protested. 'If you would let the *Rose* trade a little further.'

She sat back in her chair and stared at me with her ice-blue eyes. 'And why should I "let" you do anything of the kind? As long as you follow the firm of Dansey, my boy, Naples is our furthest port. Between London and there we can find all that we need.'

But her eyes as they lingered on my jewels had a thoughtful gleam. With the right proposition I believed I might just win her over.

I pestered Uncle Bennet for openings at revels and mummeries, audiences, maying, processions, pilgrimages, feasts … He was a hard man to catch up with, that summer; he was involved in Wolsey's great visitation of the abbeys, that squeezed so much gold from the abbots and raised so many angry murmurs. Nevertheless, he obliged me when he could, half out of liking for me, I thought, and half to prove his importance to my mother.

As winter came, the Court stayed out of London. The plague was running fiercely, and we crept about, all of us, with herbs clasped to our faces, keeping well clear of anyone we saw on the streets. 'The King is keeping Christmas in the country at Eltham Palace,' Bennet told us. 'The Secret Christmas, they are calling it. Still, I believe I can smuggle you in, if you have a mind to it.' I arrived there by night, and Bennet helped me to slip into the Great Hall, mingling with the servants who were serving gold cups and bowls of wine. I stopped in the doorway in amazement. The hall was a forest: trees of green damask stood in groves, and from their branches hung leaves of beaten gold and bunches of gilded acorns that flashed in the glare from the burning torches. Between the trees were wondrous beasts, antelopes and oliphants and lions made of canvas with gold crowns and tails of iron wire, and jesters dressed as wild men who leapt about in masks draped with ivy, letting out shrill shrieks and hoots. Laughter and music filled the room. Round the forest were bowers of silken roses, and through these the King and his courtiers danced to the sound of shawms and violins. They were in masks too, gilded and smiling, the men all with beards of gold thread. The couples dipped their heads beneath the hoops of the arbours, the ladies' pearl chains clinking on their bosoms. It made me burn with longing as I watched from my place among the butlers and pages, and the bowls of steaming wine. Why should I be apart from all this? What iron law kept me a tradesman in bales of woad and boxes of spice, while these golden creatures taunted me with their laughter? In an instant I grabbed up a mask that was lying by the wine, and slipped among them. The dancers separated and whirled beneath the arbours, and I was swept after them, the fiddlers skipping among us and the wild men chattering, the men and the ladies gasping and laughing.

One girl especially I noticed, wilder and freer than all the rest, flinging her head back as she spun round, the black hair streaming from beneath her hood. She was strong-hipped and tall; her breasts pressed against the white cambric stomacher stretched across the opening of her sea-blue gown. Around her neck she wore two ropes of good pearls of the Orient, which descended her bust and vanished down beneath her bodice. When the dancers separated briefly I darted after her through the glittering trees and caught her hands. Her eyes, dark brown behind the gold of her mask, sparkled with surprise. We swung together between the trees, while the shawms bayed and the violins sang. I was, in that instant, one of them, a blessed, golden being in a world of beauty and gems. I swung her fast, and she put her head back and laughed. But the music was dying already, and the dance swaying to a halt. We stopped at the foot of an arbour of paper roses. They had become torn by the violence of the dance, and lay scuffed underfoot.

The girl said, 'Are you not going to let go of my hands?'

Already I was behaving like a fool, and showing I was no courtier. 'Only if you show me your face.'

I released her hand, and just as she lifted off her mask, so I did mine. Her face was round, soft, alight with excitement: an excitement so far from the world of trade that it made me gasp. She cared for nothing, nothing but the pleasure of the moment and the delight of being alive. She gave me a sense of infinite promise. With a girl like this beside me I could go anywhere, become anything. Even as I was thinking these thoughts, I saw the girl's face change, and take on a curious smile. And yes, I saw it too. I had not seen that face for six years, but there was no doubt whatsoever. The girl was Hannah Cage. She threw back her head and laughed.

'The boy who played in the street! What, have you inherited a dukedom?'

The music began again, I slipped my mask back on to hide my annoyance and took her hand. We whirled together back into the figures.

'Not yet,' I told her. 'And you? You left home? Married?'

My heart began to pound as I asked it. She laughed.

'My father bought us a finer town house. Away from the stink of the river. Married! To marry me they would have to catch me. And courtiers are so horribly slow.'

'But I caught you. Did I not?'

'For a short time. But I am going somewhere I do not think you will find me.'

A jester tumbled and shrieked in front of us with a jangle of bells. I relaxed my hold for an instant and Hannah broke away, to vanish back into the dance. I ducked under the trees and ran after her; in a clearing I looked left and right, darted to the left towards the door of the hall, and then ran right up against my Uncle Bennet. He frowned in displeasure, and shook his head. I was furious and shamed. He was right: if I was caught, he would be the one to suffer. The chase was over. For the moment.

After Christmas, the plague began to ease. Bennet told me the King was moving his Court a little closer to London, and would be holding a great joust for all the nobility at his palace of Greenwich on Shrove Tuesday, to mark the beginning of Lent. 'But this time,' he added sternly, 'you must be discreet.' I thanked him. My meeting with Hannah Cage had made me greedy for more. And besides, if I was ever to break into the Court world I knew I had to keep watch, and follow the King in all his doings the way a thief follows his prey. So there I stood, on the morning of the sixth of February 1526, in the midst of the crowd at the Tiltyard, the open field that runs all down the eastern flank of the palace of Greenwich. Behind me rose its towers and pinnacles, while beyond began the low houses of the village, crouching like beggars at the King's gate.

Down the centre of the field were the barriers, built some six feet high of stout planks, to separate the jousters. To my right was a huge cluster of tents. I saw squires and armourers moving between them carrying tongs, hammers and bags of rivets, stablemen in their particoloured tabards and gentlemen waiters in white satin carrying steaming hot wine. There was the King's great lodging pavilion, its conical roofs topped with gilt dragons and lions, where men must now be helping King Henry into his armour. Further off were the cook-tents, with smoke rising from vents in their roofs, and the camp of the King's mariners who had come off their ships bringing capstans and cranes to set up all the various pavilions. Some thirty trumpeters and drummers on horseback stood waiting.

At last I saw the flaps of the great tent drawn back, and out rode King Henry. He was in full armour from head to toe, brilliant steel where it could be seen, but draped all over with surcoats of cloth of gold and silver, on which was some device in crimson, and a motto or poesy snaking round it. His horse too was in armour, with crimson ostrich feathers on its brow. The King held his lance upright in his hand, gilt and painted, a tremendous length, yet cunningly hollowed for lightness and ease. Eleven other riders came out from among the tents and fell into line behind him, all in the same colours, and they came trotting forward, their horses kicking up clods of the muddy turf. With a tremendous sudden clangour the drums beat and the trumpets sounded. The crowd around me took off their hats, and I cheered with the loudest of them and cried, 'God save you! God save King Harry!'

A second line of horsemen gathered at the lists at the opposite end, all in coats of green and crimson satin. Both troops rode to the Queen's pavilion halfway down the field, where they dipped their lances in salute. Beyond them I scanned the courtiers ranged on either side of the Queen, searching for signs of Hannah, but without success.

I saw the armourers helping the King lower his lance into position. This was no simple matter. The butt end of the lance was secured to the body armour by clips, and the King's right gauntlet was hooked over the lance and locked by more fastenings to his left arm. Another pair of clips caught the lance firmly in the crook of his left elbow, resting on the notch in his shield. Then, with legs straight, and his jousting spurs reaching up on their long steel wires to touch the horse's flanks, King Henry set himself in motion.

His horse's hoofs tumbled forward in turn, never breaking into a canter or a gallop, in the peculiar, rolling gait called the amble that is proper for the joust: for only with this steady gait can the rider hope for any kind of accuracy in his hit. Like a stormcloud the King rolled forward, not fast, but with an immense, calm strength, and his lance dead level. The Marquis of Exeter, one of Henry's oldest childhood friends, launched himself into an amble on the other side of the barrier, closing the distance with the King. He was skilful too, but the sway of his lance showed that he lacked King Henry's strength and control. When the pair met, the King's lance struck full on Exeter's shield with a bang. The lance shattered, Exeter swayed and his own lance swung clear. I cheered and huzzaed for the King, whose broken lance marked him as the victor. He rode on, wheeled round and then came slowly back up to the top of the course. He passed by not ten feet away from me, and I had my first clear view of the design on his coat. I stared after him. My palms began to sweat, and my pulse beat in my ears.

What I saw, repeated on the King's back, on his shield, and on his horse's flank, was a crimson heart in flames. This heart was trapped in a press, perhaps a wine-press or the sort that book-binders use. Beneath it curled the motto, DECLARE JE NOS. *Declare I dare not.* This was the heart of a tortured lover, caught in the agony of a secret and unrequited passion. Four years ago, when I had just returned from my first venture to Lisbon, the King had ridden to a joust wearing just such an emblem. His badge then was a wounded heart, and the other jousters sported a variety of matching symbols, hearts shattered, hearts chained, hearts in prison. Their mottoes had groaned in concert: 'Without remedy', 'My heart is broken', 'Between joy and pain'. No one at the time read the meaning in it; but shortly afterwards it became known Henry had begun an affair with a new mistress. Mrs Mary was a niece of the great Duke of Norfolk, married to a certain William Carey, the King's distant cousin and another of his childhood friends. She had been at the French Court, and now she was one of the Queen's ladies, while Carey became an obliging Court cuckold.

I had watched the progress of this affair from Goldsmiths' Row, where I saw in preparation the gold lockets, the crystal scent bottles, the crosses and pendants bloated with rubies and pearls. I cursed my luck that I was too young and too poor to share in the profits of King Henry's love. In time the flow of jewels from Cheapside to the King's various palaces slowed. Indeed, according to Uncle Bennet, the King had recently handed Mrs Mary back to her husband, pregnant with Henry's child. The King's wounded heart of four years ago had healed. But now this: a heart once more in flames, and *Declare I dare not.*

A fresh pair of riders thundered past, their lances wavering and failing to hit, and the audience groaned in disappointment. Who was she, I wondered. One of his wife's ladies, perhaps, as Mary and his previous mistress, Bessie Blount, had been? But whoever the woman was, I was in no doubt that this, at last, was my moment: the chance, the piece of fortune I had been waiting for. The spoils for those who supplied jewels to feed the King's passion would be immense. And this time I was determined to have my share.

As I travelled back up to London, squeezed on a bench between the tiltboat's other passengers, to the rattle and bump of the oars and the splash of riverwater against my back, my mind hammered at the problem before me. It was exasperating. I had waited a long time. I had schooled myself, trained my senses, my skill and my judgement until they were fine tools, ready for use. But if I was to make a serious attempt I had to have funds on a scale beyond anything I could raise on my own. There was no way round it: I would have to ask my mother. My pride rebelled against it, going to her begging. I would have to fight her old distrust of the bewitchment of beautiful stones that had cost her husband so much money down the years.

I found my mother sitting at her table in the counting house, with stacks of glittering coins before her: French écus, Portuguese cruzados, Genoese ducats. All these she would weigh before taking them to the Royal Mint to be changed for English crowns. She still looked young. Her hair was dark and waved, and always protruded somewhere or other from beneath her black widow's hood. A fire burned in the small hearth, and the scent of cloves from the warehouse below mingled with the tang of burning charcoal. William Marshe was hunched on the high-backed settle with an account book open before him, his long face wearing its usual melancholic expression. It was growing dark. A number of tin lanterns stood on the floor, unlit, for the use of our watchmen at night. I sat down by the fire facing William.

My mother spoke without looking up at me. 'And so you have something to say.'

It was harder to begin than I had expected. There was no use in trying to excite her over my ambitions, by painting for her the pomp and seduction of the Court. That would only turn her against me at the start. And so I went straight to the crux of it, the King's device and motto, and the signification I read in it: the flames of passion ignited once more, to replace the discarded Mrs Mary. While I spoke, her eye rested on me like a jeweller's, probing intently for the flaw in a stone.

'A new mistress,' said my mother, leaning back. 'Really? Then why have you heard nothing of it, you with your long ears for Court news? The King's lovers are commonly the very first to boast of their advancement.'

I leant forward from the fireplace. 'I told you: *Declare I dare not.* He is still wooing her: he is on the chase. He is teasing her, tantalising her, just as she may be tantalising him. The motto, the heart in the press: everything indicates she has not yet surrendered.'

Miriam Dansey put her arms behind her head, yawned, and then laughed. 'Not surrendered! Now, there is a wonder! Why should she not? I would, if King Henry came and heaped me with jewels.'

I clapped my hands and jumped up, delighted that she had played right into my hands. 'There! You have said it. What will a king do when he is thwarted in love?' I strode around the room, letting my long shadow dart out in the firelight. 'He will bathe her in sapphires, he will pile her with diamonds, he will buy all Persia and the Indies and lay them at her feet. And I ...'

My mother let out a shrill laugh. 'Now I see it! You think that you will be the one to sell the King his jewels! Oh, my mad, mad boy! The King will buy from Mr Cornelius, and Mr Christian, and Morgan Wolf. The men he knows and trusts. Why should he trouble himself with you?'

I turned on her. 'My jewels will be better.'

'Hm!' It was a grunt of amusement. 'How, in the name of all the saints, will you accomplish that?'

I swung myself down on to a stool and crouched towards her table. William, I noticed, had his eye on me. He was sharp, for all his dropsical appearance, and he was measuring me up just as surely as my mother. 'The stones that flow into London come to us from Antwerp or Bruges, and before that from Genoa or Venice. The Italians and French keep the best for themselves: Heyes and the others simply sit on Cheapside and wait for what the traders bring them. I shall not do that. I shall go to Venice, and catch the gems as they land from the East. I shall bring back such stones as have not been seen. I shall ...'

'Why not go further?' said William, with his half-smile. 'To Cairo, or even to Serendip or Golconda?' He was testing me, trying out just how fantastically high my plans might soar. I shook my head.

'There is too little time. To make my profit, I must be in with the first. When the lady succumbs to the King's charms, the flow of gifts will slow. Henry will no longer want what is most rare and fine. A few little tokens will do. Like the New Year's gifts he still sends to Bessie Blount.'

William sat back and nodded. 'I see I am to lose you, Mr Richard.' He glanced across at my mother, who tapped the table with her fingers in impatience.

'I shall be the one to decide that.' She turned back to me. 'And so you are asking me for a loan. A very, very large one. That is it?'

I stood before her and nodded. The Widow of Thames Street frowned. She rapped the Dansey seal on the table and said, 'I shall settle nothing until the *Rose* comes home.'

Mr William was due to set out any day, and myself along with him. I had hoped to avoid this voyage. I put my hands on the table. 'But that will be too late: speed is everything. Surely you see that?'

My mother stood up slowly and rested her hands next to mine. She said softly, 'I see you are running ahead a little too fast.'

I looked back at her, angry. 'Very well,' I told her. 'Let the *Rose* sail first. But I am not going with her. My place is here, where I can watch the Court.'

My mother drew in her breath and lowered her brows for a fight. But then she appeared to change her mind, and smiled. 'As you prefer.'

I turned and walked out of the room. It was two weeks before the *Rose* at last dropped downstream from the Tower with the tide and vanished out to sea, carrying her usual outward cargo of dank-smelling English woollens. It might be months before her return. I waited with impatience. I tried to believe that my mother intended to use some of the profits of the *Rose*'s venture to fund my own; but more likely she hoped to weaken my purpose through delay. I spent the time moodily patrolling the town for news. I had to know I was right: and I had to know the lady's name. I needed to have a face, a form, a mode of beauty in my mind before I began to buy: for stones are as varied and fickle as women themselves. But my Uncle Bennet could tell me nothing of any new royal mistress. All the news from

Court was of the ambassadors from France, and the new Holy Catholic League that the Pope was forming to fight the overreaching ambition of the Empire and fling the Spanish and German armies out of Italy. His Holiness had been joined in this alliance by Florence and Venice, and then by France, and these states were busily employed in raising armies. But our own King, after swift deliberation, had decided on strict neutrality. That way, said Bennet, Henry could be the peace-maker, the one all the other powers came to, begging for help and offering favours in return. With this pleasant thought, King Henry had left London to spend the summer hunting. The Court vanished into the deep country, and news dried up completely.

I might almost have thought Henry's new love was a chimera conjured only from my own fancy but for the flow of jewels out of Goldsmiths' Row. In April there was a gold brooch in the figure of a heart, black enamelled and set with five rubies and five diamonds, supplied by Morgan Wolf; the next month a rope of sixty pearls, and the month after that a gold frame for a portrait miniature, garnished with a falcon with eyes of emerald. All these objects disappeared into the King's hands. Each time I brought the news to my mother, as fresh proof. I was convinced that I was right. But who was she? No one could tell me of a woman who had received these jewels, or been seen wearing them.

In July the *Rose* returned at last and anchored below London Bridge. I stood on the wharf, watching the boat come in with Mr William in the bow. He took my hand briefly and went straight up to the counting house. I paced the wharf anxiously, glancing repeatedly up at the window, while the men unloaded the goods from the lighters, nutmegs and pepper and casks of sack. Dusk was gathering, and mists rose from the river. Then I saw William peer from behind the diamond panes and beckon me up. I walked quickly through the dim aisles of the warehouse, climbed the wooden stairs to the counting house and stepped inside.

Still my mother made me wait. In one hand she held a paper covered in figures, which she was checking rapidly, her lips working, while the sands ran through the narrow waist of an hourglass framed in ebony. She grudged time spent checking her underlings' accounts, and used the glass's discipline to make herself read fast. Her other hand rested on the respected Dansey seal, a broad disc of brass with a polished wooden knob, which she toyed with as she read. I sat down in a chair facing her. My heart was beating hard.

Suddenly she put down her figures, took hold of the hourglass and laid it on its side, halting the flow of time. She looked at me a moment with her head tilted, still playing with the seal. Then she tapped it on the table three times, and pushed towards me a sheet of paper. I snatched it up and ran my eyes greedily down it. *At sight of this bill I request that you pay to the said Richard Dansey, merchant, of Thames Street in the City of London, for value received, the sum of one thousand marks in Venetian ducats or bonds as shall be agreed, on or before Michaelmas in this year of Grace 1526*. It was a bill of exchange addressed to the Venice branch of the great Nuremberg banking house of Anton Fugger, signed at the bottom, Miriam Dansey, next to a large red disc of wax pressed with the rearing wyvern of the firm. Finally I had it: the thing I had longed to hold in my hands for all those months. And the sum was ample, more than I had dared hope for. I let out a whoop of delight. 'So you are really funding my venture.'

My mother nodded, but did not smile.

'You may not be so thankful soon. You have not seen what else I have written for you.' She pulled the bill back and slid towards me a second paper, which I took and quickly read. It was a bill of sale: one of those crafty instruments by which usury was conducted without sin, so that the business of the City could go on, while keeping itself free from the Church courts. By this bill, I acknowledged the receipt of a thousand marks, and sold to her in return a twelve hundred mark chunk of my business. At the bottom was the space for me to sign.

Twenty per cent interest to my mother, that was the meaning of it: only after that would I make a profit. It was a steep rate. She had made not a single concession to the fact I was her son. She was investing in a venture, that was all: and a venture in which she had very little trust. Anger rose up in me as I set the paper down. I had prepared myself for her refusal, but not this. In a single move she was both helping me and throwing up another barrier in my way.

'You are right,' I told her. 'I am feeling a good deal less thankful already.'

She sat back in her chair, stroking the polished wooden knob of the seal, her face wearing a faint smile.

'Having second thoughts?' she said.

I reached for one of the goosefeather pens that stood in the pewter inkpot, and tapped off the excess ink.

'By God, no.'

'Wait!' She put the seal down and leant towards me. 'Dear Richard. You are taking a very great risk. And you are asking me to share in that risk too. Would it not be far, far better to stay with me? Work for the family business? Go where I advise, with our dear, trusted old Mr William to look after you? Build yourself up little by little: that is the best way in trade. You cannot swallow the whole world in one bite, my Richard. Why do you want to strike out fresh paths of your own, when there is so much for you here?'

Her voice was soft and seductive. Before her on the table lay the two documents: one threatening me with its brutal terms of repayment; the other, I suspected, intended to daunt me with the sheer size of the loan. I saw plainly what she was up to. If I embarked on my venture and succeeded, she made a handsome profit; the thought of those two hundred marks doubtless attracted her. If I failed, I would be in her debt, and entirely in her power. I would have to work for years to pay off what I owed her, travelling where she sent me, and buying what she told me to buy. She would be able to remind me forever after that she had been right and I had been wrong. I would become her creature, a humble minion of the house of Dansey. Even if she never saw her money again, power like that was cheaply bought at a thousand marks. There would be no question of my ever affording another venture on my own.

That was if I failed. But to succeed: to be my own man, to escape the Thameswater stink, the murky family world that had become a prison to me, and rise into a sphere my mother could not guess at, that was worth any risk.

The ink on the pen tip had gone dry. I forced myself not to show my rage. I said, 'Do you have any other conditions to add before I sign?'

She rapped the seal on the table, suddenly irritated.

'Only that you take along a family servant, whom I shall pick for you. I would not like to think of you entirely alone on your wild errand. That is acceptable?'

'Very well.'

I dipped the pen once more in the pot, angrily splashing ink on its pewter rim. 'You will have your twelve hundred marks,' I told her. 'And I shall make my profit, I promise you.'

I signed the document with a quick flourish, *R. Dansey*. It was done. I had mortgaged myself: there was no going back. My mother pulled the paper towards her and handed me the bill of exchange. She looked at me, thoughtful, and a little surprised, as if she had not expected me to accept her bargain. I stood up.

'Listen to me, my Richard,' she said. 'You have a sharp eye for gems, I will grant you that. But, by God, you have the heart of a child. See that you do not go the way of your father.'

I looked back at her levelly. 'I am following in no one's footsteps. Not his, and certainly not yours.'

She looked back up at me with a faint frown. 'I am very much aware of that.'

I folded the bill of exchange crisply in three, and stooped to kiss her on the cheek. Then I walked quickly out of the room, down the stairs and through the warehouse. I was fuming. That second document seemed to drag at me like a stone about my neck; a bargain with the Devil that one day I would be forced to pay. But as I emerged into the moist air of the riverside, my anger and fears left me, and I felt only exhilaration. That night, as I lay in my bedchamber, unsleeping, I worked out the various conversions and began to conceive all that that money might mean. A mark is a measure of silver, worth two-thirds of a pound, and so a thousand marks are six hundred and sixty-six pounds thirteen shillings and fourpence sterling. At the current rate that made two hundred and ninety-six ounces of gold, or a little over three thousand Venetian ducats. Sufficient, I reckoned, for some fifteen good diamonds, or else maybe twenty diamonds of poorer water, and twenty of the finest opals. Or a hundred Oriental amethysts. Perhaps I might even stretch further, if I bought wisely. How to choose? A dozen different schemes for a collection of jewels of intoxicating wonder presented themselves to me.

In the days that followed I counted out my own modest savings and changed them into bills, while Christian Breakespere and even William Marshe volunteered small loans of their own. I made a last effort to discover the mistress's name, going round all my trade connections and pressing Uncle Bennet to use his wiles at Court. But to no purpose. It was galling: without that knowledge my whole venture was at risk. I considered putting off my departure. But I had waited far too long already; if I was to have any chance of success I must sail now, even in my ignorance. I was convinced the mistress's name would not stay secret long. I begged Uncle Bennet to discover it, and write to me as soon as possible. He nodded his bald head in assent.

'Well, well, I will do all I can. And in return you must promise to send me news of Italy: her politics and the progress of the wars. Send me rumours, send me secrets. I have a particular reason for asking this of you, my Richard. See that you do not fail me, and I shall do my best for you in return.'

On the night before I was due to sail I folded my various bills of exchange inside my casket and nestled it down next to my skin. My great venture was about to begin.

Scythian Emerald: a Courtesan among Stones

Venice, 12 August 1526

My enterprise is slow and late in coming,
My hope unsure, while my desire mounts and grows;
To abandon or pursue, alike I grudge.

PETRARCH, *CANZONIERE*

PART 2

Scythian Emerald:
a Craftsman
among Stones

6

A month later I stepped up on to the great wooden bridge that spans the Grand Canal in Venice. I was swelling with pride and excitement. Crowds pressed round me, noblemen with their servants, girls selling nuts and oranges, and merchants of every nation, Venetians and Turks, Jews and Greeks. Beside me trudged my servant, burly Martin Deller. He was the last person I would have chosen to accompany me. Many was the time in my childhood he had caught me in the forbidden depths of the warehouse, and dragged me out by one ear. But, 'No servant, no thousand marks': those were the Widow's terms, and she insisted on the right to choose. He called me 'master' now, he wore a dagger at his side as well as an oak cudgel nine inches long, with a leather wrist strap at one end and some lead shot hammered into the other for weight. He was here to serve me and guard my goods: or so I was supposed to believe.

'Master,' he whispered, 'do you think this is wise? Carrying so much coin?'

I paused at the highest point of the bridge and glanced at him in irritation. We had just come from the Fontego dei Tedeschi, the Exchange House of the Germans, a vast building of white stone with jagged crenellations like some Saracen fortress that rose five storeys high out of the water of the Grand Canal. Here, in the office of the agent of Anton Fugger, banker to emperors and popes, I had presented my mother's bill and asked for a quarter of my sum in gold, and the rest in smaller bills of exchange. The agent unlocked one of the chests that stood against the wall and lifted out a large canvas bag. From this he scooped out gold, and gold, and more gold. It thrilled me to see those shimmering stacks of ducats, which the clerk marshalled into ranks, counted and then counted again: thirty stacks and more, of twenty ducats apiece, like the towers of a golden city. Seven hundred and seventeen coins in all, stamped on one side with Saint Mark and the Doge, and Christ seated in His glory on the other. I had the coins gathered into a leather purse, which I fastened to my belt beside my dagger. It was a fair burden: nearly four pounds' weight of gold.

'We shall not be carrying this for long, my Martin. We are about to begin to spend.' Before us lay the Rialto: the richest two hundred yards of ground in the world. It formed an island, with the Grand Canal wrapping itself round it, north, east and south, while lesser canals cut it off to the west. All along its waterfronts vessels were constantly landing, a fresh one putting in just as soon as the last had discharged its cargo. Behind the canal, the Rialto's lanes and squares were filled with myriad warehouses and shops, the *fonteghi* and *botteghe*, where you could buy anything that grows or is fashioned under the sun. I saw rich tapestries and carpets, ostrich eggs garnished in gold and coral, and backgammon tables inlaid with jasper and chalcedony and ivory, carved with heads and heraldic shields. There were painted playing cards crusted with gold leaf, and the most wondrous printed books with woodcuts on almost every page, for the best books in the world are Venetian; and of course all manner of marvels woven out of the gold thread which goes by the name of Venice gold. I could have filled the *Rose* seven times over with treasures.

I strode forward, down off the bridge, and at once caught sight of a goldsmith's shop. It had as its sign a gold chain painted on a board, and several steps led down to its door from the street. I leapt down those steps and pushed open the door. For many a night I had dreamt of this, and I was here at last. But, as I stood in the dappled light that glimmered in through a barred window from the canal outside and looked round, I was puzzled. On the shelves of the shop were gold chains: nothing but slender gold chains, of a wonderful fineness, some enamelled, others set with pearls, others bearing the repeated SS of the *spiritus sanctus*. I questioned the jeweller as he came out from behind his workbench. It was then that I learnt the vast scale of the trade in Venice. There was no Goldsmiths' Row as in London, with its fourteen shops, each one selling a little of everything. The goldsmiths of Venice were divided into twelve separate guilds, each encompassing dozens of craftsmen and shops. The establishment I had stepped into was of the branch that dealt only in *catenelle d'oro*: small gold chains. There were other shops for basins and chalices in silver, others for gold and silver cutlery; there was another guild for trinkets, another for the larger gold chains as opposed to the smaller, another for filigree and one for the setting of jewels; another for embossing and engraving and work with the chisel and stamps; there was even a guild all of its own for buttons made of fine gold wire. And that was not to mention the *diamanteri*: the jewellers, who are themselves split in two: those who trade in diamonds, and those who sell gems of colour. There was even a guild for sellers of imitation jewels and false pearls. 'Then finally,' the shopman went on, 'there are those who carve rock crystal, and those who specialise in faceting, or casting gold in moulds of clay, with or without the use of clamps.'

He stood smiling and blinking at me. I did not wish him to see just how dismayed I was. It was the first hint that this world I had stepped into was a great deal wider than I had supposed. I thanked him and bowed my way out.

After that began days of searching, of trudging alleys and climbing bridges, pushing through the bustle of the fish market and the streets of the butchers, the spicers, the druggists and the poulterers, then past the flour and grain warehouses, past the rope-sellers and the sail-makers near the Grand Canal, and the crowds around the four great banks of Venice, two for the nobles and two for the citizens. Everywhere we asked after gold and gems. In those days we spent many an hour, Martin and I, in those damp underground rooms, while I ran my eye over the goldsmiths' work and surveyed stone after stone. I saw wonders there: emeralds of Persia weighing as much as three scruples; a wine-coloured amethyst, as large and precious as any diamond, that shot out a ruby's fire from a heart of purple; a set of blue-green sapphires of Pegu beyond India, rare and evenly matched. I saw turquoises and cornelians, rings, basins, dishes for sweetmeats piled with diamonds and pearls. My head swam at the richness of it. But all their gems were dear, much too dear. A thousand ducats could vanish on a single stone.

Some of the shopmen curled their lips, detecting the narrowness of my purse. 'Perhaps the signore would prefer something cheaper?' They showed me the trays of lesser stones, the pale garnets and small yellow topazes and chrysolites that sold for fifty ducats and less. But that would not do. I had set myself to buy stones that had in them the seeds of obsession: deep stones, stones with hearts, stones to reflect a mighty, kingly passion.

By the seventh day I was beginning to think I had made a fatal mistake in coming here. I would have only one chance in my life at breaking free of my mother's empire. I had made my attempt too soon, without enough funds, and I was going to fail. These were the thoughts I tormented myself with as I walked the alleys in the heavy, late summer showers. My cloak was sodden with water, and my hat, a flat woollen cap of the kind worn by apprentices in London, drooped from my head. And if Venice was not for me, where else could I go? If I returned home, it would be to defeat and shame; and

I would still owe my mother those twelve hundred marks. I might travel further, to Cairo and beyond, but the time needed for a venture of that sort would stretch into many months, or even years, and my expenses would rise and rise. All hope of a quick success with the King would be gone. No, my fortune must be secured right here and right now, or nowhere and never.

My impatience came near to leading me to ruin. I had just crossed another bridge over another canal. On the far side of it was a small grated doorway; over it hung a wooden sign showing a gold ring set with a dark green stone. It was a goldsmith's: and one who dealt in gems. With a fresh surge of hope I pushed open the door and went in. Sapphires and turquoises flashed in the dim light, as if from the walls of some fantastic mine. I caught for an instant a blood-red glint from the deeper part of the shop, where I found a great fiery ruby resting on a white silk cushion. The shopman was at my elbow, his eyes glinting, murmuring low.

'A ruby of Serendip, signor. A higher colour or more life in a stone you will not find. Not in the rubies of Calicut, or Bisnager, or Pegu. Look on it. Weigh it. A full fifteen carats. For you, two thousand ducats.'

I picked up the stone and turned it in my fingers, letting it stain them red. It flashed like a burning coal, and its colour was strong, from the centre right to its extremity. It was flawless, smooth but uncut, with an uneven, bulging outline. I tried it on my tongue, and felt the coldness that is the mark of the very best rubies. As I turned it in my hands I could feel its magic seducing me. I knew I could beat down the goldsmith's price. Suddenly Martin was beside me.

'Does it not please you, master?' he whispered. 'Is it flawed?'

'No,' I said. 'On the contrary.'

'Then buy it, for God's sake. Why should you need more than a single stone? Buy it, and let us go home to England.'

Buy it, the voice of temptation whispered to me in concert with Martin's. It would be so easy. It was my mother's voice too, teasing me. *If you say you are such a great merchant,* she seemed to murmur, *let us see you make a purchase. But you are a dreamer, and a hesitator. You never had the backbone of your brother.*

'I shall cut it for you myself,' the shopman offered. 'A pyramid cut. It is too rounded for a table. A plain ring, perhaps. I promise you it will look superb.'

I turned the stone in the light, forcing myself to think coolly. What would its worth be, when cut and set, and carried home to England? More than two thousand ducats? Perhaps. But after the cost of cutting and all my other expenses there was every chance I would go home to the fate I dreaded more than all else. I would follow in my father's steps, and make a loss. And whatever its worth, it was only a single stone. It was not enough to snare and enchant the King; not enough to outshine Breakespere and Heyes. I glanced sideways at Martin, who continued to peer at the gem: whether in genuine wonder, or out of a desire to lure me into a purchase, I was unsure.

As long as I remained standing there I was in danger. I made myself lower the ruby back into its place. On the white cushion its gleam tormented me, so that I closed my eyes and turned from it. Without a word I walked back up the steps to the street. As soon as I was back in the bright sunlight the spell of the stone fell away from me, and I thanked God for my escape. I was angry with myself for having come so near to so great a mistake, and I strode on fast. All I wanted was to put as much distance as possible between myself and that treacherous stone. I heard Martin's voice behind me.

'Master! Why did you not buy that ruby? You said yourself it hadn't a flaw. When are we going to buy something?'

I could have kicked him for his obtuseness. Or was he not as dull as he seemed? I was in no doubt that Martin was under special orders from the Widow. At the very least, he must be my mother's spy. And what if he was more? What if he had delivered that near-fatal advice on purpose?

'But, in God's name, master!' Martin called after me again. 'We have seen all the goldsmiths' shops: every one. What do you intend to do?'

I turned on him. I saw in his eyes my mother's view of me, her scorn at my childish confidence, and the naïve pleasure I took in pretty things: 'So like your father.' Thomas was the one with steel in him, she always said. His mind was sharp, an accurate tool that weighed and calculated, just like the Widow herself. She did not see the Thomas who sang in the moonlight beneath a girl's window, or the Thomas who leapt across the eaves of a church roof with just as much recklessness as myself. Nor did she see the fine judgements I had taught myself to make in my quests for gems. She was mistaken, deeply, about both of us: so I told myself. But that ruby's fire had burnt away a good part of my self-assurance.

I faced up to Martin and said, 'I am here to buy gems, gems in quantity, gems of wonder and obsession, gems to kill for and die for. And that is just what I propose to do.'

I turned and kept on walking. How, though, was I to pursue this venture? It would take all my ingenuity and nerve. I knew that every great city has its depths. Most go no further than the warm shallows, but it is in the darker waters, where the fiercer fishes swim, that fortunes are to be made, for there the prices are low, and sales are quick and dangerous. I had seen the connections my father and Mr William had set up in the underworld of Lisbon, over years of patient intrigue. I must do the same in Venice: and I had very little time to do it in. And so we walked, hour after hour, day after day.

The Rialto was not only the richest and most wondrous market-place of all Europe. It was also a crossroads between the city's different quarters, and between multifarious worlds. Southwards began the great palaces of the nobles, with their rows of windows cut in strange traceries in emulation of the rich cities of Islam. By night this district rang with the sound of balls and serenades. I saw gondolas steered by moorish slaves, and veiled ladies stepping inside their closed cabins with a flash of jewels. There were opportunities here, no question. But this world was closed to me.

North and west were the districts of the spicers, and then the silk-dyers and scarlet-dyers. Further still, over the Grand Canal, lay the old foundries, the *jactum* or Ghetto. Here the authorities had permitted the Jews to settle who had been expelled from Spain by our Queen Katherine's parents, Ferdinand and Isabella, thirty years before. The Jews were allowed to practise no craft or profession, and that turned them into masters of finance and trade. And so I learnt my way around the Ghetto, and asked from tavern to tavern, and began to make friends. They knew everything, I was sure, but their lips were tight sealed on their customers' secrets. I visited the Angel, too, the inn near the Rialto Bridge where the Turks in their enormous white turbans and red felt caps were permitted to lodge. They spoke to me of their trade in ginger and aloes and coral, and of the markets in Beirut and Aleppo. One or other of these connections, I hoped, would bear fruit soon.

Even from the window of our lodging, on the narrow little square called the Campiello del Sol just a few lanes away from the Piazzetta of the Rialto, I made fresh discoveries. Every morning before dawn, I saw an old man and a boy of about fifteen come trudging up from the canal at the end of the square, each carrying a pair of buckets on yokes over their shoulders. They poured the contents down the well in the middle of the square, then went back for more. After six or seven trips they vanished. One morning I went down and asked them what they were doing. The old man told me they were *acquaiuoli*, who carry water from Terraferma, as Venetians call their territories on the Mainland, to fill the various wells of the city. Every morning they crossed the lagoon in the mist, past the great ships lying at anchor, and crossed back again to the city.

I said, 'And do these great ships pay a toll to the Republic on all their goods?'

The old man looked back at me unblinking. 'Not always.' I gave him half a ducat, and asked him to remember me.

One evening, after the gates of the Ghetto had been shut, Martin and I were making our way back home. I was feeling tired and cast down, and that made me miss our usual path. Dusk was closing in. Lights burned in front of some of the doorways, but long stretches of the alleys were dark. The next canal, by my reckoning, ought to have been the Rio di San Cassiano, and we should cross it by the small wooden Ponte dei Morti, the Bridge of the Dead, that leads past the cemetery and bell-tower of San Cassiano itself. But the alleyway twisted and turned, and then came out at a narrow bridge which I had never seen before. From across the canal came a burst of feminine laughter. There, in a blaze of light from cressets in the walls, I saw a sight to make me stand still and blink. In every window of the houses opposite there were women: naked, beautiful women. Some of them were leaning out over the canal, cradling their breasts, whose nipples were picked out in carmine. Others stood full height, looking up and down the alley, their hair decked in pearls, while their more intimate charms were shaved in the Oriental fashion. A few were even perched on the window ledges, their bare legs dangling in the air. When they caught sight of me all of them began calling and beckoning to me to come up, come and have a taste of Paradise.

I climbed the steps up to the centre of the bridge, bowed and swept off my hat. It was time, I thought, to drown my worries.

'Ladies,' I said, 'I am entirely at your service.'

I crossed over the bridge and knocked at the doorway beneath the dangling legs. A stately old woman answered it, and looked me up and down suspiciously. My clothes did not speak of great wealth, and she was about to shut the door on me. I lifted up my purse with a chink of coins, loosened the strings and handed her half a ducat. Her face broke into an avaricious smile, and she bowed to let me in. I pushed past and bounded up the curving stone stairs.

'What about me?' came Martin's plaintive voice from below.

'Amuse yourself,' I called back, and burst into the room overlooking the canal. There was a chorus of little shrieks, and the girls rushed to cover themselves with a variety of silk veils and shifts. About the room were four daybeds ornamented with scrollwork and piled with cushions and bolsters, each enveloped in a silken canopy like a tent, hanging from hooks on the ceiling. There was not another man present. I looked from one girl to another, scarcely able to believe my luck. They stood with their eyes cast down, timidly smiling: the picture of modesty, as if they were virgins just arrived from the country who had been innocently airing their nakedness at the windows on account of the excessive heat. I swept off my hat and bowed.

'Richard Dansey, of London.'

They looked up at me.

'Dardania.'

'Ippolita.'

'Angelica.'

'Armida.'

Their names spoke to me of the ancient paradises of the gods; their looks, the slight bows and curtseys they made, still holding the shifts up to their bodies, all enflamed me beyond endurance. All the frustration of my search for gems translated itself instantly into desire. I looked from one to the other. How to decide? Ippolita was tall, like the Amazon queen she took her name from. She stood resting a long leg on an inlaid coffer. Armida was delicate, Angelica round as a pudding, Dardania slender and proud. In the end it was the challenge in Ippolita's eyes that decided me. I beckoned her to me. She smiled coyly, and led me to one of the daybeds. She lay down on her side at one end with her light blue veil covering her, like a lazy Venus in a painting, waiting for me. A little chain of pearls in her hair, drawn up in a curve, gleamed in the lamplight like water drops. I tossed my purse down next to the pillow with a loud jingle of gold, and my dagger along with it: defying them to try to steal. Then I undressed to my shirt, while Angelica poured sweet wine into two glasses which she placed on an inlaid table, and Dardania and Armida set down a variety of meats intended to inflame our passions: eggs dressed with truffles, asparagus tips, and almonds and pine nuts in aniseed and honey. Ippolita ate with delicate nibbles and tiny sips of wine, darting provoking glances at me from her large, dark eyes. At last I could bear it no longer. I threw aside the plate of nuts and yanked on the gold tasselled ropes of the canopy. The curtains fell closed. I pulled off my shirt and knelt in the near-darkness opposite my Amazon, naked. Her eyes shone, wicked with danger and untried possibilities. She twitched aside the veil, rolled over like a cat and crouched facing me.

'Now,' she said, 'let us see what you can do.'

She sprang at me. She dived, she wriggled, she clasped and foined, she drew back, she leapt, she bit, she licked, she laughed. I gasped in amazement; I was out of my depth. Ippolita was a different creature entirely from the bored trollops of Stew Lane, or even those gaudier creatures of the back streets of Lisbon. But I set myself to learn fast. I answered caress with caress, attack with attack, and for each new device of hers I made sure to invent two more of my own. As we wrestled and grasped, the pearls in her headdress shook and clicked. They were fine, I thought: very fine. I promised myself a closer look, but even as I formed the thought she leapt upon me to play the cavalier, digging her heels in my thighs and sitting upright with a rhythmical swing of her breasts that mesmerised me as we approached our desire. Then, after we had refreshed ourselves with wine, I took the saddle myself. I pressed my face into her musk-scented hair, and so I found my eyes brought suddenly up against those pearls. They were of a good size, perhaps three carats or more, well rounded, with a pinkish-blue blush. That sheen proclaimed they were still in their bright youth: for pearls, unlike true gems, decline and wither with age. Persian, I judged, from the rich fisheries of the Straits of Ormuz. There were seven of them. I paused in my assault and lifted myself on my arms.

'Where did you get those pearls?'

'From a noble,' she gasped. 'Who couldn't pay. God curse you! What's the matter? Will your sword not fight?'

I sprang back to the attack. The smell of her, the gleam of the pearls, woman and pearls, woman and pearls, the delight of Ippolita and my greed for her treasure merged in a single exquisite emotion. As my mouth drew close to her ear I whispered, 'I'll give you a hundred ducats for them.'

She arched her back, bit my neck and hissed, 'Two hundred.'

I twisted and swooped. 'A hundred and twenty.'

'Oh! Oh! Oh! And fifty.'

I rolled her on top of me to drink the last drop of delight and whispered in her ear, 'Done.'

7

I went home euphoric. The smell of Ippolita was still about me: and
I had made my first purchase. But lying in bed back in our lodging I
began to doubt what I had done. What if it had only been the spell
of the wine, the exotic foods and the delicious taste of my Amazon
that had seduced me? By the light of a single candle I opened the
casket again and got out my scales. They were true jewellers' scales,
which I had bought before leaving home. They had no stand; instead
they hung from the finger and thumb, with two pans, on to one of
which the tiny weights were lifted with tweezers. My pearls were of
a good, even weight, some three and a quarter carats each, and of a
good roundness. They were pierced, of course; but it surprised me
to see that they had not been drilled right through their centres in
the usual fashion, but in a shorter line across the base. Drilling pearls
is always dangerous work; this must have been infinitely harder. It
was this oddity that had caused the pearls to hang in so bewitching
a fashion in Ippolita's hair.

I crossed to the window, still holding the pearls. Dawn was beginning to break. I heard the water-carriers making their usual way up
from the canal, and then the whoosh of their buckets emptying into

the well. As the sun rose, for the first time I saw the pearls' true glory. They had a deep and subtle sheen, like cream tinged with rosewater. The light played on them, hinting at transparent depths. And yet there were none, for the entire mystery of a pearl, unlike a gem, lies in its surface. I had been right: they were worth many times what I had paid.

'Martin!' I called, as my servant came padding through from the outside room, bringing hot water. I held out the casket and let him see them, seven silver orbs against the blue silk I had folded inside to keep the stones I bought safe and separate.

'What do you think of that?'

Martin leant over and sniffed. 'You bought from the whores?'

I snapped the lid shut in annoyance. 'I'll buy from the Devil if I have to. Do you doubt me?'

'No, master,' said Martin with reluctance. 'If you say they're real, I believe you. That's all very well. But what next?'

'Today we walk,' I retorted briefly. 'And tonight, back to the Bridge of Nipples.' That truly was the name of that narrow little bridge: the Ponte de le Tet'; and a better-named bridge I have yet to see.

'Is that your plan?' Martin asked me in disgust. 'To lie with a different trollop every night? For how long? Until all your money is gone?'

It was my mother speaking, loaded with disdain. For a moment I wavered. What if they were right? What if all I was capable of was squandering her money and creeping home, the chastened prodigal, never to attempt to rise again? But then anger welled up in me: anger at the slander and injustice of it, and at this hulking spy who dogged my every move. I walked up close to Martin, took hold of a fold of his shirt and flung him back against the wall. 'I hope my mother is paying you well,' I hissed at him. 'Because you are taking a risk. What were her orders? To force me to make a mistake? To drive me home again as soon as you could? Well?'

Martin looked back at me stolidly. 'I am here to guard you, master. And to be of service.'

I let him go. Of course he would admit to nothing. I should have kept my temper. I said, 'I will lie with as many courtesans as it takes, and do whatever more I have to, until I find what I am looking for.'

On my daily prowls through the city, I mixed with the merchants in the Piazzetta before the ancient church of San Giacomo; I walked the Merceria, that wound up from Saint Mark's towards the Rialto. And as I walked, I heard rumours that unsettled me. That summer, war had returned to northern Italy. Pope Clement had raised a force of eight thousand men, and sent them north to join with the armies of Venice and France. This confederated army had captured Lodi and Cremona from the Emperor's Germans and Spanish, and was set to march on Milan, the Imperial stronghold in the North. For some days there was great excitement, and everyone talked of a quick victory for the League. But I heard other news too, whispered by merchants who had returned from the western fringes of Venice's territory. There were great disagreements, it was said, between the Duke of Urbino, Venice's general, and the Papal commanders. The Duke wanted to advance at once and crush Milan; but the Pope's generals feared that would open the way for the Imperials to move south. In fury, the Duke had written to His Holiness to have his own orders approved; and meanwhile the army could do nothing. All this news I relayed to Uncle Bennet in ciphered letters. I hoped I might be raising my uncle's importance in Wolsey's eyes: and any increase in Bennet's standing at Court was good for my chances too.

Then came word that the Pope's army had suddenly detached itself and marched back south. Left alone, the Venetians and French had been obliged to retreat. At the same time, the Emperor's great general, the Duke of Bourbon, had landed with an extra ten thousand men from Spain. There was fear and dismay everywhere. The League was finished, some said. Pope Clement was notoriously indecisive and treacherous. He might make peace with the Emperor at any time, and leave his allies in the lurch. France was weak,

Florence would surrender if the Pope did, and that left Venice to stand alone. The older folk remembered twenty years ago, when Venice faced an alliance of the Pope, Emperor and sundry other states.

'But the city can never be captured, surely? The lagoon and the war galleys protect us?' I put this to Matteo Pasini, the old barber-surgeon who was the host where I lodged.

'Venice cannot be captured!' he echoed. 'True, but she can be ruined. In 1510, when the Emperor smashed our armies, there was not a merchant left on the Rialto. The state banks closed. There were three million ducats on their books, owed to the people of Venice. But the money was gone: spent on armies that lay dead from the fight to defend our territories. You could see the burning towns over on Terraferma from the bell-towers. Bills and bonds were worthless. It could happen again, believe me. Whatever it is you have come here to buy, my friend, I advise you to work fast.'

I wrote letters; I fretted and fumed. I was half inclined to go straight back to the Fugger agent and cash the rest of my bills, while there was still gold to be had. But I would be a fool to load myself with two thousand ducats more, when I was still unable to spend what I had. It was more urgent than ever that I keep up my search. Even now, on my hard, profitless journeys through the city, I thanked God I was not in London, and that I was free, for the moment at least, of the House of Dansey. But I wished more than once Mr William had been here, or that I had his experience.

The courtesans' world teased and inflamed me. I was fascinated by the thought of noblemen who could part with pearls for so far below their true value. I went back again and again and saw them in their gondolas, gliding up below the ladies' windows by the Ponte de le Tet': true courtiers, I thought, with their jewelled sword hilts and crimson doublets slashed with gold. They stood in the prows and gazed up with one finger keeping the place in a book of Petrarch's sonnets. 'What feeling is this,' they crooned, 'if it be not love?' and 'I swear to God you are cruel!' and 'My lady, will you murder me, when I am so loyal a slave?'

When I met them later, drinking with the ladies before retiring inside one of the canopies, they looked me haughtily up and down. I saw the rubies on their fingers, the diamonds in their hat badges, the pearl buttons. Ippolita watched my eyes with a smile. When I was alone with the ladies she said, 'You want to buy, and buy cheap? The place you want to be is a casin.'

'And what,' I growled, 'is a casin?'

'A casin, in the Venetian tongue, or casino, as they call it on Terraferma, is a place where nobles go to gamble. But looking as you do, they would not even let you through the door.'

'You need to lose that hat,' said Armida, standing up and casting it aside with distaste.

'And this cloak is more like a pedlar's,' said Dardania.

'And what a poor little dagger you have,' said Angelica. 'Gentlemen carry swords.'

'This shirt disgraces you,' said Ippolita, pulling it off. I tried to fight her away, but Armida came up behind me and took a firm grip on my breeches.

'So do these.'

'And these,' added Dardania, peeling off my hose.

'And most certainly these.'

I tried to dodge aside. 'What in the Devil's name is wrong with my drawers?'

Ippolita gave the final pull. 'They should be of silk. Embroidered.'

They had stripped me. Ippolita dropped my undergarments on the pile along with the rest, with a grimace of distaste. I was angry, but I was laughing too: I felt strangely cleansed, as if my old life had been peeled away from me along with those clothes, the brown jerkin, the kersey breeches, the wool stockings and unadorned linen shirt. Before me lay the unknown. The courtesans evidently thought the same.

'Look at him,' Armida smiled. 'Naked he stands, before the entry to a new world.'

I stooped down to my purse and tossed them a scatter of ducats. 'Ladies,' I said, 'I would take it as an honour if you would be my guides.'

And so they began. Two days later it was the Feast of Saint Michael, Michaelmas, as we call it, at the end of September. On a church holiday no courtesan may practise her trade, and so the ladies conducted me to Saint Mark's. The great square was packed with fine folk pressing for a view of the Doge as he passed in procession, dressed in crimson with an ermine mantle on his shoulders and the pointed cap on his head that is known as the Horn. Over him, keeping off the sun, was held a vast ceremonial umbrella all of gold brocade. This was the legendary Andrea Gritti, with his short white beard and fierce scowl, who had been the captain-general who fought Pope Julius and reconquered Padua for the Republic. Now he was leading Venice in her war against the Emperor. The bells rang, and along the piazza tapestries hung from every window. Monks dressed in white followed the Doge up to the five lead-sheathed doors of the church, before which flew three vast banners all of gold thread, depicting Saint Mark and the lion.

Together with my ladies I pressed through the crowd inside the church. I stood and stared at the mosaic-work and gold on every wall, the columns of coloured marble and pulpits roofed in gold, the statues of the saints too many to count. As Mass began, I looked about at the greatest wonder of all: the ladies of Venice. They sat high above us, in the galleries for the nobles. It would cheer a dying man's heart to behold the quantity of diamonds they wore, the emeralds and sapphires of such size as I had hardly seen, the pearls about their necks and in their hair, and most of all the flash of the gems in their rings when all in a single movement they put their palms together to pray. A single one of these ladies might wear five hundred ducats on her fingers, and another thousand about her throat. My own four guides wore not a single jewel, as the law commanded of courtesans when they go abroad: so jealous are the Venetian ladies of the adornments that mark them out as noble.

Dardania plucked my arm and hissed in my ear to leave the women alone. It was the men I was here to watch: how they stood, how they sat, the hang of their cloaks, the way they doffed their hats, the cut of their doublets, the way their sword scabbards swung as they walked. They were dressed mainly in black: black stockings, black doublets and gowns slit at the elbows to allow their arms to come free of the long, trailing sleeves. Everything about them was elegant, with just a few flashes of true opulence: the gold buttons here, the silver lining showing through the slashed doublet there, the gold medal in the hat, the jewelled ring on the finger. That, said Ippolita, was the true polish I must cultivate: not the raffish carelessness of the men who visited my ladies at night.

Early next day, before the courtesans resumed their trade, we met again. They ushered me into a gondola. As we skimmed along the Rio di San Cassiano, I amused myself trying to steal kisses from the ladies. But their minds were entirely elsewhere.

'Do the three Milanese women at the sign of the Angel Raffaele still make the best lace?' asked Dardania.

'Of course they do,' said Armida. 'And close by is the place for the best cambric.'

'You mean the Calle dei Preti?'

'Naturally. And we shall need a silk-draper, and a hat-maker, and a cutler.'

I gave up. When we put in at the Rialto Bridge I let the ladies guide me from one shop to the next. I ordered a black velvet doublet, slashed with cream-coloured silk, maroon silk hose, a cap with short ostrich feathers frothing all round its brim, new shirts with lace at the collar, and a rapier of Spanish steel, for which I chose a silver guard and a black leather scabbard. All this, you may imagine, required a shower of ducats from my purse. Martin looked on with apprehension.

'They are using you,' he told me, late that night as we walked home from yet another session above the bridge. 'Their only chance of real comfort is to find a patron, someone to set them up on their own. Someone like you. I warn you, master, they will bleed your purse dry.'

I shrugged him off in annoyance. Soon I would be a nobleman, to all appearances. And to those who dress richly, it seemed to me, riches must necessarily come. I worked hard at the accomplishments that completed the part: including Italian as it is spoken in Venice.

'Not "angelo",' said Armida. 'Anzolo.'

'And not "Venetsia",' Dardania corrected me. 'Venezzsia – zzs.' When I tried to copy it, that sound which Venetians spell with an 'x', they all fell back, laughing. They made me stand on a napkin, too, and practise my bows. I swept off my hat, overbalanced and broke a glass, at which they laughed more than ever. Late at night when the clocks struck three, and all courtesans were bound to shut their doors, I made my way home, tired and bad-tempered.

One morning, when I had not been asleep more than a couple of hours, I was woken by Martin shaking my arm. At his side I recognised the water-carrier's boy.

'Come at once,' he whispered to me, 'and you will see something to interest you.'

I grabbed my purse of gold. In a few moments we were out in the early dawn twilight. The shadows were thick in the narrow lanes, and we followed the boy with his lantern like a will o' the wisp. We ducked through an archway and down to the canal, where the old water-carrier was waiting in his boat.

'So there is a ship,' I prompted, as the boy began rowing us out past the fish market in the direction of the Grand Canal.

'There is a ship,' the old man confirmed. 'The master of it is in debt, and he wishes to sell some of his goods at once, before his creditors hear of his arrival, and before the officers of the Customs come out to search. He has already parted with certain rolls of silk: dark work, without lights.'

'And from where has this ship come?' I asked.

The old man turned back to me, and I saw in his eyes for a moment the excitement that all Venetians feel at the mention of the East. 'From Egypt.'

We were drawing away from the city, out into the Lagoon. The early morning mist lay in swirls over the water. Rising from it was a ship: a great ship of good tonnage, with a high, gilded stern and the figure of a triton at her bow. It had rained in the night, and her sails were spread in the slack air to dry. We had perhaps an hour's grace before her arrival was known. To come aboard before the officers of the Dogana was a crime of seriousness. I must finish whatever business waited for me on board, and get away with dispatch.

I climbed the ladder, and clasped the hand of the ship's master, a bearded Neapolitan with a scar running down one cheek. He nodded and led me astern into the great cabin. I saw Martin come in after me and look round with a scowl, his hand on the hilt of his dagger. Only now did I realise how imprudent I had been. We were at their mercy out here, in the morning mist, unknown to anyone. And they knew that we carried gold. Robbery and murder would be easy. I jumped as the master shut the door behind me. But then he walked over to a table spread with a white cloth beneath a hanging lantern, and nudged towards me a leather pouch. I sat down and tipped out a scatter of stones.

I thrilled to see them tumble out in front of me. There were fifteen or so of them, all uncut, some larger, some smaller. The light in here was poor, and in the morning's hurry I had forgotten my scales. This would be a stern test: I was about to find out whether I had profited from my hours in the shops on Cheapside; whether my eyes and ears had been open, or whether, as the goldsmiths say of a stone that is dull and admits no light, I had been deaf and blind. I held the first stone up to the lanternlight. It had a pallid yellow gleam like a young oakleaf, and yet it was oddly darkened; whichever way I held it, it refused to shine. In its depths were flecks of gold. I was almost sure this was a chrysoprase, of India. This kind of stone must be cut with care, most commonly into a six-sided figure; too often even this fails, and it appears dull, blunt, quenched of all its fire. Only time would tell. If I was right, this stone could be nursed into a surprising and uncommon glory.

I put it down, forcing myself to seem unconcerned. The captain was stooping over me. 'Well? Come, you must be quick.'

I turned to another of the stones. This one, grey-green and lumpish, sat against the cloth as dark as a common pebble. As I held it up to the lantern its gloom deepened; but then it must have caught the tiniest gleam, and it erupted suddenly into life. A shaft of pure forest-green shot out of it, leaving the heart of the stone still a mystery. I stood for a long time, gazing, turning the stone in my fingers, entirely forgetting where I was. A stone of this depth must, I thought, be an emerald of Persia. You might gaze on it every day of your life, and never understand it. There was no question it was a stone worthy of a king.

Just then one of the sailors burst in at the door and said something to the captain in a rapid Neapolitan dialect which I did not catch. The captain hurried to the window, and swore. Martin peered out beside him.

'It's the Customs officers, master. We're in trouble.'

I looked round. Through the stern windows a boat could be seen, pulling out from the city through the clearing mist. It was being rowed by several men, and from the bold streak of its wake it must be closing on us fast. I turned back to the stones.

'Master! Please! We must go!'

I picked up a white stone of the soft colour of skimmed milk. A sapphire, not a doubt. And I saw a scatter of Oriental amethysts, and several large garnets of a good red flame. I longed to gaze inside each one. But the danger now was pressing. I looked up at the captain, who kept his hard eyes fixed on me.

'So?' he demanded. 'What will you offer?'

I stretched, as if there were all the time in the world.

'Difficult to set a price,' I said, 'without scales, and in this light. If you would bring your stones ashore to the Rialto, perhaps this afternoon?'

'By Christ,' the ship's master growled, 'I will sell these stones here or not at all. A thousand: and then I want you off my ship. Or are you asking to have your throat cut?'

Three or four sailors had come in through the open door, and were murmuring together, and pointing out through the window at the rapidly approaching boat. I saw they had knives at their belts.

'You are too late for that,' I told him. 'Our bodies would be found, and you would be hanged at the columns of Saint Mark's.' I considered rapidly. This purchase would be a throw of the dice. The emerald was worth two hundred ducats or more: if it could be made to shine. The sapphire, I thought, a hundred. The amethysts: I could not say if they were perfect; if so, perhaps the same again. The chrysoprase might be worth much, or little or nothing.

'Five hundred.'

'Master, please!' Martin shook my arm. 'There is a law against even being here. Leave them! If we are found here with gold, and these stones!'

The captain rested his fists on the table. 'Eight hundred.'

Another face appeared at the door: it was the water-carrier's boy. 'My grandfather says we are leaving.'

I stood up, and tossed Martin my purse. 'Martin, count out six hundred ducats. Sir,' I said, turning to the captain, 'I regret we cannot continue our discussion further.'

Martin tipped out a shower of gold. He sorted the coins rapidly into mounds of twenty ducats apiece, which he pushed across the table to the captain. I swept the gems back into their pouch, picked up the purse and dropped the company a bow as Martin and the boy rushed for the door. The captain was cursing and muttering, mounding the pile of coins together. 'A bag for this gold! Get it hidden! And you, get off my ship!'

I turned and ran out on deck. Martin was already disappearing down the ladder. The ship had fortunately swung round at anchor, so that the side we had boarded by was hidden from the city. I climbed down, and the boy shoved off with an oar and pulled away into the mist. There was not a breath of wind. The sun was rising, an orange fireball hanging over the city. The boatload of Customs officers was heading for the great ship, not expecting to see anything else. There were six men at the oars, and a man in a feathered hat kneeling up at the bows with one hand on his sword. Suddenly there was a shout across the water, and I saw his arm stretch out. The boat changed its course and began bearing down on us.

'Faster, Zuane,' the old man urged. The boy let his oars splash in the water in his panic. With a growl, Martin pushed him aside and took them from him. His strokes were strong, and we heard the water streaming past beneath us. The mist curled round and about, folding us in blank whiteness one moment and revealing many furlongs of calm, open water the next. Each time the mist cleared, the Customs boat was nearer. I pictured myself now losing everything I had, and being thrown into a Venetian prison, where the fevers breed and condemn you to a death as certain as hanging.

'Look!'

The boy was pointing ahead. I turned, and saw another boat through the mist, its single sail furled on its yard, moving slowly across our bows.

Martin turned his head, and paused at his oars. 'God damn them, now we're finished.'

'No,' said the old man. 'Row! Keep rowing!'

Martin pulled away into a fresh bank of mist. When we came out of it I saw another boat, and another.

'Thank God and Saint Nicholas for the fishing fleet,' said the old water-carrier. 'Turn and follow them.'

Martin did. We could still see the officers behind us, skimming in among the boats. We were in the midst of them. There were the larger round-bottomed *marciliane* with masts, but also a good many rowing skiffs the same size as ours. When I looked back next our pursuers were hanging at their oars, scanning among the boats, unsure.

'Hah!' crowed Martin. 'Let the whoresons puzzle that out!'

'Quiet,' I whispered. 'Sound travels. Just follow those boats.'

We were approaching the edge of the city. You could see the wharves and warehouses, and the towers of the churches rising behind. We slipped in between the houses after a line of fishing boats, down the Rio di San Girolamo. This way led us under the frowning walls of the Ghetto, where the guards in their boats were rowing home after their night's work protecting Christendom from the inmates. One of these boats came abreast of us, a stern officer in feathered hat and black doublet in the prow. He doffed his hat and bowed. I returned the courtesy. Then we turned south, down the Grand Canal, and put in along with the horde of other vessels all landing their night's catch at the fish market, on the north shore of the Rialto. Here no one spared us a glance. We were clear: and our escape had saved the Neapolitans as well. No one could prove we had been anything more than a fishing boat, passing too close to a great ship in the mist.

I stepped ashore at last and gave the water-carriers three ducats, and another three to Martin. He rubbed the coins in his hands, and cast a sideways glance at my purse, into which I had hastily dropped the pouch of jewels.

'I hope, master, you know what you have done.'

8

We walked swiftly back up from the fish market, with the rising sun glinting on paving stones still wet from the night's rain. Maids were coming out of the houses to dip their pails in the wells; handcarts rumbled past, carrying goods to or from the markets. When we got back to the barber's house I locked myself in my bedchamber and told Martin to guard the door with his life. I would be a man in torment until I had opened that pouch again and gauged just what I had bought. I peeled the bed back to its sheet and spread out my hoard.

First I lifted up the emerald and peered at it through my perspective glass, a disc a couple of inches across that had the wonderful property of magnifying any object held just beyond it. As I turned it, the stone allowed me yet another glimpse into its wondrous secrets, and then again it went dark. I put it on the scales. It weighed four and a half carats, just under a scruple: an impressive weight. I still believed this was a stone among thousands; its worth in the end might be three hundred ducats or more. But it would take a masterhand to cut and mount it so that the ordinary eye could see its beauty. I put it down and turned to the others. The chrysoprase too would reward me, but would require skill. The amethysts were a mixed bunch.

Some were dull and pale as crystal; others were too dark, like heavy wine. But between the two extremes were a few that were pure peach-blossom, and another one or two, sky-blue, that flashed with a pale flame. Amethysts of this kind come from the mines of India. They are prized highly, and are worth nearly as much as diamonds. The white sapphire pleased me, and so did most of the garnets. I parted the stones into two piles: those fit for a king, and those not. I took the rejects to one of the underground goldsmiths' shops and sold them for eighty ducats. It was a beginning: but I could not stop there.

I went that morning to the tailor's, and found that my new clothes were ready. I dressed myself in all my finery: my black doublet, the silken hose and silver-edged cloak, and my new velvet hat with the ostrich feathers. Then I took possession of my sword. It was a beautiful piece of steel, with a large cross hilt and curved guard over it. The blade slid with a satisfying swish into its scabbard. With this strapped to my side, tugging at me with its unfamiliar weight, I felt myself beginning to be a gentleman. When night fell I set off with Martin for the Bridge of Nipples.

When I stepped inside the room with the four daybeds I bowed just so, with a backward swish of my cloak, holding my sword hilt in my left hand, while I doffed my hat with the right.

'Most noble ladies,' I said, 'will you do me the honour of accompanying me to a casin?'

The four replied with Ahhs of appreciation. I straightened up, gratified, and presented them with some trinkets I had bought earlier.

'Such the fine gentleman,' Armida laughed, unstopping a bottle of scent.

'But is he ready?' said Dardania.

'He is ready,' said Ippolita with decision. 'But only one of us can take him.'

Ippolita prepared herself. She dressed with care in a gown of yellow satin, with sleeves of green velvet embroidered with Venice gold. Armida braided her hair, and Dardania brought out a gold chain with a large, green jasper set as a pendant, and fastened it round her throat. Ippolita stood before me with poise and restraint, and yet with that *leggiadria*, the grace and lightness, that Venetians so prize. She was no courtesan, but a lady.

She led me out into the street and down to the bridge, where a gondola was waiting. The water swirled past, and I saw from the curtained window that we made several turns into other narrow canals. In a few minutes we bumped against a pier. There were twenty or so gondolas tied up here, many with silver or gold trim and coats of arms blazoned on their cabins, and servants or slaves squatting in their sterns. Behind the pier was a yellow stuccoed building with Moorish arched windows. From inside came the sound of music, and loud voices and laughter. We climbed the stairs to a door guarded by a pair of strongly built servants wearing swords and daggers. I gave them each a supercilious nod, twitched back my cloak to show my bulging purse, and we were through.

We were in a long sala, filled with richly dressed men and women. Some were walking up and down, arm in arm, talking and laughing. But most were sitting at tables over cards, silently intent, then bursting out in sudden shouts of triumph or despair. At one end stood a group of musicians, two playing shawms with their flared mouths in the air, one holding a violin low over his chest, another beating on a drum. Silk hangings, blue and white, shimmered from the walls. From the whole room came a drench of sweat, mingled with ambergris and musk.

Ippolita touched my arm and pointed. 'Over there. That is Giacomo da Crema: the man who gave me my pearls.'

We moved through the crowd until we stood behind one of the tables. Three men were sitting at it, each holding cards. In front of them were piles of ducats, which they tossed into a heap in the middle. The cards were objects of wonder themselves. They were exquisitely painted and gilt, and had on them coins and swords, knights and ladies. I understood nothing of their play.

'The game is primiera,' whispered Ippolita. 'Watch.' The men, I took it, were staking gold on the quality of the cards in their hands, which they were continually rejecting in dissatisfaction and exchanging for others, and throwing in fresh gold from their store. Da Crema was sweating. When one of the others called, 'Go!' and laid down five cards each bristling with swords, da Crema burst out 'The Devil!' and threw his away. The winner leant forward with a burst of taunting laughter and pulled in the pile of gold. The third man dealt a fresh round. I watched in fascination. The thought of staking gold in this fashion horrified me, yet drew me with a powerful attraction. I swore I would never give in to it. My venture was too much of a gamble already.

Da Crema lost again, and the last of his gold was gone. With a trembling hand he reached inside his doublet, pulled out a small purse, and tipped out on the table a scatter of ten or eleven small, blue stones. The other men blinked, and I leant forward to see. They were sapphires: rough, clouded things for the most part that would need severe trimming and discarding, like half-rotten pears. But I liked their colour. It was the pure blue of a summer sky: the most prized shade in a sapphire, and not often to be seen.

One of the other men scoffed. 'These! What are these? Well, play with them then, if you must. A ducat apiece.'

I dropped my purse on the table, so that it fell with a heavy clink. 'I will buy them. Five ducats each.' Da Crema looked up at me like a man saved from hanging. I counted him out fifty-five ducats, and pocketed the stones. Well pleased, I led my Ippolita to a long table where couples were sitting down to a banquet of roast pigeons and Tuscan wine. The wine and my success made me feel amorous, and I was running my hand along Ippolita's leg and trying to persuade her into a balcony or a sideroom, when da Crema came up to us, tossing a large purse of coins in the air and laughing.

'You have brought me Fortune, my friend,' he said, sitting down. 'I desire better acquaintance with you.'

Ippolita gave me a warning look, but I rose and bowed. 'Richard Dansey. Of London.'

He looked at me narrowly, and then at Ippolita, whom he plainly recognised. 'But I do not think you are a noble.'

I bowed again. 'Merely a lover of life, and beauty, and precious stones.'

He laughed and clapped me on the back. 'If that is the case, follow me.'

He led us back down to the quay, to a gondola with a silver dolphin on its door. He stooped into the cabin and called out to the Moorish gondolier, 'Home.'

Ippolita and I followed in ours. As we skimmed down a wider canal the moon came out and shone like quicksilver on the water. The great bell of Saint Mark's struck two in the morning. We put in at last at a row of pilings before a square-set palazzo on the east bank of the Grand Canal. Lights glimmered from its traceried windows. A servant came to meet us with a lighted candelabrum and led us up a broad staircase, through the echoing vastness of a large sala, to an intimate study. Its walls were inlaid with many-coloured marble, against which were set clocks, pictures, statues and books in gilt bindings. But there were many gaps on the shelves. The place had an air of sadness. Da Crema told his servant to lift down a leather-covered box, which he opened.

As the lid came back, a glow of flame leapt from the box. Inside was a ruby: a great ruby, uncut, and of the flattened shape that is the most prized in that variety of stone. It was pale at its extremity but a dark violet within, like the heart of a deeply banked fire. It had depth and it had mystery. I believed it must be from Serendip, that island kingdom of treasures south of India that is also known as Zeilan. It must have weighed a full two scruples, that is, twelve carats or a twelfth of an ounce. I would have killed to possess it.

'My father,' said da Crema, 'collected such things. He would never have his stones set. He said he wanted to see them in their virgin purity. Poor, poor Papa. His stones make me so sad.' He gestured to the servant. 'You! Wine!'

I was gazing still on the ruby.

'Papa was our ambassador to the court of the Grand Turk in Constantinople. It would have made you swoon to see the treasures he brought back. Now most of them are gone. When he died, he made me swear I would never let these last stones see the inside of a shop. But I find I have a need for funds. And you: you are not a shopman.'

I met his eye. 'Indeed I am not.'

The servant came back with the wine and silver goblets, which he set out on a table inlaid with precious woods.

'Well then,' went on da Crema, 'would you care to see more?'

That night, in addition to the ruby, I came away with an emerald of a vivid meadow green. I judged it was of the kind known from ancient times as Scythian, from the land of the Cossacks: the rarest and finest, and most dangerous to mine. I also acquired a small collection of jacinths. These were angry gems that flamed red out of a glare of yellow; from these stones, so Scripture says, will be fashioned the armour of the horsemen of the Apocalypse, who will destroy a third of all men. The ruby alone cost me three hundred ducats: and worth it. I thought back to that first ruby that had tempted me so sorely: a beautiful, obvious, shopman's stone at two thousand, that would have put an end to any further buying. How well I had done to wait. I could imagine myself at last kneeling before the King with these; having men of rank raise their eyebrows in surprise, and turn their heads and murmur when I passed; making women like Hannah Cage breathe quicker when they saw me. Da Crema embraced me as we parted. With the bag of gold I had given him in one hand, he hurried back into his gondola. As we pushed off over the black water I heard him call to his slave, 'What are you waiting for? Back to the casin!'

In the closed cabin of our own gondola, Ippolita lifted one eyebrow. 'And now? Are you pleased?' I had a twinge of sadness, I admit, as I thought of da Crema and his addiction, and the easy way he would lose my gold. But I had my stones, and a bewitching woman was smiling at me from the purple velvet cushion across the tiny cabin. I sprang across to her, making the boat rock. While the gondola glided on, at last we had the sport I had been longing for. I left her at her door, five ducats richer, and walked home across the Rialto.

It was too late to sleep. As dawn rose over the city I opened up my casket and lifted out the stones, turning them over in the clear, pale light to catch their every aspect, greeting the fresh arrivals, and probing the old ones for new discoveries and new approaches into their secrets. But the question of their treatment tormented me. To cut and set them worthily would be a labour of Hercules.

Night after night I returned to the casin. Ippolita often accompanied me, and more than once she left in the company of someone else, some young noble with his gold chain round his neck and his six or seven lackeys at his heels. I smarted at this, but I was not such a fool as to part with the vast sums of gold it would require to make Ippolita all my own. She had her plans, and I had mine. And so I let Giacomo da Crema slip his arm through mine and lead me from one casin to the next, silk-draped halls by shadowed canals thronged with gondolas. The same mad hilarity reigned in all these places, the same air of mingled triumph and misery. Da Crema introduced me as Milor de li Diamanti, the great English aristocrat. While he played I glided from table to table, summoned back when da Crema fell into difficulties by his cries of 'Milor, Milor! Price me this topaz!' Every man and woman there was loaded with precious stones. I watched for my chances, and when luck ran against them, and the fine ladies tearfully began unclasping emerald earrings, or taking ropes of pearls from their hair, I struck. Many of these trinkets were of no use to me, and I sold them to the goldsmiths for a profit. But I acquired a handful of gleaming cats' eyes, and a pleasing addition to my amethysts, each exquisite of its own kind.

One night towards the end of October, when a chill wind was whining in from the sea, I was hurrying home along one of the many narrow lanes of the Carampane when I felt a hand suddenly grab me and swing me back into a dark opening. I tried to reach for my sword, but a foot landed in my stomach and I fell back, to be caught and pinioned by another man, gasping for breath. Martin, I saw, was struggling against another two of them. His lantern, rolling where he had dropped it, darted its light over the paving stones. A fifth man approached me, black-cloaked and hooded, and in his hand was a dagger.

'The Englishman who buys jewels,' he sneered. 'They say you carry all your wealth on your person. Is that true?'

'Who would be such a fool?' I snarled. The casket pressed into my chest. I was sweating. In only a few moments, when they searched me, I would lose everything. I gave another kick and tried to get my arms free, but they gripped me tight. Martin, I noticed, was lying back in the two men's arms, slack and heavy. He appeared to have given up completely.

'We shall see,' the cloaked man replied. 'Perhaps your servant will be the first to talk?'

They dragged us back into the shadows of a blind alleyway. The man with the dagger walked up to Martin, who hung, lifeless and seemingly terrified. I was right about him, I thought with a sense of disgust. He was clever enough at blocking my plans, but in a moment of need he was useless. The leader of the band stood facing him, and menaced him with his dagger. The two men holding him laughed. Suddenly Martin gave a mighty wrench with his thick arms and twisted free. With his left hand he pulled out his dagger. Before he could use it the two men had pinioned his arm; but this did not dismay Martin in the least. I saw his right hand come up, and in it was his cudgel. I had laughed at him for carrying it, this blunt, bully-boy's weapon. He brought it down on the side of one man's face, felling him to the ground with a crunch of bone; the other man let him go. I shouted and tried in vain to struggle loose.

The leader slashed at Martin's face with a knife. Martin dodged, flouted his cudgel in front of the man's eyes, and at the same moment slipped the dagger between his ribs. He fell with a long sigh across the first man, who was on his knees, groaning and holding his face. Their blood began to spread out over the stones. There was still one man facing Martin, fear in his eyes and a short knife in his hand, circling and looking for an opening. I felt my two attackers loosen their grip, and with a sudden jerk I managed to pull myself free. They both drew their knives. One lunged at me, another scuttled round to take Martin in the rear. Clumsily I drew out my sword. The rasp of the steel was loud in that narrow space as it came clear of the scabbard, and the blade flashed in the lanternlight. They turned to face me, and it was at this moment I realised I had not a single idea how to use it. But at the mere sight of that sword the three men backed away out of the alley, turned and ran, their footsteps dying away down the lanes. Martin and I left the two wounded men lying and hurried away, our blades still drawn, until we came out into the open square of Sant' Aponal. Then I sheathed my sword and turned to him.

'Martin, but for you ...'

He looked aside. 'No, master, no thanks. I couldn't have seen you killed, or robbed of all your stones.'

He sounded as if he meant it. I felt a twinge of shame at my earlier unfriendliness and doubts. But he was still my mother's man, and after all he had fought for his own life as well. I reminded myself to be careful. Brushing some of the dust from my cloak, I said, 'That was a pair of good strokes you delivered.'

'I've learnt a few things from working on the London docksides that you never knew: that's all.'

Soon after that I joined a fencing school. The maestro was an old soldier who had fought in the wars against Cesare Borgia, and in his retirement had opened an *accademia di scherma* in a long vaulted hall off the Campo di San Silvestro. On the first day he had me stand with my rapier held out while he feinted and darted round me. I was not to attack: only watch, and wait. 'Patience,' he said. 'Readiness. Alertness. Decision. And speed!' He aimed a swing at my head, and I parried it only just in time. Then he drew suddenly back. 'Good,' he said. 'Your sword is also your shield: it covers you in all parts. Keep your sword point level, and let it not sway. Choose where to strike, and strike there. Never take your eye from your adversary. Never turn your back. If you hesitate –' he closed with three ringing blows, which I parried '– you will pay for it. Decision. Decision, and speed!' I lunged at him, and he parried and swiftly tapped me on the arm with his blade. 'Above all else,' he whispered, 'you will learn to touch without being touched.'

I set myself to my new discipline with determination. As the weeks passed, I learnt the six cuts and the one true thrust, the *punta* that strikes like a scorpion. I learnt the dragon's tail, and the half-time strike, that parries and attacks all in an instant. Then there were the various positions of guard: the iron gate, the falcon, the woman's guard, the crown. These you must fall back on when pressed, and yet be ready to spring out from them suddenly. I learnt how to hide my art, too, and not reveal the number of strokes I could give. I practised the false strokes as well as the true: there is the feint, and the void, and the fool. To fence, I learnt, is to be the master: of yourself, and of your adversary; to control your own fears and his, so that your mind is lucid and calm, and the next stroke is known to yourself only, while your enemy slips into a mist of confusion and terror.

I learnt to fight with other weapons too: the two-handed sword, the short pike, the sword and shield and the dagger and sword, and even with axes and clubs. I learnt to strike with a sword whose tip is tempered and sharpened like a razor, so as to pierce armour. Finally,

I was shown something of how to box and wrestle. Martin was my frequent partner in these exercises. He was heavier than me, and skilful. But I was quick, and I learnt fast. As autumn turned into winter, I managed at last to throw him on his back. He smiled up at me in surprise. 'A lucky grip, master. Still, I would not wish to meet you in a dark lane.'

'Nor I you,' I answered, and pulled him to his feet.

At night, when I could, I went back to Ippolita. I whispered to her of my ambitions and dreams as we lay together in the half-darkness beneath the green silk canopy of her bed, waiting for the three strokes of the bell that would part us.

'We are the same, you and I,' she whispered back. 'We gaze on the higher world of glitter and gold, and we long to be part of it. Oh, you will rise as high as you choose. I have not a doubt of that. And so shall I.'

Later that night, after trudging home, I unlocked my casket. First I always took out the Scythian emerald. It was like Ippolita, I thought: beautiful and alive, filling and glutting the eyesight with pleasure. But it puzzled me. It was like no emerald I had ever seen. It was too swiftly transparent, had a brilliant sparkle, and was altogether too ready with its charms. A courtesan among stones. I set it aside with a hint of suspicion. From the Scythian emerald I turned to the Persian. Here was a stone that obsessed me. I turned it in my fingers night after night trying to see inside its heart. Some nights it was blank and surly, and refused outright to shine. At other times it suddenly opened and revealed itself, took me by the hand and led me into a dark and undiscovered country. Moonlit nights were best for this; and that quality of the stone amazed me, and made me a little afraid. Another woman came into my mind as I gazed on this stone; a woman I knew I should try hard to forget.

All this time I continued to buy. I was well known now. I had no need to scour the warehouses: the merchants came to me, and sea captains just in from Cairo, Constantinople or Tunis. In this way I added several large stones of the kind called balasse or palatius: the red-violet rock that is the palace or womb in which rubies are born, and which nourishes them with its blood. Also, for two hundred ducats, I acquired a pleasing collection of opals. An opal is a wonder. Its colours are innumerable, flaming like a ruby, green as spring, sulphurous, dark as dusk, milkish, clear. They tease you and laugh at you, and change, and change again. Their glow is not the bright flash of a diamond or a ruby. It is a ghostlike sheen that seems to hover, deep within. I fell in love with these stones, even as they drove me mad.

December came. The winds blew up from the Adriatic, and the rain fell, making the brick paving on the alleys shine and beating the water in the canals a silver-grey. At Christmas I had a letter from my mother.

When will you be turning back? she asked. *You may wish to know there have been all manner of revels, masquings and disguisings at Court, and dancing with great companies of ladies. The King smiles equally on them all. So you see you are mistaken: there is no new mistress. I fear I have indulged your folly much too far. Come home, and we shall see what can be done for your debt.*

I put the letter aside in annoyance. Despite myself, I felt a stab of doubt. What if there truly was no lady? It would be my ruin. Who but a king in love would pay what my stones were worth? With my mother's letter came a second, from Uncle Bennet, and I snatched this up, hoping for better news. I consulted the cipher we had agreed, and set to work to decode it.

Your news is of value, Bennet wrote. *Now I shall give you mine. Of your supposed royal mistress I can give you no word, but there are other strange stories at Court. They say the King's conscience is troubled. He fears his marriage to Queen Katherine has broken God's law. He speaks of the curse of Leviticus:* He who marries the wife of his brother does what is forbidden: he has uncovered his brother's nakedness: they shall be childless. *True it is that all King Henry's*

children have died as infants, excepting Princess Mary. These scru-
ples, people say, will end in the King's remarriage. And there are whis-
pers already who the new Queen shall be: the Duchesse d'Alençon,
sister to King Francis. So where is your royal mistress? And I tell you
this: there is a new craftsman come to Court, in the train of Sir
Thomas More. His name is Hans Holbein. He is a man of vast skill,
and he is taking an interest in goldsmithing, and is friendly with Mr
Cornelius. So you see, you have rivals.

I put the letter down in astonishment. No royal lover: and a new
Queen! The thing was impossible. But who would know better than
Bennet? If only I were in England, and could listen to the gossip
myself. I was still convinced the King was in love with a new mistress.
I would hazard all my wealth on it. But would that love survive
Henry's new plans for marriage, if that was what he truly intended?
I wrote back, begging Bennet not to give up his search for the
mistress. Who was she? I had to know.

And then there was Holbein. I had passed through Basel on my
way across Europe, and had seen many of the wondrous wall-
paintings with which Holbein had beautified the outsides of the
houses there. The motion, fire and life in these depictions were extraordinary. If Holbein were really in league with Heyes I had a pair of
rivals to fear. I had to find a goldsmith worthy of my stones, a man
who stood above all the craftsmen of his age. But who? What great
men were there, nowadays? Everywhere in Venice I saw only pale
imitations of Raphael; florid compositions crowded with fat cherubs
or else nymphs, fauns, tritons, muses, nereids, dryads and every
other form of mermaid and fairy known to ancient learning. I had not
come this far to have men such as that work on my jewels. I began to
think of leaving Venice. Genoa would be my goal. It would be
dangerous, crossing the battlefields of Piacenza and Milan, but
Genoa was a capital of the gem trade too: there would be craftsmen
there in plenty. Perhaps, away from Venetian luxury, I might find a
simpler, cleaner style. Besides that, it was a step closer to home: from

Genoa I could strike direct into France. But every time I almost made up my mind to leave, there came another seller with another gem. After all, I still had bills unspent. Just a few stones more. Just another week, I told myself. Another month.

One day in early January, while I was practising strokes of the double-handed sword against a leathern quintain, a stooped old man came up beside me and coughed. He had the air of a nobleman. He was dressed in a long, furred gown, and had an ostrich feather in his hat; but he wore neither a gold chain nor any kind of rings. He bowed.

'You are Messer Richard Dansey?'

I lowered my sword and wiped my brow. 'I am.'

'My name is Lorenzo de' Bardi.' He hesitated. 'I have a gem I wish you to see.'

I was used to this. From the old nobleman's nervous manner I did not expect much. I looked him up and down. His accent was Florentine. I said, 'And what brings you to Venice?'

He laughed sadly and looked down. His poverty was there for all to see. 'I am a ghost. Revisiting the scenes of my former pleasures. Please. Come and see my gem.'

I felt pity for him. And so Martin and I followed him, a long and winding route west into the district of the silk-dyers, where he had rented a set of rooms. The furnishings were poor, and his servants' green velvet liveries were worn and old. Two of them closed the doors and stood in front of them. He motioned me to sit down at a table spread with a white cloth, and then sat down facing me. One of his servants unlocked a domed iron-bound coffer, took out from it an inlaid jewel box which he also unlocked, and laid on the table a red velvet pouch. Another servant meanwhile poured us both wine from an earthenware jug: rough country stuff that I would normally disdain to drink. De' Bardi pushed the pouch towards me, his eyes gleaming. This was a lot of ceremony, I thought, for goods that could hardly be worth much.

I reached inside and pulled out a single stone. Its surface was smooth as ice, rippling as if in gentle facets, with a dull, leaden gleam. I turned it in my fingers, wondering. It had neither shine nor depth. I could not place it. It could have been a drab white sapphire, or a mere lump of rock crystal. It was large, perhaps thirty or forty carats; about the size of a hazelnut. Then, suddenly, the milky surface of the stone parted. The light plunged in, down, down, into deep blue waters, alongside a snaking white flaw. As I turned it the colours gathered, darting back up in flames of orange and sulphur and shafts of green that broke over my skin like a waterfall. I let out a cry. For an instant longer the colours danced for me, and then, as I turned it a fraction, they faded like smoke, and the stone lay once more in my hand, dull and grey, a lifeless pebble. I felt a stab of grief at the vanishing of that light, and I turned the stone again, searching until once more the gleams flickered and shot out. It was a diamond, and of the rarest kind. I had seen a stone of this sort just once before, in the shop of Bartholomew Reade. It had been tiny, less than five carats, but all the goldsmiths of the Row had come to his shop to gaze on it. Not one of them had dared try to cut it.

I looked up at de' Bardi. He was looking at the stone, unblinking, his deep eyes aglow. He said, 'Do you know what it is you hold?'

I could hardly speak. I said, 'It is a diamond. A diamond of the Old Rock of Golconda.'

He nodded. I looked back at the gem. For a long time I turned it in my fingers. De' Bardi spoke.

'It is the last treasure of my house. I had thought to leave it to my heirs. But my son ...' I looked up, to see his face harden. 'My son has disappointed me. He would sell it in an instant. But if I could pass it to someone who understands ... I heard stories about you, Englishman, and the sorts of stones you buy.'

My eye was on the diamond again. De' Bardi leant forward. 'You see how the flame first kindles, then leaps ...'

'And then,' I murmured, 'while you think it is all on fire, how it suddenly turns to water, and is gone.'

'Yes. Yes!' Our eyes met, and we laughed. We understood each other.

'But to catch that light, to trap it, to open its secrets …' I continued to gaze on it.

De' Bardi looked up sharply. 'That would mean having it cut. But would you dare? You see the flaw.'

I did indeed. I had seen such stones shatter. A diamond is of such incomparable hardness that it can only be cut by another diamond; and a prudent craftsman will only use a stone from the self-same mine. But he would find no other stone born from the same vein as this. A lesser diamond must begin the cutting. That would be the time of danger. Not all diamonds are equal, and the most beautiful are not always the strongest. Some invisible crack or line of weakness might suddenly give way, and the whole thing fly into a thousand splinters.

But it would have to be done. At the moment the diamond was wild, fickle, teasing, even cruel. Cutting would tame it. The diamond would learn what at present it did not know: how to be faithful. It would shine out with constancy, not just for those with the patience and the skill to coax it into catching that gleam of light. How I wanted that diamond. I looked up again at the nobleman.

'I am presuming that you are offering me this diamond for sale.'

De' Bardi started, as if stirred from a trance. 'Sale! Yes. Yes. Indeed … if you will tell me how much it is worth?'

The smooth, native polish of the stone's faces sent pale shivers of light darting across the cloth. It was a different creature entirely from the four table-cut stones I had bought from Messer Aaron in the Ghetto four days earlier, though at the time I had been well pleased with myself. I picked it up, turned it again, and nodded, forcing myself to appraise it coolly. The stone had absolute nobility. It had none of the common defects of a diamond. It did not incline to yellowness, or blackness. There was no sign of greasiness on its surface, nor of the common inclusions that could mar its clarity: the flecks of brimstone, or those impurities known as the ice, the salt, the plumbago; no clouds, no shadowing at all. A well-cut diamond of a good colour was reckoned at forty to sixty Venetian ducats the carat; flawed, or otherwise marred, it might only be ten to thirty. If the cutting went well, I could be left with a flawless stone of twenty carats' weight. Multiplying this by the stone's worth per carat, and then by its weight again, according to the usual formula, gave a value of twenty thousand ducats: almost ten times the capital of my venture. It made my palms sweat to think of it. But then again, what if it shattered?

I glanced up at him. 'It is uncommon. I will give you a thousand ducats.' It was far more than I had ever offered before for a gem.

'A thousand?' He tore his eyes from the stone and looked up at me. I could see the doubt and indecision in his face. Plainly he was imagining what my gold might mean to him: relief from debt, perhaps, or from the surly looks of unpaid servants; or a temporary return to the life of honour and ease he once had known.

'Is it enough?' I asked. You see the madness this stone had already driven me to: I was haggling on the old man's behalf, upping the price before he had even spoken.

'It is enough,' he said. 'Enough for my needs, which are pressing, God knows. But this stone …' His eyes rested unblinking on the diamond. 'In a hundred years,' he murmured, 'when our family perhaps has recovered its fortunes, my heirs should have this stone. This one single thing to remember me for.' His face creased, and he began to weep.

I said gently, 'But will the stone still be with your heirs, in a hundred years?'

He looked up, wavering. 'If I sell you it, who will cut it?'

'I will find the man. Trust me: I will find him.'

All the time I had my eye on the diamond. Its lustre tantalised me. The secrets it hid were deeper even than those of my emerald of Persia. The stone breathed with confidence in its own beauty and power. It was a stone for those who command in the world; a stone for a king; a stone to reflect a kingly passion that is so much stronger than the loves of ordinary men because there is no power on earth to restrain it, not fear, nor law, nor shame. I turned the stone again. I was considering what I could do with it, what thickets of gold I might weave round it, what nymphs, simple and delicate, I could have carved in relief, poised to step inside its cool waters.

Suddenly de' Bardi darted forward and put his hand on the diamond.

'No,' he said. 'No. I cannot. It is the last treasure of my house. I cannot part with it.'

He took the diamond from my hands, dropped it back in its pouch and stood up. I jumped to my feet. I could not conceive he could now deny me.

'But, most noble sir, if we said twelve hundred ducats?'

Again he paused. I set my purse down on the table and loosened its strings. There were only some two hundred ducats left inside. That was ill luck: I felt certain that a sufficient pile of gold would cast an enchantment on him to outweigh that of the diamond.

'Martin,' I called. 'Quickly! Run to the Fuggers' agent at the German Fontego and change me another bill.'

I began to reach inside my doublet for the casket where I kept my bills of exchange as well as my jewels. The nobleman put a hand on my arm.

'No. Truly. I see how wrong I was now. My heirs will have it. They must. But, sir, I have taken such pleasure in our meeting. Will you not sit with me? Take a little more wine, perhaps look a while longer upon the stone?'

One of his servants hovered behind with the jug. I was beaten: but I did not have to take it with humility. I snatched up my purse, and, with a quick bow, walked straight out of the room. Martin came running after me down the stairs. 'Master! Perhaps if we stayed and drank with him?'

I turned on him.

'No! Did you not see his face? We have lost it.' I walked out into the cramped street and began walking fast for home. Where had I slipped up? Did my mistake lie in being the first to mention money? Or in giving him time to think, while the stone bewitched me? Or in my use of that word, 'uncommon'? Never flatter the goods before you buy: so said Morgan Wolf. But that was a meanness, to my mind, when in the presence of beauty. For a moment, I had been a hair's breadth from having it: the finest diamond I would ever see in my life. I stopped in the middle of the Campo di San Silvestro and looked around. A cold wind whipped up from the Grand Canal. A light drizzle was beginning. As Martin caught me up I said to him, 'Pack our things. We are leaving Venice.' He stared at me. I turned and crossed the square to the fencing school, to let out some of my frustration with my rapier.

Even so, it was a hard matter to make myself go. After six months here I almost counted myself a Venetian. I was a different being from the bedraggled London apprentice who had trudged the Rialto back in August. I had learnt to bow and murmur with the Venetian's incomparable deference, '*Schiavo su*': Sir, I am your slave. Or, as the nobles shorten it, '*S'ciao*' or simply '*Ciao*'. I had made grand acquaintances: not only Giacomo da Crema, but older and more substantial men. The senator Ludovico Falier, whose ancestor was the only doge to lose his head for treason; Alvise Pasqualino, one of the procurators of Saint Mark; and the little-loved Imperial ambassador, the Spanish grandee Alonso Sanchez. From all these men I had bought the odd stone. I had sold to some of them too: and so I had made a tidy profit during these months, in addition to filling my casket.

On my last night above the little stone bridge I brought the four ladies flasks of musk and lengths of vermilion and lemon-coloured silk that I had bought from a Turk just in from Damascus. Angelica sat and sniffed the musk, while Armida and Dardania wound their silks round them with cries of delight. They had cost me dear, these four. But I would miss them. Ippolita pressed herself against my arm.

'But you cannot leave, with the Carnival so near? There will be masquing, and plays in the streets, and bull races, and balls.'

The temptation was strong to obey her. The pull of the pure, cool, easy Scythian stone was upon me again. But I knew how it would end. If I stayed much longer, I would turn all Venetian. I would lose myself. My trade and my ambitions would cease to matter, and I would become another Giacomo da Crema, sinking slowly under the weight of Venice's delights. Better to leave now, while the pleasures were still sweet. That night our love-making was of the simpler, gentler kind. Afterwards I lay on my back, thinking. Ippolita stirred in the crook of my arm. She whispered, 'Do you love me?'

'Surely.'

She sighed. 'There is a marchese who is mad for love of me,' she whispered again. 'He will give me a palazzo, on the Grand Canal.'

'I have no doubt of it.'

She reached beneath her pillow and handed me something. It was a book, bound in yellow leather.

'Here. The *Canzoniere* of Petrarch. Read his verses. They will be the last touch to turn you into a courtier. And some woman will love you all the more for it.'

I smiled, and lay for a long time with her in my arms. When the distant bell of Saint Mark's struck three, I leant over and kissed Ippolita on the cheek, waking her from a light sleep. Then I parted the silk canopy of the bed, got dressed and walked down the stairs.

At the street door, Martin was waiting for me. I had never asked what he did while I was employed upstairs; I now saw that he had made a conquest of his own. A young girl of about sixteen turned from him in tears and darted back inside one of the rooms. I put my hand on his shoulder and together we stepped out into the lane.

Martin lifted our trunk. In my casket I had a fresh sheaf of bills of exchange, drawn on the Bank of Saint George in Genoa. As dawn rose we set off across the lagoon, rowed by our friends the water-carriers. Behind us floated Venice, her domes and towers soon swallowed in a soft, white mist.

Chrysoprase: the Lantern in the Darkness

Ostia, 27 January 1527

Love,
That from the right path led them off
To labyrinths and wandering ways;
And all the good that ever they had done
Was in that moment ugly and defiled.

LUDOVICO ARIOSTO, *ORLANDO FURIOSO*

Chrysoprase:
the Lantern in
the Darkness

9

On a grey, drizzling morning towards the end of January 1527, the great ship *Speranza* turned between the star forts at the mouth of the Tiber and began to make her way upriver towards Ostia, the port of Rome. A chill breeze was blowing in off the sea. I reached up to touch the gold medal pinned to the brim of my hat below the ostrich feathers, to check it was safe. It was entirely on account of that medal that I had embarked on this latest voyage. Martin glanced up at it uneasily. I suspected he would gladly have thrown the thing in the sea.

Six days earlier, I had still been walking the back streets of Genoa, looking in every goldsmith's shop I could find. The city's wealth was recovering after the Emperor's troops had sacked Genoa five years before. In the shops there were diamonds of India and opals and emeralds in plenty. As I toured the counters, Martin whistled at what we saw, and tugged my arm. 'Master! This one? Or what about that sapphire?' His eye for gems was improving: I had to grant him that. But I was no longer in the market for stones. I was looking at the gold bracelets, enamelled and chiselled, at the brooches, the intaglios, the bronze reliefs. I was on the hunt for my craftsman, the man who would be worthy to set my stones in gold.

At the end of each day I trudged back through the lanes to the Angel Inn behind the Arsenal in a worsening temper. Soon it would be the Carnival: Shrovetide, as we call it in England. It was a year since I stood at the tiltyard at Greenwich and saw the marks of the King's passion. Far too much time had passed already. Soon, if I could not find a craftsman to please me, I would have to take my stones home, naked and unmounted, and hand them over to Christian Breakespere or Morgan Wolf. Night after night as I lay awake I tried to convince myself that this was the right course. They would do a good enough job; the stones would still shine through. But I doubted such stones as my dark emerald or those opals had ever been seen in London. I pictured old Breakespere shaking his head over the emerald, at a loss, making a guess which angle to favour as the route into its secrets, and putting it to the polishing-wheel. I imagined the stone with its light trapped and dulled, its mysteries hidden forever. But then again, my vain search here in Genoa meant yet more delay: and lost time might ruin my prospects just as surely as common workmanship. To my surprise, I found myself unfolding my problems to Martin. His advice to me was plain.

'Please, master, go home. I beg you.'

'That's what my mother wants, isn't it?'

He looked down awkwardly at his feet. 'It's true. She meant me to get you home as soon as possible. Never mind if you lost the money. She told me you were just a child, and the lost gold would shock you into sense.' He stirred uneasily. 'And I believed her.'

So there it was, out in the open at last. I bit my teeth together in anger as I thought of the Widow. To Martin I said, 'And what do you think now?'

He glanced up. 'I think you are going to prove her very much mistaken. But please, master! Only if we turn back at once. Soon it will be spring, and the armies will be back on the move. Even for you there's a limit to luck.'

I said nothing. Every night I fought both sides of this battle, and every night I vowed myself to just one more day's search. Tomorrow, I repeated: tomorrow might just be the day.

There came a morning when I was walking the streets behind the fish market, up above the Mole where the rope-makers worked. I had passed through this district some four or five times before. But this time I noticed a shop I had not seen on my previous visits, nested in behind a silk-maker's. In its window were silver chalices and platters, pattens and pyxes for the Mass: nothing to tempt me. But out of duty I stepped inside. Martin followed me, and we split up to go sniffing along the shelves in our usual manner. At the back of the shop was a tray of medals, gold discs about three inches across, of the kind noblemen like to wear in their hats. I glanced along the tray. Most of them were fussy things, crowded compositions of saints clutching the emblems of their martyrdom, or the usual groups of Muses, Victories and Cupids. Then my eye stopped. I was looking at a Virgin and Child. The design was deeply incised, simple and bold. The mother had her eyes cast down with a look that was both sad and tender, as if she had a full awareness of the Holy Infant's destiny. The child himself gazed straight out of the medal with a look of calm certainty. It was alive: there is no other word for it. My heart began to beat fast. I glanced up at the shopman.

'Who made this? You?'

The goldsmith smiled and shook his head. He was honest; or he knew how different this medal was from the rest of his stock, and how impossible it would be to deceive me.

'No. I bought this from a churchman. An envoy from the Pope who was caught short of funds.'

I was turning the thing over in wonder in my hands. The positions of the figures' limbs and the draperies of their clothes were so full of motion and life that you would think the pair caught in some instant of change, and about to break out into fresh movement: the child's arm would carry on swinging down, the mother's fingers clench.

Even the back was beautifully finished, with the fastening done as a looping rope of gold that looked as if it should be slack as the real thing, but in fact was solid.

'But can you tell me who made it?'

'I was told it was a very young man, who has just opened a studio of his own. A man named Cellini. Benvenuto Cellini, in Rome.'

I frowned. 'Rome!' It was far, much too far.

Martin caught my eye, and started to move to the door. 'Too bad, master. Let's go.'

I still held the medal in my hand.

'How much?'

The shopman detected, perhaps, my keenness. 'Eighty ducats.'

I did not argue. I ordered Martin to count out the money, and pinned the medal in my hat. From that moment, the medal began to work its enchantment on me. Prudence spoke against it, and for two days I wavered. But I knew that Virgin and Child would reproach me forever if I turned for home now.

And so here I was, springing down the ladder of the *Speranza* to be first ashore at Ostia. My spirits were high. I had been to Ostia before, on ventures with Mr William, when the *Rose* had coasted from Genoa down as far as Naples. But I had never travelled those extra thirteen miles inland to Rome. Martin and I left the Fieschi brothers and the rest loading up their silks and velvets on to packhorses, and with a couple of hired horses and a guide we set off.

The road crossed a desolate marsh, filled with pools, reeds and the cries of herons. For a time we rode along an ancient causeway, but this soon turned to ruin, and we struggled along by the side of its broken arches until these too ran out. The rain had been falling steadily, and in places our guide had to range about over the flooded ground before he could be sure where the road ran. Martin grumbled and cursed continually. 'We might be over the border in Savoy now. Or crossing into France. All this journey just in search of one man?' I rode on in a worsening temper. Repeatedly I touched the medal in my hat.

After two hours or so the road began to rise up out of the marshes. Before us stretched the Campagna, a vast, empty plain with here and there a small farm or a ruin perched on a hill. Long-horned cattle and goats wandered across it. It was a dismal sight, with the rain blowing continually and the mountains dim in the distance. But before us, sprawling in a vast circuit of walls and towers, was the city. Rome. I took my hat off and shouted, and attempted to spur my horse to more speed. Martin looked sourly at me, the rain dripping from his cap. We reached the walls, and there I saw as massive a city gate as you could find anywhere in the world. Its two round towers bore ranks of cannon ports, with more over the narrow gateway itself. It was wise for the Pope to keep his city so well protected. The Kingdom of Naples belonged to the Emperor, and its frontier was only forty miles away to the south-east. As we passed inside the gate, I swept my hat off to the captain of the guards, and he replied with a bow full of satisfying deference. Very different, this, from my arrival in Venice six months before, an insignificant boy fresh from the Thames. I rode inside the city of the Popes with all the pride of a conqueror.

But once through the gate I looked round in astonishment. Here was no city at all, but only more emptiness: the same pastures and orchards we had been crossing for miles, with yet more ruins, the odd small farm, a lonely monastery. Left and right, enclosing these vast tracts of ground, the city walls stretched in an arc. A quarter of a mile ahead, beyond a small rocky hill, we at last approached the beginnings of a city, mean houses climbing among the ruins, and hints of larger palazzi beyond. And so here was Rome: shrunken and weak within the walls of the ancient city of the emperors, like a crumpled old man going about in the clothes that had fitted him in his youth. Martin darted me a look, as if to say, 'Do you expect to find a goldsmith in a place like this?'

We passed in among the houses. We rode down streets that were broad and grand, and others cramped and sunless, with the shops crowding into ancient colonnades or under the shelter of some half-ruined theatre or bath-house. Here and there we saw tremendous new-built palaces that must belong to the Roman nobles, square-set and imposing, without any of the Oriental flourishes of the palazzi of Venice. My spirits revived at their grandeur. I asked the youth who was guiding us to bring us to a good inn. And so we dismounted in a long, rectangular piazza, the Campo dei Fiori, filled with the bustle of marketeers, and fronted by palazzi and several almost equally grand-looking inns. Their signs, painted on the stuccoed fronts of the buildings, shone in the winter sun: the Ship, the Angel, the Moon. I chose the Ship, as a fitting emblem for a successful venture, and when Martin had set the trunk down in a chamber there we set off at once through the streets on foot, following the directions the innkeeper had given me for the quarter of the goldsmiths.

As we walked, I looked round at everything. We passed down a street of crossbow-makers, another of locksmiths, another of hatters; signs of wealthy commerce that pleased me. Even the ground beneath us was paved with good, smooth stones, and this was an amazement to me. In Venice, the streets had been paved with bricks, set in the earth unevenly on their sides, while in London all but the grandest streets have no other surfacing but the filth of ages, and gravel must be strewn if a grand procession is to pass by without wallowing in the mud.

We turned a corner on to a street that stretched away into the distance, wondrously straight and wide. This was the Via Giulia, that had been laid out fifteen years ago by Pope Julius. It cut its way deep into the mercantile heart of Rome, with new-built shops on either side, and a half-finished church dedicated to Saint Eligius, patron of the goldsmiths. On our left lay the river, while ahead and on our right began the district known as the Banchi. All the various banking firms were here, the Fuggers, the houses of the Medici and

Chigi, and the great Roman family, the Orsini. There was the newly built Papal Mint too, with the arms of Pope Clement carved on its façade: six red Medici spheres on gold. At the Fuggers' agent I changed a bill for gold; I had a strong belief in the power of coin as being more persuasive than paper.

As we came out of the office I looked up and down the narrow street. 'Now, my Martin, we begin our search.'

The shops of the goldsmiths were scattered all through this district. It should be an easy task to find the man I wanted. But the first shopman I asked had never heard of Cellini; nor had the second. This chagrined me. The man I had chosen to work my stones should be nothing less than famous. The third shop was a large, well-run affair, with a display of huge silver cups and vases, a roaring fire in the furnace, and half a dozen apprentices busy about different tasks. When I mentioned Cellini the goldsmith wiped his hands and scowled.

'Do you hear that? He wants to find Benvenuto!'

All the apprentices laughed.

'Good luck to him!'

'Is he tired of living?'

'Ask the Bishop of Salamanca, whose servant he nearly shot in the face!'

I stood facing the goldsmith, angry. He was a big man, with a full iron-grey beard. 'What do you know about Cellini, and where is he?'

'I know he's a Devil,' said the man. 'My name is Lucagnolo da Jesi, goldsmith to the Pope. Until a few years back Benvenuto was a poor little apprentice of mine. What's your business, friend? I promise you, this shop is the only one you need to visit.'

I detected Martin fidgeting at my side. This was a prosperous shop, with many hands at work. I could be sure my commissions would be attended to with speed. I looked along the ranks of burnished silver vessels. Their sides were sprinkled generously with cupids, fauns and swags of flowers and leaves.

'But do you also make smaller works?' I asked.

Lucagnolo's face darkened. 'Little trash like Cellini makes? You think I can't? Go, then! I tell you, you can buy this vase for less than one of his little whorish jewels. Go to the Devil! Get out of my shop!'

The apprentices went back to their work: as if studiously trying not to smile. I turned my back and walked out into the street.

'Now what will you do, master?' said Martin. 'You heard him. Cellini's no better than an apprentice. Steer clear, master, I beg you. You can plainly see that he's trouble.'

I rounded on him, and snatched off my hat with its medal. 'The man who made this is no apprentice. As for trouble, I'll wade through a good deal more of it before I give up on this venture. Come along!'

I led him back along the Via Giulia, and then the Old Banchi, and all the various alleys leading off them. I asked in every shop I came to, until at last I came upon an old man by the name of Pagolo Arsago, who nodded and smiled. He too had once been Cellini's master. 'This is a city of slanders,' he told me, with his finger to his lips. 'Do not listen to any of them. You will find him three streets down, on the Vicolo di Calabraga. His is the ninth door, with an old stone shield over it.' The name did not inspire much confidence. Drop-your-drawers Street, or Pissing Alley.

We turned into the lane, narrow and sunless, with buildings towering five storeys high on both sides. Arched doorways lined the street, cramped shops with a single barred window each. The place did indeed stink of piss. I stopped beneath a weathered coat of arms, its design long since disappeared. There was no shop sign; nothing to indicate that a goldsmith worked within. I knocked at the door, and when there was no answer I went in. For a few moments I stood still and stared round me in bewilderment. It seemed to me as if I had blundered into some kind of abandoned lumber room by mistake. The walls were lined with shelves, and these were stuffed with wooden boxes and untidy stacks of papers. In between I saw ends of green or crimson silk, slabs of dark brown wax, a bundle of chisels tied up in string, earthenware pots whose lips were daubed with paint, vials and bottles innumerable and gleaming offcuts of brass and lead, a dish of sulphur and a pile of yellow tallow candles. Beneath the shelves ran a workbench that was similarly loaded with bits of wood and rolls of papers, with here and there a dirty wine cup or two and a glazed dish with some scraps of chicken and bread. On the floor lay a spaniel, asleep, and beside it stood a harquebus and powder horn. Lying on a table next to that was a lute, its round back uppermost, covering a pile of sheet music. I stepped deeper into this marvellous and surprising chamber. Further in, rising up from the midst of the debris, was a figure that made me start back in shock. It was carved out of wood, some three feet tall, and depicted a naked youth with a vicious short-sword in his right hand, while in his left he held up a woman's head. The flow of blood from the severed neck so arrested me that I stood for some moments staring, while Martin shifted behind me and coughed.

From beyond the figure there was a movement, and I saw a man there, sitting at the bench by an elaborate wooden candelabrum and peering at me. He looked to be in his late twenties; he had a bristling black beard, and was scowling from beneath heavy eyebrows.

'Who are you, and what in the Devil's name do you want?'

He spoke in the rolling accent of Florence, which they say is the purest tongue of all Italy. I took a few steps further into the room. I saw clear signs that I was, after all, in a goldsmith's shop: there was the furnace in the far corner, burning with a throaty purr; the crucibles standing beside it and a bucket of charcoal; the ironbound chest; and, on the workbench in front of the man, the slender anvil like a cobbler's last, the fine knives, hammers and drills, and several curling sheets of gold that had been cut into different shapes. But there was none of the boastful display that I had seen in so many dozens of shops before: no trays of medals or racks of rings, no white cloths with pretty stones and trinkets set out teasingly to seduce one to buy. I picked up a small wax figure of Narcissus, gazing lovingly at his reflection, and I glanced at a drawing of Jupiter wielding a thunderbolt, roughly sketched out in charcoal; a Hercules binding three-headed Cerberus, who raged and foamed at every mouth; then a design for a brooch in the form of a lily, set with diamonds and enamels. They had the same spirit and life as my Madonna and Child. It was as if the very next moment they would leap into motion, Jupiter would hurl his thunder, Cerberus would snap, the lily shiver in a breeze. This was the workshop of a visionary, an artist who despised appearances, and let wine and chicken bones and divine inspiration mingle together in equality.

I said, 'I am looking for Messer Benvenuto Cellini.'

'You have found me,' said the man. He put down the file he had been holding in one hand. 'Well? Have you come to buy?'

'I have come,' I said, 'to put you to work. I have some stones that are calling out for you to cut and set them.'

He turned the wooden candelabrum a few degrees to the left and held up a cone of beaten gold against it. I saw that the candelabra had scrolling leaves running up it, and deer leaping from among the foliage, all cut in relief. This was the model for a masterwork in gold.

'When?'

'At once. I must leave Rome again as soon as may be.'

'Impossible. Entirely impossible.'

'That I will not believe.'

He did not look up. 'I have work enough for three months, maybe more.' He tapped the model with his file. 'This candelabrum is for Cardinal Cibo, the Pope's cousin. After that I have a ewer to make for the Apostolic Datary. You see, you have wandered into the wrong shop, my boy. What is it, a ring? Setting stones is childs' work. There are three or four little places down the street that will see to your needs. Now, if you will kindly step out of my light? And leave?'

I walked up to the workbench, leant on it with one hand and tapped the medal on my hat with the other. 'Do you recognise this?'

He glanced up, and then put down his file and peered at it more closely. 'By God, I believe I do. I made that medal for the Bishop of Grosseto, over a year ago. The swine, to part with it. Did he give you it?'

'I bought it.'

'Doubly a swine. How much did you pay?'

'Eighty Genoese ducats.'

'Hm! I see I shall have to put up my prices. And you travelled to Rome to find me? What are you? Venetian?'

I could see I had flattered him; and his mistaking me for a Venetian flattered me in turn.

'No. I am English. My name is Richard Dansey, of London. And I think when you have seen my stones you may change your mind.'

'Well, I shall run my eyes over them.' He stood up. 'Paulino!'

A boy came in, of perhaps sixteen or seventeen years old. He had curling black hair and a finely cut face, and bore a striking resemblance both to the wooden youth holding the severed head and the wax Narcissus. His face wore an expression of deep and classical melancholy.

'Bring us some wine – the Florentine. Oh, and Paulino, be a delightful boy and fetch us some of those candied figs.'

Cellini cleared a space on the workbench by the gory statue of the youth. I saw that beneath his feet the figure was trampling on the headless body of a woman. Runnels of blood spurted from the stump of her neck above perfectly rendered breasts. The severed head which the youth held up was wreathed in snakes.

'Perseus,' said the goldsmith, indicating the figure, 'slaying the Gorgon Medusa. I hope to fashion it one day, in marble or in bronze, if a patron will pay me. They say the blood from the Gorgon's head, as it dripped on the ground, gave birth to Pegasus, who made the spring of the Muses flow. I like to think that Medusa's blood falling on my work gives it an extra fire.'

Paulino came back in with a stubby bottle and a couple of glasses, and a plate of dried, sugared figs. Then he sank silently down on a stool near the furnace and watched us with his heavy eyelids half-closed. Martin sat some distance away and folded his arms.

'Now,' said Cellini, 'let's have a look at these stones. But I promise you nothing. Paulino: light.' The boy came languidly forward, set five candles in the sockets of the exquisitely carved candelabrum and lit them. Then he took a fig from the plate and went back to his place.

I loosened my shirt and pulled the casket out round my neck. Then I set it down beside the wine and unlocked it. I would have only one chance to make an impression. I lifted out first the pair of emeralds and set them side by side, the one shimmering, pale like a meadow, the other opaque, taunting us with its sullenness, yet harbouring a secret gleam somewhere out of sight. Cellini darted forward, then drew back, his eyes fixed on both stones. I saw that I had his attention. I laid out next the four cut diamonds I had bought from the Jew; and after that the amethysts, dark as wine after the rushing water of the diamonds. I followed the amethysts with the fiendish yellow of the jacinths; then the garnets and the balasses with their deeper flame, the golden chrysoprase and the white sapphire. I glanced at the goldsmith's face. He gazed, unblinking, still with the air of a judge who was listening to the witnesses and had not yet made up his mind. Next was da Crema's majestic ruby, wine-red and lustrous, at which Cellini sat up and let out an 'Aha!' Paulino and even Martin leant forward to see. After it came the sparkling cats' eyes, and then in a row the bewitching colours of the opals. Cellini squatted down on the floor so that his eyes were on a level with the workbench. 'Yes, yes, yes,' he murmured, as he gazed into the opals' hearts. He had the air of a huntsman, or a swordsman sizing up his adversary, searching for a line of attack. I almost had him. There were few stones left in the casket. I prayed that they would be enough. The clouded sapphires were next; things of little worth, but of a fine colour, and a few stones that I had bought on the ship in the mist and liked, but had never been able to name. Cellini raised his eyebrows and nodded, as if appreciating the eccentricity of my taste. Last of all I set down in a row Ippolita's seven pearls, and closed the lid of the casket with a snap.

'Holy Mother of God,' Cellini murmured. 'My friend, you do need me. And who is to have these marvels?'

'They are for a great king: to give to the lady he loves in secret.'

The goldsmith took a sip of wine and moved round the stones, nudging one with a finger, darting to one side and drawing suddenly back. I watched him, breathless. Suddenly he said, 'Your pearls have been to China.'

'China? I took them for Persian, from the Strait of Ormuz.'

'In origin, perhaps. But look at how they have been drilled.' He lifted one up. 'Across the base, not through the centre.'

'I know. Well?'

'No European would drill a pearl in that fashion. It would render it useless for the purpose we most prize, stringing them in ropes round the neck. The Chinese do not wear their pearls like that.'

'No?'

'They sew them upon their clothing. I have seen them. Oh yes, all wonders come to Rome. Now, I'm no friend of pearls. Fish bones, that's all they are. They do not last like stones. Women pay thousands of crowns for them, only to see them turn old and blind, and wear away into the shape of a barrel. But these: these are not common. We shall find a use for them.'

A wave of exhilaration swept over me. So, I thought: I had him. But I kept silent, in case the fish was not thoroughly hooked. He continued to circle the gems, and then swooped on a pale stone which had been among the collection I bought on the ship out in the mist. He lifted it up. It was almost without colour, a swirling, livid thing like a lightly overcast sky at sunrise. It fascinated me; I had never seen anything like it, and could not give it either a price or a name. This stone Cellini turned in his fingers in front of the candle flames.

'Of course, you know what you have there? That is a ruby.'

'A ruby!'

'A white ruby. Have you never heard of such a thing? Most white rubies have no value at all. They are as grey and dull as filthy bathwater. The only way you would know them for rubies is by their hardness. But this is of a very different order. Have you held it in the dark? I promise you, it will shine.'

He handed it to me. True enough, it was a wonder the way the light caught and flowed over its surfaces. I had gazed into it on many a night. But the steely sheen of this stone only made me long for the cool waters of that diamond: the diamond I had held so briefly in that cramped room in the silk-dyers' quarter of Venice. There was not a day went by when I did not think of it. I put the white ruby down and sighed. I said, 'If you could only have seen the stone I let slip.'

He looked up at me with a sideways smile. 'The one that got away – is that it? I would like to know what could beat these.'

'It was a diamond: a diamond of the Old Rock of Golconda. Do you know that kind of stone?'

Cellini's face turned serious. 'I know it.' He brooded for a moment. Both of us knew how the stones on the table before us would have longed for that diamond as a companion. Then he clapped me on the back and laughed. 'Regrets, regrets! What you have here is quite enough. The Cardinal's candlestick can wait.'

And so we began. All that day and the next morning Cellini and I remained at his workbench with the stones set out, gazing at them. I sat through this in impatience. 'Great works do not begin rashly,' Cellini said. 'Believe me, we are not wasting our time.' He lifted up one of the opals. It flashed with different shades, now amber, now sea-green, now dark as wine. He shook his head and sighed, and instead picked up a sapphire. 'What colour are the lady's eyes?'

I looked down. I hated to confess my ignorance. But I could not afford to lie. 'That I do not know.'

Cellini put the stone down on the bench and looked at me in indignation. 'Not know! How can you not know?'

'If I had waited to find out, I would still be in England,' I retorted. 'Even now, few men even know that our King is in love. My chance of success lies in speed.'

Cellini waved his arms in exasperation and walked round the bench.

'But do you understand nothing? How infinitely diverse are women? Consider this ruby. Suppose I set it in a cross to hang about the neck. Will it sit in splendour like a cathedral on a plain, or will it be pinched and shaded between two mountains? And these pearls, suppose we make a rope of them: though the way they have been drilled makes that nigh impossible. Will they hang straight like a long cascade, or tumble, as it were, and break their fall against rocks? And what colour is her hair? And her skin? Does she blush? Does she wear paint? You tell me you know none of these things! Santa Maria Vergine!'

'I know all that. And so what are you telling me? That I should give up? I know very well what risks I am taking. You must compensate for my ignorance with your art.'

Cellini sat down on his stool again and pushed the stones aside in annoyance. 'Supposing the fine Signor with the Venetian accent tells me what his own ideas are for his stones.'

My ideas. Night by night, notions and fantasies had woven themselves round the stones as I held them up to the candle, though to that moment they had refused to settle into definite forms. I lifted out one of the clouded sapphires. Its blue was exceptional, pale and lucid; but over its surface forking down into its depths ran blemishes, mists, blurs. To cut these out would mean leaving little behind. I put it back down with the others, and set them out in a line. There were eleven of them. I said, without even realising it, 'The sea.'

'The sea?'

'Yes! Do you not see it?' A picture was forming before me. I swirled the stones with my fingers. 'These sapphires: do not cut them. Keep them as they are, clouded and raw. They are the waves, and the flaws in them are the foam. Their faults are their virtues. Above them is tossed a ship of gold, guided by the stars. Use the diamonds for that. A brooch: you understand?'

Cellini was catching my fire. 'Ingenious. Yes. Yes, the King's love, tormented on a sea of passion, following the stars of hope. By God, it is a sonnet.' He began striding up and down. 'At the centre there must be a great stone. But which? Which? We shall find out. And there will be enamels, and chiselled decoration on the ship, everything in detail. You will see her falconets, her capstans, her topgallants. She is under full sail, bearing onwards, onwards.'

He snatched up a piece of paper and began to sketch. Then he looked up with a sudden glare. 'Of course, you have money?'

I tossed down my supply of golden Papal ducats and double ducats, bearing the Coronation of the Virgin on one side, and Pope Clement's Medici coat of arms on the other. 'Here is my purse.'

Cellini looked up at me with his impish smile. 'It is time, my friend, to open it.'

10

Day by day, I watched in impatience as Cellini worked. He began by modelling in wax. I saw him chisel the fine details of the ship, the waves with the sockets left for the sapphires, and the raging clouds where the diamonds would shine through. 'Nine sapphires,' he told me. 'There is no room for more. The others you can throw away. No one will ever find another use for stones like those.' I noticed he had also left a space for a stone at the centre of the ship, just where the helmsman stands in the steerage-house with his eye on the lodestone needle of the compass. Cellini tapped the socket with his scalpel. 'That is for the chrysoprase. Do not worry if it seems dull now. It will shine, it will shine. It stands for fire: light, the lantern in the darkness. The illumination that passion makes in the lover's soul, and which guides him in one direction only. He never loses that; never swerves. He will do anything for her. Anything.' There was a fierce light in the goldsmith's eye. I wondered at that moment what it was that drove him, and gave him his own fire. But to me he was like my Persian emerald: shadowed. I could not see far inside.

First thing every morning we sat together and simply gazed on the stones in that lucid morning light, and turned over ideas. This was the time when I felt my ignorance concerning the lady most keenly. One day, about two weeks after my arrival in Rome, I received at last a reply from Uncle Bennet. It was addressed from the Palace of Hampton Court; it had been four weeks coming, and had followed me from Venice to Genoa to Rome. I ran with it to Cellini's workshop and left him to gaze on the stones while I unfolded the letter and took out my cipher.

My dear Richard,

It appears that you were right. Everyone at Court is whispering of the King's new love. The lady's name, however, is still a close secret, though there is much guessing. Perhaps Bess Holland, one of the Queen's ladies; perhaps even his old love rekindled, Mrs Mary. But I fear she will not last long in the King's favour. Cardinal Wolsey is labouring night and day for the King's divorce and remarriage. The Great and Secret Affair: that is what he calls it. For Queen Katherine still knows nothing. This match with the Duchesse d'Alençon will be the crowning of Wolsey's policy: an alliance with France, and a break with the Empire. But my master has many enemies. Chief among them is the Duke of Norfolk. The Cardinal had thought he had pushed that blundering old warhorse out of Court, to rot quietly on his ancestral estates. But he is seen more and more round the King. He has even dared challenge the Cardinal. 'The King has a new man in Rome. Now we shall see!' Those were his words, spoken before all the Court. You may picture my master's rage at the affront.

Many of us, his servants, dismiss the Duke's words as a mere idle taunt. But my lord Cardinal is troubled. He has become convinced that there truly is some sort of secret emissary to the Pope, and he believes it concerns this matter of the divorce. I have heard him murmur, 'There is a web spread against me.' And he talks of the Night Crow. But who this is, I cannot say. I beg you, Richard, find any news you can of this man in Rome. I shall be evermore in your debt.

I put the letter down, my mind in a whirl. I was exultant: I had been right, from the very first. The King's love was no chimera. The French marriage: yes, that troubled me. But I hoped it was a mere dynastic match, a union of nations that would leave the King's heart free for his lover. Still, I knew I was guessing in the dark. *There is a web spread against me.* What did that mean? And who was this man in Rome? I took paper and my cipher, and wrote back to Bennet at once, informing him of my arrival in Rome, and promising to do all I could to discover the identity of this mysterious emissary. *In return you must find for me the lady's name*, I went on. *Who she is, what she looks like in every particular. If word of the affair is spreading, surely you can find it out. Go to Cornelius Heyes, who has supplied so many love-trinkets to the King. Offer him money: I will repay you. Be quick: I shall leave Rome as soon as I may.*

My hours spent in the workshop drained and exhausted me, and my impatience would not let me sit still when I left it. Sometimes I took Martin away with me and wandered the city. We walked all that district until I knew it backwards: the lanes behind the Banchi, the grand shops, the church of the Florentines and the great buildings of the Papal government. Further down towards the Campo dei Fiori and my inn, the palazzi of the nobles clustered thickly, often with shops beneath. And always, every few yards, it seemed, there was a church or convent with some saint's tomb, pilgrims pressing to get inside, and beggars and sellers of holy relics crowding round them. There were Englishmen among them, but these were no royal envoys. They had travelled for weeks, perhaps, to bring their prayers here where so many saints lay at rest. I could see the need and the hunger in their eyes. They were like me, I felt: souls in quest, urgent and dissatisfied, though I was a pilgrim of a worldlier kind, in search of fame, and beauty wrought in gold.

When I felt more oppressed than usual I led Martin up the Via Giulia and crossed the river by the Bridge of Sant' Angelo. On the opposite bank was the Castle of Sant' Angelo, the forbidding citadel of the popes with its vast drum-shaped tower, built of rose-coloured stone. It was here the Pope kept his treasury, his arsenals, and his dungeons of heretics and those with whom he had become displeased. To the west stretched the Borgo of Saint Peter, the walled suburb around the Pope's palace. I was headed for Saint Peter's church: the very centre of the Christian world. Surely, I thought, if I could find peace from my racing thoughts anywhere, then it would be here. The first time I walked up from the river and stood before the labyrinthine mass of buildings that made up the greatest church in Christendom, I stopped and gazed in astonishment. What lay before me was really a trinity of churches. In front was the truncated shell of Old Saint Peter's, roofless and half demolished, the nave broken off short, arches left stranded in mid-air, with the centuries-old bell-tower still standing before it. Beyond the old church, soaring high above it, was the incomplete vaulting that might, one day, support the dome of the new building. It was to be immense, and eclipse all other buildings ever conceived. But for the moment, weeds and trees grew from half-built walls that had stood untouched for twenty years after work on it was abandoned. Everyone knew that Pope Clement VII would do nothing towards completing it. His money, what there was of it, was spent on war and on luxury. Yet a third building, a plain barn-like affair of grey stone, rose over the roofless sanctuary of the old church, keeping the rain off the high altar and the tomb of the Apostle Peter himself and the crowds of pilgrims flocking round it. To me, that first time I saw it, the effect was of one church caught in the act of devouring another, a monstrous instant frozen in time.

Here I pressed along with thousands of others to hear Pope Clement say Mass. His Holiness stood at the altar behind the four giant twisted porphyry columns, and raised the host above his head. I gazed at him, this man who was Christ's own Vicar, and who had stirred up a war that had brought all of northern Italy to blood and desolation. He was about fifty, young for a pope, clean-shaven with elegant features and heavily lidded eyes. He glanced around with an expression of noble disdain. I thought of all the things that were said of him, his fabled deviousness, his pride, his malice and cowardice that together made his intentions as unreadable as if they were written in cipher. When Mass was finished I stopped to light a candle at the chapel of Saint Petronilla, patroness of friendly relations between emperor and pope, and prayed that the war would keep its distance until I was many miles on the road for home.

As I was hurrying away down the steps, a voice hailed me from behind. I turned and saw the Fieschi brothers coming towards me. They looked tired.

'Still chasing our Indulgence,' Piero explained. 'And it is a difficult run, I can tell you.'

'Fifty ducats we've paid to the Datary,' put in Federico, 'another hundred to the clerk to the Apostolic Camerlengho, an audience promised with His Holiness yesterday, and the day before, and the day before that, but none forthcoming.'

'They say the Pope can decide nothing, with the war to think about. But we have not given up.'

'*Sempre la speranza*,' I said, punning on the name of their ship. Always hope. They smiled wanly. True enough, the Pope had no interest in small morsels like the Fieschi brothers. They would be picked over by the lesser officials, and if they could find no patron to help them to an audience they would go away empty-handed. That could so easily be my own fate too, once I got home to England. It was a problem that weighed heavily on me, my insignificance, and my lack of a patron at Court. When I had raised the question with Bennet once he had whistled and shaken his head.

'My dear Richard,' he had said, 'finding your brother a place at the college is one thing: there are a hundred places to fill, after all, and he is a good scholar. But to bring the likes of you before the King? That is a different matter entirely.' Before long, this was just what I would be forced to confront. I bowed to the brothers and led Martin back down the hill to the bridge, and the little studio on the Vicolo di Calabraga. I did not like to be away from my gold and my stones for long.

Three weeks had passed since my arrival in Rome, and Cellini had moved on to the next stage of his work. Paulino took down a pair of large earthenware jars and removed the stoppers. Both contained fine, white powders. 'Gesso in one,' Cellini explained, 'and in the other the dust of old clay that has been fired once before.' He took equal scoops from both jars and mixed them in a third, adding water until he had a smooth liquid. Next he took out a small flask and poured a greenish stream from it over the wax mould of the ship. Then he wiped it into all the crevices using a fine ermine-hair brush. 'Olive oil,' he murmured. 'Not too much.' He straightened up and looked at me with a devilish smile. 'So much for the cookery. Now for the work in earnest.' He took some stiff clay from a nearby tub and made a rim around the mould. Then he poured the white gesso mixture on to the wax. I watched in excitement as Cellini smoothed it out over the surface with a brush that was slightly larger than the first.

'And when the plaster is set?' I prompted. 'We are ready for the gold?'

'Not so fast,' Cellini growled. 'Do you want a quick, botched job, or a work of mastery? First I trim and smooth the plaster cast with a knife, and bring it to perfection. Then we shall use this model to make the last mould of all, which will be of bronze. Only then shall we begin to play with gold.'

Every evening, when the light began to fail, he put down his tools and damped the fire. Then we set out together to see, as Cellini called it, the real life of Rome. The Carnival was just beginning. In a couple of weeks it would be Martedì Grasso, Shrove Tuesday, and Benvenuto promised me a night of madness such as I would never forget. Even now, crowds poured out into the streets with the setting sun, gentlemen and nobles, ladies in litters, their masked faces peering from behind the curtains, and pageboys carrying lighted torches before them. There were even cardinals riding their Spanish mules that cost more than a good horse, all decked in scarlet velvet and gold, with Moorish slaves holding silken umbrellas over their heads and their dozens of attendants and guards. They were bound perhaps on some pilgrimage to a nobleman who owned a particular statue of a saint, where there would be music, and dancing, and even some singing boys and a courtesan or two. Darting in between were groups of musicians, acrobats, zanies or dwarfs, all fantastically dressed as Saracens or particoloured fools, who stopped suddenly to perform ribald plays and interludes. The crowds gathered to watch and laugh, and then moved on. In the dark back alleys, the brothels were in full swing. Outside them in little wooden booths were the petty clerks and moneylenders who had bought the rights to sell indulgences where they were most needed. As we passed we heard their hoarse cries, 'Sodomy, twenty ducats!' 'Adultery, fifteen!' 'All sins, past and future, only three hundred ducats!' The money from these indulgences, most of it, went back to the Pope's treasury; but of course the vast organisation who marketed these documents also took its share. Who else? The Fuggers.

Every night Cellini led me into a fresh kind of madness. There were visits to the sumptuous houses of the courtesans that were scattered freely throughout our quarter; there were wild supper parties at the houses of his friends. Here I met Francesco Berni, the poet who could turn you a satire or a sonnet on any subject you threw at him. And there was Michelagnolo the Sienese sculptor, and three or four of the foremost painters of Rome. These were employed on the Pope's various villas, or on the frescos in the Apostolic Palace; they had all been pupils of the great Raphael. There were noblemen there too, young blades, mostly, but older men as well sometimes, patrons of the various artists, who fancied a taste of their free-spirited world. Each one had a woman on his arm: courtesans, plainly, some of whom gathered together in little knots to discuss in giggling whispers 'How I first went wrong'.

After a few hours' sleep we were back in the workshop: myself bleared and half-asleep, but Cellini burning with his usual fire, his hand rock-steady at his scalpel. I looked again at the plaster model of the ship under full sail, which he had broken free of the wax. Every line of it, the clouds, the stars, the waves, breathed with life. I sensed that without those riotous nights, none of this would exist.

The bronze, when he cast it, searing hot from his furnace in a brilliant stream as bright as the sun, was better yet. Word was spreading that Benvenuto was engaged on a work worth seeing. Most days there were three or four nobles in the shop, sitting over wine and watching. I had thought Cellini would fly into one of his rages at these distractions, but instead he found their presence flattering. He was young, not yet thirty, but he was the maestro, and he was executing a work worthy of the greatest.

One morning he put down the file and scalpel he had been using on the bronze mould and held it up. 'Finished.'

There were murmurs of approval from the men in the shop, 'Bravo, Benvenuto,' and applause.

'Now, Messer Richard from London, what do you think we will do next?'

I licked my lips. I had waited night and day, through all Cellini's careful preparations and wild debaucheries, for just this moment. 'Time for the gold.'

'Gold! Ah, yes. But what gold? Any gold? You think you know a lot. Well, we shall take a plate of gold that has been *ricotta*. Yes, gold twice cooked, like the cheese. And gold of a certain fineness. Under twenty-two carats and a half, and the gold will be hard, sluggish, unwilling to work. Above twenty-three carats, and it will be too sweet, as we say: too ready to oblige. It will flow where we do not want it to flow, and lie there like a trollop, fat and without spirit. Paulino: bank up the fire.'

Benvenuto unlocked the large iron chest in the corner and took out a tablet of gold. He weighed it, and recorded the result down to the last grain. Then he set down on the workbench a flat, black stone and a clutch of gleaming needles, threaded together on a string. I watched with attention. They were touch-needles; the first was of pure silver; the next, twenty-three parts silver to one part gold, the next twenty-two to two and so on, until the twenty-fifth was pure gold. Cellini rubbed his lump of gold against the touchstone leaving a streak of colour, and then tried the different needles against it until he achieved a match. Then he weighed out a tiny knob of silver, while Paulino brought out a crucible, well cleaned, and tongs, and opened the door of the furnace. Cellini himself set the gold and silver inside. All of us in that room waited in reverence, unspeaking, while the gold transformed itself into a liquid, brilliant in its beauty, deadly hot, ready to serve Cellini's will. When it was properly molten he lifted it from the furnace with the tongs and poured it out into a disc-shaped iron form to cool. Then he tested it again using the needles and stone. I watched, hardly able to breathe.

'It is ready.'

He laid the thin disc of gold over the bronze mould and set to work, massaging and pressing it, now with a chisel made of heather-wood, now with a scalpel, easing it with infinite gentleness into all the figure's folds, taking care always to draw the metal into an even thickness, and guarding against cracks. Gold, for all its beauty, is soft: you could have twisted that disc of metal with your fingers. Having pressed the gold into shape all round, he began a second massaging, where he knew the pattern was finest, teasing the metal into the fissures in the bronze with a forward and then a backward pressure. It was the work of several hours, but Cellini did not once pause or look up. At last he laid down his tools and said, 'Now let us see if I have been wasting my time.'

He prised the gold away from the dull brown of the bronze and lifted up the finished disc. The room fell silent; I gazed at it in wonder. The ship leapt through the curling waves, sails and ropes taut. It was less than three inches broad; but it was urgent, driven, haunting, obsessed. Beneath the ship were nine small sockets for the sapphires. Above it was space for the four diamonds, and at the very centre, in the ship's hull just beneath where the helmsman stands, was a single large gap that would take the chrysoprase.

'Well?' said Cellini.

'It is magnificent,' I said. But even as I said it, a malaise was spreading over me. The noblemen in the studio came past me and clapped Benvenuto on the back.

'A miracle!'

'Superb!'

'You are a master!'

The goldsmith kept his eyes fixed on me. I glanced aside. 'Martin!' I called. 'Run to the tavern down the lane and bring us back a jug of their best wine.'

Martin, who never ran, gave me a sombre look and set off. I looked again at the wondrous ship. It daunted me: it made me angry at the lowness of my rank, compared with the beauty of the gold. I felt that I myself was such a ship, carried on, on, through winter seas. Where to? What lay waiting for me at journey's end?

Martin poured the wine, and I joined the circle about Cellini's bench.

'You are a match for Raphael,' one man was saying. 'Almost divine. Your fortune is made, Benvenuto. The Pope's other goldsmiths will burst their spleens with envy.'

There was laughter, a raising of glasses, more wine. But Cellini still kept his fierce eye fixed on me. 'Englishman. What is the matter with you? You look like a man about to be hanged. My work displeases you?'

I looked up at him. 'It pleases me, all too well.' I glanced round the circle. There were five of them with us, aristocrats with their gentle smiles, neat beards, pearl earrings, rakishly tilted feathered hats. And that was just the trouble. Here in Rome I mixed with counts and marchesi, but in England I would come down to earth hard. I knew no one. I would be the Widow Dansey's son, of Broken Wharf, and that was all.

'Forgive me,' I said. I was unwilling to speak; but Cellini's eyes bored into me, and he deserved my honesty. 'It is nothing of your doing, Benvenuto. But in London it is not my good fortune to mix in such exalted company as here. No one will believe that such a one as I could have such a treasure to show the Court.'

Cellini snorted. 'This man's improvidence astounds me. Do you truly know no one at the English Court?'

I hung my head, readying myself for their laughter. But the nobles did not laugh. They leant forward, and all began to talk.

'My dear Messer Richard, there is no difficulty in that.'

'Sir John Russell is in Rome, to negotiate for peace with the Empire. King Henry's ambassador: we can present you to him at any time.'

'And Thomas Wyatt is here, Sir Harry Wyatt's son: no courtier is more perfect.'

I looked up. 'And you know these men?' I was almost gasping with amazement.

Cellini laughed and clapped me on the shoulder. 'My friends know everyone. Alessandro here even has an English courtier lodging in his house. He has been here for months, with his wife and daughters. What is his name? You would present my friend to him, would you not?'

My head was ringing. Russell, King Henry's most trusted diplomatic agent. And Wyatt: poet, connoisseur, and was he not also clerk of the King's jewels? The influence these men possessed staggered me.

Alessandro del Bene, a perfumed young noble in a crimson doublet, kissed his hand to Cellini. 'I would do a thousand harder things, Benvenuto, to please you.' Alessandro belonged to one of the great banking families of Rome. His ancestors had been driven out of Florence over a plot, and so Cellini liked to tease him and call him 'that damned exile'. He had a lucrative post in the Papal Treasury, and owned a part share in the sheep-pasturing monopoly throughout the Patrimony of Saint Peter; sinecure jobs which left him a good deal of leisure for the pursuits proper to nobility. But he was a shrewd courtier for all that. He turned to me. 'The man's name is Stephen Cage. But what his business is here, I really cannot say.'

The name stopped me dead. My mind jumped back a year to that grove of paper flowers in the great hall at Eltham, and Hannah Cage's words: 'I am going somewhere I do not think you will find me.' How wrong she would find she had been.

I said, with inward relish, 'Stephen Cage.' Why did I care so very much for that black-haired girl who had laughed at me? She was the essence of the world I hankered for. Her ease, her pride, her disdain; they were qualities she shared with the finest gems. And I had the chance to step into her world, into her very family. A Roman nobleman would present me to her with proper ceremony and I would make my bow to her as an equal. I felt my palms sweat, and the colour rise in my face. But her father? Could he present me to the King? What did I really know about him?

Martin started towards me. 'Master,' he whispered. 'Surely, Thomas Wyatt, or else Russell ...?'

I shook my head. 'No. Stephen Cage.' I faced towards Alessandro. 'If you would be so kind?'

He bowed, and Cellini sealed it with his ringing laugh. 'Then that is all settled. Paulino! Another bottle! It is too late to go back to work now.'

11

Next afternoon I set out with Cellini down the Via Giulia. It was Sunday, the third of March, just two days before the Tuesday that would mark the end of the Carnival. There was music everywhere, and actors in masks danced through the streets. My heart was beating hard. The last time I met Hannah I had been nobody, and she had treated me with little more than amusement. But this time things would be different. I had mixed with nobles, both here and in Venice. I had the courtier's bow and the courtier's clothes: with my black velvet Venetian doublet, my silver-hilted sword and my hat with its feather and medal, I could cut a figure in any company.

Before long we turned left into a small, crooked piazza. On our right, forming almost two whole sides of the square, was a yellow stuccoed building four storeys high. Between each line of windows ran a frieze of ancient Roman battle scenes, painted in fresco. We stopped before the door.

'The Palazzo del Bene,' Cellini said. 'Those friezes were done by Polidoro da Caravaggio a couple of years back. You remember him? Another one of Raphael's boys.'

A servant let us into a spacious vestibule paved in white marble with a staircase leading up from it to a pair of balconies. It was grand, and careless of its grandeur. I drew myself up and brushed back the feather in my hat.

'*Benvenuto!*'

Alessandro del Bene was coming down the stairs towards us accompanied by a man of about fifty, tall, lean and quick in his movements, and clean-shaven in the English style. Alessandro embraced Cellini, and then gestured to me. 'Here is the man I have told you of, who has brought Benvenuto such wonders.' I bowed carefully, graceful and low. 'Richard Dansey, merchant of London.'

Alessandro continued, 'And this is Messer Stephen Cage. A great man at the English Court.'

The man before me was expensively dressed in a doublet of Venice gold and scarlet, and in his hat he wore a gold medal resembling my own. Inside I was exulting. This was it: I had as good as arrived at King Henry's Court, and the impression I was creating was surely exactly right. Stephen Cage looked at me a long moment, then returned my bow, swift and offhand, and waved a deprecating hand at Alessandro.

'Great man at Court? Hardly that, hardly. A pilgrim, merely.' He spoke good Italian. He touched the medal on his hat, which showed the two saints Peter and Paul, one with his keys, the other with a drawn sword: the emblem of a visitor to the two tombs that are the holiest places in Rome. I gazed at him, calculating. What if I had blundered after all, and in my keenness to have a fresh sight of Hannah Cage I had allowed myself to be introduced to an Englishman who had no influence at Court at all?

Mr Stephen ushered us up the staircase to the right-hand balcony, and stopped before a grand doorway with another slight bow.

Alessandro came up to my side. 'I have given Messer Stephen half my palazzo for his household,' he whispered. 'Tonight we dine at his table, not mine.' I stepped through the doorway, and had to suppress a gasp. We were in a grand sala that stretched the whole length of that wing of the palazzo. Enormous tapestries shimmered from the walls with riots of pagan deities, shepherds and cornucopias all picked out in gold and silver thread. In the centre of the room was an L-shaped arrangement of tables, spread with rich Turkey carpets and white linen cloths over the top. Beyond it I saw a carved walnut credenza from which silver flagons and basins glimmered, of the kind I had seen destined for the King on Goldsmiths' Row. A fire burned in a vast hearth carved with busty nymphs, while four musicians sat on silk cushions in an alcove, playing a rapid, cheerful air on recorders and a violin. The whole room breathed with comfortable, easy opulence.

Suddenly I heard a peal of female laughter from beyond a door in the far wall. The door flew open, and five or six spaniels ran yapping into the room, chasing after a monkey dressed in a scarlet-and-yellow coat. Round its neck was a rope of large and valuable pearls. A group of women pressed through after the dogs. And there she was: Hannah Cage. Her lips were pulled back from her teeth in a wild smile, while her eyes, dark brown and sparkling with mischief, followed the monkey as it ran round the room, pursued by the pack of dogs.

A second girl ran past and then turned on her. 'Hannah! Stop it! Make it give them back!' She was younger, perhaps only seventeen; slight and fairish-haired where Hannah was full-figured and dark.

'First you'll have to catch it, sweet Susan.'

Susan threw herself down and disappeared under the table where the monkey had taken refuge behind the cloth. 'Come here, Beelzebub, come now, do.'

The monkey ran out in front of my feet and I grabbed at its chain. Yanked backwards, the beast hopped in front of me, baring its teeth while the dogs snapped round it.

'So you really did follow me here. I am rather impressed.'

I looked up to find Hannah staring levelly into my eyes. She had spoken softly, so no one else could hear. I handed her the monkey's chain and bowed: formally and low. Susan at that moment crawled out from beneath the table and snatched the necklace from the monkey.

'Susan! Stop that immediately!' A lady advanced towards us. Stephen put a hand on her arm, ignoring his daughters, as if the affair of the monkey were a common occurrence and not worthy of his notice.

'Meet Richard Dansey,' he introduced me. 'A dealer from home.'

'Merchant,' I corrected him in annoyance. 'Of London.'

'Merchant,' Stephen repeated, with a politeness that I found even more irritating. He turned to the lady at his side. 'My wife, Grace Cage.'

Mrs Grace smiled at me, with rather a forced quality. She was some years younger than her husband, with an ample figure and hair that was still thick and dark. I sensed I was in the presence of a real aristocrat with Mrs Grace. I found out later that she was a cousin of the Duke of Norfolk, and of a shade finer breeding, therefore, than Mr Stephen himself. She curtseyed and came forward to be kissed in the good old English style of greeting that even the highest-born observe: a custom that the French and Italians look upon with astonishment. She just touched her cheek to mine, and drew back.

'And these are my daughters,' Stephen finished in a tone of resignation. 'Hannah and Susan.'

I caught Hannah's eye and she smiled archly. It was our secret, those times we had met before. I bowed to her again, with a sweep of my hat and my left hand on my sword. Then, how did I dare it? I came forward for my kiss. And she gave me it, full and willing on the cheek. I caught the momentary scent of musk from beneath the crimson silk of her dress, and then she stood back with a look of wicked amusement.

'What sort of merchant? Not salt fish, I hope?'

Before I could reply, little Susan darted in front of me for her kiss, lips puckered comically in her flat, freckled face. She gave me a peck at the edge of my mouth and then turned away with a grimace, as if she had tasted something nasty.

Servants came flocking round us carrying silver basins and ewers. I looked round uneasily, and did my best to copy the others, holding my hands out while a servant poured warm water over them, and a pageboy waited on bended knee with a towel to dry them. All this ceremony was an amazement to me: I knew it ought to be done, and was done in the houses of the noble-born or the royal. But I had seen nothing of this sort at the casins of Venice or the artists' parties of Rome. Cellini, on the other hand, seemed perfectly at his ease. Having claimed the 'English liberty', as he put it, to kiss the ladies all round, he was washing his hands and joking with Mrs Grace. Hannah brushed past me and whispered, 'This time you really do look like a gentleman, Mr Richard. I wonder if you can keep it up.'

I bowed to her. 'Mrs Hannah.' I knew the correct form of address for a young gentlewoman. I would prove myself to her, right enough; and for a start I was determined she would not detect a single lapse in my manners.

Stephen Cage took my arm and guided me to the table. He seated each of us in turn, placing the ladies inside the L and the men facing them on the outside, in the fashion common in Rome. I found myself on Alessandro's left hand, close to the angle in the table, looking straight into Hannah's shining eyes. On my left sat Cellini, facing little Susan, while on the other branch of the table were Mr Stephen and his wife, as well as a priest who must have been the Cages' almoner, with responsibility for the family's charity. He set down a little silver dish to receive the first loaf of bread for the poor, and murmured a few words of benediction in Latin, which thanks to the music, which was still playing, no one save God could hear.

'Messer Dansey, Richard Dansey,' Stephen mused, looking me up and down with sharp eyes. 'Merchant. I ought to know you: or your family, at any rate. Now I have it!' He snapped his finger and pointed at me. 'The Widow of Thames Street?'

I nodded, annoyed. To be recognised even here, and marked with the taint of home: it was galling. 'She is my mother.'

Stephen smiled. 'Oh, she is known. Her business dealings are ingenious, most ingenious. Spice, dyestuffs, even a little usury on the side.' He turned to me with his half-closed, mocking eye. 'And you? Are your ventures of a similar kind?'

The subtlety of his contempt stunned me. How was I to make any impression on this man? I saw my introduction at Court vanishing into air, along with any interest Hannah might ever have had in me. I said, 'Mine are ten times more ingenious than hers.'

Stephen grunted, and Grace glanced in my direction with a slight smile. The dishes were brought in, a dozen of them at least: fowls and small game birds and pies all on silver platters. At the centre of them, just beside a vast gilded salt cellar modelled as a group of bathing nymphs, was set down a majestic heron. Its grey wings were spread wide, its head and neck bent round as if in life, with the black crest quivering behind its lifeless eyes. 'Slain by my own hand,' Mr Stephen was explaining. 'Crossbow: in the marshes.' One of the servants leant forward to carve the bird's breasts into slices in a few effortless strokes, executed in perfect time to the music. I gazed on this spectacle like a man struck dumb; there were nuances of luxuried living here I had never even dreamt of. Susan, seeing me, put her hand to her mouth and laughed.

I met for an instant Hannah's gaze, but she betrayed nothing. She ate with perfect confidence and ease, casting a bored glance over the table. When she wished for a drink of wine she summoned a servant with a lifted finger, took the cup, drank, and returned it. She used her fork just as if she had been accustomed to this curious Italian device all her life; she wiped her full lips on her napkin after every mouthful, she took salt from the gilded nymphs with only the very tip of her knife, and sampled just a little from each of the many dishes, missing none of them.

I was determined to keep pace, and show myself no mere trades-man. But the meal was a trial by ordeal. After drinking I had placed my cup on the table in front of me: my first false move. I looked down at the dishes before me in dismay. In between the platters bearing the various joints of meat and roast birds were silver dishes holding a dozen different sauces. The green verjuice, sharpened with pepper and garlic, was apparently meant for the heron, and the mustard was for the pig's brawn, but where did the ginger jelly belong? I saw Susan solemnly spooning it over the black lampreys, and did the same, only to have her fall back in her chair and point at me in laugh-ter. Hannah gave her sister a kick under the table. She leant forward and said, 'It is really no disgrace to be ignorant, Mr Richard. That one is for the sugared herring.'

Stephen's voice suddenly boomed at me from the head of the table. 'And how is trade in Italy? Do the prices please you?'

I glanced back at him, but I could not reply for rage. At last, at long last, I was sitting down with the choice and high company I had watched for so many years. And they despised me. I had relied on the manners and clothes I had acquired in Venice to give me the stamp of nobility; but with the Cages this counted for nothing. Susan, clearly, had marked me down as a clod who could be made to believe anything. She had even seized a spaniel from under the table and ostentatiously wiped her fingers on its coat, glancing at me archly to see if I would follow her. Hannah was watching me with her provoking smile. She leant across the table to me and murmured, 'You must forgive my family. I feel sure there is rather more to you than there seems.'

I leant towards her. 'By God, you will find out that there is.'

'In that case, amuse me,' whispered Hannah. 'You have no notion how dull life is here. Surprise me. I do not think you can.' She leant back with a lift of her eyebrows and a witching smile.

I wiped my lips with my napkin, put it back on my shoulder and looked Stephen Cage in the eye. 'My thanks to you for asking. My trade is flourishing.' I turned my gaze to take in the rest of the table. 'Perhaps you would care to see.'

The servants were removing the dishes. The heron departed, its wings broken, its sides stripped bare, its neck collapsed on to the edge of the platter. Its substantial remains would be offered to the poor, who were doubtless already lining up at the door on the piazza. In its place the servants set down little custard tarts or doucettes, steaming dishes of almond cream, sugared dates and raisins, and offered us cups of hot hippocras.

Everyone turned to look at me. Hannah moistened her lips with her tongue and leant forward, folding her arms beneath her bosom with a faint clinking of her pearls. Cellini lowered his thick eyebrows and shook his head at me in warning. I ignored him. My blood was up. Stephen's insults and Hannah's disdain burned like a knife in a wound. I was not going to let these aristocrats beat me. I pulled at the chain around my neck, hoisting my grease-polished casket from its hiding place under my clothes. My fingers shook; I was aware of the indelicacy of what I was doing. But then I had pulled it clear of my collar and laid it down on the table among the dishes.

Mrs Grace looked down the table at me in surprise. Stephen's expression was bland and impassive. He expected nothing from me of any interest. I retrieved the little key from my belt, inserted it in the mouth of the cupid and opened the lid. My various stones were wrapped in folds of silk to keep them apart, for not all gems are of equal hardness: a ruby will mar a sapphire, and a sapphire scratch a jasper. The first to meet my fingers were the four blue-white diamonds. I lifted them out and set them on the table beside a dish of ginger comfits. They had been well cut. They sparked and flamed, while beneath that outward dance of colour their native water shimmered, icy cool. Hannah's eyes were alight. From the upper end of the table, Mr Stephen peered down for a better sight, suddenly arrested.

The next stones I set down were larger than the diamonds, and flashed with many several points of flame, amethystine, sulphurous, lightning-blue, changing from one moment to the next. The sight of them thrilled me, as it always did. I stroked my chin, winding my finger into the strands of hair I had been trying to cultivate into a beard in the Italian fashion. Hannah, to my satisfaction, let out a long-drawn 'Ohhh'. Even gawky Susan craned forward on her elbows for a look, making the trestle table wobble.

'What are they?' asked Hannah.

'Opals. Do they please you?'

'So many colours.'

We gazed on them. The reds, the golds, the greens: one grew into another; and while it lasted, each shade appeared so real. I looked up at Hannah. 'But if you break an opal, all its colours are lost.' Grace's eye was turned on the stones, sharp, acquisitive, precise. She was valuing them; and, I hoped, revaluing me. I lifted out next Ippolita's pearls.

'So round,' Hannah murmured. 'So smooth and fine.' She was leaning towards me over the table. I became aware of the brightness of her eyes and the closeness of her body, her arms drawn together in front of her, the fall of her hair from beneath her hood.

'They are in their perfect youth,' I replied.

'Oh!' She darted me a glance. 'Do pearls grow old, like us?'

'Surely they do,' I answered, looking straight into her eyes. The pupils were black and bright as a table-cut diamond, their irises as brown as sardonyx. 'If they are not teased forth from their homes by those who love them, in the end they yellow and die: unadmired and alone. And that is a terrible thing.'

For a moment Hannah held my gaze, and her mouth broke into a smile, showing her strong teeth. Then she lowered her eyes to the pearls, which she began rolling lightly on the tablecloth under her fingers. I glanced along to the top end of the table. I had their utter attention. I sensed, after this, that it was time to display my pale Scythian emerald. Like a garden, an emerald of this kind will always refresh the eye, no matter how glutted it is by other glories. It shed

157

its cool, green rays over the table. After the excitement of the other stones, I felt their mood shift to a more tranquil wonder. I let them look on it for a minute, and then, like a green-gold sun, I brought out my chrysoprase, and then my scatter of pebbly, clouded sapphires, as it were a shower of hail. I held that whole table of noble men and women in the palm of my hand. I had stolen from the stones a part of their enchantment. It was time to sweep them on in a rush of wonders, and so I set out the grey-green cats' eyes, the dark Persian emerald, the white ruby, the amethysts, the jacinths, the balasses, the garnets. Each stone was hotter and brighter than the last, and was met by a fresh murmur of delight. I kept my greatest treasure until the end, the brilliant ruby, as large as the end of your finger. I set it down among the others, and let its fire shoot out across the whiteness of the cloth.

There was silence. Our doucettes and our hippocras steamed on the table, forgotten. Even Cellini leant forward, gazing without blinking. Hannah glanced from the stones to my face, and down again. Her eyes shone. She breathed fast through her nostrils, and sweat glimmered on her upper lip. She had set me a task, a challenge: she had thrown up a barrier between us and I had smashed it down. There was a nakedness about her as she looked at me. If there had been no one else present I swear I could have reached across the table and kissed her, and she would have been mine.

'By Saint Anthony!' Stephen exclaimed at last. 'That ruby alone must be worth five hundred crowns!'

'It will be worth very much more than that when I have brought it to its full perfection,' Cellini said. 'It must be cut and set: then you will see a wonder.'

Little Susan still peered forward at the stones, her hard, green-blue eyes unblinking. She said, 'Give me one.'

Grace frowned down the table. 'Susan! Be quiet!'

Hannah glanced from her mother to Susan, and then back at me. Her eyes were laughing, her chin puckered to hold herself in: as if she could barely wait to see what I would do, and how I would go about suppressing her sister. I raged at what this nasty girl had done. My enchantment was broken. The barrier between Hannah and me was back: a new challenge had been set. And what was I to do? To give in would show weakness and make me Susan's creature. But to refuse would prove me a mere merchant, small-minded and mean. My eye swept over my stones and rested on the very least of my sapphires, a cracked and clouded pebble fissured like mouldy cheese. I picked it up and flicked it across the table towards little Mrs Susan. She whooped and swatted it with her hand as you would a fly. I saw Hannah's eyes light up with surprise, and she laughed. I had passed the test: I had shown in a single instant an aristocrat's disdain and an aristocrat's greatness of spirit. Then I selected one of my four diamonds, a stone of Bengal of the purest pale-blue water, and a rose-pale amethyst that was its equal in value, and a vivid Bohemian garnet. I pushed them across the table to Hannah.

'Choose. Whichever you please.'

She smiled with a flash of her teeth. I had her: surely, surely I had her. Or so I thought.

'But, Mr Richard,' she said, 'if I am to accept a gift you must offer me something that is worthy of me.'

She pushed the gems back towards me. I stared at her in disbelief. She was free of me again, off and away. She smiled at my confusion. I had mistaken altogether the depth of her resource; she was not a creature to be caught so crudely as that. Susan looked up from admiring her sapphire and pointed a finger at me. 'Ha, ha, ha! Did that sting?'

At this, Grace and Stephen exchanged uncomfortable looks, and Stephen waved a quick hand at the almoner, who bowed his head and murmured the words of the grace. *'Benedictus Deus in donis suis, et sanctus in omnibus operibus suis ...'* The dinner was over. Mrs Grace rose abruptly from the table and bore down menacingly on the two girls. 'Susan. Hannah.' They stood obediently and turned away, to run across the sala to where the spaniels were curled in front of the fire. Almost blinded with rage I began pitching my stones back inside the casket. Grace glided up to my side with a gracious smile.

'Please forgive my girls, Mr Richard. We brought them to Italy to acquire polish. I fear we shall need to stay somewhat longer.'

I stood up and bowed. 'Please do not think of it.'

The servants brought the ewers, basins and towels for yet another ceremony of hand-washing. Mr Stephen beckoned to one of the pages. 'My good boy, another cup of hippocras for Mr Richard.' As the pages brought the wine and fresh wafers, he guided me towards the fireplace with an arm on my shoulder. Plainly, in his eyes, I was no mere tradesman any longer but a person of importance and interest. I ought to be building on this, hinting at my pressing need for an introduction to King Henry; but at that moment all I wanted was to break away.

The two girls were rubbing the spaniels' ears, whispering together and laughing. How could I approach Hannah now, after my defeat? We were separated by ten feet or so of shimmering russet-and-blue Turkey carpet, but she might as well have been a hundred miles away. She bent over the ears of her dog, murmuring, 'Sugar comfit, poor little lady.' Beneath that indifference no doubt she was savouring her triumph. Or was she waiting, maybe, or even hoping, for my next attack? No, I was just flattering myself to think so. I raged, looking at her. My gems had worked their enchantment on everyone else at that table. Even Susan was sitting and holding her misty sapphire up to the light. Hannah alone had slipped free.

Stephen still stood at my side. 'Dansey,' he pondered. 'Dansey, let me think. Your mother was born a Waterman. You have an uncle? A secretary to the Cardinal of York?'

I looked at him in surprise. 'Yes,' I answered. 'Bennet Waterman.'

'Hm! A position of great trust.'

'I believe it is.'

I stood looking at Stephen, suspicious. Was he a friend of Wolsey's, or did he belong to that group of courtiers who opposed him? My skin prickled at the thought that I might just be face to face with the secret 'man in Rome' of Bennet's letter. If so, he was my family's enemy. But that was far too great a leap to make. I decided I would say nothing of this meeting to Bennet. At least, not for the moment. Stephen's face took on an impenetrable expression, as if he was keen not to say too much. He nodded slightly to his wife. Mrs Grace came bustling up to my side.

'You must tell us all about your venture. You have your own ship?'

'My mother owns a ship,' I answered. 'I do not need one. A merchant in gems does not carry bulky cargoes.'

'Of course he does not.' Mrs Grace moistened her lips with her tongue. 'And is this your first venture, Mr Richard?'

'Not my first. But my first venture alone.'

'How very fine. You are staying in Rome long?'

'I shall stay as long as I need to,' I replied, with my eyes on Hannah.

'Good! Tomorrow evening is the racing on the Corso: the wild Berber horses of North Africa. There will be scaffolds set up for persons of quality, to afford a better view of the ground. Perhaps you would join us in ours?'

My heart jumped, and I turned to look at her. 'It would be a delight to me.'

I darted another quick glance at Hannah. Her eye was on mine, thoughtful and challenging. The chase was on once more.

12

'Are you completely and utterly out of your mind?'

Cellini slammed down a bundle of chisels, files and knives on top of the papers piled beside the gorily dripping head of Medusa. 'You would have given away a diamond? Does our work mean nothing to you? Where would you find another to match the three that were left? Or is the ship to be guided by three stars, and one empty hole?'

It was early the following morning. Martin and I had just stepped into Cellini's workshop, to find him sitting before the polishing wheel. He was holding up the gold disc with the image of the ship at sea, turning it so that it caught the light in different ways. I was not prepared for his anger.

'If it had worked,' I growled, 'I would have won something of much greater value than I had lost.'

'Indeed! And did you never think how mad it was, to throw your stones about like that? How many people now know that you carry a fortune of jewels around your neck?'

'A family of English courtiers. What of that?'

He took several small pots and jars down from the shelf and set them beside the tools.

'About forty servants, and all their friends, and their friends' friends. You are a marked man. You had better know how to use your sword.'

I put my hand to its hilt. I was growing annoyed, and felt more disposed to fight than to argue. 'Do you want a demonstration?'

'Later. Now I have to work. Let us see what can be done with this chrysoprase, while we still have it. Hand it to me.'

I took the casket from round my neck and opened it up. Inside, the stones were in confusion. Benvenuto was right: I must have been mad last night. I nested them properly in their different wrappings, and handed him the chrysoprase. It shone with a pale springtime green that showed its kinship to the emerald, mingled with those shafts of gold that gave it its name, *chrysoprasos* being, Benvenuto told me, merely Greek for 'the golden leek'. Cellini set it on its place in the ship. In that early morning light it had a ghostly sheen: as if the helmsman were following some marshlight or jack-o'-lantern, that would lead him into danger and dismay.

'Women,' he said, as if reading fresh wisdom in the stone. 'You should forget them, my friend.'

He picked the chrysoprase up again, turned it a few more times, and then put it down.

'Well! In the ordinary way I do not call a chrysoprase a gem. They are soft, misty things, like milk, not water. Diamonds, sapphires, emeralds, rubies: those are the stones for princes. But this one will do very well.'

He opened up one of the jars and removed a little pinkish-yellow powder with a tiny bone scoop. This was tripoli-earth, such as I had seen used many a time in London. I leant forward. He mixed the powdered earth with a few drops of oil to make up a paste, and rubbed this over the surface of the polishing wheel. Then he inserted the chrysoprase in a *tanaglietta*, or dop, as the jewellers call it at home, a rod with a soft leaden grip to hold the stone. He set the wheel spinning with the foot-pedal, cranking it up to a furious speed, took a last look at the uncut stone on its rod to judge the point of attack, and lowered it over the wheel.

This stage of the goldsmith's work always filled me with a mixture of wonderment and fear. Moment by moment you saw the brilliant gemstone emerge and shake off the dull, even roundness it had borne for untold centuries underground. But it was fraught with danger. I had seen Christian Breakespere's old hands fumble, and an emerald of price slip from the end of the dop in a splinter of fine powder: ruined. Every few minutes Cellini lifted the stone from the wheel, then gently put it back again. He was grinding the single flat surface on its crown that is called the table. I watched, breathless, impatient for the gem, and for my coming meeting with the Cages.

All that day he worked, until the light began to dim and we heard sounds of music and the shouts of masquers from outside. Cellini let the wheel slow to a halt.

'That's enough. If we do not hurry, we shall be late.'

He lifted the gem, still on its dop, and held it up to the last rays of evening sun. It was only half-faceted. The clouds about its surface were parting, allowing seductive glimmers of green-gold from within. I tore myself from it with difficulty. Benvenuto crossed to his chest and locked the gem away.

I stood up. 'You are coming too?'

'To the race of the Berbers?' Cellini smiled his devilish smile. 'I would not miss it. Paulino!'

The boy got up from his corner near the furnace, went out and returned with a tray of small white balls.

'Tonight is the Battle of the Confetti,' said Cellini. 'I would not like you to meet your enemy unarmed.'

'Confetti?'

'Comfits, master.' It was Martin's voice. I turned in surprise. I had not realised he understood Italian that well. 'Almonds, in a coat of hard sugar. The Cages' servants told me about them. Every household in Rome has been preparing them for tonight. It's a rough sport.'

Paulino held out the tray with an enquiring lift of his brows.

'Put them in a bag,' I instructed Martin. 'Benvenuto, my thanks.'

We left the studio together. As we stepped out into the darkening street Cellini murmured in my ear, 'Be warned, my friend. She is a dangerous woman.'

'I have known that for a long time.'

I turned to find Martin close behind me, frowning. Disturbed, I strode quickly on down the street. It was a mild night, carrying the promise of spring, though cool gusts still fanned up from the river.

All round us was laughter and the sound of lutes and shawms and drums. Great numbers of people were out, cardinals on their mules, noblewomen in litters and great streams of young gentlemen masked as devils or long-nosed satyrs swathed in black capes. They all of them carried bags of comfits, which they hurled at one another in stinging showers. Children darted everywhere underfoot to retrieve them. They were as hard as slingstones, those comfits, and hit with a smart. I started angrily at these attacks, but I did not retaliate. I was saving our weaponry for a very special foe.

As we came out of the lanes into the Piazza Navona, Martin caught me up. His voice was accusing. 'So you know her.'

'What if I do?'

'Master, I haven't followed you God knows how many miles to see you play the fool now. A fine parcel of folk you've fallen in with.'

I turned on him. 'Listen to your impudence. You think because I forgave you for being my mother's spy, you have the right to say anything.'

He fell silent, and trudged on a pace or two behind. 'Stephen Cage,' he muttered. 'A pilgrim! He's not that, whatever else he may be. Of course, you don't want to listen to what I have to say.'

'No, I don't.'

'Or what I've found out?'

I stopped. Angry as I was, I knew Martin had sense, and long ears for gossip. 'Well, if you know something, then tell me it.' I dodged as a devil-faced masquer flung a volley of comfits at us.

Martin leant close. 'Very well, then. While you were showing off your wares, I got friendly with their man Fenton, the chamberlain. None of them know what Mr Stephen's doing here. But he sees the Pope almost every day, and after every meeting he comes away in a sourer temper than the one before.'

I shrugged. There was nothing to trouble me in that. On the contrary: it only went to prove that Mr Stephen was a man of real standing, whatever he might say to deny it. I said, 'Then he is some sort of ambassador to do with the war. More secret and trusted than Sir John Russell, but with the same mission.'

Martin lowered his voice. 'But Russell is in the best of humours, they say. He's delighted at having stopped them from making peace without his agreement.'

I looked at Martin with surprise, and new respect. He saw more deeply into politics than most Italians, who had complete faith in our King's desire for peace. 'Yes,' I granted. 'The more Pope Clement and the Emperor squabble, the greater the power of King Henry.'

'So if Mr Stephen is on the same business as Russell,' Martin pursued, 'what makes him so out of sorts?'

I did not answer. I thought of Bennet's letter. *The King has a new man in Rome.* And that man, Wolsey thought, had something to do with the divorce. But Wolsey was working for the divorce himself. If this truly was Stephen's business, why was it kept secret from the Cardinal, who was King Henry's most trusted minister? And then there were Wolsey's words: *There is a web spread against me.* I frowned, and quickened my pace.

The crowds were growing thicker. Cellini was calling from ahead. We caught him up, and soon came to the Corso, longest of all the streets of Rome, reaching straight as an arrow nearly a mile out to the city walls. Every window and balcony was filled with people, and the houses were hung with tapestries and bundles of pine boughs and paper flowers. Looming over us was the Palazzo San Marco, a vast residence belonging to the Pope, where Clement himself sat in state on a balcony, in a scarlet mantle and skullcap. Round the square beneath the palazzo were wooden scaffolds draped with heraldic banners of the noble families of Rome. I saw women in masks, their silk gowns cut away to the waist to show their bare breasts beneath numerous ropes of pearls. Courtesans: or perhaps not. Just as the courtesans ape the manners of fine ladies, so ladies in turn copy the courtesans; so that these women might just as easily be among the highest-born in Rome.

Cellini pointed to a pavilion bearing the black on white of the del Bene family, from which Alessandro called out to us. I climbed its wooden steps and bowed. Seated in a row, with tapestries behind them and a pan of hippocras steaming over a low brazier, were the Cages. They were dressed, all of them, in black capes. Mr Stephen had in his hand a white mask in the form of an owl's face. He rose to take my hand.

'Mr Richard! How very pleased we are you have come. Take a seat, do, between me and my wife.'

I pressed behind Alessandro and Mr Stephen. Mrs Grace tilted her head for a polite kiss on the cheek and sat down again. Beyond her sat Susan and then Hannah. Mrs Grace's chair blocked the narrow passage, taking away all possibility of a kiss of greeting with Hannah. I sat down, displeased, between the two elder Cages, and peered to the left on the pretext of leaning out and craning for a view of the Pope, high up in his balcony. Susan was glancing all round with an air of bitter boredom, and returned my glances with a glare. Beyond her, Hannah held in one hand a mask of moulded wax, covered in gold leaf and shaped like a cat's muzzle with slit-eyes. A strand of black hair wound down from her hood across her cheek, and her mouth curved in a smile. Our eyes met for a moment, and

167

then her lips pouted and she lifted the mask to her face. I sat back again, fuming.

Mr Stephen turned to me with a jovial air.

'Now tell me about your ambitions. Your jewels: this is no common trade you are engaging in. They are fit for a king.'

I looked back at him levelly. 'I believe so too.'

'But kings are hard to see, for young merchants.'

'True enough.' I held my breath. He had seen right into my deepest needs. He held me in the palm of his hand.

Stephen smiled. 'Well, I dare say when we are all home in England we can do something about that. Now tell me about your uncle. Bennet Waterman. Has he been with Cardinal Wolsey long?'

So there it was: the chance of that longed-for introduction at Court, and, along with it, the price I would have to pay. I answered warily, 'About five years.'

'A secretary, did you say?'

'A lawyer, in origin.'

Stephen took a sip of hot wine, his pebbly eyes fixed on me. 'Indeed? Tell me more.'

I hesitated. I did not like to be squeezed for information in this fashion. If Stephen was who I suspected, then I should be learning his secrets to feed to Bennet. Instead was I to tell Bennet's secrets to Stephen? But he was Hannah's father, and my route to the King.

I said, 'He has been helping the Cardinal to dissolve a number of smaller monasteries, which he needs to fund his new college at Oxford.'

'I know that,' returned Stephen, rather too quickly. 'And does your uncle take part in any of the Cardinal's more ... confidential business?'

I looked back at him, my heart beating fast. Here, I guessed, was the question of the divorce. I knew little; less, I presumed, than Stephen himself. But it would not do to admit that. Mr Stephen had to believe he needed me. I said, 'He takes on any work that is asked of him.'

Stephen returned my gaze. 'What an extremely valuable man.'

'You should see the horse I have entered,' Alessandro said to Cellini. 'I've staked a hundred ducats on it. Wild as a lion! They say no man has ever managed to mount it.'

I turned to peer out over the street, relieved to seize an opportunity to turn the subject aside.

'Surely,' I commented, 'a serious defect in a racehorse?'

Alessandro caught Stephen's eye, and both smiled.

'Ho!' said Mr Stephen. 'He will see, won't he?'

At that moment we heard the loud report of a cannon, and a distant roar from the crowd far up to the right along the Corso. Galloping towards us came a confused mass of horses. Not a single one of them had a rider. They stampeded forward, bucking, twisting, shying off in the direction of some side street, colliding and going down on the stones in a confusion of flying manes and squealing, foaming mouths and then picking themselves up and running on. The din of the crowd was building, and the horses were careering closer. I could not conceive how they could be made to run in the right direction, until I saw men in blue livery darting out from behind the canvas with pots of steaming pitch, and ladles with which they flicked the boiling liquid on to the horses' haunches, driving them into a fresh, crazed charge. As if this were not enough, each horse had a ball tied to its flanks set with spikes, that acted as a kind of spur as it ran.

'Minotauro! Minotauro!' yelled Alessandro, as the first three horses dashed into the square, then turned at bay and bolted this way and that. 'Where are you?' Several more ran in after them, bumping and falling together. 'The devil,' shouted Alessandro. 'Look at him, tumbling in the dust, after eating my gold.' Men ran out, darting round the whinnying, stamping horses and snatching at their bridles to catch them. I heard their shouts as they tried to keep clear of those hoofs, and the screams of others as they were thrown down to the ground.

'This is the Recapture,' said Stephen. 'The finest part of the race. Also the most dangerous.'

I glanced along at Hannah. She was holding her mask by its edge, tapping its golden rim against her chin. Her face was rapt with wild excitement. I cursed my luck that I was not sitting at her side.

'Over too quickly,' said Stephen. 'But there are more races to come.'

'Horse races?' I asked.

'I believe they are races of ... other sorts.'

'They are hardly proper,' said Grace. 'Persons of quality watch the race of the Berber horses, and then they go.'

For a moment husband and wife looked at each other. Tension flared between them. Mrs Grace's eyes, dark like Hannah's, shone above her pinched nostrils, while Mr Stephen drew in his breath, his lips parted from his teeth. Then Stephen looked down with a grunt. 'Hm. Indeed. In fact, I do have some papers to read. But we shall meet again, Mr Richard. No doubt of it.'

Grace turned to me, brushed back a wisp of her black hair and smiled her exquisitely elegant smile. This was my dismissal, it seemed. I rose and bowed, and climbed back down the wooden steps to the street, where Martin fell into pace behind me. The sun was close to setting, and a chill, misty air was creeping through the city with the twilight. But I did not have the heart to return to my inn. I was nervy, ill-tempered, wound to breaking point with disappointment, and turning over in my mind how I could contrive to get back to see Hannah. And so I wandered the city. The streets were still filled with rowdy masquers, calling out to each other from behind the faces of foxes or goats, guessing at one another's names or hurling comfits. Without a mask I felt strangely naked and without defence.

'Messer Dansey!' It was a woman's voice, hailing me from behind, almost drowned by the music and shouts of the masquers. But surely, surely I could not be wrong. I turned and scanned the crowds, black-cloaked or particoloured, in turbans, crimson hoods or silver paper crowns. The groups parted, revealing for a moment a stationary figure in a black cape down to the ground, and a golden mask shaped like a cat's muzzle with slit-eyes. A strand of black hair wound down from her hood across it. I sprang after her, but a group of acrobats dashed across my path, doing handstands and high leaps into the air, followed by a troop of buffoons on stilts. When they were out of my way, the cat mask had gone.

'Mr Richard!' She was standing across the street this time, in the shadow of a colonnade. We were in the Via delle Botteghe Oscure, the street of the dark shops that are all built into the ruined foundations of an ancient theatre. I darted over the road and ran along the overhanging wall with its dingy orange stucco dropping off the ancient stone, peering into every one of its green, mossy recesses. Martin stood still, watching me with a frown.

'Don't stand there!' I snapped at him. 'Help me to look!'

'Mr Richard!'

I spun round. She was over the street again, calling from the colonnade of a palazzo. This time I ran straight across to her, caught her by the arm and pulled down the mask. I was staring into Hannah's mocking smile. She was alone: wherever her parents and their grand household were, Hannah had somehow given them the slip.

'Where were you hurrying off to?' she teased me. 'All the amusement is back at the Corso.'

'And you came to fetch me?'

'Why not, Mr Richard?'

'My dear Mrs Hannah. So something about me is worthy of your notice after all.'

'Do you think so?' Her smile took on a gleam of danger. 'Anything is possible. But really I simply hate to see anyone go trudging home like a whipped dog when the best part of the entertainment is just beginning.'

She glanced at my hand where it touched her gown. Then she lifted the mask back to her face, becoming infinitely wild, a golden beast in a black pelt. I told Martin, 'You may go back to the inn.'

Martin, however, was immovable. 'Master,' he murmured. 'If you had heard the way those men of the Cages talk about you and your jewels, you would not wish to be out alone. You're the man made of diamonds, the man with a million ducats round his neck.'

'Go back,' I snarled at him. 'I'll be safe enough.' He looked as if he were about to argue, but I turned my back. Together, Hannah and I pressed on through the crowds. It was almost dark now. Along the Corso hundreds of torches flamed, making an alley of fire. Hannah turned to me and lifted her mask.

'The horse race was the tame one,' she said. 'If you want to see something truly wild you have to stay up for it.'

From the northern end of the street we heard the roaring of many men, together with a tremendous animal bellowing. Suddenly we saw rushing towards us in the torchlight a dozen wild bulls, each as black as night, tossing their long, curved horns this way and that. Hannah came forward to the very edge of the roadway where the canvas barrier had been torn down beside an ancient column, watching fearless as the bulls came rushing towards us. I was proud then to be standing at her side, just as motionless as she was. They were nearly upon us, when a single bull broke away and began bucking along the edge of the street, tossing its horns, looking for someone on whom to take out its rage. Still Hannah did not move. Its rolling pink eyes picked us out. At the very last moment I took her by the shoulders and pulled her back behind the column. As the bulls thundered past, I pressed her against the stone. The noise of their hoofs was deafening. Her face was alight and alive, with just a slight smile of mockery, maybe, that I had been the first to draw back. I leant towards her and pressed my lips against hers. She was surprised; her wide open eyes stared into mine. Then they slowly closed. The sound of the bulls' hoofs diminished. I could feel her lips soften, and as my tongue pressed they parted, and a little flick of her tongue darted out against mine. The touch of it enflamed and astonished me. If I had never loved her before, I loved her then. But even in that same instant there was a doubt. What if that lick was a tease, a taunt? I could not say if she had truly abandoned herself, and if this was a moment of shared intoxication and delight. There is only one cure for these kinds of doubts. I put my arm behind her back and ran it up into her hair. I felt her mouth beneath mine twist into a smile, and she stepped away from me to one side. I moved closer, putting my arm round her again. She wagged her finger at me in reproof.

'Dear Mr Richard! Before you take any further liberties you ought really to tell me who is my rival.'

The word stopped me dead.

'Rival?'

'The lady who is to have all those jewels. Or are you telling me you really are just a tradesman? You buy, you sell, you make a profit?' That face of hers, so close to mine, was maddening: the slow pucker of her cheeks, the spreading smile, the dance of those deep brown eyes.

'Oh, I shall make a profit. Never fear.'

All about us the crowds were surging northwards along the Corso. Hannah swung herself round the pillar and set off after them. I ran to catch up. She cast me a disdainful look over her shoulder.

'And you put all that passion merely into making money? How you disappoint me.'

I hesitated. Since arriving in Italy I had kept my plans secret from everyone save Cellini. But how could I let her see me either as a dirty tradesman, or as a lover of anyone but her?

'No,' I said. 'You are right. There is a lady who is to have them.'

'Aha!' She smiled. She had me now, she thought: she could tease me without end for wooing her while I bought gems for another.

'But the lady is not mine. She is the King's.'

Hannah clapped her hands and laughed with glee. 'So that is it! What a very clever man you are, Richard Dansey. And if I know the lady in question, she will be exceedingly well pleased.'

I stood rock still and swung her round to face me. 'You know?' I whispered. 'You know who she is?'

There it was: everything was out now, not only my innermost ambitions, but the appalling fact of my ignorance as well. Hannah's eyes opened wide, she put her hands to her mouth and she drew in her breath as if she had just heard the most tragic news of her life. 'Oh, my poor Richard Dansey.' Then she laughed out loud, doubling her body over at the waist. 'And you really, truly do not know? But everybody knows who the King's new love is!'

'Who is it?' I asked urgently. 'Hannah, tell me who it is.'

Still she kept laughing and wiping her eyes. 'Mercy. No more. You will kill me with laughter.'

I took her hands in mine. I kissed those hands, three, five times. 'Dear Mrs Hannah, sweet Mrs Hannah. Tell me who she is.'

'What,' she said, mastering her laughter a little and looking into my eyes, 'betray a secret? Oh, no.'

I clenched her fingers. 'But you said yourself it was no secret at all.'

She leant her soft, teasing face close to mine so that our noses almost touched. 'Everyone may know,' she whispered, 'but no one is supposed to tell.'

I gazed at her: astonished, enraged, and loving and desiring her all the more for the way she tormented me. Feet raced past us. Dimly I heard voices shouting, 'The dwarfs! The dwarfs!'

Hannah put her finger on my lips, and slipped past me and out on to the Corso. With a glance back she called, 'Quickly, Mr Richard! We cannot miss the dwarfs.'

I followed her, steaming with impatience, until at last we reached the Piazza del Popolo. The crowds were thicker than ever here. The city wall ran along the far side of the square, with a strongly fortified gate set in it; beside it was the handsome church of Santa Maria with its slender bell-tower, that had been paid for by all the people of Rome. In the middle of the square were gathered forty dwarfs, dressed in the liveries of their masters: for there is not a noble house in Rome that does not keep one or two. Hannah was standing already at the front of the crowd.

'There, look!' She pointed. 'Do you see that one in white and black, with his beard stained red? That is Morgante, Alessandro's dwarf. How much do you think I should bet on him?'

'Whatever you please.' The last thing I cared about at that moment were dwarfs. Hannah took out a few ducats from the small pouch at her side. She looked up at me in reproach.

'Mr Richard! This is Rome, the capital of the Christian world! The least you can do is show a little interest in its traditions. Or do you think my money would be safer on that tall one with the crimson lions, the one with the bells?'

Some of the dwarfs were dressed as jesters, and served their masters as buffoons, singing and dancing and doing tricks. Others, serious and proud, were almost aristocrats themselves: they could dispute with cardinals on theology, they knew all the courtier's graces, his compliments and bows and witty speeches. Many of them, plainly, were well known and loved. They strutted round waving and kissing their hands to the crowd, who frantically chanted their names.

'Moretto! Moretto!'

'Carafulla!'

'Tattamella!'

'No,' said Hannah. 'I shall bet on Calandrino. He is the most handsome. He belongs to Jacopo Cardelli, the Papal Secretary. Cardelli keeps him as a chaperone for the daughter he has had by his concubine. He says it's just as good as having a eunuch: no girl could be seduced by a dwarf. I think the man's a fool, don't you?'

'Hannah!'

She slipped away and ran up to a man in a feathered hat who was standing on a scaffold near the centre of the square shouting out odds. She handed up to him her ducats and took away a slip of paper. Almost at the same moment there was the crack of a whip, and the dwarfs were off, sprinting down the Corso in the same direction as the horses and the bulls, while the crowd cheered and shouted them on. Despite myself, my eyes followed them as they ran off, bells jingling, feathers nodding: bizarre and yet strangely thrilling.

I turned to find Hannah peering down the Corso after the dwarfs. She had her mask down again. She appeared to have forgotten me completely.

'The King's lady. Please. Tell me who she is.'

She turned, and eased aside her mask for an instant, just long enough to utter a single word.

'No.'

'If you will not give me her name, at least tell me what she is like. Is she tall or short? Quiet? Witty? Does she wear pearls? Rubies? Diamonds? And her eyes, sweet Jesus, Mrs Hannah, you have to tell me the colour of her eyes!'

'Poor Mr Richard, so driven by his ambitions. Can you not forget them even for a moment?'

From the far edge of the square came a confused sound of laughter and cheering, and calls of, 'The old men!'

Hannah pulled me by the hand deeper into the crowd. 'Come on, come, come, come, come. A new race!'

Laughing, yet angry, I allowed her to lead me. The man in the feathered hat called out, 'Calandrino! Calandrino the winner of the dwarfs!'

Hannah went up and collected her money, then came back to me with an arch smile. I said, 'Have you bet again?'

'Not this time. I always stop while my luck is good.'

The old men jostled into line, shoving and cursing each other, white-bearded, bald and deadly serious. The crowds screamed with laughter as they set off hobbling down the Corso. At once we heard a braying and screeching from behind, and suddenly the square was filled with wild donkeys, dark bristly creatures with bared teeth and mad eyes. Grooms struggled to keep hold of their halters, and then off they went, bucking and kicking after the old men. Hannah and I laughed with the others. I was catching the exhilaration of this, the madness of making any living thing race that could be caught and forced into line and goaded into moving. But still I had to know that name.

'Tell me,' I said to her.

She turned on me, a frown gathering on her forehead. 'Why should I tell you?'

'Because you love me.'

She shook her head slowly, comically sympathetic. In exasperation I reached into my bag of comfits and flicked one at her forehead. She let out a cry. 'Oh! Mr Richard!' But even as she spoke she dropped her mask over her face, dipped her own hand into a bag and pelted me in return. We flung the small, hard sweets at each other wildly. Hannah ducked away from me, laughing, and I ran after her down a side street. Ahead I could see the glitter of the river in the lights of the torches that moved everywhere, carried by the masquers. I had nearly caught her up, and I made a grab for her cloak, when suddenly we were hit by a stinging hail of comfits. Hannah stopped with a shriek and covered her head with her hands.

A voice came from the shadows over the street. 'Messer Dansey?'

I turned in anger. 'Who is there?'

A group of men approached in masks with hooked beaks like eagles, and feathers sprouting from their heads. 'Don't you know me?'

'A filthy old chicken like you must be Benvenuto Cellini.'

'Of course. Look after your lady, Messer Richard!'

He reached into his bag and began pelting us afresh. Hannah ran, and I after her. We took shelter behind a low wall. The goldsmith and his four friends were casting about along the riverside, looking for us. I heard the voice of Francesco Berni, the satirical poet, among them. 'Sing, my muse, the beard of Messer Dansey; not large, perhaps, but finely curled, and fancy. Where is that Englishman?'

I looked at Hannah. She was out of breath, her mask raised on to her forehead.

'Ready?' I whispered. Hannah nodded. Together we stood up and began pelting Cellini and the others with rapid accuracy. Cursing us, they ran off up the street. We slumped behind the wall, laughing. When our laughter died away we remained there. I gazed at her, wondering. Soon I would discover all the bewitchments of her secrets; not just that name I so badly needed, but the dreams and the longings, the hidden things that drove her. She looked back at me, and for once her eyes were thoughtful and calm.

'Dear Hannah, all my success is for you. You know my ambitions. Wealth, renown, the favour of the King. But I no longer want them only for myself. Together we can take King Henry's Court in our hands, and have our triumph. I took a great risk, coming to Italy after gems without full knowledge of the person they are for. If you tell me now, while Cellini is at work, I can have him craft works that will go right to her heart. Please, Mrs Hannah. Tell me the name of the King's mistress.'

She looked down. My speech had surprised her, and for a moment she looked shy: almost innocent. I waited several heartbeats. Then she lifted her eyes to me again, and they were sparkling with mischief. She laughed and clapped her hands.

'I know what we will do! We shall play cards for it.'

'Cards?'

'Yes.' She jumped to her feet. That wild smile was back. 'Tomorrow, on the last day of the Carnival: Martedì Grasso, when everyone is at the height of madness. What could be better?'

I had a morbid distrust of cards. They were thieves and deceivers.

And as for Hannah, though I desired her, I trusted her less than any person I could name.

I stood up and faced her. 'What card game?'

She smiled at me, swinging her body from the hips, her hands behind her back. 'One of my choosing.'

Still I said nothing.

'Don't be so afraid!' she coaxed me. 'There's no pleasure in life without a little spice of danger.'

'If I win, you will tell me?'

She went on smiling, her body swinging, swinging. 'Yes,' she said. 'I will tell you.'

I hesitated. Like a swordsman who was almost beaten, I stood cautiously in the position of the guard. I could not read her different moves, her feints, her thrusts. But I had to have that name.

'Then I accept.'

Hannah ran a few steps away from me along the river, then turned, looking back at me. 'Only watch out you do not lose. For if you do, Richard Dansey, merchant of London, then God help you.'

She placed the golden cat-mask back over her face, turned away and was gone.

13

I lay that night in my bed at the inn unsleeping. I could not guess
why Hannah was playing this game with me. Just as with Mr Stephen,
there was more at stake than met the eye. What did she really feel for
me? I felt over and over again the touch of that kiss; but each time it
was different, now passionate, now mocking, now hot, now cold.
Like the diamond that had teased me so in Venice. Hannah had
come looking for me, after the horse race. Surely that must mean she
wanted me just as much as I did her. But with her, nothing was
certain. In irritation I threw back the coverlet, lit a candle and took
out my book of Petrarch, most elegant of poets, whose verse is the
finishing gloss of the courtier. With the bells striking midnight
outside, I began to leaf through it. And I found that Ippolita had
presented me with a monster. Beautiful verse, yes: but this was a poet
of mad and hopeless passion, a man who burns and freezes, who
loathes life, who wanders like a storm-racked ship guided by no
stars, through the night, in a maze, blind, frightened, shamed, fed by
love and destroyed by it. I would never let that happen to me.

I threw the book away. There was no question of sleep. I thought
ahead to my meeting with Hannah next day. She had challenged

me; and I was pitifully ill-prepared. I shook Martin until he woke up.

'Get out the cards, and teach me everything you know.'

He yawned and stared in amazement, then took out his battered pack, grumbling. Up until now I had kept well clear of cards. I had a horror of becoming sucked in, the way I had seen happen to others, until, as the poet Berni said, I would not care if I gambled away my eyes, or wagered my own blood, one pint at a time. Martin, on the other hand, was a demon player, and had turned cards into a profitable side-venture. I had the rest of the night in which to learn.

And so we began. Primiera was the game. I was convinced that this would be Hannah's choice. All Venice and Rome were obsessed by it. It was a true courtier's game, more taxing to the mind than chess, so they said; devious, subtle, full of bluffs, feints and swift overthrows. For the first hour I lost. Then luck and skill began to run my way, and I slowly regained almost to the point of breaking even. When the bells all round Rome struck three in the morning, Martin yawned. 'Well, master? You're a quick learner, I'll grant you that. Have we done enough?'

But I was not content. 'What other games might she choose?'

Martin blinked blearily. 'Well, there's gleek, and maw, and noddy, and picardy, and gagne-perde, and ruff and honours, and cent ...'

'Teach me them.'

Martin shook his head in weariness and dealt the cards. It was the very deadest part of the night, silent out in the city, and cold. Martin, though half-asleep, played by instinct and long years of practice. I began to lose steadily. By the time dawn showed through the shutters, I no longer knew whether the six of swords in my hand was worth eighteen points and should be matched with a seven and an ace in primiera, or whether it was Tumbler in gleek and beat Towser, or with another six made four in noddy; and whether it should be thrown away, or hidden, or turned into trump. Our game passed insensibly into nightmare, and I saw Hannah standing over me, throwing down bizarre cards that held no meaning, her smile breaking into a peal of excited laughter.

I opened my eyes slowly. My head was resting on the hard board of the table. The shuttered windows let in piercing glints of daylight. I lifted my head painfully. Across from me Martin was slumped back in a rush-seated chair like my own, snoring. I shook his arm to wake him.

'What? What? I'll vie the ruff.'

'We're finished,' I told him. 'What's the reckoning?'

Martin blinked, and peered at the row of chalk marks on the edge of the table. 'You owe me two hundred and ninety-six baiocchi.'

I frowned, and rapped the table in irritation. A baiocco was a slim silver coin, worth roughly the same as one of our tiny English silver halfpennies. At a hundred and nine baiocchi to the Papal ducat, I had lost nearly three pieces of gold. Martin accepted the money from my purse with a satisfied gleam in his eye: to him, this was several months' pay. The gold to me was nothing. I could afford to lose it; but Hannah's secrets I could not. Martin stretched, and stamped off downstairs to fetch my morning dish of frumenty, wheat boiled in milk with cinnamon, and a fresh jug of wine.

'Another game, master?'

I shook my head. Confidence and decision would serve me better than six more hours' fretful practice. 'It is high time we went to visit the stones.'

After breakfast we set off. It was a bright day, though cold. I took a roundabout route, walking to clear my head, past the Apostolic Chancellery and down on to the Via Giulia. The streets were strangely deserted. Just beyond the church of Saint Eligius, where the quarter of the goldsmiths begins, I passed a group of soldiers in puffed jerkins with blue and red feathers in their hats. They carried harquebuses, and they were clustered around the doorway to a house. With them were six or seven men with axes and two-handled hammers. A shopkeeper was arguing with the soldiers, and two of them pushed him back inside with the butt ends of their weapons. I saw the workmen wrench the door off its hinges and throw it down in the street. The soldiers pushed their way into the house, and soon there was the sound of furniture being thrown down and smashing earthenware. I slowed down, peering sideways for a better look, but Martin pulled my arm.

'Keep walking, master.'

Further along we passed other openings without doors, and three more troops of soldiers. We saw the swing of the axes and hammers, and frightened faces that appeared at windows or balconies and then ducked back inside. We hurried on and slipped into the shop of Cellini. The goldsmith looked up at me with a serious air as I walked over and sat down on my usual stool. I said, 'What is going on?'

Cellini let the polishing wheel slow to a stop and looked up.

'War, my friend, war. The Imperials are moving south. There are new proclamations out: all foreigners must register their weapons, all stores of grain are to be declared and recorded, and those suspected of leaning towards the Emperor will have their doors taken off their hinges, so that their houses can be searched whenever the authorities please. And this district –' he nodded down towards the Banchi and the Via Giulia '– has a great many Florentines.'

'But Florence is allied to the Pope.'

Cellini gave me an impatient look. 'Let me explain it to you. Until four years ago, Florence was ruled in person by Giulio de' Medici. Then he became Pope: our present Holy Father, Clement VII. He left Florence in the hands of his relations, Cardinal Cibo among them.' He nodded in the direction of the candlestick. 'Yes, my generous employer. Now, of Florentines there are two sorts: friends of the Medici, who are pretty few and growing fewer, and the rest of the city who would like to see the Emperor come and kick the Pope and all his family into the sea.'

I accepted the wine that Paulino set down on the workbench. My head was pounding after last night. 'Then, in God's name, what are you doing sitting there? The soldiers will be here at any moment.'

Cellini laughed. 'They know not to come here. His Holiness and Cardinal Cibo value my services. No, I am a Medici man, like my father. Long live black Alessandro and whoremaster Ippolito! Down with the Republic!'

He bent once more over the polishing wheel, and I sat down to watch, my mind spinning through dreams of cups and swords and trumps, the gem's fire, Hannah's kiss. Benvenuto had already broadened the chrysoprase's principal face to his liking. He was working on the lesser facets around it, that juggle the light and deflect it down, down into the stone's heart, until, meeting the underside, illumination is sent rebounding up again and out. With every cut my excitement quickened.

At last he lifted up the chrysoprase in triumph. It was fully cut. The play of light through it was exquisite. It was paler than an emerald and faintly milky, like a misted morning with the sun shining strong and diffused; so that instead of sending out sparks and flashes the way a hard gemstone does, it possessed an eerie green glow that seemed to light the stone from the inside, with shafts of gold cutting through it. When you turned the stone it became unstable, fickle, beyond any man's guessing. I looked on it for long minutes, and put it down at last with a shiver of pleasure.

I said, 'Will you set it now?'

Cellini shook his head. 'First I must fire the enamels. And before that I must pound them. But not yet.' He stretched, and pointed up at the ray of sun slanting into the shop through the window. 'It is time we made further plans. Well, out with your stones, quick, quick. We cannot count on light like this every day, not at this season of the year.'

Paulino spread a white cloth. I pulled the casket out and unlocked it, and once again we arranged the stones in a line where the early spring sun could fall on them, making them dart out their various shades in long streams of vermilion, sea-green or gold. For all my absorption with Hannah, I thrilled to see them. Benvenuto crouched down to be on a level with them, then lifted each in turn. He sighed. I too was gazing on them, nudging them with my finger into patterns. I drew aside the balasses. There were seven of them, uncut. They had a fair share of the blood-red and purple of rubies, though they were paler and more dilute. But they were strong, striking stones nevertheless, and of outstanding size; some of them as large as hazelnuts. To assemble rubies of that weight would have cost tens of thousands of crowns. I put them together until they formed the shape of a heart, and dropped some garnets into the gaps. They glowed with a deeper purple fire, making the heart appear swollen with blood. I formed a crack between the stones, and into it I slid the white sapphire. Cellini opened his eyes and leant forward.

'Good: your heart, I like. And the dart piercing it to its centre: it is an old conceit, but a good one. But not the sapphire. It is too tame. No, that will not do.'

He was right. The sapphire's gentle, milky sheen made it no fit symbol for the violent shock of love. I longed more than ever for the diamond I had lost in Venice, the diamond of the Old Rock, with its chill, blue glints and secret heart: noble, beautiful, exquisite. Like Hannah. No, without that diamond the heart and thorn must remain an unrealised dream. The ray of sun slid slowly up the bench. We pulled the cloth along. Soon the light would be gone for the day, and we would have learnt nothing new about the secrets of my stones. We both drank. As the sunlight spilled off the end of the bench it settled for a last moment on the opals. They flared all at once with every conceivable colour. They were mad, fickle, dangerous. I began to pace up and down, excited. I was seeing visions. Cellini turned to watch me.

I said, 'Consider this. The King has given his lady the brooch with the ship on it. He has declared himself: his love is a madness, an obsession. He is driven on, over winter seas, following her eyes as if they were stars. She accepts the gift. She wears it. She is on the point of surrender. But she is afraid.' I darted back to the workbench, arranged the opals in a line and then joined two more on each side, forming a cross.

Cellini frowned. 'A cross? Are you mad? As a love-gift from a man setting out to commit adultery?'

'No,' I said. 'It is perfect. Do you not see? The cross is a promise: just the promise she will want King Henry to make. It will say to her, "You can trust me. I am a man of honour and religion." So a cross: but a cross set with opals, the most fickle and devious of stones. Because she is also a lover of danger. They will say to her: "This is humanity. This is you, and this is me. Beautiful, fallible, passionate."'

Cellini shook his head. 'You really are mad. You do not even know this lady.'

I walked over to the window. By God, I would know her soon enough. In the meantime, there were a few things at least I could see. I said, 'If she listens to the King's courting for more than a minute, then she surely loves danger. And believe me, she must be afraid.'

The goldsmith stretched and scratched his beard. 'Hm! An opal cross. I have never seen or heard of such a thing. The symbol of Salvation done in the stones of witchery and sin. It is a true piece of wickedness.' He leant over the opals and smiled. 'Messer Richard, you are a man greatly to my liking. We shall do it. Only do not let the Pope or his cardinals see it. I do not think they would approve of your theology.'

I clapped him on the shoulder. 'Hurry and finish those enamels. There is still a lot of work before us.'

I led Martin back out into the street. It was just past noon. Together we walked back along the Via Monserrato and turned into the little square where the Palazzo del Bene nestled in a corner as if waiting for me. Its stucco, which before had seemed so drab a yellow, today flamed almost blood-red in the sun. I let Martin rap on the door, and when Alessandro's chamberlain opened it, stepped inside.

It was plain at once that something out of the ordinary was taking place. The usual cluster of servants in the spacious vestibule was swelled by six or so men in scarlet carrying halberds. My first thought was that Alessandro had somehow fallen foul of the authorities. But these halberdiers were not the rough soldiers I had seen on the Via Giulia. They were the guards of a very important personage, and with them was a pair of monks each bearing a silver cross on a pole some eight feet long, which indicated that the visitor was a great churchman.

At the head of the stairs Mrs Grace came out from the sala where we had dined two days ago, smiled her perfect smile and kissed me on the cheek.

'Mr Richard! How very fortunate.'

I returned her kiss with a little extra warmth. The closer I drew to Mrs Grace, it seemed to me, the closer I drew to Hannah.

I heard distant voices and girls' laughter. 'I would not have troubled you,' I assured her, 'if I had known you had an important guest.'

Grace cast her eyes towards the deeper parts of the palazzo, with an expression that mingled reverence and irritation. 'Stephen is with Cardinal Campeggio. But I believe the girls are in the loggia.'

She led me into the sala. Even as I was nerving myself to meet Hannah, the name Campeggio sent my mind spinning. Though an Italian, he was Bishop of Salisbury by the gift of our King Henry, and Cardinal–protector of England. He was the man who stood between the Pope and the King, as mediator or ambassador; loyal to His Holiness, naturally, but also very much beholden to the King. Where his loyalties truly lay would be hard for any man to say. He was a powerful man, but a peaceful one; a man of deep understanding who had been married once, before he was a priest, and loved the delights of the table. I well remembered the stir in London when he had arrived to seek support for a crusade against the Turks some nine years earlier. I had been just twelve, and had gazed in wonder on his barge as it passed up the Thames with its scarlet banners and crosses of silver. His presence here was yet another sign of the weightiness of Mr Stephen's business.

I followed Mrs Grace through a grand door beside the fireplace. Cool air blew against my face. We were in an arcaded gallery with a balustrade and a row of columns running along its edge, overlooking the garden with its marble statues. The walls and curved ceiling were painted with scenes of heroes, shepherds and misty seascapes and woods. I heard Hannah's laughter mixed with snarls and yaps. At the far end of the loggia three spaniels were running in tight circles, leaping up at a ball which Hannah held just above them on a string. Susan was sitting closer to me with an enormous viol cradled between her legs. Her knees and elbows stuck out in four grotesque angles; she held the bow in her palm, slanting back across the strings, and on her face was a furious scowl of concentration. The bow touched the strings, which responded with a dismal howl. At her feet Alessandro's dwarf, Morgante, was throwing sweets to the monkey, which caught them in its paws and grinned. Susan looked up.

I said, 'Is the monkey really called Beelzebub?'

'That's my name for it. Hannah calls it Piccolino or something such. The nasty beast.'

I frowned down at her. 'Hannah, or the monkey?'

'As you like.'

I walked past her. Hannah saw me, and her face broke into a smile which warmed and delighted me. She tossed the ball away in the direction of Susan, which sent the spaniels barking and jumping round her feet. Susan let out a cry of anger, stood up and began stamping at them and calling them every kind of Satan and devil.

'Susan!' warned Mrs Grace. 'Try to be a civil creature.'

Hannah glided towards me and offered her cheek for a kiss.

'You will be with us for dinner?' said Grace. 'Tomorrow will be Lent: this is the last night of the Carnival.'

At my side Hannah whispered, 'And I hear it is the cruellest and wildest of all.'

'But dinner is not for two hours,' Grace continued. 'An awkward length of time, is it not? If we had longer, I might suggest a trip to the grottoes, or over the river to the Belvedere. His Holiness has made us welcome there at any time.'

Hannah said, 'Perhaps Mr Richard would be diverted by a little game of cards.'

Her eyes on me were loaded with challenge. I said, 'What a charming thought.'

Grace smiled. 'Then let us go to the saletta.' She led the way to a door at the end of the gallery. Beyond was a room far more intimate in size than the sala. A single window looked out south-west across the Via Giulia to the river. The walls in here were painted a deep green, overlaid with swirling flowers of every kind, giving the impression that we were inside some rustic temple with a flowering wilderness all round. Three older women sat near the window with embroidery frames, workboxes and scissors round them. They looked up as we came in, and bowed their heads. These were gentlewomen, I took it, kept by the female Cages as companions. A door on the right must have led back into the sala; from another, on the left, came the murmur of voices, one of which I recognised as Mr Stephen's. That would be his anticamera, or studio, a place for receiving the most honoured of guests.

Mrs Grace went over to sit with the gentlewomen, and peered with bright interest at their work. Hannah led me to a small table with its legs carved in the form of naked-breasted sphinxes. A white cloth covered its top and three chairs stood round it. She motioned me to sit. One of the Cages' silent, impeccable servants set down wine. Susan came in, laid her instrument on a bench with a deep-voiced twang, and sat down at one of the chairs. She stared at me with a look of deep significance.

'You don't mean that Susan is playing too?'

'The game we are going to play is for three.' Hannah opened a chest and took out a stack of cards, which she set down on the table.

They were large, almost as long as my hand, and the stack was thick. I looked at them in suspicion.

'What are these?'

'They are Tarocchi. What the French call Tarot.'

I looked on, dismayed, as Hannah shuffled the cards and began to deal them out in batches of three. The game of Tarocchi was of notorious difficulty, played mainly by the aristocracy. It was of Italian invention, unknown in England; I had watched in Venice, but never played. Martin, of course, would not know it, and in any case I did not possess the requisite cards.

I said, 'I shall play you at anything you please. But not Tarocchi.'

Hannah went on dealing. 'You allowed me my choice.'

'I trusted you to choose within reason.'

She gave me a look of indignation. 'What did you think I would pick? Primiera, maybe? Even our servants are playing it. What do you take me for? Some wench in a tavern?'

Mrs Grace looked up from the embroidery frame which she had taken over from one of the gentlewomen.

'I hope, my sweets, you will take care of those cards. They cost your father a good deal of money. They were made by Messer Padovano, the Michelangelo of card-makers.'

Susan sang back, 'Have no fear, *madre mia*.'

She snapped up the cards as fast as Hannah dealt them, spreading them in her hand and peering at them with grunts of pleasure. Already I felt this game was slipping away from me. I said, 'What does Susan get if she wins?'

Hannah lifted one eyebrow. 'I hardly think that is very likely.'

'But supposing?'

'If she wins you, she can have you.'

Susan snorted, and darted me a look of utter loathing. Grace peered at us again.

'You are not playing for high stakes, are you, my pet lambs?'

Hannah went on dealing. 'Nothing of any importance.'

I looked across at her, the faint smile about her lips, the lifted brows and the intensity in her eyes. She was playing with me as a cat does with a mouse. Still the cards kept coming, with their plain light green backs, shot across the cloth by Hannah's quick white fingers.

I leant over and spoke in a whisper. 'Dear, sweet Mrs Hannah, is this fair? To play me at a game I do not understand?'

'Poor Mr Richard,' said Hannah. 'It seems to me this is not the only game you do not understand. In the life you have chosen you will have to become a fast learner. Or are you saying you will admit defeat right now?'

Fuming, I threw myself back in my chair. 'No.'

All the cards were out. I picked up the pile in front of me. As I spread them in my hand I saw that the face of every card was coated in gold leaf, with the designs richly painted over the top. There were the four familiar suits that all Italian cards share, coins and cups, batons and swords, though these cards were so ornate that they were not always easy to read. That pair of vine stocks, for example, with grapes hanging down from them and a fox reaching up to eat them, must be meant for the two of batons. Then there were the Triumphs, the winning cards. Each had a picture on it that was its own exquisite little work of art. I saw in my hand a naked woman holding a star; a man handing a flower to a woman, with a cupid hovering over their heads; a skeleton mounted on a horse grasping a scythe. They bore neither names nor numbers.

'You must remember the pictures,' Hannah prompted me, 'and which one conquers which.'

I hissed at her, 'You are mad. I cannot remember what I have never been told.'

Susan said, 'I suppose we ought to have a little pity on him?'

Hannah frowned, as if she were trying to judge just how great an advantage she was handing me. Then she said, 'Well, we shall tell you: but not too much. There are seventy-eight cards, though we only play with seventy-two. Twenty-one of them are Triumphs, that beat all the other suits. Highest of these is the Angel.'

'They also call it the Day of Judgement,' added Susan. 'Sometimes even God.'

'Below that is the World.'

'Then Sun, Moon, Star.'

'The Devil and Death, and the Traitor.'

'After him is Gobbo, the Hunchback: then the Virtues.'

'Below those,' Hannah said, looking me in the eye, 'is Love, and all the other troubles of life.'

'Then Emperor and Pope, Empress and She-pope.'

'Last is the Bagattino: we call him the Conjuror.'

'We have forgotten some,' said Susan. 'Oh! Shall we tell him about the Fool?'

Hannah shook her head. 'Oh, no. Let it be a surprise.'

'Good idea.'

'I think that is all we have to say. Do you still want to play?'

'And win,' I told them. Inside I was seething. They could keep me in ignorance if they pleased. I was going to beat them, no matter what it took.

Hannah took four of her cards and laid them aside, face-down. 'Everyone else throws out one. Then we play.' She darted a glance at her sister. 'You are first. And no helping the enemy.'

'You are the enemy just as much as he is.'

Susan took a card from her hand and set it down. It bristled with swords: three curved blades interlocking with three more. I was next. I decided to begin boldly. I laid down a young man holding a sword.

Hannah immediately placed on top of it another youth wielding a sword, mounted on a horse. 'Mine, I think.'

She pulled the cards in front of her, laid them face down and immediately played a new card. It was the king of swords. Susan played an eight. I held the three and the four. Most likely I was expected to sacrifice one of these, and lose yet another trick to Hannah. But this appeared altogether too tame and obvious a course. Instead I chose out an old man in a hood with crooked shoulders, carrying an hourglass and a staff. This must be the Gobbo, I thought, the hunchback. I laid it down on top of the other two. Hannah creased her brows.

'You must have a sword. I cannot believe you do not.'

'What if I have?'

She leant forward and spoke in an angry whisper. 'If you hold a sword, you must play it. You are not allowed to play a Triumph until your suit is bare.'

I said, 'If you will not tell me the rules, you cannot be angry when I break them.'

Susan pointed at her sister, with a 'Ha, ha, ha!'

Hannah frowned, then waved her hand in dismissal. 'Take it, then. Five points for the king. The hunchback counts for nothing. But don't think you're going to win.'

After that we skirmished a little in the low-ranking batons, and I had some good success. I looked up at the two girls with a smile. But Susan shook her head. 'You poor dupe,' she said. 'Those cards are worthless, and the tricks only count one each. You will have to do better than that.' Then Hannah played a ten of cups on my three, and began pulling in the cards.

Susan's hand came down on hers. 'Not so fast, big sister.'

Susan turned to me. 'In cups and coins, the suits run contrary. A two beats a three, and a three certainly beats a ten.'

Hannah glared at her. 'No, they don't.'

Susan laughed in astonishment. 'By God, they do.'

'Mr Richard,' said Hannah, 'who are you going to believe? This little liar or me?'

I looked between them. Susan had her mouth open, the amazed and angry child, while Hannah wore on her face a look of deep and beautiful guile. 'No contest at all. I believe Susan.'

Hannah pushed the cards at me in annoyance. 'You've chosen a dangerous friend.'

'My dear Mrs Hannah,' I said, 'I will gladly surrender the game, if you only tell me the name of the King's mistress.'

Susan looked up sharply, eyes widening. 'Saint Jennifer's arse! Is that what we are playing for?'

'No,' said Hannah. 'Because I am not going to lose. We are playing for Mr Richard, heart and soul.'

'But you would not really think of telling him?' persisted Susan.

'Don't be foolish. I told you, I am not going to lose.'

I turned to Susan. 'You could save your sister a lot of heartache if you simply told me yourself.'

Susan snorted. 'Why should I?'

'Besides,' said Hannah. 'Susan is so fond of telling lies.'

Susan opened her mouth in outrage. 'Fine talk, coming from you. Oh, I shall enjoy this. Play on!'

Hannah took my ace of batons with the Emperor, and threw down a card bearing a great silver tower with lightning flashing round it.

'The House of the Devil,' murmured Susan. 'None can quench his flame.' She twisted her face into an ugly squint, peered at each of us, and then with a gesture of carelessness let fall a card. It had on it a man in a broad-brimmed hat, standing at a table with dice and a scatter of cards.

Hannah let out a whoof of indignation. Across the room, Mrs Grace looked up briefly from her sewing. Hannah turned to Susan and lowered her voice. 'Dear sister, if I thought you were helping Mr Richard to win, I would do something extremely unpleasant to you.'

Susan sat back and folded her arms. 'Think what you like. You know what a little fool I am at cards.'

Hannah turned her eyes on me. 'Susan is handing you the Conjuror: the lowest of the Triumphs, and the only one besides the Angel to carry a score. It is one of the Seven Tarocchi, and counts five points. If you can beat my card, you can have it.'

I pondered hard. I had to beat her. Hannah's card, the tower or House of the Devil, had not been among those the two girls had mentioned. I looked at my remaining Triumphs. I held the Star, Love, Death, and a pair of females who must be Virtues. Where in the sequence did Hannah's burning tower stand? Fire falling from the sky, divine vengeance, consigning man to the devil and damnation. This, surely, was the card that linked heaven to man. I would gamble my Star was higher. I eased out from my hand the naked woman bearing over her head the silver star, and set it down over the Conjuror and the Tower.

For a moment no one moved. Then Hannah nudged the cards towards me, with a glacial look at her sister. 'Take them.'

I lost for a while, then took back the lead with my king of coins. We were playing fast, all of us, driven as if by some devil to win. From Hannah came the Angel, highest card of all, carrying off my Death and Susan's Sun. Susan struck back with some wily Triumphs. Her Traitor, hanging upside-down from a tree, brought down my cavalier of cups and Hannah's queen.

'Traitor,' murmured Hannah, as Susan greedily scooped in the cards. 'How very apt.'

Then Hannah's queen of batons came up against my king. He was shown seated, white-bearded in a green mantle, holding in his hand a rugged club. I could not resist a yelp of delight. But Hannah's hand covered the cards before mine. My fingers were on hers, and our eyes met: hers stubborn, and with a hint of that wild smile of amusement.

'Come, come, Mrs Hannah,' I said. 'Let me have them. A king is master of his queen.'

'Not in this game,' said Hannah. 'The kings of swords and batons are the two Pilgrims: *i Pellegrini*. They are sad little things that wilt before their women.'

I still held her eye. 'Mrs Hannah, you are inventing every word of it.'

'No,' said Susan. 'She's not. That trick really is hers.'

Slowly I released my hand. Hannah took the cards with a smile. We were down to seven cards each. I had a fair-sized pile of won tricks in front of me, but I had been prodigal with my high cards, and I had few left. I won the next trick and played my cavalier of coins, counting on both of the others still holding coins. But Hannah's She-Pope beat me. I cursed under my breath. Susan took the next two tricks; then Hannah took back the lead and put down a nine of coins. I swooped across the table and grabbed her by the wrist.

'So you do have a coin in your hand, and yet you trumped my cavalier! You are a cheat, Mrs Hannah, a cheat, a cheat.'

She looked at me with an amused smile. 'So you noticed. I didn't think you would. Now we are even.'

I released her hand. We had only two cards each. Hannah, without a pause, snapped down the ten of batons. Susan trumped it with a woman in white holding scales and a sword: Justice. I still held one Triumph. It had on it a woman, blindfolded, and a wheel with one figure climbing it, another falling. Fortune and her wheel. But did it rank above Justice, or below? If I played it and won, I had a chance at catching all those last six cards. The cautious path would be to keep my Triumph for last. But when did I ever opt for caution? And I had a shrewd notion that the inventor of these cards believed luck reigned high. I set down my Wheel of Fortune on the other two cards. Hannah and Susan looked at me. Hannah's brows furrowed.

'Hm! You continue to surprise me, Richard Dansey. That is yours.' I gathered them in, chuckling. I looked down at my last card, bearing a goblet wreathed in roses. The ace of cups. Hannah caressed her own single card, running her finger along its edge. 'Let us see what you have, Mr Richard. Play!'

I slapped down my golden ace. A lovers' cup. Hannah hesitated. Then, with a huff of irritation she tossed down her card. It was a queen: noble and warlike, robed in crimson and silver. In her hand was a sword. I smiled.

'Not so fast,' said Hannah. 'Susan, show us your last card. And let it be a Triumph.'

Susan raised her left eyebrow, looked at us each in turn, and slid forward a jester in cap and bells, playing on a pipe and beating a drum. I let out a cry of anger. I had lost the trick. The reckoning must be close. I was convinced that that queen of swords would make the difference between victory and defeat. But then Susan whisked her card back again, and put it on her own pile, leaving the other two behind.

'The Fool,' said Susan. 'No, he is no Triumph. He can neither capture nor be captured. He joins the party, makes his excuse, and leaves. But he is valuable, even if he has no power. The Fool is the Seventh Tarocco: five points to me.' She nudged the queen and the ace towards me. I gathered in the cards, and glanced across at Hannah. She was frowning and biting her lip. We all looked down at our three piles of cards, pale green against the white of the cloth. Hannah reached for my pile.

'No. I'll be the one to count,' said Susan.

Hannah let her, but kept an eagle eye on her quickly moving fingers as she counted off the cards in batches of three, picking out those that scored. I watched, jealously, though I understood little of the bizarre reckoning system.

'Thirty-one,' said Susan. 'Agreed?'

Hannah gave a slight nod. 'And yours?'

Susan went through her own pile. 'Twenty. Misery me.'

Hannah turned over her cards and counted them out, while Susan peered at her in suspicion. When Hannah had gone through the last of them she put them down and said nothing.

'Twenty-six!' said Susan. 'You've lost, you've lost!'

I leant forward with my elbows on the table and smiled. 'And now, my sweet Mrs Hannah, you are bound to tell.'

From Mr Stephen's private anticamera the murmur of voices grew louder. Mrs Grace and the gentlewomen laid down their

197

sewing and looked up. Hannah squared up the cards with angry flicks of her hands. 'You cheated,' she hissed at me. 'You're a cheat, cheat, cheat. We take off five for that king you stole. Those points are mine.'

'Since we're talking of cheating,' I whispered back, 'what about my cavalier of coins? Give me that and take the king. You'll see I still come out ahead. Isn't that right, Susan?'

'Not at all,' whispered Hannah. 'If I had won that king the whole course of the game would have been different.'

'What about me?' interrupted Susan. 'I cheated too. You were both too wrapped up to notice.' Hannah turned on her, mouth open in outrage.

The door to the anticamera opened and we heard slow footsteps approaching. Mrs Grace moved into the middle of the room and swept a deep curtsy, drawing back the edges of her skirts with both hands.

'My lord Cardinal.'

We rose hurriedly from the table. Cardinal Campeggio was a tall, stooped man in his mid fifties, with the long, sad face of a bloodhound. He wore a scarlet mantle and biretta. Round his neck hung a jewelled cross on a gold chain. His eye picked me out immediately as the stranger in the room. I approached him and went down on one knee. He offered me his hand, and I kissed the gold ring on his swollen fingers. I recognised on it the Medici balls and Florentine lilies of Pope Leo X, our present Pope's cousin, who had advanced Campeggio to the cardinalship. On his little finger was a very fine citrine in a ring, carved with a face in profile. It was an exquisite work. He must have detected my eye on it.

'Ancient Roman,' observed the Cardinal. 'Nothing we moderns do can equal them. And so you are an Englishman too, and I believe you understand something of stones.'

'I have some knowledge, your lordship,' I admitted. *Vostra signoria* was the correct address for a cardinal; I thanked Ippolita for that piece of instruction. I went on kneeling before this man who had been a great churchman and Papal Legate while I was still a child. His mild, sad eyes, I thought, missed very little. His gaze rested on me.

'And I believe also that your family is close to Cardinal Wolsey: a man for whom I have the very highest regard.'

This, I knew, was some way off the truth. Campeggio and Wolsey were old rivals. Wolsey had taken the opportunity of Campeggio's visit to England to have himself made a legate, and by that means had stolen a good deal of Campeggio's power. But I guessed Campeggio was privy to Mr Stephen's hidden business, and Stephen must have told him I was close to Wolsey's secrets. To be seen like this with Stephen Cage by one of Wolsey's men was possibly a deep embarrassment for the Cardinal. He appeared anxious, at any rate, for Wolsey to be pacified, and that only stirred my suspicions all the more. Was this gentle, sombre old man also a part of the 'web' that Wolsey feared so much? Stephen, behind the Cardinal, watched us with a cold smile.

Campeggio withdrew his hand and I got to my feet. Mr Stephen came up behind him. He stopped beside me for a moment and gave a private nod. Hannah picked up the cards and crossed to the chest to put them away. 'Cheat,' she whispered as she passed.

We walked through to the sala, where tables were set out and the minstrels playing. Dinner was more stately and sumptuous than ever. Trumpets sounded, and the dishes entered in procession – capons stuffed with whole cheeses, pigeons in verjuice, pork in ginger and a pie made out of the lungs of kids – a final day of feasting before the austerity of Lent. As the last of the platters were set down, talk turned to the war. The Duke of Bourbon's Imperial army had left Piacenza, it seemed, and advanced to the foot of the mountains north of Florence.

I felt my heart beat faster and my palms sweat. Florence! So the war had moved down into central Italy, pushing right past Venice and the Pope's other allies in the North: a thing no one had believed could happen.

Alessandro del Bene laughed nervously and dabbed at his mouth with his napkin. 'But the Imperials are still two hundred and fifty miles off. They are hungry, the rain has swollen all the rivers, and there is snow in the mountains. They are in no condition to cross them. Thank God they are so far from Rome, with Florence in between, and the Venetian army in the field too. And then again, peace is certain to be made soon.'

'Well!' said Mrs Grace brightly, taking a morsel of roasted piglet on her fork. 'It is so gratifying to hear good news.'

I saw Campeggio look aside. I said, 'I perceive that your lordship suspects more than he is saying.' I spoke before I had realised. The whole table turned to look at me: Stephen and Grace shocked, Alessandro freshly alarmed; while Hannah for the first time in the meal turned and looked at me with interest. Campeggio's face wore a faint smile, as if he were pleased that someone had seen through Alessandro's comforting half-truths.

The Cardinal nodded slowly. 'The Emperor's army is unpaid. It cannot possibly be disbanded without money, and where is it to come from? They know Rome is rich with treasure. Bourbon's army numbers thirty thousand, Lutheran mercenaries from Germany and Spanish moriscos, many of them Muslims from Alicante; all of them hate the Pope. Believe me, we are in greater danger than most of us care to admit.'

We sat in sombre silence. Campeggio's talk chilled me. How long did I have before I should cut Cellini's work short, and bolt for England? If only the army would keep away until he had finished, until I had that name, until I had Hannah. I leant close to her and whispered.

'Hannah. You have heard what the Cardinal said. Will you not tell me the name?'

Without looking at me she whispered back, 'No. I won't.'

'Why don't you play again?' suggested Susan.

Hannah turned on her. 'And have him cheat again? No. Impossible.'

I lost all patience. If we had been alone I might have hit her. Instead I hissed at her, 'Why, Mrs Hannah? Tell me why!'

Instead of answering she signalled for wine, and drank deeply. As she handed back the cup her eyes suddenly lit up and she clapped her hands. 'I know! We'll settle this tonight.'

Susan twisted her face into a squint of disbelief. 'You don't mean the *moccoli*?'

'Just so,' said Hannah, turning to me with a smile that sparkled with mischief. 'We shall let the *moccoli* decide. Oh, and, dear Mr Richard, bring a candle.'

I looked from one to the other. 'A candle?'

'Just a candle,' said Hannah.

Both girls smiled, met one another's eyes, and burst into laughter.

14

As I came away from the Palazzo del Bene it was already growing dark. I walked quickly through the streets, oppressed by a sense of urgency. From down the alleys off the Via Monserrato Martin and I could hear occasional shouts and running feet, and there was the glitter of torches passing along a street end, or across the opening of a piazza. The city seemed to brood with a sense of expectation. I headed straight to find Cellini.

As I stepped inside his studio I was hit by a blast of heat. From the deepest part of the workshop came the roar of the furnace and a momentary flash of flame as Paulino opened the iron door with a hook. Cellini strode about in the glare of the fire wearing his leather apron and holding a pair of iron tongs, which he slapped against his leg.

'More coal! Don't slack now, damn you! I'll not have your slowness mar my work!'

I laughed. 'Benvenuto, when you are dead you will make such an excellent devil!'

'I shall see Lucifer one day, I promise you,' Cellini growled. 'I know a priest who can raise him up. He knows the charms, and the amulets, and the perfumes to burn. He can call out all the demons of Hell any night he pleases. By God, I dare stand before the Devil face to face. Does any man say I do not?'

He turned on us, beard bristling, eyes red from the smoke.

'Not I,' I answered. He turned back to the fire, peered inside its depths and grunted. Then he used the tongs to pick up an iron plate from the workbench. On it was the golden ship. In the indentations of the pattern were deposited the tiny heaps of coloured powder that would melt into enamel in the heat. He brought the plate nearer to the furnace, and nearer, then held it steady, while the glare of the fire glanced off the gold, and the powders started to fuse. I watched, struck silent.

'Be ready with the bellows!' he shouted to Paulino. He slid the disc of gold into the furnace. I caught my breath to see that thing of beauty go into the flames. I knew that for this stage of the work the fire must be just as hot as the enamel and the gold can bear, and that a moment's misjudgement would ruin the whole work.

'I hope to God you made that fire fresh?' murmured Cellini. 'The charcoal clean?'

'Yes, master,' answered Paulino. He darted him one of his looks replete with devotion and sadness, hurt to the quick that his master could have doubted his care.

'Just be ready with those bellows,' said Cellini.

I peered past him, straining to see what was happening inside the fire.

'Ready as I take it out!' roared Cellini. 'Now!' He whisked the plate from the furnace and held it in front of the boy, who went to work furiously with the bellows, sending out creaking gusts of air that blew puffs of smoke spiralling off into the room while Cellini lowered the plate on to an iron grille. After a few minutes he told Paulino to stop.

'Good,' he murmured. 'I don't think even old Arseface himself could have done any better.' Caradosso, or Arseface, had been the nickname of Ambrogio Foppa, the greatest craftsman in gold and enamels of his generation. He had died last year, a very old man. I peered in eagerness at the brooch. The waves beneath the ship glowed with the glassy blue of cobalt, all the more brilliant for its background of gold that shone through the half-transparent enamel like sand in shallow water. The ship's timbers had been picked out in streaks of orange and red, while the sails were a ghostly pearl-white. Cellini had left the sky as virgin gold, deeply scored with incisions to mark the angry clouds boiling around the four stars. Only the sockets for the gems remained to be filled.

'Perfect,' I breathed.

'A little polishing with tripoli,' said Cellini modestly. 'That is all it needs. And now!' He wiped his hands and took off his apron. 'It is a windless night: perfect for the *moccoli*. Paulino: the candles.'

I saw to my alarm that Cellini was putting on a padded doublet, of the kind worn to protect the body against dagger thrusts. I tapped at his chest. 'Just what is this about? Are you afraid of assassination?'

'In a manner of speaking,' said Cellini. He waved his hand. 'It is the *moccoli*, the *moccoli*! A *moccolo* is a candle-end. Everyone carries a candle tonight. It is the last game of the Carnival. You have to dowse the other man's flame, by any means you like, and keep your own alight.'

I nodded, perceiving at last Hannah's challenge. At this sport, cheating was impossible, because absolutely anything was allowed.

'So,' said Benvenuto. 'Take these, then, and join us.' He held out to Martin and me a pair of masks, hawk-nosed and evil-eyed, and Paulino handed us each a long candle which he lit with a spill from the furnace.

Out in the street we saw eight or nine people heading towards us, fantastical characters in masquing costume, shouting and waving. Each of them carried some form of light: a wax taper, a long church candle, even a three-branched candelabrum.

'Ah!' said Cellini. 'And here are our friends. Tonight, it is safer to hunt in a group.'

I saw one in a sheepskin like a brigand; another an emperor in purple velvet and cloth of gold, with a feathered pasteboard helmet. There were courtesans too, one dressed as a she-fool with bauble and bells, another an Amazon, naked-breasted with bracelets in the form of wild silver serpents round her arms. This was Pantassilea, who had once been Cellini's mistress. A lady smothered in silken flowers gave me a roguish smile which I began to return, until I recognised her as a Spanish boy named Diego, who sometimes worked for Cellini as a model. There was Berni with his wicked grin, Bacchiacca, a Florentine painter who specialised in vast scenes for wall paintings and tapestry designs, and Polidoro da Caravaggio, with a number of young noblemen: Cellini's whole crew. All of them wore masks, grotesques in gold or silver plaster with beards or horns and staring eyes and grimaces.

We set off, heading away from the river. Masquers swarmed in the streets, each with a candle, or two or three. The balconies on all the buildings were crammed with life, young people and old, who shouted down at the masquers and threw water, or lowered handker-chiefs on strings so as to quench their flames as they walked past underneath. Everywhere was laughter, and sudden attacks, and street-vendors walking between them holding out candles for sale and calling, '*Moccoli*, buy your *moccoli*.' Over it all there went up the savage chant, 'Death, death, death if you lose your candle-end!' We fought as a band, roving among the crowds, darting up upon groups of men and girls, knocking the candles from their hands and then flourishing ours at them.

I took no part in this. I was scanning the crowds for any sight of Hannah. On every side there were the shouts and screams of the beaten and the hoots and laughter of the victors. I saw groups of boys, their candles spent, hurling oranges and eggs into open windows, while those inside tipped showers of flour out over them in revenge.

We passed the church of Santa Maria in Vallicella and carried on, out into the Piazza Navona. Down all the length of the piazza, round the abandoned booths of the meat and vegetable markets, the lights darted and struck. As I stood and looked around, a masked figure stole up to my side. I jumped back, ready to defend my flame.

'Messer Richard.'

The eyes glinting behind the mask were those of Alessandro del Bene.

'You!' I said. 'Hannah Cage: is she –'

'She is waiting,' said Alessandro. 'At the Ruins.'

'But which?'

'The Campo Vacino.'

'To the Ruins, to the Ruins,' the others picked up. We headed east, down narrow lanes and past rearing columns, and along the blank wall of the ancient theatre where Hannah had accosted me after the horse race. I peered into every shadowed doorway, convinced her attack would be sudden. Perhaps Alessandro was in league with her, and was leading me into an ambush. Before us rose the Campidoglio: a rocky hill on which the ancient citadel of the Romans had stood. A thousand years ago this had been at the city's heart. Now, crowned with drab houses and the tall bell-tower of a church, it marked the very edge of modern Rome. We circled the foot of the hill past an old, weathered triumphal arch, mired up to its knees in soil and filth, with trees growing out of its top. Beyond it, desolate and haunted, stretched the barren marsh known as the Campo Vacino, or Cow Pasture. Beneath its damp grass lay the Forum of the Romans. Here they had held their markets and worshipped their gods, and their statesmen had delivered the orations which our master on Old Fish Street had tried so hard to beat into us. A second triumphal arch stood further off with a church built into its wall, while behind loomed the broken curve of the Colosseum, vast and forbidding.

Across the marshy grass candle flames moved in the darkness, darting in and out between columns and the broken-down walls of temples, suddenly casting a tiny illumination over some ancient carving, or a solitary white ox, lying on the grass, watching. There came shouts and shrieks as someone was caught and his light extinguished. The scene resembled some haunted revel of spirits. As Martin came up beside me he crossed himself.

I peered about for any sign of Hannah. At least, I thought, our band gave me some protection against sudden attack. But at that moment Berni snuffed out the flame of the boy-woman Diego with a whisk of his cloak, and ran ahead over the grass, singing, 'Lost his candle! Lost his candle!' Diego let out a shrill shout and ran after him.

The rest of Cellini's crowd, laughing, chased them towards a low wall of marble blocks. Our band, that had fought so far as one, turned on itself. Pantassilea pushed Berni and swooped on him, leaning out and blowing at his candle. Berni, extemporising his verses all the time, danced round her like a fencer: not to blame if he snuffs her flame; play the game. Benvenuto feinted at me and dived round Pantassilea, as the courtesan rapidly lost her temper. A girl dressed as the huntress Diana who had been clinging to Polidoro's arm darted towards me with her little candle. She was a slight, dainty thing, with a bow slung over her shoulder and a silver moon in her hair. I dodged her, whisked round, and knocked her candle from her hand. She let out a small cry, and I laughed.

Suddenly from over the wall behind us there was a fiendish yell. I turned to see some six or seven shapes leaping at us, masked as devils and wearing heavy cloaks. In their right hands were flails, roasting spits, streamers of cloth, while in their left they carried their candles, full-length church lights that burned strong. They plunged among us. The older men, Polidoro and Bacchiacca, stepped back from this new fight, but Alessandro, Cellini and some of the others joined in with a will. The space in front of the ruined wall turned into a whirling dance of masked figures and flames. I dodged a woman who thrust her candle at me, and jumped back in time as she shot out two yards of crimson silk which nearly caught my flame. All the while I was scanning among our attackers. Most of them were women, but they fought like demons. I saw one slice through the air with an iron spit and lop the head off the candle belonging to Giovanni Balbi, nephew of the transvestite Bishop of Gurk. Balbi let out a cry of dismay and fell backwards into a reedy pool with a splash. The woman tipped her head back and laughed. I knew that voice, with its throaty purr of excitement. Hannah's black hair streamed from behind her horned mask, which grinned, pale as a skull. I moved round the fighters to get nearer.

Already many of the skirmishes were over. Cellini's flame was still burning but Alessandro's was out, and so were several of the women's. I saw a skinny she-devil who was the image of Mrs Susan wandering about with a smoking candle-end, saying, 'Give me a light, a light! God damn all of you!' Diego danced round her, chanting, 'Lost her candle, lost it, lost it!' Others of them were taking their masks off, the fight over, kissing or exchanging playful buffets of revenge. I recognised two of the Cages' gentlewomen talking together, their faces animated; they were younger and more spirited than I had thought. Martin's candle was still burning. He sat down next to a girl who looked like a maid and slapped a hand on to her knee.

Hannah, left without an adversary, drew back into the shadows. I followed her. Just beyond the pool Balbi had fallen into were some more ruined buildings: dark, looming shapes jagged as dragons' teeth, with odd blocks of masonry strewn about everywhere underfoot. I picked my way cautiously forward. It would not do to stumble and lose the contest through my own clumsiness. Holding my candle behind me to keep it safe, I peered round a corner into the darkness. At the end of a short passage between two walls I saw Mrs Hannah. She was sitting on a fallen section of column, and to my astonishment I saw that Cellini was with her. He was sitting with his right arm round her shoulder. In his left he still carried his candle. Hannah held her own, also still burning, cautiously out of reach. Her mask was lifted from her face, and she was smiling.

'Come now, Signora Hannah,' Cellini was saying. 'I have known you a lot longer than Messer Richard has. Why do you not allow me just one single kiss? Is that not what English girls do when they meet their friends? Why so very cruel?' He stroked her hair. Hannah was regarding Cellini with just that same wild smile of danger she had worn last night after I pulled her clear of the bulls and kissed her. It was a smile I considered mine, and mine alone. I sprang forward in a rage, swapping my candle into my left hand ready to draw my sword.

Cellini drew his arm from round Hannah's back and sighed. 'She loves you, Englishman: it is the only explanation. Women do not say no to Benvenuto.'

My anger cooled at this, and I looked at Hannah. Her cheeks were puckered in a near-smile, and her eyes flashed with amusement. She was enjoying the spectacle: she would neither confirm what Cellini had said nor deny it. While the goldsmith kept his gaze on me, gauging whether his soft words had had an effect or whether he was going to have to fall back on his sword, Hannah's hand came up, still holding the spit, and whisked his candle out of his hands. Its flame vanished in the grass. She let out a wild laugh, jumped from the fallen column to the top of the wall and was gone.

'Ten thousand devils!' roared Cellini. 'Take her! I want no woman such as that!'

I hurried past him and vaulted over the wall, blindly into the dark. I landed heavily on the grass and bumped against a body. Hannah was right there: she had been waiting for me. Before she could react I pinioned the hand that held the spit against the wall with my body. Her right arm, with its still-burning candle, was stretched out straight, beyond my reach. I had my own candle in my left hand, held at full length for safety, while my right clutched her shoulder. It was stalemate: neither could reach the candle of the other. I brought my face close to her ear.

'My dearest Mrs Hannah. Why do you not simply tell me the mistress's name?'

She looked back at me, defiant, breathing hard. 'Because I choose not to.'

'Then why did you not just say no? Instead, you go to all these lengths. You challenge me. You fight me. You trick me. Mrs Hannah, I think you are in trouble. The more you battle against me, the more you are ensnared. Very soon, you will be mine.'

'You are wrong!'

She tried to pull free. Her face was twisted round just in front of mine. I saw to my amazement that she was afraid. Something was driving her, pursuing her, goading her into her mad attacks and escapes. But in her deep soul she wanted to be free of it. And I was the man who would free her. I leant forward and pressed my lips against hers. She was surprised; her wide open eyes stared into mine. Then they slowly closed. Her breaths came quick. I felt her lips part, and moved my mouth closer over hers. But even as I did so, my hand stole further round her back, over her shoulder blades, down her arm, seeking for her elbow; next would be her wrist, which I would grip, and shake that candle from her grasp.

From far away over the city a bell rang out, one, two, three times. There was a pause, and it rang three times again, and then three times more. It was the Angelus: the end at last of the Carnival and the start of Lent. I let my pressure on her mouth ease, while my hand stretched out to reach those last few inches down her arm. I was almost there. Suddenly, with a jerk of her head she broke the kiss, and her hand with the candle swept round. With the butt-end of her candle she aimed a blow at mine that dashed it out of my hand and put it out, while her own flame carried on, up between our faces, until all I could see was fire. I heard the fizzle of her flame as it caught the thin hair on my cheek and went out, and I smelled the stink of burning flesh even before I felt the pain. I gasped and fell back against the wall with my hands to my face. The last chimes of the bell echoed round the ruins, and I heard Hannah run away, laughing.

PART 4

The Golconda Diamond: a Thorn in the Heart

Rome, 17 March 1527

My galley charged with forgetfulness
Through sharp seas in winter nights doth pass
'Tween rock and rock.

SIR THOMAS WYATT, SONNET V, AFTER PETRARCH

15

Light fell slantwise from the plain glass windows of the little church of Saint Thomas of Canterbury, sliding down over the terracotta tiles of the floor and gleaming off their pale gold decoration of angels holding scrolls. The choir of some two dozen boys and men, seated in two ranks just below the altar, began to sing.

'*Reminiscere miserationum tuarum, Domine ...*' Remember, Lord, thy mercies. May our enemies never master us. Save us from all our straits. Into the church advanced in procession the Master and Brethren of the Hospital of Saint Thomas, the hostel for English pilgrims in Rome that adjoined the church. This place formed a private domain for English visitors to the city of the popes, where they could meet and exchange news of home. The Master of the Hospital, an English priest named Paul Ballantyne, was dressed in the violet chasuble and stole proper for the season. It was the second Sunday in Lent; the Sunday that is known as *Reminiscere*. Remember.

It was impossible for me to forget. The pain was there to remind me, whenever I moved my face, despite the poultice of ambergris and lard applied by the apothecary from the Spicery in Trastevere, the best place in all Rome for medicines. I glanced up the aisle towards the stone altar that was spread with a white silk cloth. In the front rank of the congregation, in a box of their own, sat the Cages. Stephen was on the left, his broad back covered in a thick cape edged with fur. Next to him, with Susan and Grace on her other side, was Hannah. She wore a russet gown embroidered in gold, and covering her hair and her hood was a veil of pale yellow silk. I saw her dip her head devoutly as the priest went by. During the responses I strained to make out her voice among the others. She was lost to me, just as surely as the Golconda diamond I had lost in Venice, which had teased and shone for me just as Hannah did, for so very brief a time.

This was my third trip to the church since the night of the *moccoli*. My first had been the very next day, Ash Wednesday, when I had knelt to have my forehead marked with the holy ashes, emblem of repentance or regret. And, by God, how I did regret. I regretted I had not moved quicker, or kept my candle higher; then again, I regretted having tried to trick her while we kissed; I regretted not having thrown my candle in the grass and given her her victory for nothing, instead of fighting for it and losing. I regretted my anger and shame, that prevented my going up right now, past where their household sat, their chamberlain, the almoner and the gentlewomen, sweeping my bow to Mr Stephen in the old, familiar way, and slipping back into their family. But I could not bear the thought of the two girls' smiles, their gloating comments, their clucking over my burnt cheek; Hannah's effortless pride. That girl haunted me. My days were blank until the following Sunday, when I knew I could see her without being seen.

As the service came to an end I slipped out into the aisle so as to be among the first to leave. If it had not been for the Cages, I would have shunned the English church entirely. It carried with it too many reminders of home. Among the pilgrims in the congregation there were a good many merchants, ill at ease in a foreign city, many of them speaking scant Italian and all of them more at home on the

Thames. Their plain, solid faces seemed to say to me, 'You are one of us after all. You never belonged with those high Court gentry. See what a fool they have made of you. Come back to us. Thameswater is in your blood.' I took a last, thirsty look at the back of Hannah Cage's head, and stepped out of the church with both sadness and relief. Then I set off at a brisk pace across the little square of Saint Catherine of the Wheel, aiming to put Saint Thomas's behind me as swiftly as I could. A chill wind was blowing up from the Tiber and a few specks of rain fell. I would go back to my inn and eat a silent dinner of dry, salty Lenten stockfish, and then, perhaps, spend the afternoon walking about Rome in the rain.

'Richard! Richard Dansey?'

I kept on walking.

'Richard? By God, I know it is you.' The voice was English, and familiar. I turned round. Hurrying after me from the direction of the church was a young man of my own age, tall and long-legged, dressed in a rather shabby blue doublet. He had a cloak and sword, and a cap of blue velvet on his head, which sported a red ostrich feather, broken halfway along its length. I stared in astonishment as he came up to me, smiling.

'John!' I shouted. 'John Lazar!'

We embraced. It was three years since I had last seen him; almost six since our childhood band of three clasped hands in the street outside our house on Thames Street. John laughed and hugged me round the shoulder. 'Now that I have you I will not let you go. A bottle? For the sake of old times?'

Tired and sick at heart as I was, I managed a smile. 'A bottle would be perfect.'

'And is this your servant?' He peered at Martin, who walked along beside him, looking at his tatty clothes in suspicion. 'Do I not know you?'

'I remember you, sir, yes,' said Martin. 'A great raider of our warehouse, if I recall rightly.'

'Good man!' said John, and put his other arm through Martin's. It appeared that John had no servant of his own. Linked like this, we carried on down the Via Monserrato and out into the large square that lay before the palazzo of the Farnese. It warmed me to be in John's presence again. His confident step put fresh life into me.

'About this bottle,' John was saying. 'We have two choices. Either I shall pay, in which case we can afford about a thimbleful of sour beer, or else you pay, and we may fare rather better.'

I laughed. 'I will pay.' John and I had been equals and rivals all our lives. It flattered me to think that my fortunes had overtaken his. Also, God knew, I needed a confidant. I did not trust Cellini to hear of my sufferings, and Martin was no use. While he was dressing my wound that night of the *moccoli* he had said only, 'She is a bad woman, master. Perhaps now you'll leave her alone.' Since then he had kept a watchful eye on me. He knew, as well as I did, that to forget Hannah Cage was impossible.

'Where are you staying?' John enquired.

'At the Ship. In the Campo dei Fiori.'

John's cheerful face broke into a smile. 'Then we'll chart a course.'

It was a relief to be guided back to my own inn, and to let my old friend do the talking.

'But you must explain to me everything,' he said. 'You are here to trade? And what clothes! Look at the silver on those buttons! And what is that stitched along your collar? Not pearls? The firm of Dansey is doing well for itself. Where is Mr William?'

'Back in London, I hope. This venture is all my own.'

He opened his eyes in appreciation. 'No! In that case, two bottles!'

I let John step first into the warm dimness of the inn. The Ship was laid out a little like a nobleman's house, with vestibule, sala and private rooms. This sala was a far step from the grand room of the Cages, though. It was long and low, with massive oak beams painted with red and yellow flowers, and ranks of trestle tables. Like many of

216

the inns in this part of Rome, the Ship was owned by a wealthy courtesan who ran it as a sideline to her other business. We sat down together at one of the tables slightly apart from the other diners. Instead of my penitential stockfish I ordered us a carp, luxuriant in oil and honey and raisins, and a sweet Sicilian wine to go with it.

'To the old band,' said John, raising his cup.

'To the old band.'

'How did the verse go? "Sweet band of friends, farewell: together we set out; but far and various roads will bring us home."'

'Something of that kind.'

'Beautiful times. Do you remember the oath Thomas made us swear? To meet again, the three of us? Well, I have been off and away in Hungary, inspecting salt mines. And, by God, what a ruinous venture that was. We got out a whisker ahead of the Turks, pater and I, with the Janissaries and the Vayvod of Transylvania on our tails, and heads rolling like cabbages.' He reached for the bottle and poured himself another full cup.

I wondered whether John was telling the whole truth. I looked at the broken feather in his cap, the frayed, stained clothes. No, he had broken from his family, just as I was doing; though his break, I guessed, had been more abrupt and less carefully planned than my own. I smiled faintly, and looked down. He leant forward across the table.

'But surely you are not here to deal in jewels?'

I took a sip of the wine, and a mouthful of carp. 'Naturally.'

'On your own account? Are you thriving? But this is marvellous! Well? Do you have something? Let me see, let me see.'

He took the bottle and poured me more wine. I looked from side to side down the long room. A couple of tables away sat eight or nine rough-looking men. They had the air of soldiers, or the idle bravos that made up the retinues of noblemen, all full of swagger and sword-fights over nothing. I did not care for men such as that to know my business.

'After we have eaten,' I said quietly. 'I shall take you to a place where I can show you.'

John's pale blue eyes gleamed. 'Most interesting.' He lifted his cup again. 'To profit.'

We drank, and John snapped his fingers for the second bottle. It was late before we set off arm in arm back the way we had come, past the English church, heading for the Vicolo di Calabraga. Martin knocked at Cellini's door. After a time we heard the drawing back of locks, and Paulino came and opened it. Deeper in the workshop several candles burned. John followed me in, looking sharply round the shop. Cellini was sitting at his bench, holding in his hands the opal cross. He had been working on this for nearly two weeks. With my moody wanderings about Rome since the night of the *moccoli* I had scarcely paid any attention to how his work had been progressing.

I said, 'What's this, Benvenuto? Working on a Sunday?'

'This is not work,' he murmured, nudging one of the stones with a scalpel. 'It is pleasure. Pure, sinful pleasure. Look!'

He held up the cross. It was only a couple of inches long, but the stones blazed with such light and colours that they stopped me where I stood. The opals teased me, shimmering in ripples of ghostly green beneath their skins, the hues shifting as I came nearer, darting out like bold words from a girl, each one promising much, then instantly withdrawn. I saw that Cellini had placed one opal in the centre that was almost black, but which flashed with sulphur, carmine, and the pale green of burning oil; as if there were a fire in it deep inside. The stones were set perfectly: not too deep, the way many goldsmiths do, thereby hiding their glory; they were clasped just as high as was safe without the risk of losing them. It was a thing of utter and hopeless bewitchment.

John, standing at my elbow, let out a whistle. 'May I hold it?' He spoke in Italian, fluently and with a Tuscan accent like Cellini. With a twinge of unwillingness I handed it to him. '*Meraviglioso*,' murmured John. The syllables rolled beautifully from his tongue. He made me feel as if I were the one who was the outsider, me with my drawling Venetian speech, the word endings cut short as in French. Cellini too had detected the accent, and turned to him sharply.

'And what manner of a man are you?' he asked.

'Another Englishman,' said John, looking up with a smile, and setting the cross down on the bench. 'A simple wanderer on the roads of life.'

'That, I doubt,' said Cellini.

'A merchant, then,' said John, waving one hand, as if grasping in the air for answers. 'With packhorses loaded down with ambergris and ivory, and many a rich argosy on the seas.'

'I think you are a damned *fuoruscito*,' said Cellini. 'An exile from Florence, an enemy of the Medici. One of those who would like to see the Pope's family kicked out. Lovers of liberty, as you call yourselves.' Cellini scowled. 'Malcontents. Rebels. I know the look of you, Englishman or not. You have fugitive written on your face, your clothes, the way you look round as if you don't know who might be coming at you. You'd like to see all the princes and bishops in the world laid low, and no grandeur or marks of rank left anywhere. That's the sort of man you are, isn't it?'

'Exile,' repeated John pensively. 'Fugitive. Rebel. I have been called all those names before.' He picked the cross up again, gazed at it, tossed it from one hand to the other and set it back down again. No, it's true about being a merchant. I did have some goods. I had been dealing in this and that; but circumstances constrained me to leave most of my stock behind in Florence and run away south. No, my friend, I'm a great lover of grandeur and rank. I only wish I had a little more of them myself.'

John smiled roguishly. He had always had charm, even as a daring, pale-haired boy of twelve, caught in the act of some petty theft or trespass, wide-eyed, talking his way clear of trouble. With the years his manners had gained in ease and poise. Cellini suddenly laughed. Well, let it be as you say. Paulino, if you please! Wine.'

We sat down together round the bench. John pointed at the opal cross. 'This is for no common customer. I am guessing at the King?'

I said, 'Perhaps.'

'Well, it is a fine beginning. It will start you on your way, when you get it home to London. Of course, if you had more …'

'But I do.'

'No!'

His incredulity flattered me. I turned to Cellini.

'Benvenuto, be so good as to show him the Ship.'

Cellini hesitated, then crossed to the chest and unlocked it with the steel key he wore on a light chain round his neck. He lifted out the finished brooch with both hands, carried it over and laid it down on his bench. There it lay, a living picture in gold, with its enamels, its gold-green chrysoprase, its four diamonds, its nine clouded sapphires. For some minutes we all gazed on it, saying nothing.

'The ship of state,' murmured John, 'the kingdom in miniature? No, I do not think so. There is more passion in it than that. This is a ship blown by sighs, watered by tears, guided by a girl's eyes. It is a lover, I think. A fine gift for one's mistress, perhaps? And they do say the King is in love.'

I put a hand quickly on his arm. 'John,' I said, speaking in English, 'if you know who the King's new mistress is, you must tell me. I am begging you.'

John spread his hands. 'My friend, if I knew I would tell you. But I have been gone from England myself this year or more.'

It needled me, his confidence that, if he were back home, he would know. But after all, I knew very little now about my old friend. His connections might very well exceed what you would expect from his appearance. I looked once more at his clothes, the threads hanging loose from the edge of his cloak, the well-worn boots.

'I know,' he said, switching back into Italian. 'I have seen troubled times. But so have you, from the look of things.' He gestured at the half-healed burn on my cheek. Cellini snorted.

'Ask him how he got it.'

'No, no.' I tried to push him away, but John peered more closely at my face.

'Merciful Jesus,' he murmured. 'It looks like you have had a fight with the Devil.'

'Near enough,' said Cellini, drinking. 'It was a woman.'

I pulled away and put my hand up to cover the wound. 'She is such a woman as neither of you two will ever touch.'

Cellini laughed. 'Listen to him! After all that has happened, he is more in love than ever. Well, this is no time for your love yarns.' He picked up the opal cross and the ship and placed them safe in one of the compartments of his chest, which he then closed and locked. 'It is high time we settled our next move.'

John gave me a look of polite puzzlement. I smiled, delighted to be able to surprise him yet again. I pulled out the casket from under my shirt, and laid it open on the bench. He leant closer to look.

'By Saint Anthony's pigs, you do have more.'

I lifted my treasures out one by one and set them on the cloth. The sight of them both thrilled and lifted me. We sat and gazed, and moved the gems into this pattern and that across the cloth, and drank the rich Tuscan wine. The daylight was poor by now; but you can learn something of a fine stone even when it is in repose.

John picked up the pure, pale Scythian emerald. 'That really is rather fine,' he said. 'The last time I saw that casket of yours it had nothing in it but a few rock crystals. You will be back home when? Before the summer?'

I frowned, tugged my lip and gazed into the stone. The emerald's cool depths were a tonic to me. I wished I could forget everything else: the need for haste, the chance that I might delay too long and miss my moment. I had hoped to be back in England long since, certainly well before the summer. Today was the seventeenth of March. I ought to be setting out, but I could not leave with Cellini not at work and half my stones still unset. And I loathed the thought of ever leaving at all. What? Sail away from Hannah, without a word? No, I was bound here, even if all I ever saw of her were those weekly glimpses in church. And so I avoided John's eye, my glance fixed on the emerald, and said, 'Maybe.'

'Summer,' said John, turning the stone in his fingers. 'The King's lady will be taking her pleasure in her gardens. I see bowers, roses, green arbours, mayblossom, fresh young shoots. All done in gold and sapphires and pearls. Yes?'

'By God,' said Cellini, and snatched the stone from him. He held it up to the light. 'And the emerald is a distant meadow. We shall have reapers round it, shepherds, fauns. In the foreground?' He lifted up the pale, milk-coloured sapphire. 'A pool. Naked nymphs, bathing, lifting their feet over the brink. I see a pendant. I hope to God this lady has small breasts.' He put the emerald back on the bench with the sapphire beside it, drew out a sheet of paper and a charcoal pencil, and began to sketch in rapid, furious lines, frowning at the stones as he worked. 'Your friend,' he murmured to me, 'is rather useful.' I turned from him, content to leave him to his work. My mind was ill at ease.

'Drink, my friend,' said John, raising his glass to mine. 'And laugh at misfortune. That is what I do. Now, supposing you tell me that love story.'

I managed to laugh. 'It has a poor ending.'

He waved a hand. 'Who said it has ended?'

And so I unfolded the story to him, starting with the first mocking glint of Hannah's eye at that dinner when I laid out my stones and she refused the gift of my diamond, passing through her challenge our fights, our kiss amidst the violence of the *moccoli*, and my conviction that, despite everything, she needed me, and a sad loneliness sat in this wild girl's heart. I finished with my last, mournful visit to the church of Saint Thomas of Canterbury earlier that day. Just one thing I omitted: her name. John gazed at me with his pale eyes. The only sound was the scratching of Benvenuto's charcoal pencil.

'My dear, dear Richard,' he said at last. 'I pity you, I do. You really have encountered a siren. Beware woman, Richard.'

I stood up in impatience. 'And so that is it? Your advice is the same as Benvenuto's and the rest? Give up on her?'

John sprang to his feet and took my arm. 'By no means! Is that what your friends have been telling you? By God, Richard, go back to her. Fight for her and win her. What else?'

'Beware woman, you said.'

'It is just a little too late for that,' John said with a laugh, leading me back to the workbench and pouring us more wine. 'By God, this Tuscan is good. No, Richard. The way with women is steer clear, or else conquer.'

I drank. I could feel the wine throbbing in my temples. 'But will she have me?'

John laughed and waved a hand in dismissal. 'Oh, she will huff, and put her nose in the air, and I dare say she will laugh at you at first, and ask which is slower to heal, your burnt cheek or your sulks at losing the game. But if you are a true lover, you must bear it.'

'And you really think I will win her?' I was beginning to feel my hopes and my courage returning.

'With me to help you?' John said. 'Not a doubt of it.' He smiled, the warm old smile that had just a hint of challenge in it, and held out his hand. 'What do you say? Do you dare it?'

I hesitated. Just how much had passed between John and Hannah during those months when I was off in Lisbon, and he and Thomas had stood and looked up at her window? It flashed into my mind how we had fought over her as boys, and John had promised to win her. But I did not think I could go back and brave Hannah's scorn without him at my side.

I grasped his hand. 'I dare it. By God, I do.'

John laughed, embraced me, and then stood back, his hand still clutching mine.

'The old band is back together,' he said, 'or the heart and bowels of it, at any rate. Trust me: I know these girls. Now, take me to this palazzo.'

I caught for a moment Benvenuto's eye as he looked up from his drawing. He could not have followed our talk, since we spoke in English. But his look seemed to say he had caught the sense of what we had been saying, and saw no good in it. I turned away from him in irritation. To John I said, 'Come with me, then. Now, at once.'

I wanted to make my assault on the palazzo while the wine and John's words still gave me courage. Because in truth I was full of foreboding. As I climbed those marble stairs up from the vestibule of the Palazzo del Bene, with my friend at my side, I could not remotely predict the reception waiting for me. One moment I came out in a cold sweat of anger and indignation at how she had treated me, the next I prayed only that she would show a little mercy with her taunts, the next I burned with shame at the humiliation of my return. It was only John, outdaring me with his easy gait, who made me reach the top of those stairs and stand waiting before the carved pilasters while the Cages' chamberlain, Fenton, knocked on the door to the sala and held it open.

Inside, the room presented an appearance of dusky calm. The shadows were growing deeper, but the servants had not yet lit the candles. A fire was burning despite the gradually warming season, and its light glinted across the marble paving and the blue-and-crimson Turkey carpets. The tapestries with their gods and goddesses hung dark and sombre, the gold thread sparking fitfully like the eyes of half-sleeping beasts. In one corner a hawk shifted on its perch with a faint ringing of bells. John cast his eyes round the room in surprise and drew in his breath. I had forgotten the splendour of the place. But that meant nothing to me. Just beyond the fireplace Hannah was sitting with her sister and a couple of the gentlewomen Susan was bending over a lute, and as we walked forward she struck a chord of surprising beauty. I saw that she knew a lot more of music than she pretended. Hannah, her feet tucked up beneath her like a coiled snake, kept her place with her finger in a small book, while her head rested listlessly on her other hand. A strand of hair wandered down from among the pearls on her head and across her cheek. At our approach she slowly turned her head, and when she saw me her face broke instantly into a smile. It was so warm, so natural, so open that I almost choked with love for her. I crossed quickly the remaining expanse of marble floor and carpet, and went down on my knee beside her chair.

'My dearest Mrs Hannah!'

She touched my cheek with her hand, tenderly. There was not a hint of triumph.

'Your poor, poor face. Will your beard grow again?'

I took her hand in mine and kissed it.

'It is growing already.'

We were lovers at last; just as if our last moment together had been that kiss among the ruins, and not the violence that followed it. I simply gazed at her, and smiled. I had not a single notion what to say. John's voice came from behind me.

'Mrs Hannah. I might have guessed Richard would not forget you.'

Hannah's eyes opened wider and she looked between us, recognising us again as a pair. Her mouth began to curl in amusement. She must be picturing us as we were, fourteen-year-old urchins capering in the street. John, though, was a master of tact. He turned to Mrs Susan and threw himself down beside her in a kneeling posture mimicking my own.

'And who is this delightful being?'

Hannah's face puckered into laughter, joined by the rest of us. Susan glared at John and swung her lute round so that its pegs nearly caught him on the nose. John sprang back on his heels like an acrobat and jumped to his feet. At that moment the door through to the saletta was opened, and in came Stephen and Grace Cage. I stood up swiftly and bowed, deeply and with all the grace I knew.

'Dear Mr Richard!' Grace bubbled as she took my hand and kissed me on the cheek. 'Why have you been so long away from us? We were all so very concerned.'

'We had begun to fear some calamity,' added Mr Stephen, returning my bow with a true Court curtsey, left leg and left hand back, right hand across the waist as the head dips. To have a man of the rank of Stephen Cage drop a bow such as that to me meant a very great deal.

'A small indisposition,' I said, with a glance down at Hannah, whose face smiled with warm mystery back up at mine. 'No more.'

'But you are back with us now,' oozed Grace. 'And your friend?'

Before I could present him, John stepped forward with a small ducking bow like an actor's, and swept off his broken-feathered hat.

'John Lazar. Merchant. Of London.'

It was an introduction so close to my own first appearance at the Cages' that I felt a prickle of displeasure. I did not like my hosts to be reminded of that moment. Only now did I see how unfitting my old friend's raggedness was to our surroundings. But I need not have worried. I, at least, was firmly back in my old place in the family.

Grace's lips narrowed, and Stephen gave John a piercing stare. His eyes registered surprise, and for a moment I would have sworn that Stephen Cage knew John from somewhere before. Then he tilted his head at John with a grunt. 'You are welcome,' he said. 'For Mr Richard's sake.'

John smiled amiably and bowed once more, as his quick eyes darted over the carved and inlaid credenza, the niche with its gold-tasselled seat, the brilliant Turkey rugs draped over the trestle dining tables stacked neatly away against the far wall.

That evening we sat together: myself, Hannah, John and the elder Cages, while Susan and her music tutor performed airs on their lutes. We played a silent game of glances, Hannah and I. I looked up at her, caught her looking at me, then glanced down. I looked again; she turned away, smiling, knowing I was watching, then turned on me, and both of us gazed for a few moments, teasing one another, then broke away.

At last Susan put down her lute. The minstrels came in and began to play on two recorders and a shawm, accompanied by the swift beating of a drum. Mrs Grace held out her hand to me, and we all of us danced. The air was a *saltarella*, with a step, a hop, and two steps, all joining together in the round, then breaking into couples to recombine in different ways. The dance went faster and faster. Mr Stephen showed a surprising talent at the quick steps, throwing out his arms in wild gestures, his face comically composed. John managed the steps with ease, taking the arm now of Hannah, now of Susan, now of Grace. I had danced scarcely at all since that night at Eltham Palace when I swept along with Hannah under the tinsel trees and paper bowers. In Venice Ippolita and the rest had laughed at my efforts, and I had given it up. But I threw myself into it now with gusto. It was really not so very different from fencing, with its quick springs and feints, then closing suddenly with your adversary.

As I linked arms briefly with Hannah she whispered, 'Do you love me madly?'

'Yes,' I whispered back, and swung into the arms of Mrs Grace.

'Dear Mr Richard. Now that we have you back with us, we will not easily let you go. You will come to us again tomorrow?'

The music throbbed and blared, faster, faster. The tune was of the kind called a *piva*, a peasant dance usually played on the bagpipes. It was a music of savage joy, employing strange tonalities unknown to the more refined musics.

'You are a fool,' murmured Susan, taking my arm in turn. 'Don't you see how dangerous we are? Isn't one wound enough?'

I whirled her round by her arm and spun her away from me, then twisted backwards in time to the baying of the shawm and the beating of the drum, back into the arms of Mrs Hannah, who smiled, and gripped my arm with a gentle pressure.

When John and I finally left that night we went reeling through the streets, drunk on music and wine, singing and dancing a *saltarella*. In the Campo dei Fiori we found half a melon left from the day's market and kicked it across the paving stones until it shattered in the gutter. We fell at last into each other's arms, laughing.

'Where are you staying?' I asked John at last.

John shrugged, with his easy smile. 'Wherever you recommend.'

'Then you are lodging with me. Come!'

16

There was dinner, most days, in the Palazzo del Bene. We ate well, in spite of Lent. The Cages' chamberlain usually succeeded in finding us either a dozen lobsters, or a fat sturgeon with its little black eggs, or oysters, or crayfish, or turbot in honey and dates. Some days Mr Stephen procured a dispensation to eat *lacticinia*, the fruits of flesh, and then we had our seafood in cream and eggs. At other times the Cages took me with them to their grand connections in Rome, to Cardinal Campeggio's four-square palazzo over the river near Saint Peter's, or to Gregorio Casale, the resident English ambassador. Sometimes there was news of the war. Sir John Russell had broken his leg in a fall from his horse; the English peace embassy had faltered, and one man alone was left to mediate between His Holiness and the army of the Emperor, which was marching rapidly on Florence. That man was Cesare Ferramosca: clever, secretive and loyal only to the Emperor. Stephen and the rest frowned and shook their heads. But what did peace or war mean to me, as I drank a private health to Hannah, which she returned, and which no one else could see?

On other days we walked in the Pope's gardens, or else the Cages set up their crimson silk pavilion out among the ruins and we feasted off their exquisite rustic maiolica, decorated with nymphs, pomegranates and cupids. Once we ventured into the grottoes, ancient banqueting rooms buried underground. We darted down those echoing caverns, holding our lanterns up to walls painted with coiling sea serpents, tritons, fishes, birds, scorpions, trick vistas of balconies and fountains, and golden statues looking down from arbours. Beneath their dead eyes Hannah and I stood and kissed.

On these expeditions John always accompanied me. It gave me an extra flush of pride to have a retinue of my own beyond just a single servant; a kind of gentleman-in-waiting, who bowed and eyed the company with a smile, and said nothing. There was a satisfaction, too, in being the leader and seeing my old friend in the position of loyal follower-on. Only his clothes were a problem. After several days I told him he must allow me to buy him a suit of clothes.

John smiled sheepishly. 'When my goods come in from Florence I'll pay you back. Just wait.'

I waved my hand. Money was nothing. I was drunk with the success that would fall into my lap just as soon as I returned home to England. I had the connections, I had the cross, and the ship, and the swiftly growing garden that Cellini was fashioning out of gold, to house both the emerald and the white sapphire. All the same, I made sure John's clothes were not quite so glorious as my own. I let him choose a black doublet with a slender silver trim, a velvet hat with a curling white ostrich feather but no jewels. I took the opportunity to fit Martin out with some more suitable attire. Heads turned when the three of us walked down the Via Monserrato heading for the Palazzo del Bene. Always at my journey's end there were Hannah's smiles, and, when I was lucky, a kiss.

It was Laetare Sunday, the thirty-first of March, the midpoint of Lent when there are flowers on the altars of every church and the priests wear rose-coloured vestments instead of violet. There was a relaxing of the fast, too. We were invited to dine with the Portuguese ambassador, and he promised us something to remember. Don Martin of Portugal, a nephew of Spicer King John himself, dwelt in a castellated mansion near the Corso. His house had a stone tower and a pair of cannon on its roof, and it was said to be the strongest place in Rome after the Castle of Sant' Angelo. We dined that day on capons, sugared and fried, pheasants roasted in the juice of oranges, and a baked young kid in cinnamon, wrapped in the thinnest pastry. Even Mr Stephen responded with a satisfied 'Ah!' as the dishes were carried in. Don Martin, a sparely built man in his thirties, ate little himself, and watched his guests with a slight smile. As the meal ended, he turned to Stephen and said, 'I have heard a disturbing report from England. I hope you will reassure me that it is untrue.'

Stephen glanced up sharply.

'I have heard,' went on Don Martin, 'that your King is seeking a separation from his wife. A wicked slander against a most pious and upright monarch.'

Stephen wiped his mouth on his napkin and put it back on his shoulder. 'It is true.'

I was staring at them, listening intently. Here it was at last: the first admission from Stephen that the divorce was more than a mere rumour, more than a secret scheme of Wolsey's among a dozen others that might be disavowed at any time.

'What?' said Don Martin. 'After being virtuously married for close to twenty years!'

'There were doubts all along as to the legality of our King's marrying his brother's widow. Remember Leviticus, Don Martin. Our King has grave scruples of conscience, which he can no longer in honesty ignore.'

Don Martin gave an exasperated laugh. 'But Pope Julius II granted a dispensation allowing it!'

Stephen leant forward. His pale eyes had taken on a look of deep and incalculable menace.

'There are questions here which your lordship overlooks. Whether the Pope has the power to dispense at all. Or whether, on the contrary, the prohibition against marrying within the degrees of consanguinity is a part of the law of God that not even a Pope can sweep aside.'

I glanced at Hannah. She too was listening hard, her eyes fixed on her father. It appeared that this talk interested her deeply. Don Martin rapped the table in irritation.

'But, Christ Jesu! My own master, King John, is married under just such a dispensation! And last year the Emperor Charles married his sister-in-law, who is also his first cousin! Are their offspring to be bastards? You will destroy all the royal bloodlines of Europe!'

'God's judgement against this marriage is plain,' responded Mr Stephen. 'Our King's childlessness is proof of that.'

'Childless?' Don Martin spluttered with amazement. 'He has a daughter.'

Stephen waved his hand. 'A daughter will not save England from civil war when King Henry dies. There must be a son.'

Don Martin suddenly smiled and leant back in his chair. 'Ah! And so the point is not divorce, merely, but remarriage. And I hear your King's eye might light on … a French princess? King Francis's sister, the Duchesse d'Alençon, perhaps?'

'You have heard more than I,' replied Stephen stonily.

I looked at Stephen in surprise. He had admitted readily enough King Henry's plans for divorce. So why this sudden reserve over his remarriage to the princess? Don Martin responded with a knowing smile, and the rest of the meal passed with that perfect politeness which courtiers know so well how to command. But I could see that Mr Stephen went away displeased. And myself? I did not like this talk of the King's new marriage. I saw all my plans for rising to wealth and rank wavering like smoke. I needed to finish the jewels, and get home fast.

* * *

I spent more time than ever with Cellini, urging him on to greater speed. It was the beginning of April. I resented the passage of time; but my casket held a good many gems still unset. Nearly a week after Laetare Sunday I was watching Cellini smoothing the gold for the emerald garden into its bronze mould when we heard the insistent beating of a drum. He laid down his scalpel and we went to the door. The sound grew louder. We ran to the end of the street. Down on the Via Giulia a column of men was advancing. At their head waved a banner, scarlet circles against gold: the Medici colours. Behind came four men with large drums strapped round their necks. After them came the soldiers. They were dressed in black: black puffed doublets and cloaks, and hats with red and yellow feathers in them. Over their shoulders they carried halberds or harquebuses. They came forward in a disorderly swagger, swords swinging, with a terrible, careless menace.

Cellini nodded grimly. 'The Black Bands.' I had heard of these Florentine troops. They had fought against the Emperor last summer at Milan, where their captain, Giovanino de' Medici, had been killed. They were masterless now, and it had been rumoured for some while that if the danger grew great enough, Pope Clement would bring them south and pay them to guard his city. After them came a second column in blue-and-yellow cockades, marching rigidly in step: Swiss mercenaries, the elite of all soldiers. We watched both columns wind northwards out of sight. Cellini shook his head, and went sombrely back to work.

That night as I lay in bed I heard men shouting and singing, the crash of splintering wood, and the occasional clash of swords. Once there was a hammering at the door of an inn opposite ours, and from the window I saw three of the black-clad soldiers beating on the wood with their sword hilts. When it gave way they plunged in, cursing and wielding their swords. Next morning I hurried off along the Via Monserrato with John and Martin. Wreckage littered the streets, smashed furniture, pottery, broken window glass. But,

God be thanked, the Cages' mansion was intact, its door solid, its lower windows barred. Anxious for my jewels, I hurried on to find Cellini.

In the Vicolo di Calabraga debris was scattered thick over the stones. Outside the workshop a cart stood, with several men standing round it with drawn swords. I saw Paulino come out carrying a roll of papers, which he stowed inside the cart next to cauldrons and crucibles, bundles of tools and the great iron-bound chest where Benvenuto kept his gold and his jewels. As I ran up the men moved to block me.

'Let him past! He's a friend.' Cellini appeared, carrying in his arms the Perseus statue, wrapped in cloth.

'What in the devil's name are you doing?'

'Doing? I am packing up, bag and baggage, that is what I am doing.'

'But what about our work?'

'It can continue in a few days when I have set up my new shop. Safe out of the goldsmiths' quarter, down by the river. By God, I'll not risk staying here, with the Black Bands out.'

I raged against the delay; but he was right. Those fiends of robbers loose among my treasures: it was not to be thought of. Somehow I must stomach this loss of precious time. I turned from him and strode quickly back through the streets to the Palazzo del Bene. Hannah must be my consolation. Inside the sala I was met by Mrs Grace.

'So very frightful. And these are the very men who are meant to protect us! What would it be to meet the enemy?'

Around us the Cages' servants were passing to and fro, one carrying a candlestick, another some package, while Fenton, the chamberlain, barked instructions. A terrible foreboding struck me.

'Surely, my dear Mrs Grace, you are not thinking of leaving?'

Grace gave a dainty sigh. 'They say the war will not come nearer than Florence. But for my part, I wish we were at sea, or better yet already in France. Stephen is in agreement. We stay only as long as it takes to conclude his business. But when that might be, the way His Holiness wavers, today one way, next day the other ...'

I saw there was no longer any pretence at being pilgrims. The door to the loggia opened and Susan came in, followed by a servant carrying her lute wrapped in cloth.

'With care, I said!' She looked up, saw me, and gave a quick nod back the way she had come. I bowed to Mrs Grace and passed through. Out on the loggia, leaning on the balustrade and wearing the crimson dress she had had on when we first met in Rome, was Hannah. I went up to her side. Behind us servants came and went.

I said, 'And so time, after all, is against us.'

She turned to me with her mocking smile. 'There is always time, if you grasp it with boldness.'

I darted at her meaning. 'Then I shall come to you.'

'Oh?' She smiled. 'How?'

I nodded down at the garden.

'You will climb the wall? Very gallant. Where?'

She was challenging me again. I scanned the garden wall. It was some fifteen feet high, built of crumbling brick. One-storeyed shops and sheds backed up against it.

'There. Where that roof hangs out, and the vine reaches up on this side.'

'And when will you perform this daring act?'

'Midnight. Will you be waiting?'

Her eyes were alight. 'You will have to try me and see.'

All the rest of the day I stewed with expectation. I saw moonlit arbours, embraces, kisses and more, much more. To keep busy, and to advance my jewels as speedily as possible, I went back and helped Benvenuto move his goods. Martin laboured alongside me, but of

John there was no sign. Cellini's new shop was on the very brink of the river, on the bend looking out towards the Borgo and Saint Peter's. The place had once been a blacksmith's, and so there was a useable forge. It was a quiet spot; there was no sign here of the soldiers.

'Tomorrow we finish,' said Benvenuto. 'Then we resume the work.'

Dusk was falling when Martin and I walked back to the inn. Already the Black Bands were out, swaggering through the streets in search of trouble. As we climbed the stairs to our chamber, a thin figure closely wrapped in a cape came out of our chamber and hurried down the stairs. My hand jumped to my sword and I half made to chase after him, but John called out to me from inside the chamber.

'Richard! Leave him, leave him. Come in: I have good news.'

I found John sitting at his ease at the table. 'My goods have come in at last from Florence.'

I looked at him in surprise. 'And where are they?'

John tossed a leather purse across the table towards me. I picked it up: it was full of gold. 'Already sold.'

I sat down. My suspicions were on the boil. These were dark sorts of goods that could change hands so quickly, and for so much gold. And I agreed with Benvenuto: John did not bear the marks of a man engaged in trade. I said, 'That man on the stairs?'

John smiled his easy smile. 'Cesare Ferramosca.'

'Ferramosca!' Most trusted of all the emissaries of the Emperor: the man all Rome was relying on to negotiate the peace treaty with the Duke of Bourbon. I said, 'And so these are the goods you have been trafficking in.'

'Of course. I did not really lie when I told you I was a merchant. But in these times secrets are a far more profitable commodity than any other.'

'And will there be peace?'

John shrugged. 'No one trusts anyone. One ambassador slanders another. One thing is sure. Whether we have peace or war, it will not be settled by the men you can see. The invisible is what counts.'

'Men like you?'

John smiled, full of impudence. It was an old familiar smile that soothed away my fears. I said, 'Well, that gold is real enough, at any rate. We must celebrate. Martin?'

'Yes, master, a bottle.'

Martin padded away, taking one of the two candles with him. In the near darkness John smiled again.

'You never believed me, did you? Ah, Florence, city of delights. But the news from there is not good. If the Imperial army comes any nearer, the people will rise up against the Medici. Freedom, that's what they see in the Empire. The Pope and the Medici mean only tyranny and serfdom. Yes, I think Alessandro de' Medici and his cronies, the Cardinals Cibo and Passerini, are shaking in their beds tonight.'

I did not like to hear this talk. Like all Romans, I had come to think of Florence as our bulwark against Bourbon's army. It might take months or years, people said, for the Imperials to conquer Florence. In that way, Bourbon's strength would exhaust itself before ever drawing close to Rome.

'But not all Florentines are for the Empire?' I pressed, as Martin brought the wine.

'All? No. But a few bold men, hot for revolution, will be enough. Men like Salviata and Corsini, and de' Bardi.'

The name made me sit up with a start. In my mind I saw once again the diamond I had held for so short a time in Venice, but which I had seen over and over again since then in my dreams. I saw its cool blue gleam and its sudden fire, and that milky veil suddenly drawn across its charms.

'Not Lorenzo de' Bardi?'

John lifted his cup and laughed. 'No! Not the old man. I mean his son. Alonso. There is not much love between the two of them: the father staunch for the Medici, the son as hot against them. They say old Lorenzo has cut him off. Won't see or speak to him. He means to die alone, with what little wealth is left to him. And that won't be long now. Days, most likely. What's the matter?'

I was staring at him. My face must have been like a ghost's. The ideas were chasing one another round in my head. Lorenzo de' Bardi. Dying alone. No heir. The old man and the diamond. Dying. Alone. I felt it was within my grasp: and I knew at the same moment that I could never be content with my other stones. I stood up.

'John, how many days' ride is it to Florence?'

'Three or four, if you ride like thunder. And if the rains have not closed the passes.'

'And how far do you think Bourbon's army is from the city?'

'By my information, about forty miles. Why?'

'Martin, fetch us horses. We are going.'

'By God's precious blood, master, I beg you, no. Not the diamond?'

'The diamond.'

'But Mrs Hannah? And Benvenuto?'

Hannah: yes. There had been promise in her eyes, no question. I almost wept to think of what I might be missing when midnight came tonight. But would she really be there? Or was I just sticking my foot into another snare, with more mockery, more teasing? If I could only get that diamond, I thought, the Diamond of the Old Rock of Golconda. That would be the conquering of her.

'You will take her a message,' I told Martin, 'and Benvenuto can work very well without us.' I turned to John. 'Will you come?'

John leant back and stretched. 'My dear Richard, you are my very dear friend, but I will not stick my hand into that hornets' nest again.'

'Very well, then.' Martin still stood staring. I clapped my hands at him. 'Be quick! We have a long road to travel. We will be back in a week, I promise. And that stone will make us rich.'

17

For two days we wound up the valley of the Tiber to Orvieto. Then came barren wastes where the road climbed to a rocky, treeless pass and the wind blew tatters of cloud across our way. Ahead we saw the stone fortress of Radicofani, outpost of the Republic of Siena. This we skirted. Siena was no friend of the Pope, or of Florence. At an inn high in the mountains I counted my remaining bills and reckoned up what I could afford while still leaving enough to pay Benvenuto and get home. I decided I would run up to sixteen hundred ducats, four hundred more than I had offered in Venice. It was an even chance, I thought. Last time I had failed. Everything hinged on the old man's frame of mind. I folded the bills away and spent a cold, anxious night, trying to sleep. Next day came the descent to Cortona in the territory of Florence, and after that the last fifty miles down out of the hills.

We came at last, Martin and I, to the hill overlooking Florence, and a fair sight it was, well walled, with the dome of the cathedral rising at its heart. It was late afternoon on the eleventh of April: ten days before Easter. John's three or four days had taken us five. We rode quickly down and into the city. The place had an air of calm affluence. Carts made their way home from the markets, gentlemen walked the streets. It did not resemble John's vision of a city divided against itself, or in fear of war. I went at once in search of that diamond.

The Palazzo de' Bardi was situated on a street leading off the Piazza della Signoria, the long square that is the city's heart. The quarter of the bankers and goldsmiths was close by, and the streets were thick with grand palazzi, with the tower of the Palazzo della Signoria rising above them all. At the de' Bardis' door I presented myself as an Englishman who was acquainted with the master of the house in Venice, and begged an interview, however brief. I paced the entrance hall, impatient, while my message was taken up. I noted the walls bare of tapestries, the plinths where statues must once have stood. Plainly the old nobleman was still short of ducats. The gaunt old chamberlain returned.

'Signor de' Bardi will see you.'

He led me up a bleak, echoing staircase and into a small saletta. I stopped, taken aback. Seated at a plain walnut writing table was a young man, elegantly dressed in black satin. He stood up, and I bowed.

'And so you are a friend of my father's?'

'I had the honour to meet him some months ago, in Venice. Is he …?'

'Still living. But in no condition to receive guests. Perhaps you will accept my hospitality in his place.'

The young man was urbane and courtly. He smiled, rang a small bell and whispered to the chamberlain when he returned. There was nothing I could do but bow and murmur thanks. But inwardly I was raging. Where was the bitter feud between father and son that should have given me my chance?

Alonso de' Bardi led me through to a smaller room, painted with trompe-l'oeil scenery. He smiled again and beckoned me to sit. The same old chamberlain brought us wine and then two or three dishes of chicken, mutton and beef, plain but excellently well dressed. Alonso drank freely, laughed, complimented me on my Italian, and questioned me closely about my business in Venice and Rome. I gave away that I was a merchant in gems, and shared an interest in them with the young man's father; but I said nothing of the diamond.

'And what a fortunate moment you choose to come to Florence. I dare say you have heard nothing of the Armistice? Peace signed and declared between His Holiness and the Duke of Bourbon.' He took another long drink of wine, emptying his cup. 'That will please a great many people.'

I sat, calculating and distrustful. There had been rumours of peace so many times before. 'But not you?'

Suddenly he slammed his cup down on the table. 'By God, not me. You know nothing of Florence, I see. What are we? Neither a true republic nor yet a dukedom, but a wretched vassal of the Holy See. The city is in the pocket of a couple of Pope Clement's father-less, base-begotten relatives.' I noticed he was swaying and slurring his words. He counted on his fingers. 'There's black Alessandro de' Medici: that's bastard number one. Son of a slave: they call him the Moor. Then there's Ippolito de' Medici, an idle young whoremaster. Bastard number two. To prop them up there's a couple of damned eunuch cardinals, that vulture Passerini, Bishop of Cortona, and stinking Innocenzo Cibo, the Pope's cousin. Did I say eunuch? I'm sorry. I forgot that Cibo is fond of futtering his brother's wife.'

I ventured, 'And so your lordship would not be sorry to see the Imperial army advance a little nearer to Florence?'

De' Bardi glared at me, suddenly suspicious. 'What is your real business here?'

I nodded back in the direction of the goldsmiths' quarter. 'Trade.'

'And does "trade" give you a reason to see my father? I am curious about you, Englishman. Well, you shall see him. Marcello! Old whoreson, lights!'

Dusk had been gathering while we ate. The chamberlain returned, and with trembling hands lit all the candles on a five-branched candelabrum. 'Forgive my poor Marcello. He is slow, old, and timid. A true Florentine.' He gave the servant a light kick on the rear. Marcello stumbled. The three of us set off through another doorway, and up a winding stair. Martin, who had watched the meal from the shadows, followed.

We passed along dim halls and came at last to carved double doors. Alonso threw them open with a bang and then strode ahead into the darkness. 'Do not trouble over Father. Night is his most wakeful time.'

As I entered the room with the candles following, I saw a large, canopied bed, still with its hangings of rich blue silk. Propped on bolsters was a small and shrunken old man, who looked back at me with the same mild eyes I remembered from Venice. His face was more yellowed and lined, and a smell of rottenness breathed from his body as I came near. Alonso hung back, leaning against the wall with a smile.

Old Lorenzo lifted a bony hand in greeting. 'And so it is the Englishman, who so nearly bought my diamond.'

I heard a snort from behind me. Alonso saw through me. And my business with the old man would have to be done in the son's presence. I said, 'It grieves me to see your lordship in such poor health. I was still further grieved when I heard your lordship had quarrelled with his son. I am glad to know that such rumours are false.'

The old man glanced quickly in the direction of his son. 'We are once more in accord. Well? You have not just come to see me. Will you have a sight of the diamond?'

He motioned to Marcello, who put down the candelabrum and unlocked a chest beside the bed. He took from it the inlaid jewel box, and from that the red velvet pouch, which he handed to his master. Lorenzo de' Bardi's long, shaking fingers drew out from the pouch the diamond. I caught my breath. I had seen it before in daylight. By candlelight its seduction was multiplied. The subtle gleam ran over its surface, half-opaque, with only a glint of sea-blue and carmine as the old man turned it in his hands. His face was alight. My fingers itched to hold it. At last Lorenzo held it out to me. I lifted it between thumb and forefinger. It was cool and smooth; as I turned it the candlelight penetrated, and I experienced once again that sudden plunge into its depths, that brilliant cascade of colours, blood-red, indigo, sea-green. It exceeded even my memories of it. There were three separate places, I saw, at which the misty veil could be made to part, and at each one the dance of light was different. I would have done anything to have it.

The old man smiled in triumph. 'What will you give me for it now?'

I darted him a look of quick expectation. 'Sixteen hundred.'

He shook his head. 'It is not for sale. Buy it from Alonso when it is his. Perhaps next week. Perhaps sooner.'

But a glance at the younger de' Bardi convinced me I would have little luck from that quarter. Alonso sneered. 'Sell a rough diamond? No, I shall have it cut. Then what will it be worth? Twenty thousand?'

I turned back to the dying man. 'I beg you to let me take it to be cut. I know the only man who can do it. You know that one mistake would be the ruin of it. Eighteen hundred.'

Lorenzo took the diamond from me. His face kindled again as he touched it. Then he grunted in pain, and lay back on his bolsters with a sigh. 'No one cuts this stone while I am alive. But come to me again, Englishman. Come in the day, when the stone truly shines. Your talk gives me life.'

I bowed, and turned to go. Lorenzo lay with the diamond still clutched in his hand.

As we walked back to our inn some streets away behind the Mercato, Martin was studiously silent. At last I could bear it no longer.

'By God!' I burst out. 'Tell me you think we've come on a fool's errand and have done with it.'

'I am not saying so, master. Only time will answer that.'

Day by day I sat in the darkened chamber that looked out over the Via dei Calzaiuoli, the street named for its shoe-makers but actually one of the grandest in Florence. Old Lorenzo talked to me of his family, of the faded glory of the de' Bardis, once among the richest bankers of Italy, until their great fall into bankruptcy in the year 1343. He spoke of the senior branch of the family, the Counts of Vernio, who still kept up a show of grandeur in their palazzo on the Via de' Benci. 'But the glory is long gone, long gone.' At other times his talk moved to the war. 'God be thanked for the Armistice. The world has more sense than to rip itself apart. Alonso is a good boy. He may talk about liberty, but if the day came, he would stand by his native city against the Imperials. We must oppose the foreign invaders. The Medici have their faults, but they are Florentines, like us. If Bourbon ever came to Florence, it would be with fire and the sword.' This speech appeared to exhaust him, and he lay panting, with the diamond loose in his hand.

I raged at the delay. I pictured the Cages back in Rome, their goods packed, waiting only on the pleasure of the Pope in order to depart. I should abandon this chase and go back. But the diamond's pull was too strong. And to go back and face Hannah without it, after the way I left her: no, it was not to be thought of. I sat and saw the doctors come. They slid their lancets into the old man's arm and let the blood drip down into a crescent-shaped dish held beneath. I saw them change the dressings on the swollen ulcers on his side, that unloosed a stink of corruption when they were unbound. Lorenzo's slow slide into death appalled me. But the old man seemed entirely content. Myself and the Golconda diamond were to be his last companions.

'For forty-three years I have gazed on this stone every night. Nothing else has lasted.'

'Sell it to me,' I whispered. 'Let me give the stone its reward. I will offer it to a great King, and he will give it to his lady. She will wear it on her breast. Thousands will see it.'

Lorenzo looked up at me. 'What lady is this?'

'The most beautiful lady in the world. Who else could wear the most beautiful diamond?'

His resolve was weakening, I was almost sure. He said, 'Did I never tell you of the day I bought it? Venice: the Rialto. In the days of Lorenzo the Magnificent. November, 1484. A dealer just in from Cairo. He dared not keep it; the temptation to try to cut it was too great. He dared not. Two and a half thousand ducats I paid.'

'I'll match that,' I whispered, knowing as I said it that I was ruining myself.

Lorenzo's fist clenched over the diamond, and from his eyes tears started. The closer he slid towards death, the further he was from relinquishing the diamond. I could bear no more of this. I straightened up and marched out of the room. I needed to walk the streets and vent my frustration; but I would be back. I knew I would be back. Leaning in the doorway, Alonso watched me go with a satirical smile.

I had been in Florence about a week when Martin came to me at breakfast and told me there was news. I jumped up.

'Dead?' This was the thing I dreaded most: to lose the old man too soon.

'There are more affairs in this world than your diamond,' Martin chafed me. 'No, the Imperials are advancing.'

'How far?'

'They say they have moved round to the south, blocking the road we travelled from Rome. They are at a place called San Giovanni Valdarno, about twenty miles up the valley.'

'But the Armistice?'

'There's news about that, too. The eighty thousand ducats that the Florentines sent to the Duke of Bourbon to pay his troops, to persuade him to move away: well, he's sent it all back.'

I felt the pit of my stomach fall away. There could be no clearer sign. Bourbon had torn up the treaty, and meant to storm Florence. This was what I had sworn to myself I would have the wit and luck to avoid: to be caught in a city subjected to the horrors of a sack. I left my bread and wine unfinished and hurried to the goldsmiths' quarter where I had made a few friends, and asked after more news. There was panic everywhere. It was too late to send any goods out of the city for safety. I heard curses of the Medici, curses of the Pope who had had the arrogance to sign Florence into the Holy League without her own permission, curses of Cardinal Passerini, who governed Florence and had not the ghost of a notion what to do.

'He must arm the people. We must have pikes and harquebuses from the Arsenal. There are enough of us to keep the walls against Bourbon.'

'Passerini will never dare. He knows if we're armed he'll be the first to feel the blade at his throat.'

'He will have no choice.'

'He'll wait to the last moment: the Duke of Urbino is coming, with the Venetians and the other allies of the League.'

'They'll do nothing. They may be our allies, but Venice has no interest in saving Florence.'

Next I hurried to de' Bardi. 'I must leave Florence,' I told him. 'Tomorrow at the latest. I beg you, if you wish to see the stone come to its glory after you are gone, sell it to me now.'

Lorenzo's breaths came slowly, and with long rasps. He murmured at last, 'It will go to my heir.'

I flung away from him in frustration. But I did not leave Florence. For the next two days I stayed away from the palazzo. It was a risk; I did not want him to die, and I blamed myself too for my cruelty in depriving him of his only companion. The next day, I thought, I would go back and let him talk his fill of the old days when he had bought the diamond, back in the eighties of the last century when he had his minstrels and his jester and his mistress. Then I would try again.

Easter Sunday came, and I pressed into the Duomo with the crowds for Mass. Whispers ran round. Passerini was issuing arms, some said. No, said others. But what I heard again and again was that the League was on its way, coming down from the north. Some said ten miles, some twenty. Florence was between the two armies.

Next morning when Martin came in to me he carried a letter. I took it with puzzlement. Not a soul knew I was here. But Martin told me it had come by carrier to the palazzo of the de' Bardis, where he had gone that morning, as always, to check on the old man's condition. I broke it open and read:

> *While you are off chasing stones, what have you left behind? I warn you, another man has his finger in the pot. If you love anything other than your pebbles, you had better return. That is the advice of*
> *Your friend (who will be nameless) in Rome.*

I sat gazing at the paper. Then I pushed it across to Martin, and stood up. I was trembling with rage. Someone was daring to woo Hannah Cage in my absence. But who? I saw in my mind that night of the *moccoli*, Cellini sitting among the ruins with Hannah's hand in his, and that smile of hers, the smile that belonged to me, directed instead at him. Hannah was still in Rome: that at least was plain. But better for her to be speeding back to England, still loving me, than this. I kicked the chair, as Martin let the paper fall.

'The devil! I should have listened the first day to that goldsmith Lucagnolo. I should never have trusted Cellini for a moment. And when I think of that last night, before we left. She was waiting for me, Martin, waiting for me!'

Not only that. I had left the finest of my stones with Benvenuto, a man who had nearly committed murder in Florence, a man no goldsmith in Rome would trust. I had grown so used to running risks, and always scraping through. But now: to think that, after all I had gone through, I had made such a fatal move. Hannah lost, my gems perhaps likewise, and myself trapped in a city under sentence of death.

'Master, will you listen to advice? Your love of that diamond is feeding de' Bardi. Keeping him alive. While you are here he will never part with it. Go back to Rome, master, and sort out your affairs there.'

I had a strong urge to do as he said. But none of my other stones could satisfy me now. Only the diamond of the Old Rock could bring me a glory worthy of the woman I loved. And there it lay, just two streets away, clutched in a dying man's hand.

I said, 'I have made my throw of the dice. We shall keep our stakes on the table a little longer.'

Martin merely sighed, and nodded.

That day de' Bardi was very low. He drew his breaths with difficulty, while the doctors in their black gowns applied poultices of poisonous yellow orpiment to his sores, and wiped away the rotten humours with a sponge. The next day he was the same, and the next. The Imperial army still held its position: thirty thousand they numbered, ill-clothed and ill-shod, desperate men hungry for plunder. Opposed to them were the Venetians under their captain-general, the Duke of Urbino, who had moved round just to the south of the city, facing Bourbon. They numbered only ten thousand; a second allied force of French and Swiss to the north made a mere ten thousand more.

'Urbino will not fight for Florence,' said Alonso de' Bardi, pouring us both wine. My pursuit of the diamond gave him great amusement, and he often asked me to eat with him after I came away from his father. I thought it wise policy to accept. 'Not without a price. The

Pope took away his dukedom. Very foolish treatment, towards a man who might be His Holiness's only salvation. The Medici are caught like rats. Passerini will arm the people. He must.'

That day and the next rumours flew round. Bourbon's army was moving closer, and the Venetians, it was said, had moved back to be nearer the French. Still I kept at that bedside. On Friday the old man opened his eyes and whispered to me once more the tale of how he came by the diamond. He unclenched his hand, and allowed me to hold it. The stone teased me with its dullness and its quick flashes of fire, and the old man's eyes took on a feverish light as he watched me. Then he held out shaking fingers to snatch the stone back again.

'Master,' urged Martin as we walked back through the streets. 'If we leave now, we might still get away.'

I thought of Hannah back in Rome, and what she might be doing, and I ground my teeth in fury. But still I replied to Martin, 'One more day. Just one more day.'

There were crowds out on the streets every day, milling about, snatching at news. Late on Friday word ran round that the Cardinal had at last recognised the danger to the city. The next morning, arms would be distributed to the people.

I rose early. The city was already filled with turmoil, as the men of the sixteen *gonfaloni* into which Florence was divided headed each to a different church to assemble, ready to be led to the Palazzo della Signoria for weapons. Martin and I walked out through the streets, north past the Duomo and the Medici palace. The sight of an entire state mobilising for war both frightened and exhilarated me.

As we came towards the city walls by the Gate of Faenza, the crowd suddenly swept back to let a procession of mounted men past. I saw Cardinal Passerini in his mule litter, with his scarlet banners, and after him Cardinals Cibo and Ridolfi, and the cortège of Ippolito de' Medici too. They were bound for the Duke of Urbino's camp, it was said, to offer him bribes in the Pope's name to come and defend the city.

'Farewell to the Medici!' someone jeered.

'Go with God!'

The crowd laughed as the gate shut behind them. For a moment, they surged like an uneasy sea just before a storm, agitated and unsure. Then suddenly someone shouted out, 'The People, the People!' Another voice called, 'Liberty!' Then the voices came in a roar. In a single instant, every soul there knew what they had to do. The tyrants had left the city, and in an act of incredible folly they had chosen the very same moment to allow the citizens weapons. The crowd began to move. They swept south, and Martin and I with them. At every church more men poured out, the cries of 'Liberty, liberty!' were repeated and doubled. The standards of the sixteen *gonfalonieri* waved here and there above men's heads. I saw young men, running, shouting; graver men with their gold chains and beards, walking with calm determination, all in the same direction. As we came out into the Piazza della Signoria, vast crowds were already gathered. Some of them, trooping up in order behind their standards, had not yet heard the call. Behind rose the palazzo, pale and elegant in the morning sun, with its corbelled battlements and soaring tower. Before it, rising over men's heads, stood the wondrous white form of Michelangelo's statue of King David. For some moments I stared at its beauty. David had been caught in the moment of resolution before he fought the giant Goliath: a piece of propaganda carved twenty years ago, meant to show Florence defying the world's great powers. Today it stood for the Florentines in rebellion against their own masters.

Around the gate of the palazzo I saw a group of the older citizens gathered round a number of the standard-bearers. Luigi Guiccardini, chief magistrate and standard-bearer of Florence, was arguing with some of the hotter young men, begging them to be calm. Suddenly there was the flash of a dagger, and one of the men darted towards him. Guiccardini staggered. The cry went up, 'The standard-bearer is dead! He is dead!' The crowd, which had been checked for a moment while it watched the argument outside the gate, pushed forward. The palace guards, a troop of men with harquebuses over their shoulders, scuttled quickly out of the way across the square. The crowd swarmed in at the gates, with cries of, 'To arms, to arms!' Among the first of them I saw the dark, determined face of Alonso de' Bardi.

Martin and I looked at each other. I said, 'Back to the old man.'

The crowd was thinning at the entry to the piazza, and we were able to push back against the tide and into the Via dei Calzaiuoli. Up in the sickroom, the din of the people came like a distant murmur through the veiled windows. Lorenzo lay with his eyes open, listening. He was alone. I stood still: I could not speak to him of what was happening. Suddenly we heard the sound of a harquebus being fired, and soon afterwards the booming of the great bell in the campanile of the Duomo: not the slow tolling for Mass, but the rapid strokes of men beating the bell with hammers as a blacksmith would an anvil, the signal of alarm. De' Bardi turned his eyes on me. 'And so it has come.'

'Yes.'

Still I did not mention his son. But I was spared the necessity. Old Marcello came hurrying in, and whispered in his master's ear. Lorenzo's breaths came quicker. 'You must be wrong.' To me he said, 'Let us talk together of old times.' And so began again the story, the trip to Venice, the music, the dancing, the nights of love: just as if I too had been alive in 1484, and had been there with him to share it. The shouts outside subsided, then flared up again. Marcello padded out and returned, bringing the doctor. All the while, Lorenzo caressed the stone in his hand.

'Two and a half thousand,' I whispered. 'I beg you.'

He smiled. 'Money means nothing to me now. Talk to me, Englishman. Tell me of your King's lady.'

And so I talked. I described to him her hair, black as the wing of a raven, her laughing lips, her breasts which, when she was dressed for masquing, presented nipples as red as cherries. I spun lies without shame, and the day darkened towards evening, and the old man's breaths grew shallow and slow. At times the pain must have come stronger, and his hand clenched on the stone. Marcello came back in, this time with a priest. He sat down in a corner. I was growing desperate. The notes of the bell had long ceased. Suddenly there came the sound of shrieks and running feet from outside. I sent Martin out to find what was happening, and a moment later a deafening crash of gunfire came from the direction of the square. Screams and shouts, further shots, and the roar of men running to the attack. Martin crept back in. The Medici were back in Florence, with the Venetians to help them: the rebels were trapped inside the palace. The old man coughed and choked, and both doctor and priest jumped forward. Then his breathing resumed.

'My son,' he murmured.

'Your son,' I began. But I could not poison his last moments. His lips moved weakly, and he drifted into a sleep. I sat back down in frustration. The room was almost dark. The shots and the repeated blows of the Venetians' battering ram ceased. I too must have dozed, before we heard heavy steps in the passage, the door was thrown open, and in walked Alonso. He was out of breath. His clothes were dusty, he had no hat, and he carried a drawn sword in his hand. Lorenzo's eyes flicked open. He stared at his son, his yellow eyes hideously wide in the skull-like face.

Alonso threw himself down in a chair. 'Devils, cowards and knaves. That is what Florentines are. Three hours ago we were masters. We were passing laws, we were a republic again, we had named Ippolito and Alessandro traitors, we had sent our own ambassadors out to the League. And now? They are back, and we are pardoned. Pardoned!'

The old man still stared at him, not understanding. I was the one who questioned Alonso, and won from him the story. The young men had swarmed inside the palazzo and set up a rebel parliament there; for three hours they had talked and argued. No one had thought of manning the walls, or shutting the gates against the Cardinals' return. No one had gone through the streets to mobilise the people. They had rung the great bell, but without leaders the Florentines did nothing. In the afternoon, the Medici marched back into Florence. They must have bribed Urbino well. His men cleared the piazza with a volley of shot and set about breaking into the palazzo. It was Alonso who found a store of building stone, which they dropped on the attackers from the battlements. That gave them enough time to enter into talks: not with the Medici, who would glibly swear out amnesties and pardons and then cut their throats in the night, but with the Venetians.

'They are the ones who have promised us our safety. But the Pope's agents know our names. When the League's army is gone, we are dead.'

Lorenzo's face was a mask of horror and disbelief. 'My son,' he murmured. The doctor felt his pulse and nodded to the priest, who came forward, reached from his clothes a small, golden flask, and began murmuring in Latin.

'*Indulgeat tibi Dominus quidquid per visum deliquisti.*' May God forgive you the sins committed by sight. The priest scattered a few drops of oil over the old man's eyes. Yes, he had looked on beautiful things, and lusted after them. The priest forgave the sins of smell, taste, touch, speech, the privy members, touching each organ in turn with the holy oil. Alonso stood up.

'Good-bye, Father.' He turned and walked out of the room. Lorenzo's face slumped sideways so that it was staring into mine. The grip of his fingers loosened.

'Take it,' he whispered. 'Take it.'

I gazed in amazement at the stone, lying unprotected in the old man's hand. I fumbled in my clothes for the bills.

His voice came lower than ever. 'No gold. Take it.'

I lifted the diamond from his hand. As I did so, his body relaxed, as if all pain in that instant had left him. His head rolled back with a sigh. The priest, still murmuring, leant forward to close his staring eyes. The stone had released him. It was mine.

18

That very night we rode from Florence, west into the hills away from the armies. Then we doubled back, south and east. The next two days brought us to Cortona, and then over that windswept pass down into the lands of the Pope. The trees were coming into leaf in the hills, and over the plain lay a warm, blue haze. I could think of nothing but Hannah, and the traitor. I had pictured my triumph when Cellini saw the diamond. Now hatred curdled me when I thought of him. It was the first of May when we finally crossed the Tiber by the Milvian Bridge and reached Rome: I had been gone almost a month. A light mist hung in the air. A heavy guard manned the gate, but these were citizen troops, slow and unsoldierly. There was no sign of the Medici Black Bands, or the Swiss.

My rage carried me to the old, familiar palace with its tawny stucco, and the twining paintings of ancient heroes that ran round above the barred windows. I hammered on the door. Two men opened it, strangers. They were carrying harquebuses. A new fear gripped me then: what if the Cages had finished their business and gone? But at the name Stephen Cage they nodded, and I went in. There were more armed men on the stairs, and a pair with halberds guarded the door to the sala. From inside came the sound of music and a man's laugh. I was shown in. There, on a gilt chair by the fireplace, sat Benvenuto. Susan Cage was with him, and both had lutes on their laps. Benvenuto was a fine player. He plucked out a lively phrase, then waited for Susan to follow, her face puckered and frowning, her notes slower but delicate. Then he laughed, and set her a further challenge, and she muttered in mock dismay. I walked up to face them. If he was this free with Susan, I boiled to think how he had been behaving with Hannah. My sword leapt from my scabbard into my hand. Susan let out a gasp. Cellini nimbly put aside the lute, and in an instant he was facing me, sword drawn.

I sprang at him. He answered my blows with ringing parries. His guard was good; but still he did not attack. Susan jumped up. 'Oh, you are fools! Stop! Stop!'

The doors flew open, and the two men with halberds ran in. I circled round to face them.

'Leave us be,' said Cellini. 'This is a mere friendly bout.'

The men doubtfully withdrew.

'You do know,' said Cellini, circling, 'that I could simply ask my men to kill you. Those soldiers are mine.'

I attacked again, and he dodged. 'Yours?'

'The Black Bands have gone. Oh, the Pope dismissed them. Their looting became an embarrassment. Besides that, they were costing him thirty thousand ducats a month.' He struck at me, powerfully and without apparent effort. I was tired, I realised, from my ride, and my parries lacked strength.

'And the soldiers?'

'Each house looks to its own defences. My friends and I guarded Alessandro once before, when the Colonnas invaded Rome. Now he has asked us back. I live here, with these charming ladies.'

'Traitor!'

I deployed the *punta*, the long lunge. It was a deadly stroke. Cellini, however, slid his blade across in the iron gate, just in time.

'Stop, please!' Susan was laughing, even as she was almost crying. 'You are too comical. Richard: you remember? "Another man has his finger in the pot." You should be looking elsewhere than Benvenuto.'

I lowered my sword and looked at her. And so the letter was hers. At that moment the door to the loggia opened, and in walked Grace and Stephen. Behind them came John. At his side was Hannah, with her hand resting on his arm.

'What! Swords!' Stephen came hurrying towards us, waving his hand as you would to part fighting dogs. 'Put them up, put them up.'

'A mere friendly difference of view,' said Cellini. He sheathed his blade. I was looking at John. My amazement and my rage had only a moment to build when Hannah detached herself from him and ran to my side. She hung on my shoulder, and the warmth and weight of her body changed all my feelings in an instant.

'God be thanked!' she sighed. 'Everyone is talking of the uprising in Florence. You escaped before it?'

'No, I was there.' My sword was a sudden embarrassment: I slid it into its sheath. Hannah's eyes shone. Her admiration, her concern and devotion: they were for me and me alone. I darted a glance at John. He strode easily forward and clasped my hand. 'Old friend. We had almost given you up. But you are like me: you always win through.'

'And you come in such good time for dinner.' Mrs Grace smiled her cultured smile. She called for Fenton, and soon the old ritual was set in motion, the boards laid on their trestles, the cloth spread; the minstrels trooped in. The silver plates, the gilt candlesticks, the tapestries, all had seemingly been once more unpacked. We sat down. With Hannah's eyes on me, and her breathless questions, the last of my anger drained away. Mr Stephen, too, treated me with grave respect, and wanted to hear every movement of the armies.

'When I left,' I told him, 'the Spaniards and the lansquenets had drawn away. With the Venetians in Florence, they will find it a hard city to take.'

Hannah broke in. 'Oh! What is a – a lanskenay?'

I turned to her, relishing her attention. 'A lansquenet, my dear Mrs Hannah, is a demon that is bred in Germany, with a sword in his hand and Luther in his heart.' She shivered with a delighted horror, and put her hand on my arm. I thrilled with glory. Still secret, wrapped inside my casket, lay the diamond of the Old Rock. But I promised myself I would not show it to Hannah yet. I would have it cut, and then I would amaze her. She would know then, for sure, how far I would rise when we returned home.

After dinner I walked with her alone in the loggia, and then at last I begged forgiveness: for running away from her that night when we should have met in the garden, for fighting like a beast in the sala, for my vain jealousies and suspicions.

She squeezed my arm. 'My dear Mr Richard. I hope your gain in Florence was worth the loss of that night.'

'It was a heavy price. But there will be other nights?'

'Perhaps.'

Cellini at this moment appeared. He murmured in my ear, 'If you have cooled down, come with me to my workshop. I think you will be surprised.'

Hannah gave me a last smile: elusive but laced with promise. Cellini and I walked out together into the late afternoon sun. We were silent until we stood in the workshop down by the river, where Cellini unlocked his chest and held up to me a gold pendant on a chain, a disc some two inches broad. There it was: the garden, just as we had planned. There were the reapers in gold relief, their sickles cutting into the corn; there were the meadows, studded with crimson jacinths, as it might be poppies; the shepherd beneath his tree; the nymphs, one undressing, two naked, their feet hovering over the pale, milky pool of the white sapphire. Round its rim hung Ippolita's nine pendant pearls. Every smallest space had been used, and yet the composition did not seem in the least crowded or constrained. Only one thing was missing. In place of the green distant fields that were

259

to have been figured by the Scythian emerald, there was only an empty socket.

'It is a marvel,' I murmured. 'And the emerald?'

Cellini wiped his hand across his beard. 'The emerald, you say. Well! I tried to cut it, and I couldn't.'

'Couldn't!'

He held up the stone in his other hand. As he turned it, rounded and smooth, it glinted with a pale, beech-leaf brilliance, shooting out glances of turquoise and amber. 'Look at it. Have you ever seen an emerald like that?'

I had to admit it, I had not. There had been something all along that was not right about it. It was too pale, too ready to shine, and with colours that were simply too fickle for an emerald. But its beauty had always shouted down my suspicions. 'You are not telling me it is fake?'

Cellini tossed the gem up in his hand and caught it. 'That depends what you mean. This is not an emerald. It is a diamond.'

'A diamond!'

'Of the rarest kind. It is a green diamond. I have only ever seen one other like it.'

I took the stone greedily from his hands. It was plain to me now. It had a diamond's temperament, its limpid depth and sudden flash of colour; yet all in an emerald green. It was a wonder. I looked up. 'Will you cut it?'

'If you want the risk. But the green in a diamond of this kind is most likely skin-deep, no more. It is a virtue which the stone drinks up from its mother rock, but which does not penetrate to its heart. Cut it, and we may have only a drab white stone.'

I gazed at it. Its surface rippled like gently flowing water. 'It is perfect as it is.'

He nodded, and looked at me with a sideways smile. 'Paulino, bring us wine. Our friend is in need of it. He went to Florence for a stone, and came back with only a bad temper.'

It was my turn to smile. I took out the casket, unlocked it, and handed Cellini a fold of silk. He unwrapped it and took out the stone: the Golconda diamond of the Old Rock. He lifted it to the light in silence, turned it, round, under, back; he paused, he rotated it again. I let him look in silence.

'Its main faces are three,' he murmured. 'After we have cut away the flaw. Its water is good: very good. Pure, limpid, silver-blue. Its shape, yes, the light already invites us where to place the table. And its flash, its fire, they will be of the finest. But it will be ticklish work. Oh, yes. You wish me to attempt it?'

I stood at his elbow, gazing along his line of sight into the diamond. Already I saw it in new ways. The hidden gem inside its smooth outer skin seemed to jump into life. I said, 'I trust you.'

Cellini laughed. 'Now you trust me! And what is your plan for this stone?'

'A thorn. A thorn to pierce the heart.'

Cellini handed me the diamond. 'You are right. This is a deadly stone. It is a stone men would kill for.' He gave me a sharp look. 'I have no notion how you afforded it.'

'Let us just say I still have enough left to pay you.' I took out the blood-red garnets and the violet balasses and amethysts, and laid them beside the diamond. Cellini, with his paper and charcoal before him, was already beginning to sketch.

That night I sat drinking with John, back at the Ship. He had ordered a bottle of the finest old romney. 'My friend,' he protested, his hands spread in appeal, 'what was I to do? Mrs Hannah was distraught. I merely kept her company as best I knew how. We spoke of no one but you. And then, when Benvenuto recruited his little army, of course I volunteered. And so Susan actually wrote to you in Florence, to warn you I was stealing your place? The little strumpet has pluck.'

I laughed. John was right. Susan was no better than a spiteful child. She envied her sister her happiness; and perhaps she would have liked some of John's easy smiles for herself.

I was impatient for Cellini to get on with his work. But he spent several hours each day at the Palazzo del Bene: Alessandro, he explained, fretted constantly over his defences. There were fifty men quartered there in all, some on the roofs, others in the two gardens which flanked the building's wings, others ready to defend the windows. Fifteen had harquebuses and the rest were armed with pikes, crossbows and swords. There was a good supply of gunpowder, which Cellini ground and mixed himself.

Of Bourbon's army there was no news. It was presumed he still lay at Siena, where he had gone to take on fresh supplies. The majority of Romans thought nothing of the danger. A ragged army a hundred and twenty miles away, that would regard Florence as unfinished business before it ever turned south to Rome? What danger was there in that? The citizen militia obeyed the call to patrol the gates and walls with bad grace. What was the point? Only a few men like Alessandro feared the very worst, and made their own private plans accordingly. Stephen Cage was another who took the threat seriously.

'We shall be out of this damned city,' he murmured to me, 'just as soon as we may. Our goods are ready to be loaded up at a few hours' warning.' Then he took his leave for yet another trip over the river to the Pope's palace.

I sent Martin out about the city for news. His Italian had become almost as good as mine; I knew I could trust him as a spy. It was Friday, two days after I returned to Rome, when Martin brought back a letter from the English hostel. It came from Bennet Waterman. I snatched at it with impatience and sat down at once to decipher it

My dear Richard,

At last I can offer you a name: a name which is on everyone's lips at Court, and soon will be known through all England. That name is Anne Boleyn. She is a gentlewoman, of Kent; her father and brother both courtiers. She is the sister of the King's last love, Mrs Mary. No beauty, but that the King's regard makes her one. Her hair and eyes, dark. Figure slight; her wit and temper both quick. Her emblem: a falcon. At last I understand the fear I see daily in my master, Cardinal Wolsey. He had a hand in breaking off the Mrs Anne's betrothal some years back, and she hates him for it. The King's love makes her powerful; powerful enough perhaps even to threaten the Cardinal. Well might he call her the Night Crow, this dark woman who murmurs against him in the King's ear when they are alone together. But he swears her days of glory are numbered. When the King has his divorce and marries the Princess d'Alençon, this Anne will be heard of no more.

For the sake of your business, hurry home. Fear is our daily diet. I tell you also, the Cardinal fears more and more what the secret envoy might be doing in Rome. And I am disappointed in you, Richard: three months in Rome and not a word of the agent sent there to harass us. If I did not know you were my own nephew, I would suspect you were concealing something from me. Well: we have discovered his name nonetheless, and it is one to watch for, and fear. Stephen Cage. He is Mrs Anne's cousin, and a strong arm of her faction, and therefore an enemy of Cardinal Wolsey and of us. I beg you, write to me soon with news of Italy, and, if you can, send me word of this Stephen Cage. He is dangerous.

I put the letter down and let out a long breath. At last I had it. A name, and with it a face. In my mind I saw Anne Boleyn, wearing on her bosom my opal cross, or my ship, or my green diamond idyll. No beauty, Bennet said, but her wit quick: so much the better. She would appreciate my treasures, and take their beauties for her own.

But the second part of the letter hit me hard. It was what I had suspected for many weeks: Stephen was the man in Rome. I had not written to Bennet since meeting the Cages, and my disloyalty pressed on me with a weight of guilt. If I did not tread carefully I would soon lose my uncle's trust, and I feared what harm might come to me if Cardinal Wolsey came to count me as one of his enemies. But that was just one more risk I would have to take. My new loyalty pulled stronger, and Bennet's own letter confirmed I was right to stick close to the Cages. Stephen was one of the Boleyns, the faction that counted on Anne's place in the King's favour to secure their own fortunes. I was one of that faction now too. I must do Stephen Cage all the good turns I could, and put him firmly in my debt. That was my surest way to Court, as well as to the girl I loved. But my uncle's suspicions and warnings still nagged at me. Just what was Mr Stephen doing here?

I repeated the letter to Martin, and he whistled. 'You're playing a dangerous game, master, when you don't know who's who, or who makes the rules. Get yourself out of these courtiers' snares, and for God's sake let us go home.'

'What, when I've just learnt the name of the lady? And who would cut our diamond? No. Not yet, my Martin. Not yet.'

The next day, Saturday, the fourth of May, I set off as usual for Cellini's workshop. As I came down towards the river I heard the ringing of bells from Saint Peter's, and from Santa Maria del Popolo to the north, and soon from all round. Benvenuto came out and we stood together, listening, looking out across the Tiber, which surged with a swift, brown flow.

I said, 'What do you think it is?'

'Suppose we find out.'

We set off together across the Bridge of Sant' Angelo and up into the Borgo. Here there was a great streaming together of people running out from the houses to see what was wrong. Through th crowds groups of soldiers were pushing towards the city walls: the few remaining detachments of Swiss and the citizen militia that had been mobilised by Pope Clement's general, Renzo da Ceri. Near Cardinal Campeggio's palazzo we climbed a stone stair to the ramparts, past men toiling up with casks of gunpowder to the cannon on the towers. From here we looked out over the marshy valley known as the Vale of Hell. Before us was an army. Its bands stretched out, miles long it seemed, to left and right. Banners waved over the different divisions; there were the clustered pikes, the longer straggle of the harquebusiers, the horsemen, and behind them the scores and scores of wagons with their canvas covers. The din of hoofs and the clatter of harness and armour were audible even here. The men around us looked out at the sight, frightened and amazed, and I too was shaken. I knew for a fact this army had been at Florence, a hundred and fifty miles away, only a week ago.

Cellini said, 'I must see Alessandro.'

As we walked back through the city we saw bands of servants and artisans being herded into companies and issued with weapons. They had a shambling, half-hearted appearance. In the goldsmiths' district, Cellini stopped with this acquaintance and that, and we heard snatches of rumour. No one seemed too much bothered.

'The walls will defend us.'

'How do we know that army is Bourbon's? Most likely it belongs to the League.'

'They say the Imperials are dying of hunger.'

'They need to be: without the Black Bands we are helpless.'

'Well, suppose Bourbon does take the city? Things can only change for the better.'

'True, Rome has been under the priests for long enough. Let the emperor come from Spain and rule us. Why not?'

We made for the Palazzo del Bene, where Cellini's men stood on nervous guard outside the doors. Bundles and packages filled the entrance hall, and the Cages' servants passed to and fro bringing out more. I felt a stab of apprehension and hurried up the stairs. In the loggia I found John, a harquebus at his side, talking to Hannah. My suspicions instantly returned, but the smile with which John met me was open and full of innocence. Hannah ran over to my side. She put her head on my shoulder and murmured, 'This frightens me.'

John, with a smile, withdrew. I stroked her arm. 'You, frightened? The girl who stood in the path of the wild bulls?'

'There is more to be afraid of than a few bulls.'

'No one in the city seems troubled.'

'But my father is.'

I was about to speak again to calm her, persuade her there was nothing truly to fear. I was enjoying my role as gallant protector. At that moment the door to the saletta opened and we stood quickly apart. Stephen and Grace came out, with Susan stalking after them. Grace squeezed my hand in silence. Stephen, his arms full of papers with dangling seals, had a fierce glint in his eye.

'The devil! Perhaps you can tell me, Mr Richard, how the Imperials covered the ground so quickly? Forded rivers in flood, marched thirty miles a day. Starving, are they? Too weak to march? Well, they have already sent their trumpeter to the gates, demanding Rome's surrender. Do you know what they carry as their standard?'

I shook my head.

Stephen poked a finger at my chest, still clutching his papers. 'A gallows. A gallows with a noose, to hang the Pope. That's how Bourbon gave his troops the spirit to march. That's what he's promising them. Lutherans, Moors and Jews. All those the Church persecutes. Well, they will have their revenge if they can. Where's the Pope's peace treaty? Ferramosca saw to that, by telling the Spanish and Germans they could never trust Pope Clement. And where is the army of the League, that should have stopped them from ever coming this far?'

'Dear Mr Richard,' Grace put in, 'why do you not come with us? Follow us home to England?'

'Then you are really leaving?'

'Just as soon as may be,' answered Stephen. 'His Holiness!' he spat out. 'He is just what the popular jibes say of him: the Pope of Ifs and Maybes, the Pope with feet of lead. Tomorrow, he says. Well, tomorrow then. And if not, we are gone.' He caught my eye for a moment, and allowed a smile of complicity to pass over his face. 'We understand one another increasingly well, I think. I shall look forward to taking our discussions further.' Then he turned abruptly away to confer with Fenton: leaving me with the uncomfortable knowledge that for the price of favour I would be called upon to make further betrayals of Bennet's secrets.

'But the roads,' I protested to Mrs Grace. 'Surely you would be safer here?'

'The road to Ostia runs down the east of the river,' Susan sighed, with the air of one who was instructing a child. 'The Imperials are to the west. If we leave now we'll be safe.'

'Consider it, Mr Richard. Please do.' Grace squeezed my hand again, and turned after her husband. I glanced at Hannah, who rewarded me with one of her arch smiles. The temptation tugged at me. I pictured myself setting out for Ostia, sailing home with Hannah, riding across France in that vast and glorious cavalcade that was the Cages' household, with the servants putting up the pavilion for one of their fantastical luncheons wherever we stopped. And Hannah: seeing her every day, and yes, with luck, by night. But then I thought of the diamond, uncut, opaque, misted, its charms still secret, perhaps never to be revealed. How many of its former owners had left it untried, had been deterred for one specious reason or another? And was I to be the same as them, to return home with jewels of wonder, yes, but without the greatest treasure of all? Cellini had set the green diamond yesterday. The Golconda diamond sat even now in his locked chest, waiting.

'Another few days, Mrs Grace. The danger from the Imperials cannot be so pressing as that. Then, God willing, I will come with you.'

I took my leave, bowing low to them both, and Hannah watched me go with a frown. It would be some time, I consoled myself, before the Cages could be fully packed and ready to go. I wanted to see Cellini, to badger him into returning to his work. But he was busy with Alessandro, discussing whether to put extra crossbowmen in the rear windows. I turned away, fuming. Together with Martin I set out to scour the city for news. We found fear in some quarters, but in most a cheerful confidence. There was no great rush to flee the city, or hide away valuables. The Imperials, it seemed, had no cannon with them at all: everything had been left behind at Siena to allow them to complete so swift a march. They would be unable to bombard the walls. This news heartened me a good deal.

That afternoon the Pope held a special Mass in Saint Peter's. He sat on his throne dressed in a violet cope staring down on us, his eyes bearing their usual expression of proud reserve. He made a long speech, urging his people in his lilting voice to fear nothing. The Imperials had not the strength to capture even a little fortress, let alone a city like Rome. After the first failed attack, they would break up and be seen no more. 'God in His mysterious providence has led the heretic Lutherans here, to the chief seat of His holy religion, in order to destroy them and make them an example to others. All those who die in defence of the Holy City will have full remission of their sins and immediate entry to paradise, as well as remunerative church benefices for their heirs. Two days: that is all we need. If we hold the walls for two days, they will be gone.'

There was fear, I thought, in the way he glanced about and licked his fleshy lips. But his hearers murmured with appreciation. His Holiness stepped down from his throne and twelve priests in white surplices formed a ring behind him. Each one carried a tall lighted candle. The church fell silent. Then Pope Clement began the terrible ceremony of the Anathema. He excommunicated the Duke of Bourbon and his accomplices from the bosom of Holy Mother Church, and condemned them all, thirty thousand souls, to eternal fire with Satan and his angels. A murmur of gratified horror ran round the people as the twelve priests dashed their candles on the ground, where they rolled for a few moments until every flame was extinguished.

PART 5

Ruby of Serendip: a Stone to Heat the Blood

Rome, 5 May 1527

Fortune is all-powerful:
That I believe,
For to fight her none has strength;
… But Fortune is God's will, as some have said?
That I cannot think.
God then would be unjust, fickle,
… Harsh and cruel as She.

ANTONIO FILEREMO FREGOSO, *DIALOGUE ON FORTUNE*

19

The next day Renzo da Ceri was seen in his plumed helmet in all quarters of Rome, issuing orders for the positioning of the reserves, pointing to decayed portions of the walls and sending up builders with wheelbarrows of stone and lime. It was a mad burst of haste; I did not know whether to laugh or be afraid, seeing men actually building up the walls while the enemy was camped before them. The men obeyed sluggishly. Renzo could not be everywhere, and when he went away the men threw down their shovels and ambled off to the nearest wine shop. Beyond the walls we could hear the drumming of hoofs and the distant murmur of many men. That army of the damned had not gone away.

Around noon there was a great stir through the city. Cannonfire was heard from the north side of the Borgo, and all the roar and din of battle. The Imperials were attempting to scale the walls. I sat in the Cages' sala with John and the womenfolk, while Stephen stayed alone in his study. We did not speak. At times we could hear Stephen pacing about, kicking the walls, murmuring to himself and then shouting out loud. He was in some great indecision, it seemed. All the Cages' things were packed. But still they did not leave.

Benvenuto, yet again, had abandoned the diamond, and sat up on the rooftop gazing north. From time to time Paulino came down with news.

'They are drawing back,' he told us at last. We laughed and cheered. The attack had lasted just an hour. It seemed the Pope had been right about the Imperials' feebleness. Mrs Grace summoned in the minstrels, and soon we were dancing, while the bells rang all through Rome, and men ran down the streets shouting, 'Victory, victory!' Mr Stephen stepped in, his face grave. Without a word he walked out and down the stairs.

'The Pope,' Mrs Grace whispered. The girls nodded. A proclamation had gone out that morning forbidding anyone to leave the city; but Mr Stephen, I had no doubt, could secure an exemption from the rule if he chose. I offered Hannah my hand. 'If you would walk with me in the garden?'

Grace smiled her approval. I had the heavy sense that my time with Hannah was short now indeed, whether Mr Stephen obtained what he wanted from His Holiness or not. We made the small circuit of the garden down the single loop of gravel path, past the Roman statues, the lemon trees, the arbour, the vine I had never climbed. She walked with soft, slow steps. We were beginning our second turn round before either of us spoke.

I said, 'I have found out the secret you tried so very hard to hide.'

Hannah looked up quickly.

I went on, 'The King's love.'

She looked guarded. 'You've found out, have you? How very clever you are, Mr Richard.'

'You must know Anne Boleyn well: she comes of Kent gentry like yourselves. You are a mystery to me, Mrs Hannah. Why would you not tell?'

She stared at me a moment, and then smiled and looked down at her feet as they scuffed along the path. 'And you are a mystery to me: why you are so much in love with your stones. First one, then another. Then that one will not do, and you need one still finer. You are a lost man, Mr Richard.'

I protested all over again that I was doing it only for her. 'When we are home again, and I have my success with the King: then you will understand.'

She stopped, and looked up at me. The skin of her forehead was creased in a frown. I could not read what was troubling her, but the concern in her eyes made her infinitely beautiful. 'Will I?'

I made no answer. Instead, I stooped forward and kissed her. She gave a little sigh and rested her hands lightly on my shoulders. Her eyes closed before mine. She gave herself up to that kiss; but there was a sadness in it, I thought, a sense that perhaps this was not just one among the first of our kisses, but the last. Suddenly she pulled away. We could hear Mr Stephen shouting from somewhere in the house.

'Fenton! Fenton! Where are those horses? I told you we needed more! And load the silver in the middle carriage. Armed men to the front and rear.'

Hannah ran ahead of me through the door into the entrance hall. I caught up with Mr Stephen soon after.

'You are not going?'

Stephen's pale eyes were fierce. 'At once.'

'Allow me to wish that you have obtained what you desired from His Holiness.'

It was a last try to tease from him some information. He turned on me. 'No, by God, I have not. But I had rather return a failure than stay any longer in this deathtrap. The Imperials will be back. If you are ever going to leave this place, it has to be now.'

He turned away. Servants ran across the hall to the pile of bundles. Outside in the piazza I could see packhorses and carts waiting.

Hannah's eyes looked at me in question.

Mr Stephen's talk had chilled me. But I would not let myself believe the worst. 'Two days,' I promised her. I was calculating. Two days for the armies to clear and for Benvenuto to cut the stone. That would have to content me. I would have someone else make up the heart in England, and fashion some rings and suchlike out of the remaining stones: I could sacrifice that much of perfection. But I must have that diamond. Hannah looked at me for a long moment, and then she turned from me with an angry toss of her head and ran up the stairs to the sala.

'Piccolino! Who is looking after Piccolino?'

She had changed in an instant. From the deep, beautiful woman, full of promise and dark melancholy, she was once more a petulant, teasing girl. I looked up at the balcony where she had gone. Over the marble balustrade leant Susan. She had seen it all. She shook her head at me, comical and commiserating. In a rage I walked out into the square. The crowd of packbeasts, men and carts was astounding; only now, in fact, did I appreciate the scale of the Cages' entourage, and the wealth that lay behind it. I saw the minstrels, the music-master and the dancing-master, the gentlewomen, the almoner supervising the loading up of a chest presumably carrying church-plate and altar vessels; the five or six pageboys in grass-green livery, the maids and men loading up chests and rolls of tapestry, table-cloths and carpets; and Beelzebub-Piccolino on his silver chain perched screeching on top of it all.

Martin was silently at my side. 'Master,' he murmured, 'I beg you. Why will you not go with them? If we ran to Benvenuto's, paid him and fetched the jewels …?'

I made no answer. Mrs Grace came out of the palazzo, and the girls, and Alessandro with a few more servants. To my dismay the Cages really were ready to go. Stephen bowed deeply to Alessandro, and then clasped him in his arms. Alessandro kissed each of the ladies, 'in the English fashion'. Grace turned to me a last questioning look, but Hannah avoided my eye and climbed into one of the covered carts with her father. Too late, I bowed, and realised I had lost my chance for that last kiss which custom allowed. The first o the carts, on which two men with harquebuses rode, moved out of the little piazza and turned into the Via Monserrato. In a few minutes, with a vast rumbling of wheels and snorting of horses and mules, the Cages and all their household were gone. I stood there in the empty piazza staring after them. Never have I felt more desolate, and angry too, both at the Cages for going and myself for my stubbornness in staying behind. Already I sensed I had made a terrible mistake.

That night I roved the streets of Rome without purpose. It was a damp night, with a chill air rising from the marshes. I reached as far as the Cow Pasture with its buried triumphal arches and columns, and then turned north beyond the Colosseum to the grottoes. Everywhere cried out to me with Hannah's absence. The very air was heavy with memory and regret: the places we had been, the things we had said and done. The streets were quiet; calmly expectant. Rome had won a victory already, and tomorrow was the day the Pope had promised for Bourbon's final, shameful retreat. Moody, I returned at last to the Palazzo del Bene. Sounds of music came from inside. When I went in, the doors of what had been the Cages' sala were thrown open. Alessandro del Bene was there, with Benvenuto sitting beside him, polishing the barrel of his gun. I saw John, tapping his feet and clapping to the rough country music of a bagpiper and a pair of fiddles, while several of Benvenuto's soldiers were dancing. The grandeur of the Cages' occupancy had vanished like a dream. Among the faces in the candlelight round the walls I recognised a good many of Benvenuto's friends: Berni, and Polidoro, Pantassilea and Diego. I saw Polidoro debating a sketch with the Florentine painter Rosso, making additions to it in charcoal, then laughing and passing round the jug. On the fire a basin of wine was steaming for hippocras. When Alessandro saw me he called me in. Martin went and sat down with a group of servants who were playing cards outside the door. Cellini held up his harquebus to me with a smile.

Its steel barrel was chased in gold, and the serpentine that held the match was carved as a rearing dragon. Naturally it was all his own work.

I said, 'It seems to me you are enjoying soldiering rather too much. When will you attend to my stone?'

Cellini waved his hand. 'Dear Richard: always so urgent. Tonight we drink to victory, and the long continuance of art, and her patroness the Church.'

'The Church!' echoed some of the artists. 'May she commission frescos and goblets and altarpieces without end. Amen.'

I took a cup of hot wine and sat down next to John, who smiled and raised his cup to mine.

'I am surprised you're still here,' I murmured.

'Oh, I would not leave Rome for the world. There are excellent opportunities here for trade.'

He caught my eye and I looked back at him, wondering. And so he was still dealing in his mysterious, invisible goods. But whose side was he working for? He had left Florence in a hurry: so I guessed he had been on the run from the Medici. He had left informants behind there, who forwarded 'goods' to him as they became known. I suspected he knew Mr Stephen, even before I introduced him. And he had dealings with Ferramosca, who was trusted by the Pope to negotiate peace, even though he was in the pay of the Emperor. John's smile gave nothing away.

The music swelled and the sketches were passed round, nude nymphs, rolicking satyrs, dainty goddesses. It seemed a profanation of the room where Hannah and I had danced, and where I had sat down to the Cages' grandiose feasts. But they were gone: I had made my choice, and put my treasures before my love. Perhaps I had been a fool. But I consoled myself by thinking how soon I would set out on the same road as the Cages. I would travel fast, and overtake them before they believed it possible: and then I would show Hannah that diamond. I allowed myself to relax and drink.

In the silence that night back in my bed at the inn I pictured the Imperials melting away, first one band, then another: their banners falling, the men simply vanishing into the mist, withering under the Pope's curse. In the end I must have slept. When I woke, I heard a noise I could not place. It was a murmur like a swarm of distant bees, mingled with booms of thunder. Martin was shaking my arm.

'Master, wake up! They are attacking.'

We hurried to the palazzo. There were men up on the roof, peering across the river. It was early, not long after dawn; mist hung in the streets in pale, glimmering strands. I found Benvenuto and Alessandro downstairs.

'We can tell nothing from up on the roof,' Benvenuto was saying. 'The mist is too thick.'

Alessandro was hopping from foot to foot in fear. 'Come with me to the walls, I implore you, Benvenuto. Not knowing is the very worst.'

Cellini's eyes kindled. 'You want to see it, at the cannon's mouth? Very well!'

I stepped forward. I knew Benvenuto's rashness. If there was any danger, I was not letting him out of my sight. So we set out, with Martin and ten or so of Cellini's soldiers carrying harquebuses. We crossed the Bridge of Sant' Angelo under the walls of the castle and then hurried up through the Borgo. We skirted Saint Peter's, from which came the sound of chanting: the Pope was saying Mass for victory. Between here and the walls was a vineyard belonging to the Pope, and the palace of Cardinal Cesi stood to one side, where I had walked with Hannah just a few days ago among the Cardinal's outstanding collection of sculpture. From three sides now, where the walls looped round, we could hear the crash of repeated harquebus volleys and the roar of the enemy army. They were attacking everywhere at once: from the Valley of Hell beyond Saint Peter's, and westward among the vineyards. We followed Cellini up the stone steps to the battlements. Dead men lay everywhere. It was about an hour after dawn, and the fog was growing thicker. Shots fell all round us. We crouched behind the parapet while Cellini, with a wild light in his eyes, loaded his gun.

'Now that we are here, we are bound to fire a shot.'

Each of us followed his lead. I had learnt the working of a harquebus from Mr William on our sea voyages, but I had never fired at a living foe. Upon Benvenuto's word, we stood up and trained our weapons over the wall. What I saw was a white blank with dim shapes moving in it, but from everywhere came the yelling of men, the clangour of their movements and the volleys of shot. I fired at random into the mist and ducked quickly down again. Bullets chipped into the stone around us, and our cannon shot answered from the towers. Alessandro crouched behind the parapet, murmuring over and over, 'I wish to God we had never come.' In some places, scaling ladders leant against the walls and the enemy climbed, one by one, to be shot down before they could reach us; but others always took their place, with their yells of 'España, España!' Cannon shots flew overhead, and one crashed into the wall at our side, throwing three men back in a welter of rubble and blood. They came from our own guns in the Castle of Sant' Angelo, firing blindly into the mist.

Cellini motioned to us and we crept further along the parapet. The Spaniards and Germans were attacking in bands, all along the walls. It was a marvel how they kept up their fury, with no cannon of their own to answer ours. But their sheer numbers gave them freshness. As one detachment fired off their shots or grew tired, another came up from behind. Around the bend in the walls we came to a place where the ramparts ran lower. Sections were cracked and decayed, and I saw that the rear wall of a farmhouse had been built into them to save expense. The Spaniards were attacking here with greater fury than ever: they had the wit to direct their strength to the weakest point. I whispered this to Benvenuto, and he nodded. We stood up to fire; two of his men were shot down. The fog was as thick as could be. We were in a world of white, where we could not see more than an arm's length, and yet death was crashing all round us. The shouts of the bands of Spaniards and their volleys of shot echoed, now near, now far, and I felt a sudden exhilaration, as if we were invulnerable. Then the fog blew apart for an instant, and I suddenly saw their ranks, the bristling pikes in dense squares, the harquebuses trained up at the walls hundreds together, and I felt the full fear of our own weakness and the terrible strength of our enemy.

The Imperials milled about at the very foot of the walls, and one of the Papal captains handed out iron balls with fuses, fire bombs, which we lit and threw down. The explosions and cries from below told us we had done some good; but more men came scuttling up through the vineyards to creep between the piles of stinking refuse that had been thrown from the walls. Out beyond their first ranks we glimpsed a figure in white riding about on a horse, shouting out encouragement. Shots fell around him, and when the fog blew past we saw him at the foot of a scaling ladder, encouraging his men to follow. A murmur ran along the battlements: 'Bourbon. The Duke of Bourbon.'

'That's the man to hit,' growled Cellini. We all of us trained our guns down into the fog. He was climbing the ladder, and the Spaniards came roaring up behind him; we fired, and then again. Next we heard sounds of confusion and the firing of the enemy diminishing, and through the smoke and the fog I saw the Spanish fall back, carrying the man in white with them, his surcoat drenched in blood.

'I killed him!' Cellini was shouting. 'I killed Bourbon!'

'Any one of us could have fired that shot,' I corrected him.

'Don't be a fool,' growled Cellini. 'None of the rest of you could hit an ox.'

I resented this; I had practised at sea until I had a fair aim. 'Benvenuto,' I hissed, 'why do you forever need to be the first and the best?' John caught my eye. He too had shown himself handy with a gun, and fired and reloaded wearing a calm smile. But there was no time to quarrel. A cheering was springing up round us, the firing was falling silent, and many of the men on the ramparts actually jumped down and began running off into the lanes between the houses, shouting 'Victory! Victory!'

'Now, in the name of God, can we go?' Alessandro picked himself up. He was still shaking.

None of us answered. I peered into the fog. The ladders were abandoned. I saw bodies scattered on the ground, plumed helmets, dead men's beards lifting in the light breeze that blew the fog in swirls, the wounded trying to rise. I did not trust what I saw. Martin was at my side. He had no weapon, but had been helping me to reload my gun. Horses' hoofs could be heard out in the fog. The cannon of Sant' Angelo still fired, their shots landing at random in the vineyards and the marsh. Martin and I looked at one another, and our looks both said the same: they will not give up.

Slowly at first the sound grew. In a moment it was a roar, thousands of throats all shouting at once, with the drums and the trumpets sounding in concert. The first volley of gunfire hit the walls, and then the Spanish were at the ladders again. We ducked back, and fired, and fired again. There was no longer any question of Cellini's troop withdrawing. We would have left a fifty-foot length of the walls unmanned: there were so few left to defend them. Those soldiers who had run off into the city with news of the Imperials' defeat prudently never returned. Soon we had thrown all our bombs, and the men round us were pouring cauldrons of flaming oil down on the attackers, who screamed and fell burning. After that we threw whatever we could, rubble, bricks, dead men's swords. Still they came on. The Spaniards fought madly, with desperation on their faces as they reached the rampart and were shot down. They knew that with Bourbon dead there was nothing to keep them together. If they did not take Rome swiftly, they would break apart, and the League and the murderous countryfolk would hunt them down. It was at this time, I think, that many of us first became truly afraid. These were the walls that Renzo da Ceri had promised were so strong, and up the ladders before us came the enemy the Pope swore was so weak. Where were the reserves Renzo had posted throughout the city? Renzo himself, in his dazzling armour and feathered helmet, could be seen at intervals, walking along the foot of the walls, well clear of danger, shouting out to us that victory was near.

I fired, and then peered down at that crumbling farmhouse that was built into the walls. A squad of Spaniards was creeping along the base of the wall there, where the refuse was piled high. They were peering upwards. Before the mist blew thick again, I thought I saw an opening in the house wall into the city: a window or a hatch, around which I glimpsed the shapes of men. I nudged Cellini, and told him.

'Are you sure?'

'No. But aim all your fire there.'

We fired off a round of shots; but we had all we could do to keep the enemy off the ladders in front of us. A young man who had danced with the courtesans last night lay with half his face shot away; Alessandro had subsided again at his side, moaning with fear.

Then, from behind us, Renzo da Ceri shouted out those words that have made him so infamous. 'The enemy are inside! Every man save himself who can!'

All round us, men who had stood before the enemy's fire for two hours, their fear growing by the minute, threw down their guns and ran for the stairways. Some ten Spaniards, no more, emerged from the farmhouse and took aim on the fleeing soldiers. More of our men jumped down, and all along the walls it was the same. A rout. Behind them, the first of the Spaniards climbed over the tops of the ladders on to the ramparts. Cellini, his brows drawing down in rage, muttered, 'We can do no more good here.'

We sprang down the walls and began running: Benvenuto, Alessandro, John, Martin and I, and some three more of the guards from the palazzo. More and more Spaniards were pouring from the old abandoned house. A burst of shot flew after us, and another one of Cellini's men fell. To our left rose the front of Saint Peter's: a vaunting folly, half ruin, half unfinished dream, its arches bleak against the fog. From the Hospital of the Holy Spirit came the screams of the sick, who were being slaughtered in their beds. Ahead of us, where the Vatican Hill sloped down to the river, we could see Renzo's plumed helmet as he ran ahead of the rest, and soldiers and townspeople streamed after him. I could hear the enemy behind us, crashing through the vineyard and round the Cardinal's sculpture garden. When I glanced back I saw they were not even troubling to reload, but were running on with their swords drawn, cutting down men in their path. Suddenly we came to the river and stopped at a twisting lane that led left and right among watermills, quaysides and villas.

'Which way?' I gasped. The mist was lifting. Across the Tiber I saw the outlines of the low houses and taverns that flanked Cellini's new workshop; but a hundred yards of turbulent, brown water separated us. The only bridge from the Borgo lay to the left, upstream, before the castle. Most of the crowd were turning right, following Renzo towards the second of Rome's suburbs, Trastevere. This had walls of its own, and from it three separate bridges led across the river to the city. But the gate was a good way off, and the road was already blocked by fleeing crowds, soldiers and townspeople mixed.

Cellini looked down towards Trastevere, and seemed to think. 'No,' he murmured. 'Back.' He led us to the left. Gunfire crashed behind us. Across the street that led back up to Saint Peter's the few hundred Swiss that the Pope had kept in his service were drawn up: true soldiers, who took aim on our pursuers and fired a concerted volley. The Spaniards were stopped, but soon they returned fire. We ran on. The crowds were thick here, nobles and cardinals on their gaudily trapped mules with their servants round them, ladies in their litters, all pouring out from their palazzi. Before us, its gaunt drum tower looming over all the city, rose the Castle of Sant' Angelo. Once a tomb for emperors; now the last refuge of Rome.

Beyond the Swiss, a party of Spaniards were firing up at the city walls. I turned to look. They were shooting up at the Passetto, the secret passage built into the walls that ran from the Pope's palace to the castle. I saw a flash of red at the narrow windows as the cardinals accompanying His Holiness ran by; all of them had been taken utterly by surprise. Over the Tiber, from out of the city itself, people poured across the bridge making for the castle. I saw old Cardinal Pucci in his scarlet knocked from his mule and trampled, and others pushed over the parapet into the river, where they were swiftly swept away. At the gate, ladies, courtiers and bishops were pressed tight, screaming, shoving, unable to move. I saw Gregorio Casale, the ambassador of England, and Cardinal Campeggio, both of whose palazzi were nearby. We too were slowing down, mired among humanity.

'Benvenuto!' I shouted above the din. 'The jewels!' Over the river in Cellini's chest were my treasures: the ship, the green diamond garden, the opal cross: and, dearer than all of them, my diamond of Golconda.

'We won't cross the river by that bridge,' he answered. 'Not now.'

Further volleys rang out. Back up the street I saw the last of the Swiss fall. They had stood their ground to the end. Ahead of us soldiers sallied out from the castle. For a moment it seemed they would rally the Pope's forces, and make some attempt to drive the invaders back from the Borgo. But instead they set about breaking down the doors of nearby shops and houses and dragging out barrels, hams and cheeses, sacks of bread: provisions for a siege which no one had foreseen. Then they pushed back through the crowd to the gate. Benvenuto was forcing his way after them, with John, Martin and Alessandro close at his side. If I followed him, the castle would swallow me up. For how long, who could tell? And my jewels: I could not leave my jewels.

I looked back. Spaniards and Romans were running down the streets together, a confused mass of killers and killed. But the soldiers had not yet reached the street along the river. Ahead, Benvenuto and the rest were being sucked in through the gate. Martin turned and stretched out his hand to me, shouting 'Master!' Then they were gone. I turned and pushed back through the crowd, and then I began to run. I passed fleeing men and women, their faces wild with terror, and then towards us came the Spaniards. They were swinging their swords, cutting down the townspeople as they ran.

'Spain, Spain! Kill, kill!'

I slipped into a doorway. I could not stay here unseen for long. In a few moments they would be level with me and drag me out. I slowly drew my sword from its scabbard. A group of men ran by, a noble-man, hatless and terrified, with his servants. I stepped suddenly out into the street, my sword raised above my head.

'Kill! Kill!' The cry felt like poison in my throat. The men darted ahead of me, and as I ran on a Spaniard came abreast of me. He was dressed in a puffed doublet and short cloak with a feathered hat, his teeth bared behind a full black beard. His sword came down on the first of the men, a sickening sound like a butcher's knife, and cleft him at the shoulder. Blood spurted across the stones, the Spaniard wrenched his sword free and ran on. It was without sense. I felt bile rising in my throat. But still I forced myself to run on and shout that terrible cry, waving my sword and slicing within inches of the pursued. I had become a Spaniard. We were almost back to the castle. The portcullis had at last been dropped, and the struggling crowd cleft in two. Inside, the bolder Imperial soldiers who had pushed ahead were being quickly slaughtered, while those Romans caught outside were darting this way and that, desperately searching for safety.

Beyond, by the bridge, the crowd paused in dismay and began to push backwards. At the foot of the walls was Cardinal Armellini, a man of vast wealth with whom I and the Cages had once dined. I had visions of that meal, the gold plates, the lobsters and the peacocks. Now he danced about, trapped outside with his helpless servants, until a basket was lowered from the battlements on a rope, and he was raised, swaying, up the wall. The Spaniards laughed and trained their guns on him, but at that moment a tremendous thunder of cannon broke from the castle, crashing into the nearby houses and throwing stones, limbs, bodies into the air. The Spaniards scattered back into the streets, and I ran with them, not looking back, not caring who was following me; back past the crossroads where Cellini had paused, and the little watermill, and the ropes that stretched across the river for the use of the ferry. I considered for a moment. The ferryboat rested on the bank, a little skiff that could hold about six people. It would be easy to jump in and pull myself across the river using the ropes. But that would be a fool's notion. The soldiers would see me; I was in plain view from the Castle too, and the Pope's gunners might take me for an Imperial. No, but those ropes, lying submerged in the yellow-brown water, invisible in the foam of the recent rain: that might be a thought. I looked back. A group of soldiers was moving towards me, but they stopped to break down the door of a villa and push inside, shouting and firing off their guns. For the moment, the street was clear. I scrambled down to the water's edge, sheathed my sword, and waded out among the reeds. Then, with both hands clenched on one of the ropes, I pulled myself out into the waters of the Tiber.

20

It was easy going at first. The current did not pull hard, and the sounds of firing, shouts and cries grew more distant behind me. What peace it was, to have water rippling over me and round me: water that had flowed down out of the mountains, past Orvieto and down the Tiber Vale, where surely the Venetians and the Duke of Urbino were marching hard for the relief of Rome. I extended one arm after the other, my head just clearing the water. Three hundred arm's lengths, perhaps, to get over. I pulled, and pulled again. But I had to rest. The current tugged harder here, further from the bank. I gasped, swallowed a gulp of the yellow, mud-laden water. Drowning would be so easy. I peered ahead. I had the odd feeling that the far bank was getting no nearer; in fact, it seemed further than ever.

From behind me I heard splashes and shouts. The boat was pulling out from the bank with ten or so men, Papal soldiers, all piled in together and yanking on the rope for their lives. The rope ran in a loop: to my horror I realised I had hold of the other strand, and they were slowly hauling me back in towards the shore of the Borgo. I set about pulling myself along with all my strength, but I could make no headway against so many strong hands. The reeds, the street with the villas and the Spaniards swarming along it, the watermill I had just left: all were growing closer and closer, as was the ferryboat itself, the men inside glancing back with fear. Then from the bank I heard shots. One of the soldiers tumbled over the side, his face pouring blood. Another dropped, and another, and then the rest all together dived over and were swiftly swept off in the current, their arms reaching up like paintings of men swallowed by Hell. The boat ceased moving. The Imperials, laughing, went back to their plunder. I was alone once more, almost back where I started. My arms shook with weakness. But I began again, pulling myself slowly, painfully, back out into the river. The current tugged stronger, and then stronger; surely I was more than halfway over, and nearing the inside of the bend where the water was swiftest. I closed my eyes, while my arms still reached, first one, then the other, and I pictured to myself my diamond, lying waiting in Cellini's shop, calling me to hang on, keep going, come and save it. And then, cursing my lack of loyalty, I pictured Hannah, and imagined meeting her when all this was over, her eyes becoming soft with concern as she listened to the tales of my pains. God grant she was well clear by now and off to sea.

I felt something snagging my foot, and opened my eyes ready to struggle and fight to the death. But before me I saw reeds, and the rope sloping upwards out of the water to its iron ring and post. For a moment I thought I was back in the Borgo, and froze. But everything here was quiet. I dragged myself slowly out of the river and fell weak and shaking on the ground. The bells of the city were ringing. From close by came the solemn booming of the great church of the Florentines. I was in Rome: I was safe. The river was a barrier stronger by far than those miserable, decayed old city walls. I stood up, laughing out loud. My purse was gone, washed away in the river. But the casket that had in it my unset stones, my dark emerald, my cats' eyes, my great ruby and my bills, was safe. It was nearly midday. I was hungry: I needed to buy food. That was my first concern. My jewels would be safe enough for the moment, locked in Cellini's chest. At my inn I had a small store of money. I looked round, and staggered up an alley that led between the houses into the Florentine quarter. On the Via Giulia there were groups of people hurrying this way and that. A merchant clutching a small casket, three or four nuns, a group of soldiers without weapons. One of them wore a sash of command. I stopped him.

'What news?'

'There has been a parley. What's come of it, I do not know.'

'But what orders have you for the defence of Rome?'

'There are no orders. No one commands. Hide yourself where you can!'

The soldier ran on. I reeled down the street, heading south. I was afraid again. As I passed the Palazzo Farnese I saw a horde of people pressing in for shelter. Others streamed north, making for Don Martin's strong-built house with its tower and cannons, or the palazzi of Cardinals Araceli, Ceserino and Piccolomini: men who were known to be loyal to the Empire, and whom the Spaniards and Germans would not harm.

I saw an aged nun hurrying across the square, her skirts lifted up, clutching under her arm a jewel-studded box of relics. She would not have left her cloister, perhaps, in forty years. She looked round in fear: the open spaces, the hurrying crowds were enough to daunt her, without the appearance of the troops. Even in the midst of this rush and panic, there were still those who lounged against the corners of buildings, watching with smiles. The Imperials would never cross the river, they thought. But who was to stop them? Renzo da Ceri had shut himself up in the castle with the Pope. There were no Papal forces to be seen. Either they were still resolutely manning the walls far across the ruins to the east, or they had simply melted away. Our only chance lay in destroying the four bridges over the river. But no one had given the order. 'Who would build them up again?' I heard one man mutter. 'Us, that's who, with our taxes. Let the bridges stand. The Imperials won't cross.'

Trumpets sounded from behind me, and the beating of drums. There was fresh gunfire coming from the south, towards Trastevere. I was almost at the Campo dei Fiori, but I turned back and ran down to the river to see. I came out just upstream from the Bridge of Sixtus. Fleeing soldiers and townspeople were hurrying across it towards me, while from over the river the drums were coming nearer. Across the bridge lay the suburb of Trastevere; our men had abandoned its walls and run. As I watched, a column of Imperial soldiers came down out of the town, and others appeared from left and right along the river. On the bridge, one small group of Papal guards halted under their banner, which bore the words Faith and Fatherland. They turned and fired, but the Imperials bore down on them, and after a short battle I saw the standard fall and the Imperials sweep forwards across the bridge. They were close: so close that I could hear their cry: 'God and the Emperor!' It was the cry that had carried them hundreds of miles down over the Alps, through the hungry campaign around Milan and the ineffectual attempt at Florence. They had had precious little reward yet for their sufferings. Now they were loose in the richest city in the world. I watched, rooted with horror, as they crossed the bridge and ran on in close order into the streets. Behind them came bands of Spaniards, greedier and less cautious, who scattered at once this way and that, harrying the pursued and cutting them down: men and women, monks and priests, merchants and nobles.

I turned and ran, back up the Via Giulia and into the lanes. It was too late to reach the inn. My one thought was for my gems. I came out, panting, on the riverbank by the old blacksmith's shop Cellini used as a workshop. Of course it was locked. I shook the bars on the windows and beat my shoulder against the oak door, but they defeated me. Well: my stones were safe. What I needed was a place to hide, not far off, from which I could keep guard. And after all, it would not be for long. The League would be here soon. The Duke of Urbino had acted with caution when Bourbon's huge force was on the march and ready for battle. But it would be an easy matter for the French and Venetians to sweep away a leaderless army, drunk with plunder. I crept behind a low shed nearby, where there was an old anvil, some split roof-timbers and other refuse. I waited. I felt weak; my clothes were still wet and I was racked with shudders. I needed to run, or fight, merely to keep my courage. From all round came the sounds of terrible cries, running feet, shots.

Suddenly a group of men burst into the lane. A dozen or so, speaking Spanish. They were arguing about the foolishness of exploring so derelict a region, where there was nothing but a few poor artisans' huts. Their captain agreed. Then they caught sight of Cellini's door and stopped. Such a well-fortified dwelling interested them. The captain ordered them to bring up one of the timbers and break down the door. I crouched lower as they approached the pile I was hiding behind. The men swung their beam, and at the fourth blow the hinges leapt from the walls. They dropped the beam with cries of triumph and streamed inside. I peered forward, seething with frustration and rage. There was nothing I could do.

I heard their captain's voice from inside. 'No! This house is mine. Go and find your own. Meet me back at the church later.'

Grumbling, the men obeyed. I watched them troop back up the lane towards the Via Giulia. The Spanish captain was alone. I crept out from behind the beams. From inside the shop came the sound of blows: he could not hear me approaching. I was at the doorway; I looked in. The Spaniard, a tall man in a green velvet doublet and a broad hat with three red feathers, was bending over the lock of Benvenuto's chest. At his side rested a harquebus. He swung a hammer: that same hammer with which Cellini had beaten out the gold to make the Ship. It was too slender a tool for the job; but he succeeded in bending the hasp, hooked the hammer behind it, and prised the lock apart with a wrenching twist. His back was to me. As he lifted the lid of the chest I stole inside the room.

'Aah!' First he lifted out sheets of thin-beaten gold, and a bag of coins. He chuckled, and then came the laugh of triumph: the laugh of a man who has found the treasure of a lifetime. He had found my emerald pendant, and the opal cross. 'So very imprudent to hide here,' he murmured, lifting them and turning them in the light. 'But I will keep you safe.' Both of these he slipped into a pouch at his side. Then he found my diamond. He lifted it slowly and turned it in his fingers, murmuring to himself: 'You are so shy. Why will you not shine for me?' There was cruelty in it; it was the soft voice of a man about to commit a rape. I paced round behind him. If I could catch him now, while my stones held him in their power. Slowly, slowly I began to draw out my sword. He turned the stone again, and suddenly he must have caught that ray of light.

'Ho!' He stood dazzled, immobile, unspeaking. My sword cleared its scabbard with the faintest rasp of steel. The Spaniard swung round, the stone in his left fist while with his right he snatched up the harquebus. He fired. The report deafened me, and the room filled with smoke. But a harquebus is a heavy weapon to lift one-handed. The shot buried itself in the floor, sending up splinters of earthenware tile. I sprang forward with a downward cut of my blade. The Spaniard jumped back and drew his sword. He parried well. I was tired, hungry, utterly drained; and perhaps he was too. But we fought like demons. The age-old temptation of man was upon us: gold, treasure, the beautiful precious things that grow underground. My diamond gave us both power. I deployed the *punta*, the downward strokes and the sideways flying strokes and the upwards wheel. He kept on the defence, sensing that I would soon tire. And indeed my arm was like lead. That rope across the Tiber had cost me much. The Spaniard lifted his left hand and let me see the diamond. He smiled. 'Yours?'

I nodded grimly. He closed his fist again.

'No longer. Now it belongs to Don Adriano de Córdoba.'

He sprang at me. His blows came fast, his wrist deft, swinging the blade now this way, now that. I was an instant behind with my replies, and he caught me on my sleeve, ripping through the cloth. He smiled. He could see his triumph coming. His eyes flicked for an instant to his left hand. He was thinking of that wonderful moment when the light glances down, down, alongside the snaking white flaw, and the eye takes in all the stone's beauties at once. He was wondering, maybe, how easy it would be to catch that moment again. My blade flowed from a parry into a thrust. We were chest to chest. I gazed into his eyes that were wide with amazement. Only the hilt of my sword was showing, the rest buried in his flesh. Slowly he fell against the coffer as my sword slid out again in a rush of blood, and he landed face-down on the floor. Blood began to spread round the body in a pool. I stooped down and prised the diamond from his fingers.

I ran to the door. There was no one in sight. Shots continued to ring out, and the louder cannonfire of the Castle. I crossed back to the body and retrieved my other treasures, the emerald pendant and opal cross, as well as the soldier's purse with a few silver coins. Then I sat down at Benvenuto's workbench, exhausted. There was the Perseus, the sketches, the model for Cardinal Cibo's candlestick, the furnace in the corner. Things so familiar, witnesses now to murder.

I took the diamond in my fingers. It was mine again. But I had to convince myself it had not suffered, and could still speak to me as it used to; like a tender virgin snatched in time from the hands of her ravisher. I turned the stone and let the light pierce down, down, rebounding, whispering, echoing, breaking into blue, green, vermilion, stroking the white flank of the flaw, then twining back up again and out. I shivered. I turned it again, and let the white mist spread over its surface, smooth, rippling, seductive. A dizzy weakness passed over me. The sounds from outside, the shots and screams, came dimly as if from a vast distance. How fortunate I was to be alone here at last; at last to have time to turn the stone, slowly and with loving care. Every time I lost that gleam I felt a stab of grief and loss, but then I turned it and caught once more that darting plunge of colours into its depths; just as when Hannah's moods altered in an instant, the warmth so much more beguiling because it burst suddenly from the cold.

But the light in the diamond was changing. It was growing deeper, more sombre, the reds and the blues gathering strength at the expense of the yellows and greens. The change fascinated me. It was a long time before its cause penetrated my brain. Night was coming. I had had no idea I had sat so very long. When I moved my arm it had no strength. Very soon it would be too late to leave. I would die like this, of all the stone's owners the most fortunate; the only one to have seen so deeply into its heart. I ought to fight this, rouse myself. But the thought of that death did not trouble me. My temples throbbed.

From outside came a scream, close by, and the sound of running feet. I jerked suddenly upright. I was alert now, and afraid. The soldiers would come back. They would miss their captain; they would find me. I hurried to hide the diamond in the casket round my neck. I lurched to my feet, swayed and went down on my knees, and then crawled across the floor to the chest. I took out the rest of my jewels, and dug deeper too. A purse of coin; the sheets of gold leaf; a pouch of mixed precious stones. These I took, meaning to return them to Benvenuto. I froze. The quick footsteps came nearer. Outside the shattered door a woman ran by with three soldiers pursuing her. Once more it was quiet. I returned to the Spaniard's body and stripped off the cloak, a short soldier's cape, black with russet trim. My own cloak with its silver edging I left behind. I threw aside my cap too, having removed the gold medal of the Virgin, and put on the Spaniard's broad, feathered hat instead. I gathered up the harquebus, powder flasks and shot. Then I looked out of the door. My head was beating. It was dusk. Cannon thundered at intervals from the Castle. A red light suffused the sky.

I ran out, round the corner and back up to the Via Giulia. Bodies lay on the stones, caked in dust and mud: nobles, women still clutching children. From the church of Saint Catherine of Siena, down the street, came the most horrible screams mixed with men's shouts and gunfire. Blood smeared the church's steps. In the street below lay a great gilded statue of Saint Catherine. The saint lay face-downwards; bloody hand-prints covered her back where the soldiers had dragged her out. Round her were chalices, pattens, jewelled reliquaries and candlesticks, crosses, vases of silver, gold reliefs of the Passion of Christ.

I gazed too long; a German came at me with his sword and I darted back, drawing mine. But he only wished to defend his hoard, shouted something and turned back. I saw him sit down on a small chest and begin pulling at a wizened, severed finger: a holy relic mounted in gold. Earlier that day the faithful had come to kiss it and pray over it. Now the German teased the dead flesh from its gold with his dagger, and threw it on the ground.

I walked on, in a dream. From every house there came the sound of shouts, breaking doors, shots. A cry from above made me jump back. A shape fell in front of me, and landed hard on the stones. It was a girl in nothing but her shift: dead. Blood poured from her head. I choked and ran on. Ahead the firing was more intense. Here was the palazzo of Cardinal Piccolomini of Siena: staunch friend of the Empire. But that meant nothing now. He had refused to pay a ransom, and the Germans had surrounded his house and were exchanging gunfire with those inside. By the English church I saw the statues and the crosses carried away on men's shoulders, bodies on the steps where I had first caught sight of John in Rome. Two dead monks, lying in their own gore; a young nun, caught by three Spaniards and raped in the street before the convent of Saint Brigida. I did not know where I was going, or why; scarcely even who I was. On the Campo dei Fiori the shop doors and windows were shattered, the soldiers handing out fruit and flasks of wine. For these were hungry men, and it was a hard question which they had the greatest greed for, gold, or women, or bread. I took a loaf, and bolted down a few mouthfuls, then doubled over and was sick in a gutter that stank of blood.

I do not know how, but I was walking again; past the Papal Chancellery, from whose windows flew storms of papers and books. I saw men and women led off bound, prisoners, with the fear of death stamped on every face. I was turning on to the Via Monserrato, drawn along the old, familiar route. I passed a house that still held out, where the soldiers had piled up sticks and furniture outside, already alight, to burn the place down. I turned into the quiet old square with the yellow stuccoed palace; the palace so impregnable; guarded, thanks to Alessandro's care, by an army fifty strong. I looked up at the walls. Bullets had smashed into Polidoro's frescos. A body hung from a window; two more lay in the street. The door stood open.

I went inside. There was the hall I had entered that day with Cellini, drawn by that name, Hannah Cage. There were the stairs where I had bowed to Stephen and said 'Richard Dansey. Merchant, of London.' Dead men lay there now. That was Alessandro's chamberlain, with a sword cut from his shoulder to his chest. Those two were Cellini's friends, their guns at their sides. The steps were slippery with blood. I climbed them, shaking, holding on to the marble balustrade for support. At the top of the stairs, where the balcony swept round, another body lay, face-down, a bloody gash across the back of his head. He had been running away, and a soldier had slashed him from behind. I turned him over with my foot, and then I cried out. It was the Cages' chamberlain, Fenton. I stared into his white face, the familiar beard, the heavy eyebrows, the open mouth, as if it could ever utter again, 'Sir, the cloth is spread.'

In horror I pushed open the door into the sala. One of the tapestries had been torn down, the credenza smashed. Chairs and stools lay scattered, and there were bodies everywhere. Close to the door was one of the Cages' minstrels, the man who had had the quickest fingers on the recorder; there beyond him was the music-master who bent over Mrs Susan as she played the lute, and tactfully corrected her fingering. The door to the saletta was open. Lying across it, her skirts pulled up round her waist and her throat slit, was one of the gentlewomen who had sported with us on the night of the *moccoli*. They were all here.

I went on. I was only waiting to find Hannah. Through the saletta where we had played cards, along the loggia, up the stairs to the more private apartments where I had never been. Up here were bedchambers, and bodies, more bodies. Each door I opened trembling. The waiting maids, the valets; faces so familiar, so taken as a matter of course, lying dead. I pushed open another door, to another bedchamber. Perhaps this was where she had slept. Perhaps, if I had not run after my diamond to Florence, this was where I might have slept too. There was an inner closet opening off it. I opened the door and stepped through.

A heavy blow knocked me to the ground. I lay there, striving to lift myself, my head clogged with dizziness and pain. My limbs no longer had any strength. I heard a voice over me:

'Kill him.'

21

I would have been dead already, if it had not been for the Spaniard's thick felt hat. As it was, the blood was running down into my face. I groaned and managed to lift myself on my hands. The voice came again:

'Kill him!'

It was useless to try to rise. Long before I could reach my sword, a blade would slide into my back. A second voice hissed, 'You kill him.'

'No, you!'

There was something strange about these voices. My right hand gave way, and I rolled on to my back. My eyes were a blur. But I could not be wrong: they had been speaking in English. Both the speakers let out shrieks; and then all at once my vision cleared, and I saw standing over me Susan and Hannah Cage, the one holding a roasting spit, the other a flatiron. Hannah dropped the iron and was down on the floor, cradling my head.

'My poor, poor, poor Mr Richard.'

Susan stepped over me into the bedchamber. 'Someone could have followed him. Can't you stop dandling him and take him up?'

I tried to rise, and with both girls helping at last I managed. I fell at once into Hannah's arms. I would not let her go; I had found her, that was all I knew. I kissed her hair, her lips, her eyes. She stood motionless, and let me.

'That's enough!' hissed Susan. 'Quickly!'

Hannah disengaged herself. The room we were in had been a dressing room, and a place for admiring little ornaments and works of art. Now it had been ransacked. Broken glass scattered the floor. Hannah led me to a ladder reaching up to a trapdoor in the ceiling. Somehow I climbed it, and the ladder was pulled up after us. We were in near darkness up here. A warren of storerooms, servants' chambers and passages wound above the two wings of the palazzo, they explained to me, reached by a number of ladders and narrow stairs.

'That ladder is the only way down from here,' whispered Hannah. 'We were on our way to look for food.'

'Until Hannah nearly murdered you,' added Susan.

'You would have done it if you'd dared,' countered Hannah.

'Quiet!' answered Susan. 'We're getting near. Another shock will kill her.'

They were leading me, bent double, down a dim passage. At the end of it opened out a room that was little more than a big cupboard, cramped under the eaves. Inside it, something moved.

Susan crept forward. 'Mother. We have found Mr Richard.'

As my eyes adjusted to the dark, I saw that the figure hunched against the end wall was Mrs Grace. Her black hair was streaked down over her face. She held out to me a shaking hand.

'Mr Richard! It is very good of you to come. You are welcome. Girls! Find Mr Richard some of those sweetmeats. The almond ones are the finest. I cannot think what has become of our servants.'

Hannah and Susan exchanged looks. I sat clumsily down against the sloping wall. My head was still bleeding. Hannah tore off a strip of her gown and set about bandaging the wound. Susan moved in the darkness and came back with a shallow silver dish. 'She's right. The almond ones *are* the nicest. But I would give anything for a loaf of bread.'

At that I smiled, and pulled from my doublet the loaf. Susan fell on it, and divided it at once in four. Eating, and with Hannah's body warm against my side, I felt my strength and my courage return. Grace heaved a satisfied sigh. 'When Mr Stephen gets back, everything will be arranged.'

Hannah anxiously caught my eye, and I looked at her in question. And so I heard the story of their flight, told by Hannah and Susan in turn. They had set off through the Gate of Saint Paul yesterday afternoon, to cover the fifteen miles to Ostia. Even though no one, officially, was allowed out of Rome, the number of people who had begged or bribed permission to go was surprising. Stretches of the road were flooded, and what with the fleeing countryfolk with their carts, progress was slow. When night fell they were still out in the desolation of the marshes. That was when Stephen had ridden on ahead to scout the road. While he was gone, a party of horsemen had swept down on them, shooting off their harquebuses and veering away, before returning to shoot once more. They might have been Imperials who had somehow crossed the Tiber, or members of the powerful Colonna clan, enemies of the Pope, or simply brigands. The packhorses bolted; some of the servants driving the carts panicked and drove off into the marsh. The whole line of carts that was jamming the road somehow reversed itself and surged back towards the city. Grace and her family were jostled along with them. Bales and boxes dropped from their carts; by the time they got back to the locked city gates they had a good deal less than when they had started. By now it was perhaps two or three in the morning. Hannah and Susan wanted to make another dash along the road to Ostia, but Grace would not hear of it. Stephen was bound to come back for them. She had always known this hasty flight from Rome was a mistake. They spent a cold, unsleeping night outside the gates, waiting. But Stephen never came. Mist crept up from the pools that lined the road. With dawn, in that thick fog that had so aided the Imperials' attack, Grace ordered them all back to the palazzo: doubtless Stephen was there waiting for them; or would be back soon and make other plans. Stephen would arrange everything.

But Cellini and Alessandro were gone, and the battle was already loud from over the river. They had nothing to fear, Grace protested. After all, England was neutral in this war; it was nothing to do with them. As the sounds of fighting drew nearer, Cellini's men began to desert them. When the Spaniards and Germans swept at last up from the bridges, there were scarcely ten armed men to stand against them. Room by room Grace and her daughters retreated. It was Susan who found the trapdoor; Hannah who snatched up the sweetmeats that had stood on the table by her bed. They had had the greatest trouble with their mother. The firing, the killing of their servants, glimpsed through the windows of the loggia: none of this could Grace truly believe. She wanted to go down to them, declare who she was, explain to the Imperials their mistake. It was only the promise of Stephen's return that had induced her to climb the ladder. There they had crouched, hour after hour, while the killing and looting went on. The soldiers had made a thorough search. They had heard them, shouting to one another and throwing down furniture in disgust; but most of the plunder, of course, was in those boxes hastily unloaded from the carts and stacked in the entrance hall, which the first soldiers had speedily hurried away; the rolls of tapestry, the silver, Mr Stephen's books, the recorders and lutes. At last it had fallen silent. Only at nightfall had the two girls judged it worth the risk of descending in the hope of finding food.

'And now we have eaten our bread, and the sweetmeats are finished too,' said Susan. 'Hannah?'

'I know there are more, down in the stillroom.'

'Be sure to bring us some of the candied pears,' put in Grace. 'The ones that were a gift from Cardinal Ceci. But I really think we should wait for Stephen downstairs. He will never find us up here.'

I struggled to raise myself. 'I must be the one to go out. I can pass as a Spaniard. Promise me you will not leave here.' My head throbbed, and I fell back against Hannah's shoulder.

Susan frowned. 'He is right. If he can walk.'

Hannah brushed my hair from my brow. 'Later. First you should sleep.' Already I was drifting into a dark blank. Fire, screams, running feet, the cannons and the drums; they beat round and round in my head, growing fainter, until all that was left was Hannah's gentle breathing, the soft warmth of her body. As I slipped asleep we were passing together through France, laughing at the horrors of Italy, just a few days' travel from home.

I woke suddenly. It was after dawn. A white light penetrated the chinks between the roof tiles above us. Hannah lay asleep on her side. Grace, slumped at the end of the chamber, looked old and drawn; as if only in sleep could she grasp the true dread of our position. I lifted myself on one arm. I felt weak, but my head no longer throbbed. Susan crouched at the end of the chamber closest to the trapdoor. She whispered, 'There is someone down below.'

I listened. There was the patter of feet, a rummaging, and a scratching sound. I held my breath. Then there came what sounded like a baby's whimpers, and low animal squeaks. Susan turned to me with an impish grin.

'Beelzebub!'

She pulled back the trapdoor, and the monkey danced up and down, baring its teeth and chattering.

'We must get him away,' I hissed. 'He will betray us.'

'Kill him is best,' said Susan.

'No!' Hannah sat up. She leant forward fiercely. 'That is what you always wanted.'

'What if it is?'

'Girls!' put in Grace. 'We shall let Mr Richard decide.'

I was buckling on my sword and taking up the harquebus. 'Stay here,' I warned them. Susan let down the ladder. I descended quickly, and watched the trapdoor close again above me. Then I turned to look for Piccolino. He could so easily be the death of us, if soldiers returned to the palazzo. But the beast had gone.

I walked out through the chambers that smelt of death, down through the sala, listening all the way. A few sweetmeats would not keep us alive. I had to find some real nourishment. Out in the square a damp fog hung, the same as the day before. Through it came the muted sounds of the Sack, cannonfire from the Castle, gunshots, screams. I pulled the Spaniard's short cape round me and ran north. Along the Banchi, I saw Spanish and German officers trying to gather up their men. But with Bourbon dead, the soldiers simply laughed. 'We have no master now.' There were Italians in the Imperial army too: Neapolitans, Sienese, Romans who belonged to the vast clan of the Colonnas. His Holiness had burnt their villages and driven away their flocks. Now these men were back. They killed with as much fury as the rest, and where they went they daubed on the walls the single word, *VENDETTA*. Vengeance.

I passed by the house of Juan Perez, the Imperial ambassador, and of Don Martin too, whose palazzo everyone had thought so strong. The doors stood open. Those cannon on Don Martin's roof had not saved him. The dead lay everywhere, new corpses falling across the old. Soldiers squatted in the streets, playing dice over their piles of gold crucifixes and bags of ducats and jewels, and even bound prisoners, a handsome woman or a rich-looking merchant. Some lost all they had in a few throws, and went back to the churches and palazzi for more. The flow of treasure seemed without end. It was an hour, or two or three, before I gathered my senses together, broke into a row of abandoned shops off the Piazza Navona and snatched up sausages and bread and wine. As I was coming back past the little church of Santa Maria in Vallicella, an officer in a crimson sash stopped me and demanded something in German. I tried to push by, but he repeated it. There was no one else in sight. I swung the harquebus from my shoulder and shot him. I murmured to myself, '*Vendetta.*'

When I got back, the Palazzo del Bene was as still and quiet as a charnel house. Flies settled on the bodies, and rose in buzzing swarms as I hurried up the stairs. In the closet I whispered to Hannah and Susan to let down the ladder. Back up in the dimness of the attic I began to shake. There was triumph, exhilaration in being back in that strange pocket of femininity, with not only my Hannah but the other two women relying on me utterly. Mrs Grace smiled. With what looked like a great effort she said, 'Tell us the news in the city.'

I paused before I answered, 'Not good.'

'You must tell us the worst,' said Susan. 'Does anywhere hold out?'

'Only the Castle.'

'You can lead us away from here,' Hannah said. 'You can smuggle us through a gate, or over the city wall? Can you not, dear Mr Richard?'

Her voice was bright and wheedling, just as if she were teasing me into letting her watch the dwarf race, or finding her a second cup of wine. Slowly I shook my head. I had been out as far as the walls, and I knew that beyond the heart of the city the army still behaved like an army. They had patrols, and regular changes of the guard. They meant to make sure no relief could come to the Pope.

'In that case,' Susan said, 'we must get into the Castle.'

I said nothing. To break into Sant' Angelo: if it was beyond the power of thirty thousand besiegers, it was clearly beyond ours.

'But you will think of something,' Hannah said. 'Of course you will.'

* * *

Day by day I crept down from the attic out into the square. First, I always made my way north to the river and gazed across to the Castle of Sant' Angelo. Squat and immoveable it crouched, with its square outer battlements and corner turrets, its massive drum tower, and the taller tower rising inside that. From the top the Papal banner still flew. The cannon thundered, their shots falling on the Pope's own city. As yet the Imperials had no cannon of their own. Soldiers returned fire with harquebuses from the shelter of house windows, but they were no challenge to the Castle's power. His Holiness refused to negotiate, trusting in the Duke of Urbino and the League. Between the Imperial marksmen and the stark castle walls was a bleak region of burnt-out buildings and corpses, the snaking river and the deserted bridge of Sant' Angelo. I saw no hope in that direction.

I turned and hurried into the city on my daily search for food. Some days I did well, and came back with a good supply; some days I found nothing. On the third day Prince Philibert of Orange, who claimed to be general of the army now that Bourbon was dead, ordered the looting and killing to stop. But the soldiers only pillaged all the more, broke into the Apostolic Palace, which the Prince had claimed as his personal residence, and emptied it of all its barrels of wine.

Amid the horror, there were odd islands of normality. Some shops were open, and sold bread for coins; boys hurried through the streets to visit their fathers in the soldiers' many prisons, and cashed bills for ransom money at the banks, until they too were sacked. The brothels were decidedly open for business. I saw a group of Spaniards driving in a column of nuns, their hands bound, and heard the nuns' cries of *'Pietate, pietate!'* Pity, pity. At the door, a grinning old bawd took them in and handed the soldiers a purse of gold.

Shooting still rang out, houses burned, and fresh bodies fell on the piles. But the soldiers were discovering that Romans could be more useful alive. The city was full of hiding places, they reasoned secret tunnels, catacombs filled with hidden treasure. How were they to find these out, except by rounding up the citizens and exercising the arts of persuasion? Certain houses turned into grisly torture chambers. I saw men and women hanging from towers by their arms, and the screams from inside spoke of torments worse by far. The poor Cardinals Piccolomini, Araceli and Ceserino, who had always been such friends of the Empire, were led in chains through the streets every day, beaten and mocked by the soldiers. Then they were made to stand on a gallows in sight of the Castle. The Germans swore they would hang them unless the Pope surrendered. But after each day's ordeal they were dragged back to their prisons.

Up in the dark of the attic we sat for long, long hours, unspeaking. There was a kind of intense but chaste closeness; I shared with Hannah the touch of a hand, the sound of our breath. Breaking the silence came the screams of the poor prisoners. To distract our thoughts, I unlocked my casket and passed round my treasures. They had not seen my garden before, with its green diamond meadow and the nymphs' shimmering pool formed by the white sapphire. Grace took it in her hands with a long sigh. She closed her eyes and felt the outlines of the figures with her fingers. She was thinking of other days, perhaps, days at Court while King Henry was still young, and Stephen came wooing her with gifts; gifts almost as rich as the one in her hands. Her face creased and she began to weep. Hannah took her arm.

'We will get home, Mother,' she promised. 'We have Mr Richard now.'

Susan was holding up the Ship. In the splintered light through the roof tiles its diamonds glittered and the chrysoprase glowed like an eye. 'Look!' she said. 'A stormy sea. Very pretty.' She pointed to the sapphires with their white flaws and blurs. 'Like mine.' From her neck she drew a chain, from which hung a single blue-white stone.

'So you had it set,' I said. 'Benvenuto could have done it better.'

'Benvenuto was busy. And those diamonds: stars?'

I was growing testy. 'Yes.'

'Then it's night. And yet your sea is blue. At night the sea is grey, or black.'

I snatched the brooch back from her hands. I had been so very proud of the thing, the conception of it, the choice of stones and Cellini's work. I had never once seen the incongruity. I said, 'Does it matter?'

'No,' said Susan. 'Not in the least. It's all fantasy anyway. I told you: it's pretty.'

'Pretty enough to make my name,' I growled. I glanced at Hannah, annoyed. She was smiling, relishing the battle just as she had that first day at dinner when Susan goaded me over my manners.

'Fantasies,' Susan murmured. 'What would I give to see a real meadow, or a real ship either.' Suddenly she sat up and turned to her sister. 'Hannah! Show Mr Richard the gift John gave you.'

I looked at Hannah in astonishment. I had dismissed all my suspicions concerning her and John. Susan, surely, was concocting another of her malicious tales. But Hannah merely tossed her head. 'If he wishes to see.'

She turned back the lace of her collar to reveal a brooch. The gold of it was thin and ill-crafted; the stone at its centre a showy, red-orange cornelian, semi-transparent. It was a paltry thing, worth not more than twenty crowns, and yet more than I thought John could afford. Indignation made me speechless. She met my eyes with cool defiance, as if she were the injured one, not I. In the end I said, 'You took this – this thing from John? After refusing from me a diamond?'

Hannah tossed her head. 'You were so very high and mighty that night. And poor John: such a hangdog look he has. He was in need of encouragement.'

'Encouragement!'

I had raised my voice. Susan leant forward and hissed, 'Quiet! Do you two want to see us killed?'

I looked at Susan, her bright, penetrating eyes glinting like a pair of flawed sapphires. Her letter had perhaps not been so mistaken after all. Suddenly I felt Hannah pressing herself up against my arm. 'I was wrong. Will you forgive me?'

I turned to her and kissed her, there before her mother and sister. I would forgive her anything, over and over. The warmth of her body at my side was proof enough she was still mine.

'You do right to make amends,' Grace announced grandly, as if she were giving her daughter sound advice in private. 'I told you Mr John was no fit match.'

As Hannah drew back with another of her mysterious smiles, I looked beyond her to Mrs Grace. This, I thought, cast yet another light on what might have happened while I was in Florence. I pictured Grace pressing Hannah to accept me, the rich jewel merchant; and Hannah, resenting her mother's meddling, throwing herself at John out of spite. It gave me a little more comfort. But I could not so easily forgive John.

'Christ and all his saints,' muttered Susan. 'You sit here cooing and squabbling and drawing up love-matches. What are we going to do? Just what are we going to do?'

I gazed into the darkness. I had racked my wits for seven days, but I had no answer.

22

Still the Sack continued, and the soldiers grew all the time more
cruel and desperate. They dug up graves in their wild search after
treasure and flung out into the streets decaying skeletons and skulls.
They even shovelled their way down into the cesspits and threw
barrow-loads of excrement out over the corpses and the blood: sure
that if they only searched deep enough they would unearth secret
bags of gold. Rats scuttled through the lanes. Already there had been
the first cases of the plague. I had seen the old plague-gravedigger
going about from house to house, and the doors of infected houses
marked with chalk. Day by day it was growing harder to find food.
The shops were stripped bare. Men who had fought one another a
few days ago over diamonds and gold murdered for a sack of rye.
They would steal bread from the hands of a man half-dead with the
plague. The poorest in Rome ate the straw and wool from their
bedding and dead human flesh: the only commodity of which there
was no shortage at all.

And the screams from the prisons. As the booty diminished, the
soldiers clung all the harder to their prisoners: as if more torture,
more pain could wring from them a corresponding amount of gold.

The officers, hoping to make their troops obey orders, massacred whole prisonfuls of captives. Some of the lucky ones, who managed to pay their ransoms, were captured again by other bands and forced to pay twice; and that only convinced the soldiers they must be men of wealth, and so they demanded more, and tortured them again. When they judged at last they could squeeze out nothing more, the soldiers dragged their captives into the markets and put them up for auction, and other bands bid for them and led them away to more torments still.

For long hours every day I lay on a rooftop by the riverbank, not far from the Papal Mint, just upstream from the Bridge of Sant' Angelo. The building beneath me had been a spicer's shop; the scents of precious cinnamon and pepper drifted up from the smashed jars, mingling with the pervasive stink of death. It was a dangerous post. The soldiers had barricades at the near end of the bridge, and there was always a troop of them there, watching the Castle and taking occasional shots at it. To them that Castle was a treasure house. The Pope and his gold were in there, and some hundreds of wealthy cardinals, merchants and nobles. It would be the last great prize to fall into their hands. But Sant' Angelo was not quite ready to fall yet. The cannon still fired, and smashed into neighbouring houses whenever the defenders saw signs of movement. I looked across at those bleak walls hungrily. Inside was safety, food, beds; a life without fear or horror. There had to be a way of getting in, and I was determined I would find it.

One night I stayed on later than usual. Just as I was about to slip away from the rooftop and head back to the palazzo I saw a movement, like a spider descending against the castle wall. It touched the ground and scuttled across to the foot of the bridge, where I lost it in the shadows. But a little later there it was again, halfway along the bridge coming towards me, climbing smoothly over the cannon-locked ruins of the little chapel where condemned men used to be taken to pray before they were hanged. It was gone again. Then another movement, a shadow vanishing along the Banchi into the city. I scrambled down from the roof and ran after it, casting down this street and that: but there was not a soul to be seen. In frustration I turned back to my watching post, and gazed and dozed until dawn. Just as the sky began to grow lighter I saw a movement once more on the bridge, and that slender figure dodging from shadow to shadow. The mist was gathering, but I could just make out the line of the rope once more let down from the corner bastion of the Castle, and the man pulled up and in. Whoever it was had come and gone.

The next night I kept watch again. It was nearly midnight when I saw that slender line down the Castle wall, and the spider-figure descending it. I climbed swiftly back through the ruined shop. The spy, quick and almost invisible, was already on the near side of the bridge. He padded lightly past the Mint and into the maze of streets I hurried after him. I saw him dart out into the Piazza Navona, where on the night of the *moccoli* candles had burned from every balcony and the boys and girls had laughed and thrown water and flour. Now the houses were dark. Stones, planks, bodies lay everywhere. On the corner of the square I stood and gazed round on the empty scene in dismay. It was no use: I had lost him.

I ransacked a baker's shop for food. I found a rat-chewed end of bread that the soldiers had missed, and turned back towards the palazzo. I was in a filthy temper. In the upstairs closet I whispered to the girls. Susan's face appeared at the trapdoor, and she began to let down the ladder. Just then, a scuffling sound in the corner made us both freeze. Out into the dim light hopped Beelzebub. He had something in his paws; it took me a moment to recognise it as a severed human hand. The monkey bared its teeth and tore off a bite. I caught Susan's eye and nodded. At least I could rid of us of that damnable monkey. I put down my harquebus and drew my sword. Beelzebub appeared to sense our intent. Taking the hand in his jaws he ran out through the doorway and away downstairs. I gave chase. Along the loggia he ran, up on the balustrade; then he jumped down and darted

through the half-open door to the sala. I pushed in after him, and
opped dead.

Sitting still by the light of a couple of dozen candles were six or
even men. They wore plumed hats, and by their sides were laid
own harquebuses and pikes. They sat like a row of seamstresses,
ith the gigantic Flemish tapestries draped over their knees, picking
way at the cloth with needles. It was an incongruous sight. Then I
nderstood. They were stripping from these priceless works the
ngths of gold thread, winding them on to spools as they went.
hey had been working at this in silence, and so I had passed them
nawares. One of them stood up swiftly and pointed his gun at me.
he monkey scampered round them and off down the stairs.

'And what manner of man are you?' He spoke in Spanish.

'A soldier.'

I had answered in the same tongue. But I knew I could pass as no
ative speaker, in a still room, when I was afraid. 'An Italian,' I added.
. friend of the Empire.'

'What Italian? Roman?'

I spat. To be a Venetian came easiest to me; but the Venetians were
e deadliest enemies the Empire had. 'I am of Genoa.'

He took a few steps towards me, still pointing the gun. 'Where in
enoa.'

'Maddalena, where the rope-makers work. The French took all I
d. In Siena I joined up and marched with Bourbon.'

'Kill him,' advised one. 'He is a liar.'

Another of the men stood up. He spoke in Italian, with the accent
Siena. 'Prove it.'

My hands were sweating. Fear clawed at me, but I forced my mind
go back to that bright January evening when the *Speranza* had
lled out from the Mole bound for Rome, and the sailors had sung
they hauled at the ropes. I sang, 'We are of Genoa, we are of
addalena, we shall never marry, as long as there's another man's
fe in the world ...'

By the time I finished they were laughing, and then I sang it again, done into Spanish as well as I could manage. Their leader beckoned me over.

'You have bought your life, and a share of bread and wine besides. The Germans we took them from no longer need them.'

I took the crusts hungrily, and sipped at the sour wine. 'My thanks. And if the beast had not escaped me, you would have been welcome to a share of my monkey.'

'Ah!' The leader wiped his mouth. 'That is the very creature that led us to this house of death. Believe me, there is someone hiding here.'

My heart beat hard. 'No, after all these days it is impossible.'

The man who had called for my death fixed me with a dark, unblinking eye. 'Not if someone was helping them.'

I shrugged.

'I heard something.'

'My own footsteps,' I offered.

'Voices. I would swear to it. Women.'

At the word every man looked up. Faces hardened into lines of cruelty and lust.

'If only there were,' I laughed. 'Gentlemen, I have business of my own. If I am successful, I shall invite you to a banquet of monkey.' I stood up and walked out of the sala on to the landing. Then passed quickly through to the loggia and ran up the stairs. My whole air must have breathed suspicion. Where was my soldier's greed? My demand for a share of their gold, my insisting that the monkey, at least, was mine? I was sure they would be after me in moments. In the closet I hissed to Susan to let me up. When she lifted the hatch I grabbed the harquebus and ran up the ladder. Then we pulled it up after us. From down below footsteps sounded on the stairs.

'Quiet,' I commanded. Beneath us the men kicked through the bedchambers, clattering under beds with swords, overturning cabinets and chairs. Then we heard them stamping through into the closet. There was a pause; then a voice came in triumph.

'Up there. There's an opening.'

I whispered, 'Is there any other way out?'

Susan shook her head. There was the sound of furniture being dragged into the closet. The Spaniards would soon be up. I looked all round the attic. The walls were solid. Through the cracks in the tiles above us the sky was beginning to show the first grey light of dawn.

'Quickly!' With my arm I knocked a hole in the tiles. They went skating noisily down the roof to shatter far below on the ground. There was the crash of a harquebus going off, and a ball burst up through the floor between Hannah and Grace. Splinters of wood sprayed over us. Hannah let out a cry, and as she cowered towards me there was blood on her face.

'Up!' shouted Susan. Together we lifted Hannah through the hole. She crouched on the roof, an arm stretched down to help us, and we next dragged Grace standing. Two more shots rang out, and holes opened further off, missing us. Grace was smiling serenely.

'Where must I put my foot, Mr Richard? Forgive me, but you see this is entirely new to me.'

We hefted her up through the roof and Hannah took her hand. They teetered upright for a moment, black shapes against the sky, and then both of them slid down with a rattle over the tiles, screaming. I yelled, and there were answering cries from the Spaniards, sure of their prey. Another shot rang out behind Susan, and a rotten beam collapsed, shedding a shower of tiles over her head. She shrieked and fell. I pulled her upright, and together we wallowed over the wreckage on to the roof. 'Hannah,' I was murmuring in my grief. 'Hannah.'

'Here!' She was clinging to the sloping tiles, her feet caught on the ragged moulding that ran along the roof edge like a miniature battlement. Behind us I could hear the Spaniards climbing through into the attic. I leant over to the hole we had made in the roof and fired my harquebus. The cry from below told me I had hit home. Susan pulled me away from the hole. We slid down the tiles to join the others. I took Hannah's hand and we set off, scrambling along the parapet. Grace followed too, lifting the hem of her gown and looking round in dismay. Susan was first to reach the corner of the palazzo, where the roof turned back for the other wing.

'Where now?'

Down below us, perhaps twelve feet lower, was the roof of the neighbouring house. To reach it would mean jumping over a narrow alleyway. Further off still, and about another fifteen feet down, were the roofs of the shops along the Via Giulia. Susan looked at my face.

'You think we can't do it.'

'I know we can't.' I looked back. Grace cowered back against the tiles, vaguely smiling. Hannah, her face bleeding, clung to her mother. Round the corner of the sloping roof ridge was a row of dormer windows. There was no other choice. We would have to re-enter the palazzo. The Spaniards were on the roof: a shot rang across our heads. They must be almost out of shot, I thought, unless they had had the wit to leave a couple of men behind to reload. One by one we climbed round the ridge, with the dizzy drop before us, until we came to the first of the dormers. I smashed the window shutters and dropped into the chamber with my sword before me. A woman lay dead in the middle of the floor. 'Quickly!' I handed Susan, Hannah and the smiling Grace through the window and we set off at the run. The layout of this side of the palazzo matched the other. Down to the bedchambers, down again to a loggia, and then out on the balcony above the grand stairs. heard a shout: a man stood outside the Cages' sala, fumbling to reload his gun. We ran on down the stairs, and burst out into th square. Ten or so soldiers were running towards us from the Vi Monserrato, attracted by the shots. I pushed the three women int the shadows and shouted in Spanish, 'Inside! The Germans ar murdering us!' My cloak and my gun marked me as a soldier, and the natural hatred between the two branches of the army did the rest. The Spaniards ran into the palazzo. I heard more firing from inside, and we ran on, down to the Via Giulia, and turned right, heading north. Susan caught me up.

'Where in the Devil's name are you taking us ?'

Until that moment I had not thought. Our only safe hiding place in the city was behind us. But I saw in my mind's eye the figure climbing the rope down the bastion. It was our only chance. Briefly I explained.

'And he will be there? He will take us inside the Castle?'

'He must.'

We were at the old Banchi, perhaps halfway to the bridge. Hannah and Susan were swaying on their feet, their legs weak after days of hiding. Suddenly Mrs Grace slid to the ground.

'Forgive me, I do not know how it is …'

I pulled them aside into an alleyway. Hannah lay down against a house wall. Blood crusted one side of her face. She smiled: and it was a smile of such beauty that it made me shiver.

'Please,' I begged her. 'We must keep going. But no more running. We are getting too near the bridge.' Wearily they stood up. 'Hands before you as if bound,' I urged them. 'Heads down.' I had seen lines of captives marched about Rome like this, many a time. In the dim light no one would see they were not tied with ropes. We set off again, slowly. We had come perhaps two hundred yards from the palazzo. Behind us we heard another shot. How long before the two bands of Spaniards joined and came after us?

Up ahead I could see the barricade before the bridge and soldiers moving in front of it. Beyond, rising through the grey twilight, was the gallows the Germans had put up right where the bridge began; here the Cardinals were made to stand every day in view of the Pope. As we came nearer my heart was pounding. The officer at the barricade turned to us and held up his hand. We stopped. He called out something in German. Behind me the three women huddled close together. I spoke in Spanish: hostages, to be made to stand on the gibbet. He smiled. Cruelty was a common language; he waved us through.

We were almost at the bridge. Mist rose from the river and blew round us in swirls. Before us was the Castle: grim, gaunt, unsurrendering. Smoke puffed from one of the many embrasures in its great drum tower, and away to the left in the Borgo a cannonball crashed home. Gunfire replied from the Imperials. We walked slowly round the gibbet, its beam and noose hanging above us like death. Hannah glanced up, and nearly fell.

'Don't look,' I warned her. 'Keep going.'

Before us stretched the bridge, its paving stones broken up by shot, stones and bodies lying scattered. I led the Cages out from the gibbet into the open. Here over the river the mist was thicker. I prayed it would screen us from the Germans. We passed the first stone pier with its broken statues, then reached the ruins of the chapel halfway across. Still no one had seen us. Then came the third pier, the fourth. We were nearly up to the Castle. The outer wall lay before us, with the portcullis where I had parted from Martin and Cellini. To the right was the round corner bastion where I had seen the rope. But there was nothing there now. We were horribly exposed. And sunrise was not far off. It was late: too late for a prudent spy to be returning. I motioned to the women to duck down below the parapet, just as a shot chipped the stonework by our side. It had come from the Castle.

'What now?' whispered Susan.

'We wait.'

Hannah looked white as death. Grace, crouched behind the stones, was trying to pat her hair back into order. I would not betray to them how desperately we were placed. We would be trapped here in the growing light. Perhaps we could crawl down beside the bridge to the riverside. But to stay hidden all day, with the eyes of both th

Imperials and the Castle on us: it was more than I could ask of my luck.

'And what, in the name of all mad and unlikely things, are you poor fools doing here?'

The voice came in a whisper, from just beyond the parapet. I peered round it in disbelief.

'John?'

'The same.' There was his open, smiling face. I had never been more glad to see him. He was dressed in black, with a black cape. His tall frame was like a shadow: a shadow, I guessed, that passed spider-like down a rope and silently into the city. He scuttled round the parapet to join us where we were hiding. I said, 'And so you are still trading in the same sort of goods. But I thought you were the Emperor's man.'

'These days His Holiness pays higher. And the Empire has a nasty habit of killing its friends along with its enemies. Mrs Grace! How delightful.' Grace took his hand and they kissed. 'And Mrs Hannah and Mrs Susan. Enchanting.'

Susan glared at him. 'You might have told us we were trusting to him for this rescue.'

'Susan,' her mother rebuked her. 'Do not be churlish. Mr John, after we have rested I believe we may walk a little further. You will join us?'

John peered round the parapet. The mist was a thick white veil over the bridge; but from the Castle we were an easy mark.

'We are late,' he murmured. 'Follow me quickly.' He set off running, bent double, round the foot of the Castle. Another shot glanced off the stones, coming from the far bastion. I urged the Cages to their feet and we hurried after John. Round the angle of the Castle wall we were safe from that lone marksman. We leant against the wall, which reached high above us through the mist to the overhanging battle-ments. John whistled softly. Like sorcery, the slender line descended. He grasped the end of the rope.

'I am sorry, but I must go first. Anyone else they would kill. I will make my explanations and then pull you all up. I am valuable to them: they will not say no.'

He jumped and clung to the rope, and was swiftly hauled up and out of sight. We waited in the silence. Above us the mist blew in wreaths. Suddenly the rope dropped out of the whiteness and hung, swaying. I said, 'Mrs Grace must be next.' I tied a loop in the rope's end for her to sit in; but Grace was shaking her head.

'Oh, no. If we go up there Mr Stephen will never find us. When we have had our walk, we must go back to the palazzo.'

'Mother,' Hannah begged. 'You must go. Mr Richard knows what is best.'

A heavy silence hung over Rome. We could hear the rushing of the river against the bridge piers, and a distant cry from a prison. Suddenly there was shouting back across the bridge: Spanish voices and German. Our pursuers from the palazzo, I guessed, were at the barricade.

'You go,' said Grace. 'I shall wait here for Stephen.'

She sat down on the ground. I knelt swiftly at her side.

'My dear Mrs Grace, if Stephen returns to Rome, and he has the power, the Castle is the very first place he will visit.'

Grace looked up. 'Do you really think so?'

'I know it.'

'Very likely he's waiting for us inside.' This was from Susan.

Grace looked at her in suspicion. 'If Mr Richard says we must enter the Castle ...?'

'I do,' I said, helping Susan to seat her in the loop of rope. I gave it a tug, and she rose up into the mist.

Hannah was slumped against the Castle wall. I said, 'The two of you must go together.'

Susan looked at me with her grave, pale eyes: so different from the laughing depths of her sister's. 'You surely don't trust him? Tha man is no true friend of yours. If we go first, you will never see the inside of the Castle.'

'I will follow you. Go!'

The mist was parting in strands. The tower of the Palazzo Altuiti, a Spanish outpost just downstream, glowed yellow as it caught the early sun. Susan stepped into the loop of rope and put her arm round her sister. Then the two of them rose swiftly up through the clearing fog. I saw where the rope vanished into a narrow window just below the ramparts, perhaps twenty feet up. Susan and Hannah were within a man's height of it when shots rang out from beyond the bridge. Bullets chipped the stone around the window, where arms reached out to pull Hannah inside. Susan hung for a moment, glanced down at me, and then leapt for the window as a shot grazed the sill. They were in.

I waited, my eyes on the window. The moments passed. Soon I would be helpless, a mark for every sharpshooter on the riverbank. I fretted with anger, dread, amazement. Susan could not be right. And yet I was learning that those pale eyes very often saw true. It began to seem possible: John would leave me to die. He had Hannah, and he had no need of his friend. He would explain with tears in his eyes that it was too dangerous to let down the rope yet again; that it would be a breach of his duty to the Pope; that he would regret it for the rest of his days, and do all he could to comfort the bereaved and charming Mrs Hannah.

On the bridge the broken torsoes of the statues were becoming visible through the blowing mist. There was a slap from up above, I turned, and there at last hung the rope. I leapt for it and began climbing at the same time as it pulled me upwards in a series of jerks. In an instant I was above the mist, the sun shone clear and from over the river came the crash of gunfire. Bullets hit around me, and chips of stone stung my face. I looked up. The window was still some feet above my head. I pulled myself higher up the rope. Another shot landed in the stonework next to me, and a lump of rock hit me on the shoulder. My hands slipped. I swung for some moments in the air. Just above my head, I saw Susan at the window. Then the rope jerked upwards. As another shot hit beside me, Susan reached out and pulled me roughly in over the sill. I fell forward and dropped against the wall. Beside me Hannah lay motionless. Her gown was soaked in blood.

23

I grabbed her hand, wiping it clean, weeping, touching her face and hair. She answered me with a ghost of her old teasing smile.

'I am not quite dead yet, Mr Richard.'

She gestured to where a barrel-chested soldier lay with a gaping wound in his neck. He was dead. Blood was pooling round him on the floor. 'They hit him just as he was pulling us in.'

John threw down the rope and knelt before us.

'My friend! Thank God. When Matteo here was shot I had not a notion how I could pull you up alone. It was fortunate Mrs Susan was here to help me. Come!'

I paused. Could he be lying? It was true, Matteo was a bull of a man, well able to hoist that rope single-handed, while John was sparely built, like myself. Again, suspicion of my old friend gnawed at me. But surely John's rivalry would not go so far?

John and I supported Hannah between us. She was weak with exhaustion; thankfully the blood on her gown, it seemed, was not hers but Matteo's. Grace and Susan followed. John guided us down a winding stair and out of the corner bastion into a small courtyard. Before us rose the great drum tower itself. Through a door at its base we entered a vaulted passage lined by massive stone blocks. John led us on, up a ramp which climbed steeply, winding its way deep into the stone. I truly felt that I was in a tomb: for the entire Castle was no more than an ancient mausoleum, the conception of an emperor who had wished to be buried like a pharoah in his pyramid. Up and up the walkway turned. Torches burned in the walls. We passed an airshaft, down which shots and voices echoed from far above. At length the ramp ended abruptly in a fresh ascent which cut in a straight line through the Castle's heart, over the burial chamber itself, which it crossed by means of a soaring drawbridge guarded by sentries. Here, and in the grain silos and even the dungeon cells let into the Castle's walls, huddled the poor Romans who had managed to press inside before the portcullis fell. Women and children, many of them; babies' cries resounded up and down the passages and shafts. This ramp led us to stairs, which turned and at last brought us up to daylight.

We emerged into a long courtyard filled with activity. Along one side stretched an armoury, from which men were carrying casks of powder and cannonballs. From here stairs led up to a curving line of battlements where cannon fired at intervals, pounding against the city. On the other side of the courtyard rose the rectangular tower at the centre of the drum, and, high at its top, the Papal banner of the crossed keys. Little knots of priests stood about, watching. I turned anxiously to Hannah. She smiled faintly. John disappeared through a doorway in the tower, and came out with a liveried chamberlain, who offered to take the Cages to the place where noble ladies were lodged. 'You will find Martin with Benvenuto,' John added. 'At the top: at the Angel. Up to the battlements, and then keep climbing. As for myself, I am overdue with His Holiness.'

I clasped John's hand, and with a pang saw Hannah led away through the door. But we were safe: I feared nothing now. I took a turn or two around the courtyard, breathing the fresh, good air which blew on a light north wind from the mountains, sweeping away the fogs and the stink of death that hung everywhere down in the city. I ran up to the ramparts, then turned and entered the tower. Inside was a labyrinth of rooms, curtained off into makeshift quarters for cardinals and nobles. Tortuous stairways led me higher and higher, until I came out on the topmost terrace, the Angel, as it was called, though the great marble statue of the Archangel Michael that had stood here, raising its bronze sword over the city in protection, had been shattered by lightning some years back.

In the clearing mist I could see far out over the river, the city, and the plain and mountains beyond. The roar of gunfire was tremendous. There were five cannon here, two of them massive demi-culverins some thirteen feet long, and three of the smaller falconets, about as long as a man, mounted so they could swivel. The shot stood in little pyramids, and men ran round fetching powder, measuring it out with ladles and then, with the aid of brass funnels, pouring it into the chambers of the guns. Between them strode Cellini, his eyes on fire, roaring at the men, then aiming the guns himself and putting the fire to the fuse. Martin was with him, and Alessandro too. As another report shook the stone beneath my feet I came up behind them. They turned and saw me. Their faces showed disbelief, then the astonishment of catching sight of a ghost, and then delight. I ran forward and embraced them.

'Master! We had you marked as a dead man, sure.'

I smiled, enjoying their amazement to the full. 'I simply went to fetch my jewels.'

'And you have them?' Cellini asked.

I patted my chest.

'Well, you have the luck of the very Devil. But that luck might yet be about to run out.'

'What do you mean?'

'Later,' said Cellini. 'We have work to do.'

He sent a boy down to fetch food, and I sat against a pile of cannonballs, exhausted, savouring the fresh bread, cheese and wine while Cellini worked the guns. Harquebus shots whisked over our heads, and heavier fire too. The enemy had brought up cannon from the Borgo, and from time to time a ball crashed into the walls beneath us.

At nightfall Benvenuto led me at last to a small chamber right by the Angel which he shared with Martin. I felt weak, and still elated with my escape. I laid before them my hoard: the finished jewels and the unset stones; and I tossed across to Cellini his own property, the sheets of gold, the gems, the coin. He raised his eyes in appreciation.

'This is more than I ever thought to see again. My thanks. But all these fine things may not remain ours for long.'

I felt a sinking in my stomach. I had an inkling then of our situation. We were besieged. The castle was full of the helpless: many hungry mouths but few fighters. I remembered those soldiers who had run out from the gate in the moments before the portcullis fell, and snatched what food they could from the nearby houses. It was proof enough that the Castle was ill-provided. After all, no one had conceived that Rome could ever fall. How many fighting men were here? A few hundred? A thousand at most, against thirty thousand outside.

'I see you are beginning to understand,' said Cellini. 'The Abbot of Najera has been here, commissioner-general of the Imperial army, treating with the Pope for terms. But His Holiness cannot make up his mind. The pen is in his hand to sign the surrender, and then your friend John, out on his spying trips, brings in a fresh rumour that the Venetians are only two days away, and His Holiness lays down the pen and begs for a little longer to decide. Some days he is all blood and thunder: he will see Rome consumed in fire before he gives in to the godless, he says. And when he has finished here, he will go and smite the Florentines. Oh yes, haven't you heard? They've had another revolution, thrown out his relatives and burnt His Holiness in effigy. Other days he weeps, and says he will be the last of the line of the Popes, and it is God's judgement on us all for our sins, and for his own folly in particular. And who is to contradict him?'

'The Venetians are always two days away,' Martin put in gloomily. 'Yet they never come.'

'Why should they?' said Benvenuto. 'Pope Clement has always betrayed them. Put away your jewels. Do not count on them as safe quite yet.'

'Only make sure you stay alive,' I told him. 'I shall call on you to finish your work one day.'

It was the eighteenth of May. For twelve days I had lived in the inferno of Rome. I raged to think all my cunning and luck might yet be in vain. That night I slept in a welter of nightmare. Early next morning I went looking for Hannah. I found the Cages in a corner of one of the antechambers at the foot of the tower. Hannah lay in a pallet bed, with Grace and Susan sitting at her side. She had colour in her face again. Over one eye I saw the cut she had got from the wood splinter in the attic. Cleaned of blood, it did not look threatening.

'She is recovering well,' said Susan.

I crouched down and took Hannah's hand, and for some time I merely gazed on her without speaking.

'Stephen went ahead,' Grace commented. 'He was only to have been gone a moment. And then we came here. It is so great a pity Stephen is not with us. It would have been a perfect time to advance his business with His Holiness.'

I glanced at her sharply. I longed to question her; for all my guessing and wondering, I had still not seen to the heart of Stephen's business.

'She remembers nothing,' Susan whispered to me. 'Those twelve days have gone.'

'If only he escaped the hands of the soldiers,' Grace resumed. 'If he got safe to Ostia.'

She was growing more lucid. I said, 'There is a good chance of that.'

Grace put her hand on my arm in thanks.

'Dear Mr Richard,' Hannah murmured. 'We owe both you and John so very much.'

I felt a twinge of displeasure. I had not come through all those dangers to be a mere sharer in the glory with John. But how could I deny he had saved us? What was more, he had saved me, when he might easily have found an excuse not to. But then, how much stronger his position was now, the generous saviour of us all. It was on the tip of my tongue to ask if he had been to see her. But that would have been to betray my jealousy and spur Hannah to yet more teasing. She smiled back up at me with a glint of mischief, as if understanding all I thought.

The days went by. In the week since I had joined the besieged I had become a soldier: I spent my hours with Cellini at the Angel. I mixed and measured the powder, I rammed the wooden tampions down the gun muzzles and carried the shot, the five-inch balls for the demi-culverins and the two-inch for the falconets, and I ran the guns forward ready for firing. Cellini was the captain, and he took to gunnery with as much zeal as goldsmith work. He sighted each gun and fired, picking off the Imperials as they worked digging trenches around the Castle. Often a cardinal or two stood behind us in their red capes and birettas, watching our guns and murmuring a blessing when one of them scored a hit. Sometimes there were nobles with them. I bowed to those I knew: Gregorio Casale, old Cardinal Campeggio, Cardinal Cesi. They returned my courtesies with sad smiles. No one had believed it could come to this. From up here you could see the whole city: the smoking ruins of the palazzi, the streets clogged with the dead, and troops swarming everywhere in their hungry bands.

One morning Pope Clement himself appeared on the terrace. His face, with its heavily lidded eyes, was crumpled and haggard. He wore a ragged growth of beard: from the first day of the siege he had refused to shave, in mourning for the Holy City. As he passed by, Benvenuto threw himself down on his knees.

'I beg absolution, Holy Father, for the many men I have killed in defence of the Church.'

The Pope bent over him and made the sign of the cross in the air, pardoning him at the same time for however many more Spanish and Germans he might send to Hell. I wished I could have begged the like forgiveness. But I had killed for more personal motives: for my gems and for love. Still the jewels sat in my casket, the diamond as yet uncut. And perhaps they would not remain mine for long.

Down below, the system of trenches and cannon ringing the Castle was almost complete. John continued to slip out, passing invisibly between the two sides, weaving over the river and back again, up to the Papal palace where the Prince of Orange and the other Imperial generals held their councils of war. The danger of it amused him vastly; but he told me that before long even his own secret sallies would become impossible. 'The trenches are one thing,' he told me. 'But we should be more afraid of the mines.' The thought chilled me: that the enemy might even now be tunnelling beneath the Castle, and could at any moment bring us down with gunpowder.

The Imperials were sure of victory. The Germans paraded about in looted vestments from the cardinals' palaces, and sat down to a mock conclave in front of the trenches. At the end they sprang up, shouting, 'Luther is pope! Luther is pope!' And indeed, anything seemed possible. There were whispers in the Castle that Clement would be taken away to Spain, a prisoner, and poisoned there. The cardinals, scattered across Europe, would never see Rome again. They might meet in little conclaves, electing petty anti-popes, one in France, one in Germany, one in Spain. Martin Luther might truly become the strongest voice in Christendom. Many put the blame on Cardinal Pucci, whose ruthless extortions, men said, had driven Germany into Luther's arms. But Pucci blamed Cardinal

Salviati, who had advised Clement to ally with France, and Salviati blamed the generals, in particular Renzo da Ceri. Renzo himself walked about the terraces upright and silent, as if to say: 'None of this is my fault. I wash my hands of it.' Every night I helped Benvenuto to light three beacons at the Angel, and we fired off three cannonades: the signal to the Duke of Urbino that we had not surrendered.

Some days I walked with Hannah in the garden that occupied a tiny courtyard beside the Papal apartments. Vines crept up over the battlements, and lemon trees basked beside the furnaces for the Pope's private steam bath. It was a little fantasy, this garden: a pretence that we were still living the life of three weeks before. We seldom spoke. I thought of the jewels that hung round my neck and the greed for fame that had kept me in Rome past the moment of safety; and Mr Stephen's mysterious business, that had condemned Hannah likewise. In a simpler world we might have escaped.

As the end of May approached, the Castle's first case of the plague was reported among the poorer folk, hiding down in the dungeons. Bread was growing scarce. The Duke of Urbino was close: eight miles off, some said. But he had no provisions, and he lost deserters every day to the Imperials. One night, just after Cellini and I had fired the signal guns, one of the Pope's chamberlains stepped into our chamber. This was a Frenchman known as Cavalierino; Clement used him for all his most secret affairs. There were two soldiers with him. He told Benvenuto he must come with him at once. I watched him go with anxiety. The Castle had become a nest of whispers and accusations. Cellini was outspoken; his enemies, it seemed, had succeeded in turning the Pope against him. I spent a restless night with Martin. We sat and listened to the flapping of the great banner in the wind above us, and the occasional crack of gunfire, and played at cards. To lose Benvenuto knocked away a good deal of my remaining hope.

It was some hours past midnight when the door opened again and Benvenuto came in. His face was pale and drained. Behind him came Cavalierino and the same two soldiers, each carrying an enormous sack, which they deposited on the floor with a heavy clink. Then Cavalierino gave Cellini a sombre nod, and withdrew. Cellini threw himself down in a chair.

'What a night's work! But it is nothing to what's before us.'

He reached for the closest sack and tipped it out on the floor. From it poured a shimmering flood of gold: cups and plates, pyxes, chalices, pectorals. From among them something rolled out and came to rest at my feet. I stooped down and picked up a hollow dome of gold, set round with three coronets and topped with a tall cross. Figures in relief chased one another round its three bands: saints, martyrs, angels. Above them were figured the three persons of the Trinity. It was the Tiara itself: the Pope's triple crown. I felt my palms begin to sweat, and my hands tremble. I held it out to Cellini, who turned it lovingly in his hands.

'Caradosso crafted that,' he said. 'Old Arseface himself. Pope Julius paid two hundred thousand ducats for it. And I have just spent half the night destroying it.'

I saw the sockets all round it that once would have held gems. The other objects were the same: one chalice alone must have carried a thousand stones.

'The wonders I have seen tonight,' sighed Benvenuto. 'The rubies of Pegu, the Golconda diamonds, the verdant emeralds. All, all gone.'

'Gone?'

'Sewed into His Holiness's clothing,' said Benvenuto, with a twinkle in his eye. 'From his drawers on outwards. The man is a walking jewel mine. But don't dare tell a soul.'

'No, I swear it. But what about the gold?'

'There begins the labour. We are to melt it: cast it into the fire and render it into formless bricks.' He sighed again. I sat down, stunned. For the first time I plainly foresaw our defeat. Pope Clement was preparing himself for capture: no one would search His Holiness's clothing for gems. But I would not be so lucky. Cellini lay down to sleep, while I lay until dawn, fuming with anger.

The next day Benvenuto began building his furnace. Men brought in bricks, and he worked round the little hearth in our chamber, building it up into a pyramid. At its heart he improvised a grate made out of shovel handles. That night he lit a fire of charcoal in it and placed a clean ash-pan underneath. Then he took out the gold. Medals, brooches, rings; all he threw straight on to the coal, and in a few minutes a stream of brilliant liquid gold began to flow out from underneath. It was a sight to sicken any man who saw it. It seemed to me then that the whole world I had grown up with, the world of jewelled prelates, princes and kings, was passing away. And what would come instead? Outlaw bands, ascetic pastors, republics. They would have no use for my jewels. Cellini lifted a brooch a couple of inches across and turned it in his hands. Around empty gem-sockets were figures of God the Father, and tumbling Raphaelesque angels.

'I made that,' commented Cellini. 'Pope Clement loved it; it was what first brought me to his notice. Well, in better times he may ask me to make it again.' He tossed it on the fire. My anger suddenly swelled and burst out.

'So Clement is beaten,' I said. 'Well, I am not. Benvenuto: we have gold. I ask you now to finish your work.'

He turned to me in surprise. 'You are that sure of yourself?'

'I have to be. I still have bills of exchange. Will His Holiness sell me a few ounces of his gold?'

'I have no doubt I could arrange that with Cavalierino,' said Cellini. 'Yours is the risk.'

I pulled the casket from beneath my clothes. My hands were trembling as I opened the lock and once more took out the diamond of the Old Rock.

'You can do it? You can cut my diamond?'

Cellini waved his hand. 'I can cut it as well here as anywhere. There are goldsmiths' tools in the small workshop below us, adjoining the treasury of the Apostolic Camera. You forget Sant' Angelo is a treasure-house, as well as a fortress and a prison.' He took the diamond and smiled. 'Well, it is a piece of noble madness. We shall do it.'

As the gold trickled down through the fire and congealed in a glimmering pool below, Benvenuto turned the diamond in his hands. He had Martin bring up the tools he needed: the lapidary's wheel, a small bench, the slender goldsmith's anvil, the hammers, files, chisels, pastes. For a long time he studied the diamond. He was finding out the entrances to its beauty, the lines of approach. Its dull, rippling surface glinted as the few openings into its heart caught the light, and the flaw deep inside shimmered.

'There,' he murmured. 'I have you now. That is your weakness.' He tapped the side of the stone. Never taking his eyes from it, he pinioned it in a vice to keep it firm. Then he took a second diamond, one of those gems of his that I had rescued from the chest. He clenched this in a dop, and using it he scored a narrow line across my diamond. I caught my breath: I could almost feel the diamond's pain. It was a virgin stone no longer. Now there was no turning back. I watched with my heart pounding as he took a fine steel blade and a mallet. The diamond waited for his blow. Cellini paused, frowned, gazed again on the line. He lowered the blade, and with one blow of the mallet struck the stone.

I jumped up with a gasp. On the bench lay glittering shards of powder. But the diamond: the diamond was there, one side struck clean away. Its flaw had gone. There it rested in its nakedness, its cool blue water washing my eyes as I gazed on it, revealed at last, beautiful and pure. It seemed to look up at us in amazement, gratitude, even love. Cellini snatched it and held it to the light.

'There! By God! Did I not tell you I was the man to do it? Did you ever see such a stone?'

I took it from him. 'No,' I murmured. 'I never have.'

Now he set about the faceting. For this he gathered up the powder, and together with oil he made a gritty paste which he spread on the surface of the wheel. This he set spinning with astonishing speed. Then, with intense care, he lowered the diamond over it, mounted on the end of the dop. A few seconds' contact, and he lifted it again, frowned and then continued. Over the following days the principal face, the table, emerged. The diamond acquired a dull, sleepy glow. You might see inside, but the light echoed around against the still rough faces, like in a dream. It seemed as if its bewitchment has been lost. At the next cuts, four sloping facets surrounded the table and the stone began to wake, and cast the light around it. Slowly it advanced, slowly: to what end, I still could not fully imagine.

But Cellini could not work on the diamond for long at a time. After a while he would look up from it, drained but exhilarated, and say, 'That is enough. The stone is tired.' Then he would stoke the furnace and throw on more treasures, and remove another of the thin, golden bricks from below, glistening, streaked with coal and ash. Sometimes he darted out on to the terrace, even in the middle of the night, and aimed and fired off one of his guns. At other times he turned his mind to the rest of my stones. There were few left, after I put aside those reserved to accompany the diamond in the pierced heart. I had my dark emerald, the greenish cats' eyes that shot out colours almost as various as an opal, and last the two rubies: the one, pale and strange, almost pure white; the other noble, majestic, fiery and deep.

I nudged the stones with my finger. 'We must be quick.' June had come. I felt time pressing against us. My refuge had become a prison. The Castle would not hold out much longer. But somehow I would leave this place. Yes, and Hannah Cage and my jewels along with me.

'Quick: yes. Then after all our flights of fancy I think we must come down to something simple. A ring?'

'Yes. The dark ruby.' It was a stone to heat the blood, to bring love and lust boiling up together. It needed no embellishing. I pushed forward the deep Persian emerald. 'Let this be a sister to it.'

'A second ring: so. And your cats' eyes, and the white ruby?'

I prodded them with my fingers. So pale they were; yet powerful. The deceitful snares of virginity. I thought of Bennet's letter, and his description of the King's lady. I pictured her dark eyes, her private smile at the way she had snagged the King and held him fast. 'Make a truelove knot,' I told Cellini. Coils of gold. The stones caught in them, like flies in a web.'

He lifted his dark brows. 'Is that your opinion of the lady? What a pity you still do not know her name.'

'But I do.' I smiled at his surprise. From my casket I took out Bennet's letter, and read out to him in Italian the portion that concerned the mistress. When I had finished Cellini stood up and stretched.

'Well, my lady Anne Boleyn, if jewels are a proof of constancy, you will have nothing to complain of from your King. And now, my dear Messer Richard, which of the Pope's valuables shall we send to the fire, to fashion the tokens of the English King's love? This?' He lifted up the triple crown itself, and held it over the furnace. The flames flashed on the points of each coronet, and lit up the faces of the saints: Peter with his keys, John astride his eagle, Mark and his winged lion, patron of the Venetians who never came. Then he lowered it into the fire, where it sat in majesty on the coals for many minutes. Finally its shapes blurred and the crown sank, formless, while a stream of gold ran down into the pan below.

Cellini worked fast. The din of the bombardment from the Imperials' new cannon batteries gave him fire, and he leapt from his guns to the furnace to the workbench without rest. In a short time the two rings were ready for their stones, and the truelove was finished. The twists of rope in the knot that bound the cats' eyes and the white ruby were exquisite; and nested among them Benvenuto crafted a repeating pattern of the letters H and A. The gold heart too was ready for its gems. He set in it jacinths, amethysts, garnets: stones heavy with blood. Just off centre, a space waited for the diamond.

Little by little, the cutting of the diamond of the Old Rock advanced. New facets extended beneath it, enfolding it all round, giving it the infinite reflections and echoes that break the light and send it flashing back up and out. When I held the finished stone in my fingers I saw that it had come at last into its glory. You could see in it the flare of the waterfall mingled with the blaze of fire and the myriad glints of colour that are possessed by no other stone, nor any other created substance on earth. It had thrown off its innocence; but it had acquired something so much greater in its place. It knew how to sparkle with every turn, without pause, yet without a moment's repetition. It darted out citrine, amber, emerald; its waters played in its depths, then resolved themselves into a sudden fire which leapt and shrank back; and then, as I turned it to gaze directly upon its table, it became suddenly a creature of dark mystery, and I saw well-like depths, brooding caverns, night-time seas about whose edges danced always that shifting mockery of flames. Finally Benvenuto set it among the other stones in the heart: a baleful, beautiful thorn.

'Superb.' On a sudden impulse, I snatched up the heart and ran with it, down the steps past the treasury, and across the courtyard to the chamber occupied by the Cages. I burst in on them. The three women were seated. Grace was reading aloud from a book of verse. It was Ariosto's epic, infinitely long, full of pursuits and escapes almost as fantastic as our own. They looked up. In my excitement I grabbed Hannah by the hand and pulled her outside into the courtyard. From the many doors of the armoury men passed in and out, carrying munitions up to the gun galleries. She was laughing as I dragged her by the sleeve. 'Why? No, why, what is it?'

'Not until we are alone.'

I pulled her towards a door in the corner of the courtyard. It was ajar. Inside we were in a small storeroom, among kegs of powder, sacks of fine hail-shot and lengths of brimstone-soaked matchcord for firing cannon. A narrow window looked out towards the Imperials' trenches. In its light, I opened my cupped hands and showed her the heart. Smiling, teased by my secretiveness, she peered forward. The heart flamed, bloodied and passionate. Slicing into it from the side ran the diamond. Its edges leapt with flame, while its principal facet remained a void of mystery. Hannah gazed at it for a long time, and then she looked up at my face. Her eyes had caught the expression of the stone. They flashed, dark and fathomless.

'Now do you see?' I asked her. 'Now do you understand?'

She put her hands up to my face. I stepped towards her, took her in my arms and kissed her. Above us the cannons bellowed, and the stonework round us shook. I caressed her hair, her throat, her neck. She slid down beneath me on to a pile of sacks, her arms outstretched. I was pulling at the strings across the front of her dress, running my hand over her shoulders and her breasts. I hurried to see to my own clothing: lifted off my sword belt, unhooked my doublet and pulled up my shirt. Hannah, smiling, helped me. She knelt then, and we kissed still while I pulled over her head her smock. Naked, she waited for me, feet curled under her, smiling, resting on one arm. Her black hair fell over the whiteness of her shoulder. She was entirely at her ease. She breathed with mysterious power, just as surely as she had when first I knew her, smiling down on us from her window, or when I first saw her in Rome, laughing at Susan and the monkey. Like my stone, with the veil removed she only teased me the more. I threw off the last of my clothes and crept alongside her. As our skin touched she rubbed one leg alongside me and put her arms around my neck.

A shot crashed into the castle wall behind us. Dust trickled down from the ceiling and settled on our bodies. Hannah laughed. If we were to die, we would die. We were strong: we would walk into the dark together. As our ecstasy began, all our moments together fused into one. Hannah lying beneath me, head tipped back, her breasts pressed against me, was Hannah standing on the riverbank in the dark, swinging on her hips, twirling her mask by its string and saying, 'I know! We shall play cards for it.' She was Hannah in the ruins, Hannah deep underground in the grottoes of the ancients, and in the dark of the attic of the Palazzo del Bene; Hannah who bet on the dwarf Calandrino and won; Hannah who told me there is no pleasure without danger.

With a long gasp she fell back against the sacks. I kissed her again and again, on the face, on the shoulders and neck. She lay and looked at me with her amused smile. She was laughing at me again: but for what? It was then that I looked up and listened. The guns had stopped. Over Rome there hung a deep and deathly silence.

24

I let Hannah step out of the storeroom first. When I left a few minutes later, with my casket safe again beneath my shirt and my sword at my side, a Papal official who had been lingering at the foot of the tower came up to me.

'Messer Richard Dansey? His Holiness wishes to see you.'

I blinked in surprise. 'You must be mistaken.'

'There is no mistake.'

I followed him, hardly knowing where I went. The touch of Hannah's skin was fresh upon me. I was still in a world of glory, far above mortal concerns such as war, sieges, death. But as I stepped inside the outer hall of the Pope's apartments, I began to be a little afraid. I could not conceive the purpose of this summons.

We passed through into a second barrel-vaulted room, where knots of bishops and cardinals stood around the walls, whispering. At the next door, a low opening in the monumental stone walls of the castle, two Swiss guardsmen stood with their halberds. A chamberlain with a gilt staff stepped out, took my sword, and motioned me in. I entered a modest-sized hall with a painted ceiling. At the far end sat Pope Clement VII, in his scarlet cope and skullcap. His fingers, bare of jewels, rested on the arms of his throne. His face above the fresh straggle of his beard was drained and grey. Standing close to him was Cardinal Farnese. He was a crafty old man who had lived a wild life in his youth. He had fathered a flock of bastards, and even spent time in the dungeons beneath our feet for forging a Papal bull. He had advised the Pope months ago to flee from Rome, and for that, perhaps, Clement was the more inclined to listen to his advice now.

I saw also the sad, old bloodhound face of Cardinal Campeggio. He was one of those who spoke loudest for conciliation, rather than further acts of war. The younger Cardinal Salviati, Pope Clement's cousin, stood beside him. There was no one else in the room. I advanced towards the Holy Father, prostrated myself before him in the proper manner and kissed his scarlet-slippered feet. He gestured to me to rise. Tears were in his eyes. He tried to speak, but his voice choked. He closed his eyes. Then he said, 'I have signed the capitulation.'

My stomach sank. I had everything: I had the world. The richest gems ever to be seen in London; and I had Hannah. All this I was about to lose. Pope Clement waited for some moments with his eyes closed. Then he looked at me again. The curve of his mouth still spoke of his old, cold cunning. I saw that after all this man was far from having given up the fight. He said, 'You are intimate, I believe, with Stephen Cage?'

I said, 'While he was in Rome I had the honour to see him often, and dine with his family.'

Clement nodded. 'Mr Stephen is gone: perhaps dead. But you, you have survived. Cardinal Campeggio tells me he believes you are a most unusual young man. So: are you ready to serve me? And serve Mr Stephen's cause?'

I bowed. 'I am at Your Holiness's command.' My heart was pounding. I could not conceive what was coming next.

Pope Clement leant forward. 'Signor Casale leaves tomorrow for Venice, and after that for England, bearing letters from us and from Cardinal Farnese, to Cardinal Wolsey and your King.' He paused. 'In the midst of these terrible crimes committed against God and the Church, we look only to England. Would that we had never trusted to the promises of our other allies.'

He fell silent again. His nostrils flared in an expression of unqualified hatred. I said, 'My master, the King of England, is conscious of the title Your Holiness's predecessor conferred on him. He will act as becomes the Defender of the Faith.'

What was I saying? I was talking like an ambassador: as if I came in the King's name, with the King's own instructions and credentials. The Pope's eyes flicked upon me.

'You understand, then, the full nature of Messer Stephen's errand?'

It would not do to hesitate. I had advanced this far into the business of princes and kings, and I was not about to turn back. I bowed. Meanwhile my mind raced, trying to piece together a clue here, a word there.

'Then you will know that he left Rome discontented, without receiving an answer. This was remiss of me.' Suddenly his eyes beneath their drooping lids took fire. 'English neutrality in this war must end. It must!' He slammed the arm of his throne with his hand. 'My friends desert me. Heretics mock me in the streets of the Holy City. And I must pretend to treat with them; pay their war expenses, speak with mildness. They even demand that I rescind my excommunication and pardon them all from Hell. And that,' he murmured, his fist tightening, 'is a thing I shall never do.'

My spine shivered as I listened to him. His hand unclenched; his face became once more without expression, hanging between a smile, a scowl, and the curled lip of disdain.

'Find Mr Stephen, if he still lives,' he whispered to me, 'and tell him this: "The time may soon come." Exactly those words. Nothing more. You understand me?'

My mind was racing. Stephen's mission, undoubtedly, was to press Pope Clement to consent to King Henry's divorce; or rather, to ask him to agree that the marriage to Queen Katherine had been null from the very start. Clement had temporised, delayed answering, kept Stephen kicking his heels in Rome for week after week in disappointed hope, until finally, just too late for safety, he had left. This divorce was a thing Clement could not easily agree to. It would be a harsh blow to the papacy to concede that a Brief of Dispensation granted by a former pope was a gross error, without validity. Only his desperation for the English alliance could drive him even to consider it.

And then I thought about Stephen, the secrecy in which he wrapped himself, the pilgrim's badge in his cap, the absence of any official status as ambassador from the King. Wolsey feared Stephen. Why, if he was labouring for the divorce just the same as Wolsey himself?

And then I saw it. It came to me in an instant, with Bennet's words before me, announcing the name that very soon all England would know. Anne Boleyn, Stephen's cousin. Stephen Cage was not Wolsey's emissary, but Anne's and the King's. Stephen's presence in Rome was a sign that King Henry no longer trusted Cardinal Wolsey to push through the divorce. Why not? Because when Henry obtained his freedom from Queen Katherine, he would not be looking to the French King's sister for a wife, but to Wolsey's deadly enemy and his own true love, Mrs Anne.

A thrill ran up my back. This truly was, as Wolsey called it, a Great and Secret Affair. And I found myself at the heart of it. If I was right, I understood more of this matter than either Wolsey or Pope Clement. Stephen Cage must have talked to His Holiness about the powers of popes to dispense, the division between divine law and Papal jurisdiction, the interpretation of Scripture. He would not have told him that King Henry was in love: in love with a woman dark-eyed, slender, with a flashing wit and temper; a woman who was not his wife. No, in all these secret debates, the name of Anne Boleyn must have remained the deepest secret of all. And so Wolsey laboured for the divorce, believing in his French match but fearing and half-guessing he was only playing into the hands of his enemy, Anne. Meanwhile King Henry had told the truth of his intentions only to the closest members of the Boleyn clan. I felt my face flush, and I fought to keep my mouth from curving into a smile. My own chances were opening up, richer and grander than I had ever imagined. I was carrying love-gifts for no mere royal mistress, but for a woman who would be queen. I looked up at the Pope. His face, expressionless, waited for my reply.

I said, 'I understand Your Holiness. But if Mr Stephen should be dead? To whom should I deliver the message then?'

Pope Clement lifted one eyebrow. 'Naturally, to your King.'

Richard Dansey, emissary to King Henry. The style of that pleased me. But all of this was nothing unless I could escape from the Castle. The Pope took up a large sheet of paper from a table at his side.

'These,' he said, 'are the terms of the surrender. I am bound to pay four hundred thousand ducats to the Imperials. Until it can be raised, hostages will remain in the Castle, under guard. But the garrison, and most of those who took shelter here, are free to go.' He looked at me with a slight smile. 'Your name, Richard Dansey, is among those who will be permitted to leave.'

I could hardly ask: 'And the Cage family?'

'They too: of course. But Mrs Grace: sadly, her wits … She cannot carry a message such as this. That is why I need you. You have nothing of value?'

'A few tokens,' I said, 'to offer as gifts to my King.'

He nodded. 'Your goods will be respected. You will leave tomorrow. And I trust you will take the quickest road you can to England.'

I knelt before him. In true gratitude and relief I said, 'Holy Father, I swear it.' He made the sign of the cross over my head and murmured a blessing. I kissed his feet again, rose and withdrew.

* * *

I came out into the courtyard in a daze of victory. I hurried to the Cages' chamber, bursting to tell. I imagined Hannah's bright eyes turned up towards me in gratitude as she foresaw the many days of our journey together: yes, and the many nights. I rushed in, and there, sitting on one of the low box beds with the three Cages round him, was John. Hannah turned from him, her face wearing that look of animation which I, by rights, should have been the one to summon.

'Is the news not marvellous?' Hannah exclaimed. 'We are free to go!'

I glanced at John, and my face must have shown how stung I was to have had my triumph taken away. He waved a hand in modesty and said, 'So you have found out too? Yes, I saw the whole thing when they were drawing it up. In fact, I am the one you should thank for it. I found out yesterday that a new Imperial army is on its way from Naples, and if the Pope did not sign now, the Castle would very soon fall.' He glanced round at the ladies. 'But today it is no longer a secret. Today everybody knows. Three bands of Imperials to escort us beyond the walls, and the Prince of Orange present to make sure no outrages are committed against us. After that, we all go wherever we please. His Holiness is to hand over Ostia, Modena, Parma and God knows where else. Some hundreds of thousands of gold to be paid, and all excommunications lifted. But the Imperials are poor simpletons if they expect Pope Clement to keep his promises.'

He folded his arms and smiled. I felt a stab of resentment: foolish, for I ought finally to feel secure in Hannah's love.

I said to John, 'You are leaving too?'

'Of course.' He glanced at Mrs Grace. 'We were discussing, as you came in, the chances of finding a ship at Ostia. We are determined to try. You are coming with us?'

Hannah's smile danced from John to myself, then back to John. My old friend's expression was mild, honest, open. He waited, eyebrows raised, for me to reply. I forced aside my annoyance, turned

344

to Hannah and said, 'Then we shall all leave together. I will meet you tomorrow, early, in the courtyard. By the armoury.'

Her smile spread, showing her teeth, and her eyes glinted with the knowledge of our shared wickedness. She said, 'Tomorrow. By the armoury.'

I turned away. I was angry: with John and with myself. But there was no time to indulge my feelings. Before tomorrow Benvenuto and I had a pair of rings to finish. When I got back up to the Angel, Cellini was already at work on the emerald. He had cut the table, and was holding it over the wheel to polish its sides. He too had heard the news. 'Tomorrow we go our ways,' he said. 'But never let it be said Benvenuto left a job undone.' I watched as the stone gradually shed its mysteries and unfolded like a tight bud into a brilliant summer green. But even when it was cut it kept a dark heart, a place from which shafts of forest light sprang suddenly and then crept back into shadow. It was deep night when Cellini bent the clasps round it that would set it fast in the ring. I stretched, and took the wine Martin offered. Almost I wanted to release Cellini from finishing the last piece; but the fire was in his eyes, and he would stop for nothing. He lifted the flat, uncut ruby I had bought from da Crema.

'Now for the passion.'

Martin at my side leant forward. He was as avid for the glories of these stones as I was. I thought of when we first came to Venice, and the attempts he had made to deflect me and haul me back home to the Widow. His loyalty to her had slipped a good deal since then. I pictured my return to Thames Street, and my mother's look when I laid before her my treasure. I could not expect her to be pleased. No, there was a battle there still remaining to be fought. And Thomas: I resolved at that moment that I would force him to give me his trust, and I would make him my ally.

Outside the small window, over the terrace with its silent cannon, the light of dawn began to show. No guns fired, and across Rome not a bell rang and barely a bird made a sound. In the prisons the noblemen and ladies, priests and cardinals stirred in their chains. The soldiers, thousand upon thousand, waited for daybreak in expectation. Tomorrow all Rome would at last be theirs. Cellini held up the ruby.

'What do you say to that?'

It was alive. However you held it, the fire in it burned, and cast out streams of blood. It was a gem for a dark enchantress, a seducer of kings. I embraced Cellini. 'If you could only come with me to England, and see King Henry.' It was much for me to say: I needed his goldsmith-work, but I was jealous of it too, as a rival to my stones. I had always wished for my triumph to be alone. He shook his head.

'No, I shall go to Florence. My father is there. I must see how he has weathered the wars. Perhaps after that I may go further. Wherever there is a love of beauty and of gold.'

He sat down at the bench and began fitting the gem into the ring. I took out my casket. Not a loose stone remained. From beneath the packets that held the various pieces, the Ship, the Garden, the Cross and the Heart, I took out my roll of bills. I paid over to him seven hundred ducats: more by a bit than we had agreed, and it left me with little. But he had earned it. Martin nudged my arm. From the lower parts of the Castle there was already the murmuring of large assembling crowds. It was time for us to be gone. The three of us descended from the Angel for the last time.

The courtyard was crammed with people. The men of the garrison were forming up, with their harquebuses and powder horns and sacks of food. Nobles, bishops, servants, poor men and women pushed among them, while Papal officials called out orders which no one could hear. I shoved through the crowd to the door of the armoury, where Hannah and I had lain among the powder casks. There was no sign of her, or of Grace or Susan either. 'Martin!' I commanded. 'Wait here.' I moved towards their lodgings, but at that moment I caught sight of John's head above the crowd. We pushed towards each other. He looked displeased.

'The Cages?' I asked.

'Already gone down. They are with Casale at the head of the column. Well, we shall catch them up later.'

I glanced at him sidelong. The crowd was beginning to move. From far below we heard the beating of drums and the clank as the portcullis was raised. It was the seventh of June: a month since the Sack and the siege had begun. We pressed down the stairs and the long, winding ramp, walking several abreast through the heart of that ancient tomb. Torches burned in the darkness, lighting up the barrel vault above, glinting on the soldiers' breastplates and their sombre faces. We were an army in defeat. A mere three hundred men at arms, but ten times that number of priests, merchants, women. We passed under the gate and across the bridge where the Cages and I had fled that misty dawn. The column stretched away ahead of us out of sight. As the last of us left, the Imperials streamed with wild shouts inside the Castle. They were not to enter the drum tower: there the Pope and his cardinals were safe, but prisoners.

Beyond the bridge we entered the ruins of Rome. Houses were burnt out and windowless. Rubble and the stinking dead lay everywhere. The three weeks I had spent inside the Castle had seen the city reduced still further to an abomination, a wilderness where men turned into beasts, a terrible mark of the judgement of God upon man. Almost every door we passed had the plague-mark on it. Mobs of ragged soldiers watched us hungrily from the street corners. Somewhere ahead of us were the Cages; but my attempts to push ahead through the column came to nothing. The bands of lansquenets assigned to guard us through the city pressed us close on either side, and with the murderous stares of the soldiers beyond them I was glad of it.

Outside the Gate of Saint Paul, where I had first entered Rome five months earlier, the column divided. One portion turned east and then north, bound towards the hills. This was where Cellini was headed.

As we clasped one another a last time, he said, 'Greet King Henry for me.'

I laughed. 'And thank your father for letting his son become a goldsmith.'

He embraced Martin too.

'A good servant you have,' he told me. 'But what bad advice he gives. Think if you had never come to Rome!'

I watched Benvenuto as he disappeared among the nodding helmets and feathered hats of the soldiers, winding north across the Campagna.

'Master!' Martin pointed: our column was on the move. We hurried on. After a few minutes we caught up with John.

'They are still far ahead.' His face showed rather too deep a concern.

I growled, 'I know very well you would like to have Hannah for yourself.'

'My dear Richard! Mrs Hannah is yours. Of course she is.' His eye twinkled. 'If you can keep her.'

I made a grab for him, but he darted ahead and looked back, laughing. 'Come, Richard, you can never be angry with me.'

I caught him up and we linked arms. 'No. Because you are right: Hannah is mine.'

Ahead over the marshes rose the castle of Ostia, and beside it the mast of the ship that would carry us home: home to a triumph more glorious than I could have imagined when I first set out from Broken Wharf those many months before; home to Hannah's love and victory over my mother; home to where King Henry waited for the sight of his diamond.

ACKNOWLEDGEMENTS

I would like to express my grateful thanks to my agent, Peter Robinson, whose tireless support, insightful ideas and penetrating comments have seen me through every stage of the conception and writing of this book. My warmest thanks also go to my editor, Clare Smith, for the enthusiastic way in which she embraced the book and her excellent judgement in suggesting ways to improve it; thanks also to everyone else at HarperPress who has worked on it. I would like to thank, finally, my wife Katie, for her unceasing encouragement, the many discussions we have had concerning the mapping of the story, jewels and Renaissance history generally, and for her skilled help in commenting on successive drafts.